C000131021

Cross-Gendered Literary Voices

Also by Rina Kim

WOMEN AND IRELAND AS BECKETT'S LOST OTHERS:
Beyond Mourning and Melancholia

Cross-Gendered Literary Voices

Appropriating, Resisting, Embracing

Edited by

Rina Kim

and

Claire Westall

palgrave
macmillan

First published 2012 by
PALGRAVE MACMILLAN

Palgrave Macmillan in the UK is an imprint of Macmillan Publishers Limited,
registered in England, company number 785998, of Houndmills, Basingstoke,
Hampshire RG21 6XS.

Palgrave Macmillan in the US is a division of St Martin's Press LLC,
175 Fifth Avenue, New York, NY 10010.

Palgrave Macmillan is the global academic imprint of the above companies
and has companies and representatives throughout the world.

Palgrave® and Macmillan® are registered trademarks in the United States,
the United Kingdom, Europe and other countries.

ISBN 978–0–230–29987–0

This book is printed on paper suitable for recycling and made from fully
managed and sustained forest sources. Logging, pulping and manufacturing
processes are expected to conform to the environmental regulations of the
country of origin.

A catalogue record for this book is available from the British Library.

A catalog record for this book is available from the Library of Congress.

10   9   8   7   6   5   4   3   2   1
21 20 19 18 17 16 15 14 13 12

Printed and bound in Great Britain by
CPI Antony Rowe, Chippenham and Eastbourne

Contents

Acknowledgements

This project emerged from an academic conference organized by the editors and held in the CAPITAL Centre at the University of Warwick in 2008. Consequently, we would very much like to thank the Department of English and Comparative Literary Studies and the CAPITAL Centre at Warwick for sponsoring and hosting the event, respectively, and Professor Thomas Docherty, Dr Elizabeth Barry and Dr Susan Brock in particular for their assistance and support. We would also like to recognize all of our friends and colleagues at Warwick, where we both spent a number of very happy and academically important years. The conference itself was a remarkable success, laying the foundation for this more sustained investigation, and a number of the chapters here have developed from papers given at that event. We would like to thank all those who participated in the conference and especially the keynote speaker Professor Marina Warner. We also want to express our sincerest gratitude to all of the authors in this collection for their vibrant and productive intellectual contributions to the debate on Cross-Gendered Literary Voices. In addition, we are also indebted to many people who generously gave their time and expertise during the production of this book. We are particularly grateful to Sabrina Anna Piras for designing our elegant front cover and to Dr Sally Hoare and Dr Lucy Treep for assisting us with the bibliographic entries. At Palgrave Macmillan we would like to especially thank Paula Kennedy and Benjamin Doyle for their efficiency and patience and the manner in which they were both helpful and positive throughout the process. Finally, we would like to express our gratitude to our respective departments – the Department of English at the University of Auckland and the Department of English and Related Literature at the University of York – for their collegiate support, funding and engaging research cultures.

Notes on Contributors

Sanja Bahun is a Lecturer in the Department of Literature, Film and Theatre Studies at the University of Essex. Her main area of expertise is international modernism, and her research interests include: comparative literature and film, theory of comparative arts, psychoanalysis, and women's and gender studies. She has co-edited *The Avant-garde and the Margin: New Territories of Modernism* (Cambridge Scholars, 2006), *Violence and Gender in the Globalized World: the Intimate and the Extimate* (Ashgate, 2008), *From Word to Canvas: Appropriations of Myth in Women's Aesthetic Production* (Cambridge Scholars, 2009) and *Myth and Violence in the Contemporary Female Text: New Cassandras* (Ashgate, 2011). Her forthcoming monograph is *Modernism and Melancholia: Writing as Countermourning* (Oxford, 2013). She has also authored two books of creative writing.

David Brauner is a Reader in the Department of English and American Literature at the University of Reading. His primary research interests are contemporary American fiction and post-war Jewish literature. He has also developed additional interests in Holocaust fiction and contemporary women's writing. As well as a multitude of articles on Jewish and American fiction, he has published *Post-War Jewish Fiction: Ambivalence, Self-Explanation, Transatlantic Connections* (Palgrave, 2001) and *Philip Roth* (Manchester University Press, 2007). His recently published monograph is *Contemporary American Fiction* (Edinburgh University Press, 2010).

Joanne Bishton is a Lecturer in English and American Literature in the School of Humanities at the University of Derby. She holds a BA from the University of Derby, an MRes from the University of Nottingham (2008) and is currently working on a PhD at the University of Derby. Her research area is the dissident lesbian voice of the twentieth/twenty-first century and she is particularly interested in the work of Sarah Waters.

Sarah Hayden is currently completing her IRCHSS funded doctoral thesis, entitled *"Intimate irritant": Constructions of Futurist, Dada and Surrealist Artisthood in the Work of Mina Loy*, at University College Cork. She commenced a DAAD postdoctoral research fellowship at the Centre for Degenerate Art, Freie Universität, Berlin, in January 2012.

Rina Kim is a Lecturer in the Department of English at the University of Auckland. Her research interests include Samuel Beckett, Theatre and Performance, Gender and Irish Studies, Psychoanalytic Theories (Freudian and Kleinian), Memory and Emotion. Before joining the University of Auckland, she taught in the Department of English and Comparative Literary Studies at the University of Warwick where she also completed her PhD and further developed her expertise in Anglo-Irish literature as well as British and European Theatre. Her monograph, *Women and Ireland as Beckett's Lost Others: Beyond Mourning and Melancholia* (2010), was published by Palgrave Macmillan.

Miles Leeson is a Sessional Lecturer at the University of Chichester and worked previously in the Centre for Studies in Literature at the University of Portsmouth. His research covers contemporary British, Irish and American fiction, specifically the work of Iris Murdoch, Ian McEwan and Martin Amis, as well as French fiction since Voltaire. He writes on a variety of philosophers including Heidegger, Wittgenstein and Plato. His first monograph *Iris Murdoch: Philosophical Novelist* was published in 2010 and he is currently working on his second, *Time and Consciousness in Philosophical Novels* (Continuum, 2013), as well as journal articles on post 9/11 fiction, postcolonial fiction and French postmodern thought. He previously held a tutorship at the University of Sussex where he completed his PhD.

Mark Llewellyn joined the University of Strathclyde, Glasgow, as Professor in English Studies under the John Anderson Research Leadership (JARL) scheme in 2011. His most recent publication is *Neo-Victorianism: the Victorians in the Twenty-First Century, 1999–2009* (with Ann Heilmann; Palgrave, 2010) and he has published widely on contemporary reinterpretations of Victorian literature and culture. He is currently completing a monograph entitled *Incest in British Culture, 1835–1908* and continuing work on the Anglo-Irish turn of the century novelist George Moore (1852–1933). From 2012 Mark is on secondment to the UK's Arts and Humanities Research Council as Director of Research.

Claire Nally is a Lecturer in Twentieth Century Literature at the University of Northumbria. She completed her PhD on W.B. Yeats in 2006 at the University of Manchester. Her first book was entitled *Envisioning Ireland: Occult Nationalism in the Work of W.B. Yeats* (Peter Lang, 2009) and her subsequent project was a co-written book with John Strachan entitled *Selling Ireland: Advertising, Literature and Irish*

Print Culture (Palgrave, 2012). She has co-edited a book with Matthew Gibson and Neil Mann entitled *Yeats's A Vision: Explications and Contexts* (Clemson University Press, 2012), as well as another co-edited volume with Angela Smith, entitled *Naked Exhibitionism: Gender, Performance and Public Exposure* (I.B. Tauris, 2012). Together with Smith, she is also the co-editor for the I.B. Tauris book series *Gender and Popular Culture*.

Bryony Randall joined the University of Glasgow in 2007 as a Lecturer in English Literature. Her first book, *Modernism, Daily Time and Everyday Life* (2007), is published by Cambridge University Press, and her other publications include articles on Imagist poetry, Gertrude Stein, the New Woman writer George Egerton, Stevie Smith, and H.D. She is currently working on a second major project provisionally entitled *The Working Woman Writer 1880–1920*, exploring the relationships between work, writing and gender in the early modernist period.

Claire Westall is a Lecturer in the Department of English and Related Literature at the University of York, having joined the department in 2010. Before this she worked in the Department of English and Comparative Literary Studies at the University of Warwick where she also completed her doctoral research. Her current monograph project is entitled *Cricket, Literature and Postcolonialism: Knowing England, Empire and the Caribbean*. Her work is concerned with the literary-cultural legacies of British imperialism, comparatively in relation to Caribbean literature and wider postcolonial and global debates and in relation to debates about England, Englishness and British Devolution.

Madeleine Wood is a Sessional Lecturer in the Department of English and Comparative Literary Studies at the University of Warwick. She is also a member of Oxford University Department of Continuing Education's tutor panel. Her research creates new psychoanalytic readings of Victorian novels with the premise that familial constellations are inextricably related to both the creation of subjectivity and narrative form. She uses psychoanalytic concepts of transgenerational transmission and trauma in her readings of the novels with Jean Laplanche's theories exerting a primary influence. She gained her PhD from Warwick University in 2009, and has worked in the English department since 2005.

Introduction: Cross-Gendered Literary Voices

Rina Kim

Referring to the crazy voice of the female persona in his later poems in *Words for Music Perhaps* (1932), W.B. Yeats claimed 'Crazy Jane poems' were 'founded on the sayings of an old woman "Cracked Mary"' who 'had an amazing power of audacious speech' in Galway (Yeats 1996: 604–5). According to the aging poet, Crazy Jane was also the product of his own 'uncontrollable energy' (605), suggesting that he melded a need to borrow a female voice he knew and could confidently mobilize with his own exuberant poetic energy. In Yeats's 'Crazy Jane poems', we see the licentious old madwoman arguing against the Bishop through her 'ballad poetics' and what Elizabeth Cullingford calls the Bakhtian 'carnivalesque insistence on the grotesque body' which disputes the 'monologic identity constructed by [the] celibate clergy' (1993: 227). For Cullingford, 'Crazy Jane was both Yeats's attempt to speak the Other and a strategy for evading his own internal censor' when resisting 'patriarchal ecclesiastical authority' (235). In contrast, Alan Michael Parker and Mark Willhardt claim that Yeats's 'Crazy Jane ends up rein-forcing gender hierarchies' (1996: 202), and thereby other socio-political patterns of constraint, rather than offering a forcefully subversive sense of female agency. In a strikingly similar example to 'Crazy Jane', Samuel Beckett's female character Mouth in his play *Not I* (1972) extends this form of provocative cross-gendering as is pertinently examined by Julia Kristeva. Kristeva's reading of Mouth in her essay 'The Father, Love, and Banishment' (1980) is, however, notably ambiguous. On the one hand, Kristeva claims that 'mad, seventy-year-old' Mouth does not refuse the discourse of the Father in 'pursuing a paternal shadow' (1980: 154), and thus is submissive to the order of the Father. On the other hand, Kristeva also argues, that Mouth 'experiences *jouissance* in nonsense through repression', and therefore disrupts the patriarchal discourse by

1

pouring out the waste of repression, and by reminding us of the images of abjection, through the very image that recalls the 'vagina with a mouth', the *vagina dentata* (ibid.). In this fashion, Kristeva reinforces Mouth's ability to signal disruption but only within a patriarchal order that maintains its view of woman as a fear-inducing hysteric. Like Yeats, Beckett described how he had known and heard the voice of female hysteria he portrays, saying 'I knew that woman [old crone] in Ireland. [...] I heard "her" saying what I wrote in *Not I*. I actually heard it' (Knowlson 1996: 522). Here Beckett points to some kind of 'reality' behind the ranting, raving and largely disembodied female voice of Mouth and connects the fragmented and violent female subject he (re)created with memories of home while also deploying this subject/ voice as a means of negotiating with his own sense of ambivalence towards woman, home and Ireland.

Clearly in both cases above, the construction and deployment of an audacious female voice by a male writer – as a means of indirectly engaging with questions about the formation of their own subject position – is linked to expressions of 'home' and recast as barely controllable hysterical outpourings. Critical responses have varied considerably in their interpretation of the poetic, aesthetic and political purposes of such cross-genderings, prompting consideration of the appropriation of, resistance to, and/or embracing of a gendered 'Other'. This is the critical point of entry of the current collection. It investigates the use of female voices by male authors, including those of the type described above, but also the creation and depiction of male voices by female authors, examining where, how and why such gendered crossings occur and what connections may be found between these crossings and specific psychological, social, historical and political contexts as well as the particular aesthetic ends of individual authors. Importantly, the collection recognizes the centrality of cross-gendering for literary composition and also works to move beyond the male–female binary that the crossing of gender may have traditionally invoked.

Gendered language

Emerging from literature's long term and sustained interest in gender and gendered identities, a number of literary and cultural studies have examined the gendered nature of language and writing styles. A notable step in this direction was provided by the *Women & Literature* series edited by Janet Todd. The first two volumes, *Gender and Literary Voice* (1980) and *Men by Women* (1981), offer useful and provocative accounts of a distinctive female writing style created by women writers including Jane Austen, the Brontës and George Eliot. As the title of the series indicates, however, the volumes concentrate on the relationship between women and literature, thereby prioritizing the female voice in the first volume and women writers in the second. When covering the topic of male characters, the second volume focuses on 'the fantasies of maleness that female writers have fashioned' (1981: 2) by exploring effeminate – as in the case of Eliot – or demonic and seductive males created by women – as with Heathcliff in *Wuthering Heights* (1857) and Rochester in *Jane Eyre* (1847). In her introduction to *Men by Women* Todd contends that these depictions derive from a misconception of, or failure to subtly read, the opposite sex, implying that a barrier between the sexes remains evident in such writing. Similarly, Elizabeth Harvey's *Ventriloquized Voices: Feminist Theory and English Renaissance Texts* (1992) solely explores male appropriations of the female voice in early modern English texts, juxtaposing them with French feminist theorizations of voice such as those by Hélène Cixous and Julia Kristeva. Harvey shows that a type of 'transvestite ventriloquism' (1) is employed by male writers as 'a powerful strategy of silencing' (142) used against the female Other even though the same male writers express a need to appropriate the female Other that stems from 'what is most desired and most feared about women' (32).

While building upon the work of Todd's important series and Harvey's study, *Cross-Gendered Literary Voices* proposes that the act of gender crossing in literary works needs to be analysed with a more complex and nuanced theory of gender, pushing past the binary model that situates the Other sex as either idealized or threatening. Cixous's model of binary oppositions and Kristeva's concept of abjection have shown how the female/femininity has been systematically situated as the Other or the abject in a gendered hierarchy of power relations premised on heterosexuality. This study sits within this feminist tradition of gender theorization and interrogation, especially in relation to the gendering of language. Recently, however, the sex–gender distinction itself, in other words the relationship between femaleness and femininity or maleness and masculinity, has been vigorously disputed by queer cultural critics such as Judith Butler and Judith Halberstam. For example, Halberstam's *Female Masculinity* (1998) challenges our conception of masculinities by exploring female masculinities, that is, versions of masculinity performed and embodied by women in and through their bodies and acts of self-representation and, importantly, it calls for a radical dismantling of heteronormative assumptions about gender. Thus, this collection repeatedly demonstrates that the crossing of gendered voice also disrupts the dualism of male and female subjectivities, creating tensions, ambiguities and double meanings that indicate the significance of slippage, hybridity and uncertainty. Such sites of tension are particularly important when texts are creating and negotiating with transgendered identities and voices. The collection extends the parameters of debate offered in the *Women & Literature* series and revisits the French feminist theory by exploring the approaches of both male and female writers and their sustained and strategic use of cross-gendered and transgendered voices in order to deconstruct gendered norms. It also places such literary works alongside theatrical examples as both are often concerned with issues of embodiment and performativity.

Performativity and gendered voice

Judith Butler's ideas of gender performance and performativity that come primarily from her seminal studies *Gender Trouble* (1990) and *Bodies That Matter* (1993) feature prominently in this collection. Her concept of performativity remains academically fashionable and widely utilized, yet there is still much to be gained from her notion of gender as '"an act," broadly construed, which constructs the social fiction of its own psychological interiority' (1990: 279), as several chapters here demonstrate. As Butler argues, 'gender is made to comply' with a heterosexual model 'against its own performative fluidity' in order to serve 'a social policy of gender regulation and control' (ibid.), and this study aims to draw attention to the voicing of the gendered Other because such speech also unsettles the ideas of stability and coherence that underpin social and sexual norms and challenges the very notion of *a* (that is singular) gendered identity. In this sense, Butler's work and influence is supplemented here with readings of the gendering of voice as negotiated through literary and related artistic examples of gender crossings. For as Parker and Willhardt point out, the cross-gendered voice 'becomes a kind of performance' offering a mask to a writer and allowing her or him 'to fictionalise and to speak freely' (1996: 194). In crossing gender, then, writers inevitably reveal the formation of sexuality and gender as largely fictional by imitating and parodying their gendered Other.

   It is well known that Butler developed her account of performativity in the context of Jacques Derrida's reworking of J.L. Austin's speech act theory. In spite of Butler's foundational understanding of the linguistically constituted aspects of subjectivity and the performative force of speech, her writings on gender from the early 1990s draw heavily on the importance of the body and bodily signification, including its force as a discursive site of power, and these have been the aspects most readily taken up by others in the field, especially alongside Foucauldian conceptions of the disciplined body and subject. Following Marjorie Garber's significant study, *Vested Interests: Cross-dressing & Cultural Anxiety* (1991), the tendency to concentrate on the physical display of gender and gender crossing is also reflected in the most recent publications on cross-gendering in Shakespearean studies, as in Elizabeth Klett's *Cross-Gender Shakespeare and English National Identity* (2009) and *Shakespeare Re-Dressed* (2008) edited by James C. Bulman. While participating in this notably current discussion about gender crossing and drawing upon the insights gained from studies of gendered bodies, *Cross-Gendered Literary Voices* interrogates the often overlooked connection between the body and the voice, especially with voices that are potentially transgendered or androgynous and obfuscate or overtly confuse the gendered (and sexed) status of the body. Indeed, as Butler herself claims, speech acts are 'excitable' and beyond the control of their originating source (1997: 15). In this light we should also recall Mikhail Bakhtin's work on speech acts, his insistence on the importance of articulation and his contention that 'there is no speech act that is not also the statement of an attitude towards the world and a declaration of the speaker's own ideological presuppositions in relation to the interlocutor' (Barta 2001: 2). A number of the chapters in this collection move forward from such an understanding of the connection between speech acts or, more specifically for our purposes, literary voice and the world.

Voice and psychoanalysis

Many other chapters take as their theoretical point of departure a psychoanalytical reading of the importance of the voice. In *A Voice and Nothing More* (2006) Mladen Dolar states that the voice was not a major topic of discussion in philosophy, literature and psychoanalysis until the 1960s, when Derrida proposed the idea of 'phonocentrism' and Jacques Lacan claimed that the voice, together with the gaze, is 'one of the paramount embodiments of what he called *objet petit a*' (127), that is, a psychoanalytic object. A similar kind of objectification of the voice is also found in Steven Connor's *Dumbstruck: a Cultural History of Ventriloquism* (2000) in which he develops the idea of 'the vocalic body', the idea of 'a surrogate or secondary body, [...] formed and sustained out of the autonomous operations of the voice' (35). What is remarkable in both studies is the way they underline the role of the voice in the psychic development whereby the infant conceives its own voice as 'com[ing] from outside', from the Other (Connor 2000: 32). Employing Melanie Klein's concept of bad objects, Connor explains that when the baby cries out of hunger, just as it projects its own frustration and anger to the bad breast that fails to satisfy its desire, it also projects its aggression onto the voice as well: 'the voice is not something other than the breast, which cannot satisfy precisely because it is other than the breast, but is the breast gone bad, the breast that refuses to feed, the breast that screams instead of yielding pleasure' (31). Therefore, the 'bad voice is the infant's own voice which has been violently estranged from it', projected onto the Other and conceived as the Other (32). Connor's idea of the bad voice that is closely associated with the persecutory fear and the super-ego's demand can be linked to Dolar's expansion of the inner voice and conscience into the ethical voice. Whether 'it is supposed to be divine and supernatural' or 'daemonic', the 'voice comes from the Other, but this is the Other within' (Dolar 2006: 102). As such, according to Dolar, the 'voice can be located at the juncture of the subject and the Other', 'placed at the intersection of body and language' in general and the moral law in particular (ibid.). The studies by Connor and Dolar, then, not only signify the 'ambiguous ontology' of the 'status of the voice' (ibid.) as between the self and the Other, but also lead us to investigate further the problems of ownership, authorship and question of identity in relation to language, especially via cross-gendered voices. In this collection, therefore, the term 'voice' is used more broadly than the way that Harvey deploys it in her *Ventriloquized Voices* in which she describes voice as referring to 'the metaphors of speaking' (1992: 1). In addition to the metaphors of speaking, narrating or writing in a text, the collection also explores voice as a psychologically significant object that plays an important part in the subject formation in relation to the gendered Other by examining the complex relationship between voice, body and subjectivity.

The scope of the collection

The use of cross-gendered voices by authors has not yet been fully explored despite its centrality to literary narrativization and characterization and other artistic forms of expression. A significant step in this direction was made by *The Routledge Anthology of Cross-Gendered Verse* (1996) edited by Parker and Willhardt. This anthology shows that writing in the voice of the other gender is a long-standing literary phenomenon. By offering a sizeable primary source of literary material, from Geoffrey Chaucer's 'Prologe of the Wyves Tale of Bathe' to contemporary poems, the anthology demonstrates the abundance and importance of cross-gendering in the genre of poetry. However, the insights and implications of this anthology have not yet been explored in critical detail nor extended to genres other than poetry. A more recent anthology entitled *Women and Cross Dressing* (2006) edited by Heike Bauer brings together a range of primary sources, from newspaper articles and private letters to literary descriptions, that demonstrate the socio-political and cultural importance of cross dressing women from 1800 to the outbreak of World War Two. However, as with Parker and Willhardt's collection, the value of such material to debates about cross gendering is only just being evaluated and the important links to the voice are yet to be explored. This collection overlaps with Bauer's in terms of periodization as it investigates the cross gendering of voice that occurs in literature and theatre from the 1850s to the present, with a notable emphasis on the novel form. While there are many examples of cross-gendered voices in the Western literature dating back to ancient Greek theatre (most famously Sophocles's *Antigone* and Euripides's *Medea*), this study moves from the Victorian period when the novel rose to dominance – and by 'Victorian' we mean, following Claire Kahane, to indicate the dominant rule of 'bourgeois social proprieties in the second half of the nineteenth century rather than the literal geotemporal boundaries of Queen Victoria's reign' (1995: ix) – through to the present, charting the intense shifts in attitudes towards gender, sexuality and artistic practice. In doing so, it traces the evolution of modern concerns with women, gender and sexuality that appeared in the late nineteenth century and became increasingly central to our understanding of self-identity and the socio-cultural world we inhabit. It also demonstrates the intersection of these issues with developments in the novel form, and changes in narrative voices and prose techniques in particular.

The way that authors speak through the voice of the gendered Other opens up 'a discrepancy in the etymological sense of "sounding differently"' (1992: 2) as Harvey claims, and also exposes their interaction with a society that standardizes and stereotypes 'different' gendered identities and related social behaviours as well as their own anxiety about or resistance to gendered norms. This collection benefits from the post 1990s rise in gender and queer studies, employing, deploying and challenging many of their key theorists and thinkers. It revisits a number of approaches to cross-gendered literary narrative and gendered language in order to shed new light on canonical and popular literature and theatre from the late mid-nineteenth century onwards. The collection is organized into four parts and loosely moves forward in historical terms within and across each section. The chapters themselves do not conform to a single reading or approach to the crossing of gendered voice but speak back to key critical questions in overlapping ways. Part 1 provides the historical and literary grounding, establishing the important gendered manoeuvring that occurred in texts from the latter half of the nineteenth century when the conventional notions of sexuality started to be challenged by the appearance of the 'New Woman' and the significant rise of feminism. This volume, therefore, begins with a chapter by Madeleine Wood who uses Sigmund Freud's construction of the hysterical female narrative in identifying a new form of unexpectedly radical feminine empowerment emerging in male-authored nineteenth-century texts, *Little Dorrit* (1857) by Charles Dickens and *Armadale* (1866) by Wilkie Collins. Following on historically, Bryony Randall examines the strategic use of the male voice in three short stories from the 1880s and 1890s by the New Woman writers, Constance Fenimore Woolsoon, Vernon Lee and Mabel E. Wootton. Noting the Victorian women writers' tendency to publish under male pseudonyms, Randall explores the female writers' liminal status alongside their inclination to borrow male voices, and asks pertinent questions about whether the women writers problematically risked effacing the power of their own voices at this point in literary history.

Part 2 concentrates on the significance of the gendered Other in relation to the formation of subjectivity in modernist and late modernist works. It is not our intention to provide an overview of the main paradigmatic moves within Anglo-Irish-American literary modernism, particularly given the intense and well-documented debates that surround the term modernism and its pluralization into modernisms in current academic discourse. However, the collection demonstrates that textually modernist techniques across the first half of the twentieth century break with the more traditional conventions of realist and naturalist literary form. This break is prominent in the experimental writing represented by 'high' modernism, as in James Joyce's *Ulysses* (1922), and the centrality of the inner-self and self-consciousness. Indeed, Joyce's writing has been celebrated as one of the very examples of *écriture féminine* by Cixous. In Chapter 3 Sanja Bahun elegantly re-examines Molly Bloom's fluid monologue, previously seen as a true *écriture féminine*, and addresses the implications of Joyce's aesthetic cross-gender performance in a densely written piece. Bahun investigates Joyce's appropriation of the female voice as home/womb in the 'Penelope' chapter of *Ulysses* linking nationhood and home through Joyce's cross-gender voicing, and explores the ambivalences created by his double appropriation of Penelope and his own wife's letters.

For Sarah Hayden, rather than the Bloomsbury modernist writers like Virginia Woolf, the Bohemian modernist Djuna Barnes's cross-gendered voice is a modernist example of *écriture féminine*. Thus Chapter 4 by Hayden examines Barnes's negotiation with the voice and body of the male transvestite gynaecologist in *Nightwood* (1936) by employing Butler's reading of drag and melancholy gender, and moving towards the thinking of Cixous and Luce Irigaray. Chapters 5 and 6 examine how two late modernists demonstrate a self-conscious employment of psychoanalytic or philosophical ideas when exploring questions of the self and the Other via cross-gendered voices. In Chapter 5 Rina Kim discusses Beckett's complex way of borrowing the female hysteric voice in vocalizing emotions, and she mobilizes recent theories of voice that shed light on the very nature of ambiguous ontology of the status of the voice as between the subject and the Other. While Beckett appears to merely exploit the culturally gendered form of the hysteria, Kim identifies his conscious use of the psychoanalytic idea in verbalizing his traumatic separation from the (m)other and in restoring his own lost Other, by comparing his cross-gendered voice in his early fiction such as *First Love* (1946) and later play *Not I* (1972). Chapter 6 by Miles Leeson studies Iris Murdoch's early fiction, including *A Severed Head* (1961), and the manner in which she repeatedly uses first-person male narratives to create an unsettling combination of traditional values and an exposure of such conservatism through the comedic destruction of those same values. As well as discussing Murdoch's use of a homosexual voice, Leeson raises important questions about the social construction of gender and power, positioning Murdoch's cross-gendered voice at the centre of her philosophical and moral stance.

Part 3 moves to consider the engagement between voices and bodies, identifying ways in which thinking about the crossing of gender, even when displayed and performed physically, is also fundamentally linked to the voice and its complex articulation of self. Opening this section, Claire Westall re-reads Angela Carter's challenging dystopian novel of transgendered transformation, *The Passion of New Eve* (1977), by rebalancing the Butlerification of this work, and Carter's work more generally, with a more explicit concern with Carter's interest in the voice and vocalization. Westall usefully identifies Carter's engagement with masculinity and her exposure of heterosexual masculinity as a continuous effort rather than a 'natural' category relating to an always already established subject position. She then explores the significance of female voices and the voice of the Mother, and establishes the potentiality of Carter's deployment of transgendered vocalization, including its maintenance of a residual masculine presence.

Chapter 8 by David Brauner maps out a number of significant examples of the appropriation of cross-gendered voices in fiction since Daniel Defoe's *Moll Flanders* (1722), and examines what he claims to be the first realistic representations of the transsexual subject published in English: *Sacred Country* (1992) by Rose Tremain and *Middlesex* (2002) by Jeffrey Eugenides. Brauner contends that these texts – each with a protagonist raised as a girl but living as adult male – allow the critical identification of a 'transgendered voice' and further challenges Butler's now dominant understanding of the body as socially constructed. In Chapter 9, Claire Nally reads Patrick McCabe's polyvocal text, *Breakfast on Pluto* (2005), where the metropolitan location of the marginal cross-dressing protagonist articulates a pointed critique of the dominant forms of national, even nationalist, identity and ideology of Ireland in the 1960s and 1970s by attempting border crossings in relation to both geographical and gender.

Finally, Part 4 brings us to contemporary fiction but also returns us to the Victorian literary-cultural concerns established in the opening section via Mark Llewellyn's engagement with neo-Victorianism in Chapter 10. Llewellyn investigates the self-consciously re-imagined female experience of gender identity in the period when the male anxiety about the New Woman who claimed women's right to education and to write reached its peak and the Victorian virgin/whore distinction of women was solidified as one of the consequences. Here Llewellyn explores Michel Faber's *The Crimson Petal and the White* (2002) focusing on the female protagonist Sugar, Victorian prostitute and aspiring writer of sadomasochistic pornography. Llewellyn further investigates the tension between the female sexual subject's voice and the early twenty-first-century writer's desire to subvert, re-invent and challenge the hegemonic social claims of the nineteenth-century realist mode. In the final chapter, Chapter 11, Joanne Bishton analyses Sarah Waters's lingering homosexual voice in her most recent novel, *The Little Stranger* (2009), set in post-war Britain. Bishton calls into question Walters's status as a prominent lesbian writer and the effects this label may have on the reception of her work and the gendered reformulations it is able to present. Bishton also asks whether Walters's choice of an authoritative male narrator – a doctor – is part of an attempt to establish a universally accessible narrative voice or is actually working to complicate our understanding of gendered voices more broadly.

By examining the kind of male and female identities to emerge from the vocalization of gendered transformation, this collection establishes new ground in the critical analysis of the way gender switching, transforming or morphing is mobilized in literature to create and recreate identities which challenge established binaries. The collection also provides new impetus for further theoretical explorations of the role of the voice, and its gendered construction and transformation, within literary and gender studies.

Works Cited

Barta, Peter I. et al. (2001) *Carnivalizing Difference: Bakhtin and the Other* (London: Routledge).

Bauer, Heike (ed.) (2006) *Women and Cross Dressing* (London: Routledge).

Beckett, Samuel (1990[1986]) *The Complete Dramatic Works* (London: Faber and Faber).

Bulman, James C (2008) *Shakespeare Re-Dressed: Cross-gender Casting in Contemporary Performance* (Madison [NJ]: Fairleigh Dickinson University Press).

Butler, Judith (1990) 'Performative Acts and Gender Constitution: an essay in phenomenology and Feminist Theory', in Sue-Ellen Case (ed.), *Performing Feminisms: Feminist Critical Theory and Theatre* (Baltimore: Johns Hopkins University Press), pp. 270–82.

—— (1990) *Gender Trouble: Feminism and the Subversion of Identity* (New York: Routledge).

—— (1993) *Bodies That Matter: on the Discursive Limits of 'Sex'* (New York: Routledge).

—— (1997) *Excitable Speech* (New York: Routledge).

Connor, Stephen (2000) *Dumbstruck: a Cultural History of Ventriloquism* (Oxford: Oxford University Press).

Cullingford, Elizabeth (1993) *Gender and History in Yeats's Love Poetry* (New York: Cambridge University Press).

Dolar, Mladen (2006) *A Voice and Nothing More* (Cambridge, Mass.: MIT Press).

Halberstam, Judith (1998) *Female Masculinity* (Durham: Duke University Press).

Harvey, Elizabeth D. (1992) *Ventriloquized Voices: Feminist Theory and English Renaissance Texts* (London: Routledge).

Kahane, Claire (1995) *Passions of the Voice: Hysteria, Narrative and the Figure of the Speaking Woman, 1850–1915* (Baltimore and London: Johns Hopkins University Press).

Klett, Elizabeth (2009) *Cross-Gender Shakespeare and English National Identity: Wearing the Codpiece* (Basingstoke: Palgrave Macmillan).

Knowlson, James (1996) *Damned to Fame: the Life of Samuel Beckett* (New York: Simon & Schuster).

Kristeva, Julia (1980) 'The Father, Love, and Banishment', in *Desire in Language: a Semiotic Approach to Literature and Art*, ed. Leon S. Roudiez, trans. Thomas Gora, Alice Jardine and Leon S. Roudiez (Oxford: Blackwell), pp. 148–58.

Parker, Alan Michale and Mark Willhardt (eds) (1996) *The Routledge Anthology of Cross-Gendered Verse* (London: Routledge).

Todd, Janet (ed.) (1980) *Gender and Literary Voice* (New York: Holmes & Meier Publishers).

—— (ed.) (1981) *Men by Women* (New York: Holmes & Meier Publishers).

Yeats, W.B. (1996[1989]) *Yeats's Poems*, ed. A. Norman Jeffares (London: Macmillan).

Part I
Empowering or Effacing
The Victorian Other?

1
Female Narrative Energy in the Writings of Dead White Males: Dickens, Collins and Freud

Madeleine Wood

> *For Each of Us Destiny Takes the Form of A Woman, or of Several*
>   – Sigmund Freud writing to Sándor
>   Ferenczi (Freud 1992: 528)

Introduction

This chapter will reassess the significance of female voices in the writings of three nineteenth-century men: Sigmund Freud, Charles Dickens and Wilkie Collins. I will argue that creating a sustained dialogue between the two novelists and the psychoanalyst opens up a far more radical space than has previously been located in the male-authored Victorian novel. By conceiving of narrative as a powerful possession, as Freud did in his discourse with hysterical women, we can identify new forms of feminine empowerment emerging in male-authored nineteenth-century texts.

Psychoanalytic theory, as it evolved throughout the 1890s, was increasingly reliant on the analysis of hysterical female voices. Freud's early 'pre-psychoanalytic' writings of the 1880s encompassed a wide range of neurological and psychological questions, but the publication of the seminal *Studies on Hysteria* in 1895 clearly positioned him as a writer and theorist of female stories. Sally Ledger links this phenomenon to a more general 'crisis in gender relations at the *fin de siècle*' (1997: 4), arguing that Freud and Breuer pathologized the figure of the New Woman as hysterical and 'frigid' (184–5). However, as we shall see, Ledger's dismissal of Freud (*The New Woman: Fiction and Feminism at the Fin de Siècle* mentions him only twice) does not account for the

15

complexities and ambivalences surrounding Freud's appropriation of this 'new' female voice: a voice that both provokes and destabilizes his own writing. Heike Bauer also emphasizes the significance of cross-gendered perspectives to the creation of nineteenth-century sexual theory. In her article, 'Theorizing Female Inversion: Sexology, Discipline, and Gender at the *Fin de Siècle*', Bauer discusses the importance of female inversion to Richard von Krafft-Ebing's seminal work *Psychopathia Sexualis*, arguing that Krafft-Ebing appropriated female experience (in this case female 'inversion') in order to construct a discursive space in which *male* sexuality could be examined in medical and legal terms (Bauer 2009: 97). However, despite the presence of female sexual experience in sexological works of the period, psychoanalytic engagement with female narratives remains specific. The 'talking cure' created by Josef Breuer and Anna O. engendered a form of medical encounter characterized by a sense of mutual seduction. The cross-gendered scene of the therapeutic praxis determined the creation of psychoanalytic narratives. This can be charted through a series of Freudian texts, including the *Studies on Hysteria, Fragment of an Analysis of a Case of Hysteria* (1905), and 'The Theme of the Three Caskets' (1913). There are two issues at stake in Freud's appropriation of the feminine which will be of direct relevance to the Victorian novelists: firstly, the disruptive presence of the (potentially hysterical or damaging) female voice within the male narrative, and secondly, the way in which the female figure simultaneously becomes the means for narrative resolution. This latter point can be related to two psychoanalytic concepts: transference and mourning. Transference refers to the transferral of desire within the analytic praxis: the subject of analysis displaces their desire or trauma onto the figure of the analyst, a repetition that ultimately enables a process of 'working through'. Transference was initially formulated within a cross-gendered pairing, that of male analyst and female subject. The efficacy of psychoanalytic therapy is therefore reliant on a concept that is dependent on the function of female voices as they relate to the male author/analyst and his discourse. Consequently, we cannot see transference as emerging solely from the female subject; counter-transference (the analyst's own investment in the female subject of analysis) is likewise central. This idea of counter-transference is vital to a consideration of Dickens's and Collins's novels because the authors and their male protagonists endow women with a unique determinate power: women are keepers of secrets, objects of desire and prisms through which all male stories must pass. At the same time, the authors alternately silence or authorize the surfacing of female voices.

Dickens's and Collins's novels typically hinge upon familial loss or conflict. This may be the primal death of the mother or father, or the revelation of secrets which undermine the legitimacy of the family, and threaten to destroy it from within. Female figures take on a peculiar significance in this context, becoming the means by which traumas can be worked through and losses can be mourned. Male mourning occurs via the knowing or unknowing intervention of the female love-object; however, Dickens and Collins retain crucial ambivalences. *Little Dorrit* (1982[1857]) and *Armadale* (1995[1866]) demonstrate how women both prohibit and enable mourning processes. This remains a narratological concern: it is the women's voices, their ability and desire to speak, or to remain silent, which determine the forms of mourning played out in the texts, and the way in which the narratives are resolved.

The psychoanalytic concepts of transference and mourning elucidate the paradoxical positioning of the female voice in the male-authored Victorian novel. As we shall see, in *Little Dorrit* the eponymous heroine herself suppresses the disruptive and peripheral hysteric voices of Miss Wade and Arthur's real mother. Amy nurses Arthur in the Marshalsea debtor's prison, and helps him come to terms with his financial and social failures, but only by simultaneously obscuring the familial trauma that determines his identity throughout the novel. In *Armadale* Collins more radically conflates the two female roles. Lydia Gwilt's transgressive voice, represented to the reader in her diary, provides the dynamism for the second half of the novel, overpowering the patrilinear story of father and sons. However, Lydia is also the only means by which the primal murder that drives the novel can be laid to rest. Both Lydia and Amy are talismans and keepers of secrets: centres of narrative energy through which the characters and the texts themselves orientate.

Freud, transference and Dora

Transference affects the progress of the analysis through the displacement of psychical affect from one object to another. The past is repeated in differential form in the analytic scene as the subject creates a 'transference neurosis' through the figure of the analyst (Laplanche and Pontalis 1988: 455–61). However, this clinical phenomenon is complicated by the fact that in the writing of his case histories Freud's persona was split into two clear roles, that of analyst and author. It is telling that in Josef Breuer's early case history of Anna O. (included in *Studies on Hysteria*) Breuer remains silent on the question of Anna's transferential desire (for himself), despite the fact that her phantom pregnancy caused the termination of the case. It was Freud who later revealed Anna's desire for Breuer to his English translator, James Strachey (Breuer and Freud 2001: 40, n. 1). Significantly for us here, we can observe that whatever the specificities of Anna's case, female desire is explicitly silenced even while it determines the very existence of the male narrative. It operates as a powerful negative space within the case history. In theoretical terms, this case provided the first (if silenced) encounter with clinical transference. Importantly, while in the *Studies on Hysteria* Freud saw transference as an unavoidable 'obstacle' (303) it was later embraced in 'Remembering, Repeating, Working Through' (1914) as an essential part of analytic procedure (Freud 2001b: 146–56). From Section IV of the *Studies on Hysteria* onwards the concept emerged as a specifically feminized concern as Freud struggled with the affective dynamics of the analytic situation. The feminization of the clinical concept is crucial to *Fragment of an Analysis of a Case of Hysteria.*

In order to construct *Fragment* Freud had to endow his own voice with a narrative authority, while translating the temporal reality of analysis. The 'Prefatory Remarks' demonstrate the importance of this case for Freud as a model of self-definition: he attempts to delimit his readership, condemning those who may read it as a '*roman de clef* designed for personal delectation' (Freud 2001a: 9, Freud's italics). However, it is precisely Freud's failure to control the story – his failure to prevent Dora from prematurely terminating the treatment – that inscribes the case with its theoretical force by enabling the subsequent discussion of clinical transference. The 'Postscript' of the case provides the first extended discussion of transference found in Freudian theory and is further annotated with Freud's cross-references added in 1923. Most importantly for us here, the cross-gendering of Dora's story – a female story told by a male analyst to a predominantly male readership – provides the dynamism for the progress of the analysis itself and its narration. The female subject is placed both at centre and the periphery of this *male* story (Freud's own story of psychoanalysis). As Steven Marcus observes in his important essay, 'Freud and Dora: Story, History, Case History', 'We begin to sense that it is his story that is being written and not hers that is being retold. Instead of letting Dora appropriate [sic] her own story, Freud became the appropriator of it. The case history belongs progressively less to her than it does to him' (Marcus 1990: 85).

'Dora' was the pseudonym of Ida Bauer, an 18-year-old girl analysed by Freud for three months in 1900. Dora was referred to Freud by her father and presented with numerous symptoms including a chronic cough and hoarseness of throat, which lacked clear somatic cause.

Her family situation was clearly conflicted: at the time of analysis she was resentful towards her previously adored father, and on openly unfriendly terms with her housewifely mother, who was sexually alienated from the father (Freud 2001a: 18–24). Freud affirms that Dora's case fitted the criteria for hysteria involving 'psychical trauma, a conflict of affects, and, – an additional factor which I brought forward [...] – a disturbance in the sphere of sexuality' (24). For Dora, this disturbance in the sphere of sexuality emerges from Herr and Frau K, intimate friends of her father. Prior to her analysis, Dora tells her father that Herr K has made sexual advances to her, and she wishes to leave the lake resort they are staying in, though Herr K denied this to Dora's family. This scene leads Freud to reveal another scene which was uncovered in analysis: when Dora was 14, Herr K had kissed her, and she felt a violent sense of revulsion and a gagging feeling in her throat.

The situation between Dora's family and Herr and Frau K was further complicated by the fact that Dora's (sexually impotent) father had a long term affair with Frau K. Dora becomes aware of this affair, and simultaneously wary of her father, whom she suspects of turning a blind eye to Herr K's advances in order to further his own illicit activities. A further layer of potential conflict is introduced by the fact that Dora adored and idolized Frau K throughout her teenage years; in addition, as Freud realized belatedly, Frau K was responsible for educating her sexually (120). Freud identifies several strands of eroticized conflict in Dora: firstly, the remainder of her childhood romance centred on her father (57); secondly, a heterosexual desire for Herr K; and thirdly, a partially unconscious desire for Frau K (62–3). Freud interprets Dora's illness as operating in a multivalent way, with each symptom heavily 'overdetermined'. Significantly, however, he interprets her loss of voice as being connected with Herr K, as the symptom only emerged when the latter was absent. Freud argues that unconsciously Dora refused to speak when the object of her love was not present.

Despite this, Dora herself consistently exceeds the restrictions placed on her narrative, as Freud's uneasy, heavily annotated, 'Postscript' reveals so eloquently. *Fragment* positions the female voice as excessive and hysteric, and in this context it is significant that Dora's was the first case history where dream analysis was placed at the heart of the narrative. Her voice barely surfaces in the 'Clinical Picture' and it is only in the dream analyses that she is cited directly. As dreams emerge from the unconscious it is implied that Dora herself is spoken *by* her dreams: her voice lacks agency. Freud argues in the 'Clinical Picture' that in addition to their somatic symptoms, hysterics suffer from a narratological ailment meaning 'communications run dry, leaving gaps unfilled and riddles unanswered' (Freud 2001a: 16). Psychological chronology is disrupted by the course of the illness and so hidden connections and meanings are lost (17). These issues are complicated, however, by the nature of Dora's symptoms and by her final visit to Freud in 1902. If, as Freud himself argued, her somatic loss of voice was related to an inability or unwillingness to speak, this is clearly significant. There is a failure of articulation inscribed in the symptom itself. When returning to Freud in 1902, two years after she terminated the treatment, Dora told Freud that her symptoms abated after she told Frau K that she knew about the affair, and when she obtained Herr K's confession to his behaviour at the lake, which she subsequently presented to her family (121). Even bearing in mind the undoubted overdetermination of somatic symptoms, her previous aphonia could arguably be seen as partly stemming from her fundamental lack of vocal agency, caught between her manipulative father, the deceitful Herr and Frau K, and even Freud himself. The female voice is bound up within a complex network of gendered relations. The aphonia dissipates – if only temporarily as we see from Felix Deutsch's account of Dora in later life (1990: 38) – when she is able to affect her reality significantly through her *voice*. Interestingly, Freud himself does not comment on the significance of this despite presenting the information to the reader.

As the title of Dora's analysis, <u>*Fragment*</u> *of an Analysis of a Case of Hysteria* (my emphasis), makes clear, the story remained unresolved for all concerned, but most notably for Freud himself. Freud interprets Dora's decision to terminate the treatment as resulting from her transferential feelings, saying 'I did not succeed in mastering the transference in good time' (2001a: 118). Freud speculates that Dora had begun unconsciously to associate him with Herr K as well as her father:

> Because of the unknown quantity in me which reminded Dora of Herr K, she took her revenge on me as she wanted to take her revenge on him, and deserted me as she believed herself to have been deceived and deserted by him. Thus she acted out an essential part of her recollections and phantasies instead of reproducing it in the treatment.
>
> (Freud 2001a: 119)

However, the language of the 'Postscript' implies more than Freud admits. His own counter-transferential investment in Dora saturates his language: he should have 'listened to the warning from [him]self'

(118); he was 'deaf' to the first warning; she 'deserted' him. Ideas of transgression and abandonment are played out in Freud's account of himself. It would of course be possible to consider the erotic dimensions of this counter-transference further. Marcus suggests Freud was sexually repulsed by Dora's repressive mode of sexuality (1990: 90) while Jacques Lacan emphasizes Freud's identification with Herr K (1990: 100). In this context Jacqueline Rose notes that 'Freud's failure to understand his own counter-transference produced a certain definition of sexuality as a *demand* on Dora, which, it should be noted, she rejects' (1990: 135, Rose's italics). Yet what concerns us most here is the way in which Dora represents narrative fulfillment for Freud: she betrays his needs as an analyst *and* as an author. Freud's wish to create a coherent case history is bound up with a complex set of desires. Clearly, Dora's decision to terminate the treatment rendered the story faulty, incomplete and failed in Freud's eyes: she did not handle her own – *his* story – properly. In this context it is significant that in the 'Postscript' Freud acknowledges Dora's power as a *reader* fully for the first time. He returns to the question of how Dora acquired access to the sexual writings which educated her: 'I ought to have guessed the main source of her knowledge on sexual matters could have been no-one but Frau K. – the very person who later on charged her with being interested in the same subjects' (Freud 2001a: 120). This detail creates an important nuance: the older woman transmits the *masculine* scientific works to the younger woman, simultaneously endowing them with homoerotic intensity. Freud himself does not draw out the implications of this detail, but clearly, its placement within the footnote shows how the female appropriation of male writings threatens the coherence of Freud's own 'story'. The belated acknowledgement of this crucial detail refracts back upon the analysis as he is forced to confess 'I was often brought to a standstill in the treatment of my cases or found myself in complete perplexity' (ibid.).

As we have seen, the counter-transferential relation is crucially double edged because it is located not only in the immediacy of the analytic session, but also in Freud's inscription of Dora within psychoanalytic theory. Interestingly, Dora's analysis dates from the same period as *The Interpretation of Dreams* (1900), which was the product of Freud's self-analysis. This process haunts Dora's history, both in the centrality accorded to her two dreams, and in Freud's own narrative investment in the figure of the 'analyst'. His personal investment in this figuration can operate as an affirmative, self-constituting measure, and as a rupturing textual dialectic. Reading Dora's case alerts us to the complexities at stake in the cross-gendering of narrative; it is not simply a case of who speaks for whom, but the place which women occupy in relation to the circulation of narrative.

The talisman and mourning

As we have seen in relation to Dora's history, the power of the female voice is bound up not only with speech, but also with silence. As Dora's 'desertion' of Freud revealed, the cessation of female speech can create a negative space that determines the process of male narrative. We can take this as a wider paradigm: the female figure has the power to stop narrative, to impede or to resolve the male story. The positioning of the female narrative within this model remains unstable, alternately surfacing, or being silenced, by the male author. Rather than seeing the silencing of the female voice simply in terms of male domination it will be more helpful to think about these issues in terms of the dynamics of narrative. With this in mind, and building upon the notion of counter-transference, we can think about women not only as 'voices', but also as invested objects: as 'talismans'. As we shall see in both *Little Dorrit* and *Armadale*, female figures become the means by which losses can be mourned, and traumatic narratives resolved.

Analytic art therapy helpfully introduces the idea of the talisman. Art therapy has been used in numerous praxes, but it is explored solely in relation to psychotic conditions in Joy Schaverien and Katherine Killick's book *Art, Psychotherapy and Psychosis*. In this praxis, the subject is encouraged to produce a picture expressing their state of mind, and this picture is then used to stimulate therapeutic sessions. Schaverien suggests that the subject has a psychological investment in the painting: 'the transference was enacted and held in the picture' (Killick and Schavarien 1997: 4). The subject's painting is described as a 'transactional object', a 'talisman', which can structure the relationship between analyst and patient (4). The painting becomes an almost magical presence in the subject's therapy, a place where conflicted desires can be safely held.

Through this idea of the 'talisman' we can see how transference and mourning could be helpfully linked. Freud's theory of mourning relies on the idea that a series of investments and disinvestments occur following the loss of a loved object (Freud 2001c: 239–58). In analytic art therapy the 'talisman' can help the subject perform a work of mourn-ing by enabling transference, or to express it another way, by enabling the affective reinvestment necessary for mourning to occur (in the case of a psychosis this lost object may relate to a portion of the self rather than an external other). I argue that in *Little Dorrit* and *Armadale* the female figures become talismanic for both the male authors and male protagonists. Victorian novels hinge upon parental loss, whether this is the physical loss of death, or the loss of parental integrity embedded in a family secret. Women are the means by which a mourning process can be enabled and these parental traumas worked through.

Freud tackled these issues in his essay 'The Theme of the Three Caskets' in which he argues that female figures bear a privileged relation to the creation of narrative. Here he analyses stories where men must, for whatever reason, choose between three women. Freud argues persuasively that women structure male life stories through their roles as mothers, lovers and daughters. Both literally and metaphorically they represent the 'fates' (Freud 1985: 247). Women punctuate the temporal progress of man's life and they impart a narrative structure to experience. Using *King Lear* as a paradigmatic (and conclusive) example of the relation between women and narrative, Freud demonstrates how Cordelia (as the female love-object and the preferred woman) determines Lear's destiny. As Cordelia is symbolically not only Lear's daughter, but also the longed-for and absent mother, Freud argues that she comes to represent male destiny in the abstract – a destiny that finally can only be death itself:

> But it is in vain that an old man yearns for the love of woman as he had it first from his mother; the third of the fates alone, the silent Goddess of Death, will take him in her arms.
>
> (Freud 1985: 247)

Freud's own analysis of *Lear* is tantalizingly brief, but we can add to it, using his premise as the basis for our reading. Furthering Freud, we note that Shakespeare correlates Lear's desire for a return to the Mother (embodied in his daughter) with a return to nothingness, a regression that represents the dissolution of the self. Lear speaks of setting his rest in 'her [Cordelia's] kind nursery' in the play's opening scene (Shakespeare 1972: Act I, Scene I, ll.123). Crucially, it is Cordelia's original refusal to speak, and to pander to Lear's transferential desire, that precipitates the drama. However, as the play progresses the dynamics change: Cordelia is endowed with authority and prestige, but her voice is denied. She is a talisman, whose death in the final act finally enables a process of mourning amidst the tragedy and disarray of the kingdom. It is clear from this that women's placing within male narratives is determined by a tense and irresolvable conflict between the woman as object of desire, and the woman as subject of desire. The way in which the female voice circulates in relation to this conflict is determinate for the form of narrative discourse produced. Women bear a privileged relation to the resolution of narrative, which is achieved through the representation of mourning, or the working-through of loss. In the 'Three Caskets' this is explicitly related to women's maternal function, and this point shall be a central aspect of the following analyses of *Little Dorrit* and *Armadale*.

Little Dorrit and the mother–son story

Before analysing female voice in *Little Dorrit* it will be helpful to recount some key plot details. The novel tells the story of two families, namely the Clennams and the Dorrits. At the point of the novel's opening, the Clennams comprise an aging, morally brutalizing mother, and her psychologically dispossessed 40-year-old son. The son, Arthur, returns to England from China after an absence of 20 years. He has spent his entire adult life there with his father, who has died just before the novel's action begins, while his mother has directed the family firm from London. Arthur lives an empty, nullified life, convinced that there is a lurking paternal guilt that demands reparation. It is only at the end of Volume II that the family's secret is revealed when we discover that Mrs Clennam is not actually Arthur's real mother, and that this unknown woman died years before. In the novel's dramatic denouement the family history is revealed: Arthur's father had a relationship with a young singer, who was mentored by Frederick Dorrit. When this was discovered, Gilbert Clennam (the father's uncle and guardian) arranged Mr Clennam's marriage with the strictly religious and pious Mrs Clennam-to-be. Mrs Clennam subsequently concealed the existence of Arthur's mother and brings up her illegitimate stepson in a state of unknowing, moralistic misery, while his real mother is incarcerated and raving. Gilbert Clennam later regrets his cruelty to Arthur's mother, and adds a codicil to his will leaving her a legacy of one thousand guineas; in the event of her death this is to be left to Frederick Dorrit's youngest female relative; Mrs Clennam purloins this legacy from Amy Dorrit, ultimately its only possible recipient. Meanwhile, the Dorrit family resides in the Marshalsea debtors' prison. The mother is dead and the father is a feckless and infantile figure. The family of three siblings and father are entirely supported by the efforts of the youngest child, Amy ('Little Dorrit') who works in the Clennam household. The novel largely charts the Dorrit family's rise and fall, and the relationship between the two families.

The narrative of *Little Dorrit* is relentlessly figured in gendered terms, and the transmission of texts is key to the novel's functioning. The third-person omniscient narration is primarily focalized through its hero, Arthur Clennam. On the surface then, the narration privileges male discourse and the masculine search for paternal origins (in this case, Arthur's conviction that there is a hidden crime in his father's history). However, the novel's structure and plot rely on female narratives. There are two disruptive hysteric voices in *Little Dorrit* that threaten to undermine the stability of Dickens's omniscient narrator, and have a formative impact upon the plot. The first female voice is that of Arthur's unnamed real mother who prior to her death wrote a series of letters, which are contained in an iron box and subsequently passed between a series of peripheral characters before being given to Amy Dorrit at the end of the novel. Significantly, as readers we never hear these letters; they seem to stand in for a principle of silencing, or the suppression of the female story. They acquire a kind of uncanny force, appearing sporadically throughout the novel in different hands. The mother figure emerges in this context as spectral – a revenant – whose very absence has a determinate role. Secondly, and perhaps more radically, Dickens provides us with the voice of Miss Wade. Miss Wade is an orphan (and probable lesbian) who wishes to revenge herself on society for its ill usage. Importantly, though, as we shall see, these excessive and hysteric voices are controlled, even suppressed, by the central female figure in the novel, by its heroine, Amy Dorrit.

Miss Wade is a peripheral figure in *Little Dorrit's* plotting. She is an acquaintance of Arthur Clennam's, an orphan woman, no longer in her girlhood, but still young. She is introduced to the reader as a 'handsome young Englishwoman, travelling quite alone, who had a proud observant face, and had either withdrawn herself from the rest or had been avoided by the rest – nobody herself excepted perhaps, could have decided which' (Dickens 1982: 18). Miss Wade's chief role in the novel is a disruptive one. She lures away another young orphan woman named Tattycoram (who as a child was adopted by Arthur's friends, the Meagles, and taken from the Foundling hospital) to live with her. Their relationship is subsequently characterized by a destructive homoeroticism, which becomes mutually persecuting and paranoiac. At the end of the novel, Tattycoram returns to the Meagles, chastened and humble, to take her place in the family, partly as daughter, but mostly as servant. Miss Wade's other function in the plot is to connive with the novel's villain, Rigaud, in his plan to blackmail Mrs Clennam by threatening to reveal her fraud (perpetrated against Amy Dorrit). Miss Wade acquires the iron box containing Arthur's real mother's writings from Rigaud. Unbeknownst to Miss Wade and Rigaud, Tattycoram then returns this box to Amy at the end of the novel. Miss Wade emerges as a destabilizing revengeful force throughout *Little Dorrit*, undermining the bourgeois family institution at every possible opportunity. What is most incredible is that this woman, seemingly antipathetic to all Victorian values, is granted a first-person narrative within the main body of the novel. Half way through the novel, she writes to Arthur Clennam, telling him the story of her life and recounting the reasons for her alliance with Tattycoram. Her letter is included verbatim as a complete chapter. Her self-styled 'History of a Self-Tormentor' (554–61) threatens to undermine the novel's ideological and affective underpinning. It starts with the powerful assertion, 'I have the misfortune of not being a fool. From a very early age I have detected what those about me thought they hid from me' (554). In the letter, Victorian virtues such as 'benevolence' (561) and charity (the only recourse for orphans in Victorian society) are lambasted as soulless hypocrisy, a reassertion of social hierarchies. Describing her first position as a governess, she observes:

> [...] the mother was young and pretty. From the first she made a show of behaving with great delicacy. I kept my resentment to myself; but, I knew very well that it was her way of petting the knowledge that she was my Mistress, and might have behaved differently to her servant if it had been her fancy.
>
> (Dickens 1982: 556)

The performance of charity was frequently the focus for Dickens's own critique throughout his writing career. Indeed, *Oliver Twist* (1838) relies on the juxtaposition between 'bad' and 'good' forms of charitable action as Oliver moves from the destitution of the workhouse, to the cosy bourgeois world of Mr Brownlow. It could be argued that Miss Wade articulates Dickens's lurking discomfort with the notion of charity and this claim can be reinforced if we consider that a similar discomfort emerges from within Tattycoram's history. Miss Wade's description of her treatment by her employers would be an accurate representation of Tattycoram's own position in the Meagles family. Tattycoram is accepted as a member of the family in regards to the duties of care and obligation she is expected to perform, but she is economically excluded by working for them as a maid. However, Dickens finally rejects the radical potential of his own thought by returning Tattycoram to her place within the Meagles family at the end of the novel.

The appropriation of the female voice, represented by Miss Wade, allows Dickens to call into question the structure of his own moral enterprise. Many things that are disquieting and unresolved in the novel are transferred onto this transgressive anti-heroine. It is highly significant that she is figured (even in her own account) as a hysteric figure. Her childhood history turns upon her obsessive, persecutory and paranoiac love for another little girl, a love that eventually leads to Miss Wade's self-willed exclusion from her school. This childhood love is the prototype for the relationship with Tattycoram. What is particularly interesting about the relationship between Miss Wade and Tattycoram itself is that it seems to repeat, outside of a family structure, many of the same conflicts we see in the Clennam and Dorrit families. Miss Wade's fierce resentment about her orphan origins provides a dark shadow to Arthur Clennam's own melancholic despair regarding his family. In Chapter 2, Arthur describes his childhood to Mr Meagles:

> I have no will. That is to say [...] next to none that I can put into action now. Trained by main force; broken, not bent; heavily ironed with an object on which I was never consulted and which was never mine; shipped away to the other end of the world before I was of age, and exiled there until my father's death there a year ago; always grinding in a mill I hated; what is to be expected of *me* in middle life? Will, purpose, hope? All those lights were extinguished before I could sound the words.
>
> (Dickens 1982: 17)

Miss Wade articulates the rage proper to Arthur Clennam himself. She acts out a revenge which should be the province of Arthur and his real mother. Her paranoia and suspicion seem to relate back to a crime which has been committed in the novel, but not in fact perpetrated against her. Looking at her letter we can see significant motifs. Most tellingly, Dickens returns repeatedly to the question of sight. Miss Wade's jealous eyes are aflame with paranoid sight: 'I would burn my sight by throwing myself in the fire, rather than I would endure to look at their plotting faces' (556). Arthur's own eyes are closed or at least narrowed throughout the novel. In contrast, Miss Wade is eager to discover betrayals and slights as both a child and a young woman, a psychotic female Oedipus, who projects the mysteries of her origins onto every aspect of her life. The connection between the two characters is redrawn through the fate of Arthur's mother's writings, which are in Miss Wade's possession for much of the novel. Rather than returning his mother's writings to him, Miss Wade sends him her own story; rather than reading his own history, Arthur reads Miss Wade's. Through this technique, Dickens is able to project a radical, rebellious, female potential into *Little Dorrit*, without entirely destroying the sanctity of the maternal.

This question of the mother's writings brings us to Amy Dorrit's tal-ismanic role in the novel. Amy herself emerges as a keeper of secrets, a destroyer (rather than creator) of narrative. The heroine of the novel, Amy (known by her friend Maggy as 'Little Mother') is chiefly charac-terized by her compulsive acts of self-sacrifice, and her assumption of the maternal role towards her father, and later towards Arthur. After his imprisonment for debt in the Marshalsea in the final sections of the novel, Amy nurses Arthur back to health and hope. As Dickens's images and language reveal, Amy becomes correlated with an all-encompassing ideal of maternal, nurturing, love:

> Yet Clennam, listening to the voice as it read to him, heard in it all that great Nature was doing, heard in it all the soothing songs she sings to man. At no Mother's knee but hers, had he ever dwelt in his youth on hopeful promises, on playful fancies, on the harvests of tenderness and humility [...] But, in the tones of the voice that read to him, there were memories of an old feeling of such things, and echoes of every merciful and loving whisper that had ever stolen to him.
>
> (Dickens 1982: 679)

As this passage makes clear, this is the love which Arthur has always lacked, separated from his biological mother, and under the strictures of his cruel and exacting stepmother. The language here is saturated with mournful potential; 'the memories of old feelings', 'echoes' of childhood resonate through this scene. Dickens's language here implies that Arthur's love for Amy would enable a process of mourning for his real mother, whose absence is felt everywhere, despite his total lack of knowledge regarding her. In this context, it seems even more perverse that Amy keeps the secret of his mother from him, promising Mrs Clennam she will not reveal it. At the end of the novel Amy asks Arthur to burn the unread letter from Rigaud which would reveal the mysteries of his family to him: his rightful inherit-ance is denied to him, just as the financial legacy from Gilbert Clennam was denied to her. The nothingness, which defines Arthur's identity from the beginning of the novel, is overwritten by a sentimental narrative, which posits (as in *Lear*) the figure of the daughter as the true mother. As Freud argues in the 'Three Caskets', the process of mourning, even death itself, is correlated with the maternal figure; however interestingly, instead of enabling Arthur's mourning by granting him access to his mother's writings, she prohibits it. As the novel's 'Little Mother' Amy becomes representative of mourning in the abstract. When Tattycoram returns the box, the narrator paraphrases Amy's thoughts:

> The secret was safe now! She could keep her own part of it from him; he should never know of her loss; in time to come, he should know all that was of import to himself; but, he should never know what concerned her, only. That was all past, all forgiven, all forgotten.
>
> (Dickens 1982: 677)

Amy binds together the various strands of the plot, in both literal and affective terms. She is the crux which joins the stories of the two families: the Clennams and the Dorrits. Arthur's Oedipal failings seem to leave him as an empty presence, a 'nobody'. His final unknowingness is one of the novel's most intriguing characteristics. Through a grand transferential gesture, Dickens displaces the parental conflicts onto the strange girl-woman Amy Dorrit. Amy is the all-knowing presence, who binds the identity of her lover through his maternal transference. A female talisman: a holding place for narrative, and therefore the means through which the narrative can be resolved. However, through his representation of Miss Wade, and the inclusion of her story, we can see that Dickens was simultaneously alert to the radical potential of the female voice. Just as in Dora's case, we can see tension emerge between the representation of the female figure as the object of a powerful male counter-transference, and the surfacing of an excessive, symptomatic female voice. Dickens deals with this problem by splitting these characteristics across the two figures – heroine and anti-heroine – Amy and Miss Wade. Collins, as the more radical author, conflates both characteristics within the same woman – Lydia Gwilt – in *Armadale*.

Female destiny: *Armadale*

Collins's *Armadale* has an immensely convoluted plot, even in relation to other Victorian novels, and for our purposes here there are several strands which must be drawn out. The novel is driven by a murder, which occurs in the pre-history of the novel. One man named Allan Armadale murders another man named Allan Armadale; they are not related (excepting a very distant cousinship), but are drawn together through the disrupted process of paternal inheritance. Briefly, the original Allan Armadale, later known as Fergus Ingleby, is disinherited and the second Allan Armadale (né Allan Wrentmore) becomes Ingleby's father's heir. Ingleby takes his revenge on Armadale by marrying the latter's intended bride (Jane Blanchard) through an act of forgery, perpetrated by Jane's 12-year-old maid, Lydia Gwilt, with Jane's knowledge and blessing. Armadale subsequently murders Ingleby by locking him inside the cabin on a sinking ship, *La Grace de Dieu*. At the opening of the novel the dying Armadale writes a letter confessing his crime to his son, who assumes the pseudonym Ozias Midwinter following his father's death (although his name is also legally Allan Armadale). Meanwhile, Jane Blanchard has given birth to a son, fathered by Fergus Ingleby, and this child is also Allan Armadale. The two sons meet and become friends, and Ozias becomes aware that Allan is the son of the man his father murdered. Driven by an obsessive compulsion, Ozias confesses everything to Allan's friend, the Reverend Brock, who, in a key letter, convinces him that he can play a part for good in his friend's life. For the first two Books of the novel, the narrative charts the relationship between the two young men, posing the question of whether the sins of the fathers will be visited inevitably upon the sons, or if Ozias can make reparation for his father's crime. The first two Books are structured around three key texts (embedded within the third-person omniscient narration): Armadale Senior's confession to Ozias; the letter from Reverend Brock; and the transcription of the younger Allan's prophetic dream. Allan has this dream when the two young men find themselves (against all probabilities) on the stranded *La Grace de Dieu*, where the primal murder happened years before. The dream is proved to be accurate on all counts as the novel progresses, and depicts Allan at the mercy of a mysterious woman (later revealed to be Lydia Gwilt herself).

It is within this masculine context that Lydia Gwilt emerges, and takes control of both plot and narrative discourse. In *Armadale* Collins self-consciously plays with the idea of fate as a feminine figure, but his fate is far from being a Cordelia or an Amy Dorrit. Importantly, Lydia is still (like Amy) the means by which the narrative strands can be drawn together and finally resolved, that is, she becomes a transferential object and the means of resolution. Her own death at the end of the novel provides a point of convergence for Ozias and Allan's mourning: Allan never discovers that his father was murdered, or that his parents were married on the basis of a forged document. Lydia's transferential role is, like Amy's, partly self-willed, as she purposefully draws together the strands of the story. However, Lydia is also a blazing narrative presence as she speaks to the reader directly through her diary. In Book III the female narrative literally interrupts the male, as the villainous Mother Oldershaw's bathetic letter to Lydia takes over the telling of the story from the third-person narrator. The two women exchange a series of letters plotting how Lydia can use her knowledge of Allan's parents' dubious marriage to her own advantage (Lydia is at this point ignorant of Ozias's role in the drama). Collins's narrative structure is imploded through the introduction of female voices. The thematic centrality of the primal murder implies the primacy of male subjectivity and the inescapability of paternal legacies. While this is initially a male problem, passed from father to son, through the radical intervention of Lydia (and initially Mother Oldershaw), feminine identity becomes ascendant. Agency is removed from both Ozias and Allan and replaced within Lydia. The question of how Ozias will respond to the overwhelming paternal demand for loyalty (expressed in his father's confession) becomes somewhat effaced, even irrelevant. The violent confrontation with personal identity becomes Lydia's concern; she gazes as herself in her diary and we gaze with her. The novel's thematic reconciliation of selfhood can only be resolved through her and her writing.

This is complicated, however, by the fact that it is Ozias who precipitates the novel's move into Lydia's diary by telling her his family history. In the light of Ozias's confession Lydia decides to abandon her letter to Mother Oldershaw and plot around her discovery alone. By telling Lydia his story Ozias transfers narrative responsibility for it onto Lydia herself. Lydia is undoubtedly possessed by the paternal narrative which Ozias transmits to her. Recounting his confession in her diary, she asks herself, 'Let me think, what *haunts* me to begin with?' (Collins 1995: 424, Collins's italics). Her subsequent methodical setting out of the novel's complex pre-history engenders her murderous and audacious plan which would settle 1200 pounds on her for life: she will marry Ozias, murder Allan, and then pose as Allan's widow at his estate (Thorpe Ambrose) so she can receive the generous inheritance granted to females marrying into the family.

Collins associates female writings with a flirtatious process of revelation–concealment, and the diary becomes a veritable narrative striptease. When Lydia places a dose of arsenic in Allan's lemonade in Naples (directly fulfilling the predictions of Allan's earlier prophetic dream), she initially refuses to impart the incident to her diary, saying, 'I won't put down what I said to him – or what I did afterwards. I'm sick of Armadale' (559). Lydia subsequently reveals it, displacing the story from herself by transcribing a conversation between her and Ozias in which she cries out to him, '*Do you think I tried to poison him?*' (562, Collins's italics).

She never directly admits, even to the reader, what has been placed in his glass. Lydia is split between self and written-self, and the diary-self begins to take on a particularly transgressive resonance: it becomes the partner in her crimes the 'secret friend of my wretchedest and wickedest hours' (545). Through the splitting engendered by writing, Lydia moves from being incapable of murder and unwilling to write, to being both murderess and authoress. It is her own rereading of her salacious diary that provokes her to take up her murderous cause once more. Writing a new entry in the diary she comments:

> No; books don't interest me, I hate the whole tribe of authors. I think I shall look back through these pages, and live my life over again when I was plotting and planning, and finding a new excitement to occupy me in every new hour of the day.
>
> (Collins 1995: 547)

She has put her diary to one side when she marries Ozias, and it is only when she is willing to return to her murderous plan to poison Allan that she begins writing once more. In her first re-entry into the diary in Book V she makes it clear that the diary operates as a replacement for both friend and lover:

> Why have I broken my resolution? [...] Because I am more friendless than ever; because I am more lonely than ever, though my husband is sitting writing in the room next to me. My misery is a woman's misery, and it *will* speak – here, rather than nowhere; to my second self, in this book [...].
>
> (Collins 1995: 545)

As this passage shows, the diary takes the place of the male lover, while also becoming the *only* feminine exchange possible in the novel. It is telling that Lydia perceives Ozias's writing (he is working as a journalist at this point) as a competitor for her affections, and looking at the dynamics of the text this is not so strange. For Ozias, the recipient of a murderous confession, writing is associated with paternal narratives, with an adherence to the word of the Father; whether this is his own father, the Reverend Brock, or God. Lydia correctly feels that there is something in this male written word which conflicts with her interests. Feeling this, she takes up *her* pen once more.

Lydia's narrative is seductive, poisonous and potentially deadly. But despite this, she herself becomes the only means by which the primal paternal crime can be expiated. The final breaking off of Lydia's diary is directly correlated with her impending death as she feels a foreshadowing of disaster approaching its final page (611–2). The end of the diary implies an end of her fateful, plotting role; events are unavoidably set in motion, and will now take their course. When the two young men find themselves in the sanatorium, it is Ozias, rather than his friend, who is asleep in the sealed room into which Lydia passes the poisonous gas, intended to kill Allan. Without Lydia's intercession, Ozias would be doomed to unconsciously take Allan's place, saving him from the deadly legacy inherited from their fathers (and making reparation for his father's crime). Yet by saving Ozias, and taking his place in the gas filled chamber, Lydia herself usurps the reparative act intended for the 'son' of a guilty father. Her fated role, in the end, is her own death. The paternal story is transferred onto Lydia, and a displaced sacrifice takes place. This can be linked back to the 'Three Caskets' and Cordelia's role in *King Lear*. Like Cordelia's death, Lydia's suicide is necessary for the paternal crimes to be worked-through, or mourned. Ozias is able to make peace with his father's guilty past through Lydia's sacrifice. Significantly for our discussion, Lydia is also linked to the mother figure via Allan's family history. As we noted, as a child of 12 Lydia was instructed to perpetrate a forgery (a capital offence at the time when the novel is set) by Allan's mother: Jane Blanchard. Collins's explicitly states that Lydia's death and Ozias's silence remove the risk of Allan discovering this crime, and 'left the memory of Allan's mother, what he had found it – a sacred memory in the heart of his son' (677). Both in terms of paternal and the maternal legacies, Lydia's self-willed death is essential for the young men to mourn their parents.

It is critical that even at the moment of her sacrifice, at the moment when her talismanic status seems most assured, Collins returns to Lydia's voice. Just before she steps into the gas filled chamber Lydia intervenes in the paternal story once more by writing Ozias a letter, on the back of the Reverend Brock's letter no less (the letter which crucially defended Allan and Ozias's friendship earlier in the novel). This is the last written legacy Ozias receives, in a novel that turns upon the complex transmission of texts. In the final chapter, Ozias seemingly reasserts the primacy of the father by quoting the Reverend Brock's letter to Allan. However, if we consider the haunting resonance of texts in *Armadale* then Ozias's final eulogizing of the Clergyman's letter pronounces a profound question mark over the end of the novel. He may be quoting directly from Brock's letter, but it is Lydia's words blessing Ozias's future that are written on the final page. Unacknowledged by Ozias at this point, they remain blazed across it nevertheless. Collins's fragmentary use of the cross-gendered voice undermines the persecutory patrilinear narrative of *Armadale*, as well as subtly calling into question the Christian story of filial redemption imposed in the final chapter. Reparation for the past does take place, but it can only do so through feminine intervention.

Conclusion

The texts considered here, *Fragment of an Analysis of a Case of Hysteria*, *Little Dorrit* and *Armadale*, are predicated on the principle of a gendered confrontation which has a formative impact on the creation of narrative. The question of where the woman is situated in relation to the circulation of narrative is the key concern in each. Freud's *Fragment* reveals the centrality of (counter-) transference to male-authored narratives, and we see this perpetuated in both of the novels. Women become the recipients of male stories, and through their relation to the maternal, become the means by which these stories can be worked-through, or losses can be mourned. In the two literary texts female figures are granted privileged status in the circulation of male stories: both Amy Dorrit and Lydia Gwilt hold the key to the family secrets which provide the novels with their dynamism. They are narrative talismans, binding the convoluted Victorian plots, as well as becoming the holding place for a series of masculine desires which remain only partially worked through. Collins's radicalism ultimately grants the female written word symbolic (and aesthetic) precedence, but it is nevertheless in his final schema hidden behind the voice of the Clergyman. Like Dora and Miss Wade, Lydia's voice is endowed with the power to affirm or challenge male narratives, and as such is the focus for a perpetual anxiety, even as the novel celebrates Lydia's seductive power. The conflict created between the representations of women as objects of desire, and subjects of desire, results in fragmentary and ambivalent narratives, where the female voice surfaces as an uncanny and pervasive force. The question of how the female voice can survive this object–subject problematic is central to an understanding of Freud, Dickens and Collins; but provocatively, despite the women's ultimate silence (whether self-willed or imposed), they preserve control of masculine discourses in each of the texts under consideration.

Works Cited

Bauer, Heike (2009) 'Theorizing Female Inversion: Sexology, Discipline and Gender at the *Fin de Siècle*', *Journal of the History of Sexuality*, 18/1: 84–102.

Breuer, Josef and Sigmund Freud (2001) *Studies on Hysteria: the Standard Edition of the Complete Psychological Works of Sigmund Freud, Vol. 2*, trans. James Strachey (London: Vintage).

Collins, Wilkie (1995[1866]) *Armadale*, ed. John Sutherland (London: Penguin).

Dickens, Charles (1982[1857]) *Little Dorrit*, ed. Harvey Peter Sucksmith (Oxford: Oxford University Press).

—— (1999[1838]) *Oliver Twist: Or the Parish Boy's Progress*, ed. Stephen Gill (Oxford: Oxford University Press).

Deutsch, Felix (1990) 'A Footnote to Freud's "Fragment of a Case of Hysteria"' in Charles Bernheimer and Claire Kahane (eds), *In Dora's Case: Freud – Hysteria – Feminism* (New York: Columbia University Press), pp. 35–44.

Ferenczi, Sándor and Sigmund Freud (1992) *Correspondence: 1908–1914*, eds Eva Brabant, Ernst Falzeder and Patrizia Giampieri-Deutsch (Paris: Calmann-Lévy).

Freud, Sigmund (1976) *The Interpretation of Dreams*, trans. James Strachey (London: Vintage).

—— (1985) 'The Theme of the Three Caskets', in *Art and Literature*, trans. James Strachey (London: Penguin).

—— (2001a) *Fragment of an Analysis of a Case of Hysteria*, in *The Standard Edition of the Complete Psychological Works of Sigmund Freud, Vol. 7* trans. James Strachey and Anna Freud (London: Vintage), pp. 1–122.

—— (2001b) 'Remembering, Repeating, Working Through', in *The Standard Edition of the Complete Psychological Works of Sigmund Freud, Vol. 12*, trans. James Strachey (London: Vintage), pp. 146–56.

—— (2001c) 'Mourning and Melancholia', in *The Standard Edition of the Complete Psychological Works of Sigmund Freud, Vol. 14*, trans. James Strachey (London: Vintage), pp. 239–58.

Killick, Katherine and Joy Schaverien (1997) 'Introduction', in Katherine Killick and Joy Schaverien (eds), *Art, Psychotherapy and Psychosis* (London and New York: Routledge).

Lacan, Jacques (1990) 'Intervention on Transference', in Charles Bernheimer and Claire Kahane (eds), *In Dora's Case: Freud – Hysteria – Feminism* (New York: Columbia University Press), pp. 92–104.

Laplanche, Jean and Jean Bertrad Pontalis (1988) *The Language of Psychoanalysis* (London: Karnac).

Ledger, Sally (1997) *The New Woman: Fiction and Feminism at the Fin de Siècle* (Manchester: Manchester University Press).

Marcus, Steven (1990) 'Freud and Dora: Story, History, Case History', in Charles Bernheimer and Claire Kahane (eds), *In Dora's Case: Freud – Hysteria – Feminism* (New York: Columbia University Press), pp. 56–91.

Rose, Jacqueline (1990) 'Dora: Fragment of an Analysis', in Charles Bernheimer and Claire Kahane (eds), *In Dora's Case: Freud – Hysteria – Feminism* (New York: Columbia University Press), pp. 128–48.

Schaverien, Joy (1997) 'Transference and Transactional Objects in the Treatment of Psychosis', in Katherine Killick and Joy Schaverien (eds), *Art, Psychotherapy and Psychosis* (London and New York: Routledge).

Shakespeare, William (1972) *King Lear*, ed. Kenneth Muir (Surrey and London: Arden).

2
'Everything depend[s] on the fashion of narration': Women Writing Women Writers in Short Stories of the *Fin-de-Siècle*

Bryony Randall

Introduction

Elaine Showalter's 1993 collection of short stories entitled *Daughters of Decadence: Women Writers of the Fin-de-Siècle* contains 18 stories, three of which – or, put another way, one sixth – have identical themes, and two almost identical plotlines, all three describing the encounter between an aspiring female writer and an established male one. The three stories span a 16-year period; the earliest story, Constance Fenimore Woolson's 'Miss Grief', was published in 1880; 'Lady Tal' by Vernon Lee (Violet Paget) came out in 1892, and Mabel E. Wotton's 'The Fifth Edition' was published in 1896. The repetition of this particular theme within this landmark anthology is striking, particularly so perhaps to the reader whose first experience of reading stories of this period by women is through this collection. What is more, all three stories focalize their narrative through the male writer figure, whether in a first- or third-person narrative – despite being stories by women writers about women writers.[1]

The popularity of plotlines involving female authors in this period has attracted critical attention. 'One of the striking features of many New Woman novels', observed Sally Ledger in 1997, 'is that they are peopled with female writers of feminist fiction' (27); Ledger gives as examples novels by Sarah Grand (*The Beth Book, Ideala*), Mary Cholmondeley (*Red Pottage*) and Mona Caird (*The Daughters of Danaus*). This observation recurs in subsequent critical work. For instance, Lynn Pykett has written specifically on the prevalence of the female artist figure in New Women writing, observing that the 'use of the female artist figure is [...] a component of the self-reflexivity that characterizes much New

Woman writing [...] by making writing women its subject New Woman fiction foregrounds the conditions of its own production' (2000: 136). Ann Heilmann has a chapter on the figuring of the woman writer in New Woman writing in her monograph published in the same year as Pykett's essay. However, these critics pay relatively limited attention to the specific narrative voice of the texts, and in particular (where it appears) to the use of a male narrator or focalizer. Certainly, this narrative choice was not uncommon in short stories by New Woman writers, frequently in order to satirize male posturing, foibles or prejudices.[2] My discussion is therefore distinct from existing scholarship in the field in its focus on narrative voice and perspective.

What is more, Pykett, Ledger and Heilmann mainly discuss novels, while I am concerned with the short story. Heilmann does discuss one of the stories I look at here, Mabel E. Wotton's 'The Fifth Edition'. But her broadly psychoanalytic reading of women's writing on women writers, organized around the metaphor of mothering, neither raises the question of the narrative voice, nor does it attend to the distinctive qualities of the short story form, which is a live issue here. Angelique Richardson's section on 'The Short Story and the Speeding up of Life', in the introduction to her collection of short stories from the turn of the last century, begins with H.G. Wells's observation that in the 1890s 'Short Stories broke out everywhere' (Wells, cited in Richardson 2002: xlv). Richardson links this proliferation in the form to a number of economic and social factors, but also considers the specific link between women and the short story, noting that it 'was easier [for women writers] to raise new subjects in a new form', and offering 'practical reasons' for the appeal of the short story to the woman writer: 'short stories, by virtue of their brevity, combined more easily with marriage and motherhood' (xlviii, l). However, Richardson is more concerned with the reasons for the development of the short story as a popular form for the woman writer, than with an analysis of the formal features of the genre and the opportunities these offer.

It was, of course, not only women who wrote about women writers at this time. As Showalter notes in the introduction to her collection, 'Male novelists of the period, like Oscar Wilde and Henry James, frequently satirized women writers in their work; and women writers returned the compliment'; indeed, Showalter notes, 'Two of the stories [in this collection, namely those by Lee and Woolson] focus on a male novelist very much like Henry James' (1993: xv) (although Wooton's 'The Fifth Edition' also features a male novelist and it is in this story that the male focalizer is most heavily satirized). The satirizing of women writers was a symptom of anxiety at the time about the feminization of literature.

Sally Ledger notes that, for example, Henry James's 'The Death of a Lion', appearing in the first edition of *The Yellow Book* (the foremost avant-garde periodical of the time) in April 1894, 'laments the feminization of literary culture at the *fin de siècle* [...] in a narrative that echoes George Gissing's *New Grub Street*, published three years earlier' (2007: 9); she describes an article by Arthur Waugh published in the same issue as an 'invective against women's writing' (10). What aroused this anxiety was the increasing number of working women writers, particularly successful ones; the increase in professional working women in this period was largely a result of the female 'surplus' identified in the 1851 census, which found that there were 400,000 unmarried women in the United Kingdom.[3] As Richardson and Willis note, these women 'posed a considerable if inadvertent threat to separate-sphere ideology: uncontained by spouses they risked spilling into the public sector, becoming public and visible' (2001: 4) – and indeed were they to choose writing as a means of making a living, becoming a very real commercial threat to established or aspiring male writers. Just as writing was starting to become acknowledged as a profession, with the establishment of the Society of Authors in 1884, so many male writers became increasingly concerned to protect it from what they saw as its infiltration by women writers. And this anxiety was itself bound up with the anti-New Woman rhetoric of the period, which sought to resist the social, political and cultural advances being made by a significant number of women who, while diverse in their beliefs and modes of activity, refused to comply with established norms of femininity, through political campaigning, personal conduct and professional career-building.[4] The question of a writer's gender identity was, then, a particularly fraught one at this time.

Sensitivity about the gender identity of the writer in this period is signalled by the fact that women still frequently published under male pseudonyms, such as George Egerton, George Fleming and Vernon Lee – though the latter was chosen more for its ambiguity than its masculinity. Note, however, that even those authors using a male pseudonym were often widely recognized as female. This is obvious from, for example, the advertisements placed in *The Yellow Book* for writing by women under male pseudonyms; or the engraving of George Egerton appearing in the fifth volume of that journal, in April 1895, from which her gender is clear (7). Marianne DeKoven's use of the terminology 'female-' or 'male-signed', in her landmark monograph *Rich and Strange: Gender, History, Modernism*, is intriguing in this context (1991: 4). Throughout her discussion of late nineteenth and early twentieth-century writers of both genders, DeKoven uses this '-signed' formulation, rather than, for example, 'text with a male/female author'. Interestingly, this usage is not discussed or addressed directly in any way in DeKoven's work, as if it is taken for granted that this is the only legitimate way to discuss the gender of the 'author' of a text – gender can only be located in the signature appended to the text in the place that designates 'author'. DeKoven's striking terminology evokes the uncoupling of gender signifiers from the physical body made possible through authorship. And the significance of this uncoupling – which in turn raises questions of what is significant about the gender of an author, and the way that gender is displayed, drawn attention to, or disguised – is intensified when discussing, as I do here, stories in which female (if not all female-signed) authors write about female writers but, to a greater or lesser extent, in the voice of a male writer.

Narrative voice and structure in 'Miss Grief', 'The Fifth Edition' and 'Lady Tal'

Brief outlines of these three stories will indicate the extent of their proximity in terms of narrative voice and structure, and highlight the narratological approach I am taking to these texts. Woolson's 'Miss Grief' and Wotton's 'The Fifth Edition' are almost identical in structure, but very different in narrative voice. In both a successful male writer meets a struggling female writer, is flattered by the woman's admiration of his work, reads and is impressed by her writing and takes an interest in helping her to get her work published, but this interest comes to nothing (for the woman, at least) and the woman eventually dies of illness brought on by poverty. In 'Miss Grief', the narrator is the male writer himself, writing retrospectively, and the narrative is characterized by the increasing accordance between the narrator and what Wayne Booth, in his discussion of possible varieties of narrator, calls the 'norms of the work' (1996: 127). Put another way, the narrator is broadly reli- *really?* able, and becomes increasingly sympathetic as the story progresses. 'The Fifth Edition', however, uses a third-person narrative focalized through the male writer, and here the focalizer of the narrative remains strongly at odds with the 'norms of the work' almost throughout. The absolute opposition between the focalizer and the 'norms of the work' is emphasized through the third-person narrative voice, which, though not dramatized, appears so vivid as almost to represent a third central character in the story. The specific effects of these different narrative approaches will be examined below; what is significant is that neither story uses the female character as either narrator or focalizer.

The third story, Lee's 'Lady Tal', similarly begins with a successful male writer meeting a woman who then reveals her novelistic aspirations, but this story is almost an inversion of the others as regards the features of the characters. In 'Miss Grief' and 'The Fifth Edition', the women are poor, old (or at least older than the male writer characters) and physically vulnerable, but clearly talented, while the men are confident and successful. In 'Lady Tal', the woman is rich, young and physically vigorous but relatively untalented, while the male writer character is successful but relatively malleable. Although there will not be space here to explore all the interpretative permutations these comparisons offer (and I devote more space to Wotton and Woolson than to Lee) they nevertheless indicate the extreme proximity, either direct or inverted, between the structures of these texts. Of most significance here is the fact that the narrative of 'Lady Tal' is, again, focalized through the male writer not the female aspirant. (There is in fact a first-person narrator, though their presence is barely perceptible, the pronoun 'I' appearing only twice, which means that the narrative reads like a third-person narrative.) My key question is, thus, about the effect of the cross-gendering of the narrative voices in these stories all of which offer a portrait of the aspiring woman writer in the late nineteenth century. By paying close attention to narrative voice, I may not go quite so far as Franklyn Leyden, the antihero of one of these stories, in saying that 'Everything depend[s] on the fashion of narration' (Wotton 1993: 148), but I will certainly argue that much hangs upon it.[5]

'The Fifth Edition': satirizing the masculine and the art/life binary

The story in which the male perspective is most clearly used against itself, to critique the masculine literary world, is Mabel E. Wotton's 'The Fifth Edition'. In this story, a successful young writer, Franklyn Leyden, intends to pay a visit to a friend, but on arriving at the relevant address, finds that the rooms are now occupied by someone else. Just as he is about to leave, he notices that one of his own books is out on the table; this, of course, arouses his curiosity (as well as flattering his ego). Thus when Janet Suttaby, the new occupier of the rooms, enters, he probes her on her interest in literature, and discovers that she too is a writer; she makes her living writing short pieces for magazines and periodicals. But she has also written a novel, and having persuaded her to show him the manuscript, he is sufficiently impressed to suggest that they collaborate on the work in order to get it published. She refuses, insisting instead that he simply take it, as a gift from her; he eventually agrees but promises to give her 30 pounds for it (she has said she thought she might get 10). He rewrites the story – using Miss Suttaby herself as a model for the refigured heroine – and it is another great success. However, he puts off giving her the full sum he has promised for several months, and when eventually – on the date of the publication of the novel's fifth edition – he visits her rooms intending to give her the balance he owes, he finds that she has gone. Unbeknownst to him, she has in fact died 'of practical starvation' (Wotton 1993: 163).

The narrative arc, as well as the unarguably repellent conduct and characteristics of Leyden, make clear the 'norms of the work' which place our sympathies entirely with Miss Suttaby. We might, then, wonder why the story should be focalized through its antihero. This narrative strategy might tend to reinforce the idea that it is men to whom we should be paying attention; that masculine conceptions of the female writer are the crux of the problem facing women writers. This is not to say that changing male perspectives on female writers was not a necessary part of improving their lot. But, arguably, keeping the text's focus on a man might mitigate the possible impact of its feminist politics. Why should our attention be given to this offensive young egotist? It is, surely, Miss Suttaby whose interior life the text wishes us to value.

The narrative strategy in this story (exhibiting a level of gender stereo-typing which stands in stark contrast to the problematizing of gender in Woolson's story of 16 years before, as we shall see) provides a means for attacking masculine behaviour but from a supposedly masculine posi-tion, on the basis that the most powerful place from which to critique a position is from within. This is effected by the heavily satirical mode of narration. See, for example, this representative instance of the third-person narrator's commentary, which implicitly condemns Leyden's self-congratulation on having restrained himself from making romantic advances to Miss Suttaby:

> Despite the stretch of years between them, the temptation assailed him to flash into those eyes the love-light their serenity had never known, but strong though it was, he resisted it, applauding himself immensely for his self-denial [...] being the man he was, that he still contrived to leave her peace undisturbed, may doubtless be counted unto him for righteousness.
>
> (Wotton 1993: 153)

So, while we are only given access to Leyden's interiority and not Miss Suttaby's, the effect is to criticize rather than arouse sympathy for him.

Further, this highly self-aware narrative, with its almost dramatized third-person narrator, foregrounds the telling of the tale, reminding us that there *is* a (real) female writer behind this story. Here, the narrative and biographical cues to align narrator, implied author and Mabel E. Wotton herself are extremely strong. While little is known about Wotton, what we do know indicates her own struggles with the literary establishment. Showalter states that 'Her novel, *A Girl Diplomatist* (1892), met with such disparaging criticism that Wotton nursed a lingering bitterness throughout her life towards the worlds of books and book-men', and argues that this anger surfaces in the collection in which 'The Fifth Edition' first appeared (1993: 326). We are, indeed, at risk of falling into the so-called 'autobiographical phallacy' as identified by Mary Jacobus, 'whereby male critics hold that women's writing is somehow closer to their experience than men's, that the female text *is* the author, or at any rate a dramatic extension of her consciousness' (1981: 520), of which more below. For the moment, let us note that the question this 'phallacy' raises, about the relationship between art and life, is of supreme importance in the late nineteenth-century era of aestheticism and so-called art for art's sake, and indeed is a theme in this story, and the way it is employed appears at times to reinforce, but elsewhere to complicate, the simple – even simplistic – alignment of women with the 'life' side of this supposed binary.

The Art versus Life debate is raised directly in this exchange (which again shows the male focalizer being used as the butt of the narrator's mockery):

> 'We may raise an altar to Art, Miss Suttaby, but neither you nor I can insist that only the worthiest shall be altar-servers. Many of them have shirked their apprenticeship, and the consequences are as disastrous as I tell you.'
>
> He was not quite sure what he meant, though he thought it sounded well. But he had often found that women made a beautiful translation from a very imperfect original, and he waited for her answer, knowing it would furnish the keynote to what she believed she had discovered in him.
>
> 'Yes, I see,' she said thoughtfully. [...] 'You mean that unless Life has taught you servitude at her other altars, – at those of duty and self-sacrifice, and conquered longings, perhaps especially, – one should not dare approach to the high altar of Art. Of necessity one

would have no fruits to lay upon it. Yes, it is a beautiful idea, and I quite see what you mean.'

'Exactly,' said Franklyn Leyden.

(Wotton 1993: 151–2)

Miss Suttaby here offers a generous interpretation of Leyden's meaning-less remark implying that he himself has served at the altars of 'duty and self-sacrifice, and conquered longings', but appears to follow the aestheticist line by placing the altar of Art above that of the 'other altars' of Life. Although the relationship between New Woman writing and aestheticism was not always antagonistic (Ledger 2007: 23), given the thoroughgoing critique of Leyden the aesthete dandy which character-izes the narrative voice here, we might have expected that the norms of the work would be set against this elevating of Art above Life. But Miss Suttaby's interpretation of Leyden's phrase also gives significant value to Life as a necessary precondition for the creation of Art. This is rein-forced if we consider how Miss Suttaby's work is described. Miss Suttaby allows Leyden to rewrite her work so extensively that it is, essentially, no longer hers. In particular, Miss Suttaby has included in her story events and emotional responses which Leyden initially dismisses as implausible (Wotton 1993: 156), although as the story progresses, he realizes that these events are based on the events and emotional responses of her own life (160).[6] And yet, even before he has realized the extent of the alignment between Miss Suttaby's own experience and her novel, Leyden observes that in her work 'she had looked into her own heart, and written of what she had found there'; this reminds him of her earlier self-deprecating statement about her story: 'There is no art about it' (154). It also implies, rather disturbingly, that it is not just Miss Suttaby's book that he ends up rewriting – not so much her 'art', it being artless – but her life.

Heilmann argues that Wotton's story 'locate[s] the binaries Woman and Art within a male discourse that is highly antagonistic to women and manifestly ignorant of their lives' (2000: 157). But the logical corollary of this according to the construction of Art and Life as binaries, namely the alignment of Woman with Life, returns us to the autobiographical phallacy. The narrative's apparent valorization of those works of literature based closely on real life – such as Miss Suttaby's – is reinforced when we discover that Leyden's great bestseller was in fact based on a true story told him, on his deathbed, by someone Leyden met while travelling; that he himself, by his own admission, 'could not create' (Wotton 1993: 146–7). But what we need then to

remember is that it is precisely the *story* of another's life that he faith-
fully copies and publishes. Even as the narrator further condemns
Leyden by revealing that his own creation is not in fact a product of
'art' but of 'life', we are reminded that the rendering of life into art will
always require the construction of a selective narrative; the telling of
this story by a vividly dramatized (if unnamed) narrator, reinforces this
point. It is compellingly tempting to read 'The Fifth Edition' as a cry
of rage direct from Wotton herself, knowing what we do about her
own lack of literary success – in other words, to become persuaded by
the autobiographical fallacy/phallacy. Yet the fact remains that this is
a rendering of experience in fiction, just as both of Leyden's novels are
versions of a story – fashions of narration – not versions of a life. Thus,
in this story, as in Miss Suttaby's subtle articulation above, the Art/Life
binary, and its gendered associations, does not hold. The various 'altars'
are not so easily separated and hierarchized, either in her statement,
or in the narrative itself, where artlessness is by implication approved
in Miss Suttaby and condemned in Leyden.

A final observation about the effect of the narrative voice forms
a bridge to my discussion of Woolson and Lee. The 'fashion of narration', while focalized through Leyden, protects Miss Suttaby from the
intrusion that she has already experienced at the start of the story in
the form of Leyden bouncing into her rooms and before long 'mak[ing
himself] quite comfortable and at home' (Wotton 1993: 145). Miss
Suttaby's 'silence', or our lack of access to her interiority, performs this
protection from those who would judge her. There remains, then, an
air of mystery, unknowability, or (to use a term we will come across in
a moment) 'unavailability' about Miss Suttaby. This unknowability is
not only directly alluded to in all three texts, but is performed through
the authors' eschewal of either a first-person narrative in the voice of
the female author, or a third-person narrative focalized through them.

'Miss Grief' and the unknowable woman writer

Each story refers explicitly to the idea that the female author is difficult
to define. In 'The Fifth Edition', Leyden comments that Miss Suttaby
'never seemed to have had any individual existence at all, since with
her it had always been bound up and dominated by "the others"'
(Wotton 1993: 153). Here, her lack of 'individual existence' is put down
specifically to her role as provider for her family. In 'Lady Tal', the
eponymous aspiring female writer is described in similar terms: 'this
woman did not seem an individual at all' (Lee 1993: 198), although

here her individuality is not obscured by her sacrifice to others, but rather by her apparent complete compliance with the social norms of the privileged and affluent. Jervase Marion (the male writer through whom 'Lady Tal' is focalized) does change his opinion of Tal, but this lack of clear definition, tendency to the diffuse and un-pin-downable is succinctly expressed in Marion's oxymoronic observation that she 'thrust her inscrutability down one's throat' (Lee 1993: 223).

Just such an air of inscrutability is also found in the eponymous Miss Grief. In this story, a woman who the narrator – an unnamed male writer – calls 'Miss Grief', presents herself at his door (his servant has misheard the name she actually gives which is 'Miss Crief'). He turns her away on numerous occasions, assuming that she has something she wants to sell him. However, when he does admit her, he discovers that she has come to him to ask his opinion about a play she has written. He reads it, finds it compelling, and promises to help her to get it published, but insists she must make some changes in order to make it acceptable. She refuses to change a single comma, and when he tries to rewrite it, he finds it impossible. Having then been out of touch with her for some time, in part while he works on her manuscripts, he eventually discovers that she is on her deathbed; he lies to her that her play has found a publisher, and after her death he keeps her manuscript as a reminder of her genius and his 'good fortune' (Woolson 1993: 190).

The title of the story signals that the ending is not to be a happy one, and thus indicates the position of the implied author – or the 'norms of the work' – namely that our sympathies are to lie primarily with the female author who will come to 'grief'. However, in this story the male writer himself grieves over her tragedy (unlike in 'The Fifth Edition') and he undergoes something of a transformation over the course of the story, from displaying conceit and hard-heartedness at the outset, to sitting anxiously at her bedside, lying to protect her feelings, and eventually lamenting her tragic death.

That he is depicted in a relatively sympathetic way is of course emphasized by the use of a first-person narrator reflecting on his own mental and especially emotional development. Why, then did Woolson not opt for a first-person narrative from the point of view of Miss Grief herself? Most obviously, this would not (without a radical challenge to the norms of narrative fiction) have allowed her to die at the end of the story, thus limiting the impact of the narrative and in particular of the narrator's behaviour – although conceits such as a found first-person narrative in the form of a diary or similar could have been employed, or a third-person narrative could have been focalized through Miss Grief. But one of the key effects of this particular choice of narrative voice, I suggest, relates to the air of mystery which attaches to the woman writer, to a greater or lesser extent, in all of these stories.

This theme of female mystery is a familiar one in the *fin-de-siècle*, indeed a cliché by 1897 when Oscar Wilde wrote his 'The Sphinx without a Secret', a short story entirely devoted to parodying the idea of the mysterious woman: 'My dear Gerald', the narrator warns his friend, 'women are meant to be loved, not to be understood' (3). However, Angelique Richardson has specifically linked the idea of women's mystery to the short story form: 'Inconclusive, open-ended, evasive short stories were a perfect fit for the modern woman, as she released herself from repressive social codes, and tried out new identities' (2002: lxvi). Richardson observes the increasing focus on subjectivity in the literature of the period, and in short stories in particular, and concludes that by 'undermining objectivity, the time-hallowed status of woman in fiction as an *object* was no longer a possibility, in the hands of either a male or a female writer: she remained ultimately unreadable', and that this unreadability was celebrated by writers such as George Egerton as 'proof of sexual difference' (lxvii).

Elizabeth Bowen's key essay on short stories identifies (as Adrian Hunter puts it) a 'change that occurred in the latter decades of the nineteenth century, a change that, as she saw it, signalled the short story's breaking free from the grip of novel and the novelistic imagination' (2007: 1). In the vanguard of this change were, Bowen argues, writers such as Henry James, who, influenced by Russian and French writers, propose the use of the 'tactical omissions' necessary in the short story to 'suggest and imply meaning, rather than stating it directly', and finding that 'the short story could achieve great richness and complexity [...] *as a result of*, rather than in spite of, its brevity' (Hunter 2007: 1–2). If, then, the short story form as it evolved in the late nineteenth century offers omissions, indeed silences, as not simply necessary evils but significant elements of how the short story *means*, it appears particularly suited to narratives which insist on maintaining a 'mystery' or unknowability around the otherwise central female character.

Certainly, these three stories offer a picture of unreadable women alongside sometimes all-too-readable men. But they also make a connection between the inscrutability of the women characters and their identity as writers; this in turn can be read as a narrative strategy which aims to evade, or protect the woman writer from, the discourses of the literary establishment, as we will see if we examine how the first-person narrator of 'Miss Grief' describes the eponymous character. There are a number of ways in which this woman's mystery, her unreadability, is signalled in the text. Here the narrator describes the figure of 'Miss Grief':

> [...] her black gown, damp with rain, seemed to retreat fearfully to her thin self, while her thin self retreated as far as possible from me, from the chair, from everything.
>
> (Woolson 1993: 169)

Woolson's syntax here mirrors the way Miss Grief's 'self' is obscured as layers of distance are built up between her and the narrator – and, thus, the reader – by the repetition of 'retreat(ed)'. Woolson's employment of chiasmus further folds the prose in on itself. The ambiguity of the adverb 'fearfully' is also significant here; most obviously it means 'very much', but it also implies not only that she is fearful, but that there is fear in the very atmosphere – perhaps the narrator, too, is fearful. This speaks to the profound level of connection between the two characters, revealed at a later stage in the story.

What is more, the narrator of 'Miss Grief' has immense difficulty in identifying her according to the usual markers of age, class or even gender. For example 'A woman – yes, a lady' (Woolson 1993: 168) is his initial assessment of her class, though he is later surprised by her failure to dress for dinner. He identifies her as having a servant, but this person later on turns out to be her aunt. He describes her as 'more than middle aged' but she reveals that she is 43 (younger than he had supposed) (180). And when he remarks that 'after all, she was a woman' (ibid.), it is with the implication that this may somehow have been in doubt. Miss Grief disturbs – and intrigues – to a great extent because she fails, or refuses, to be easily recognizable in terms of key social, and thus largely patriarchal, markers.

Her mystery in large part arises from her problematic gender identity, and this gender ambiguity is indicated not only insofar as she is described as unattractive, and thus unfeminine, but specifically because she is a writer. When he makes this realization, the author inwardly exclaims 'An authoress! This is worse than old lace' (171) – the use of the feminized term implies an abomination.[7] The two identities, of woman and of writer, are separable for him: 'It was the woman that impressed me then, more than the writer' (175). Emphatically, however, they are not separable for her. While she insists that she values his opinion so much that if he had not responded positively to her work, she would have committed suicide, saying 'if your sentence had been against me, it would have been my end' (177), she nevertheless resists any suggestions he makes to change the text. Thus her sense of self is entirely bound up with her writing. The total interconnection between the two is indeed ultimately confirmed by the narrator where, reflecting on his attempts to 'improve' her work he says, 'At last I did unravel the whole, and then the story was no longer good, or Aaronna's; it was weak, and mine' (185). The work, once modified, loses what made it good, which is that it was emphatically a product of Aaronna – that is, Miss Grief.

This use of Miss Grief's first name brings me to a key point about her 'mystery', which is that the narrator literally does not know what to *call* a woman writer. Miss Grief's identity (including her gender identity) is further undermined by the layers of names that stand between the two characters. Having been led to believe by his servant that her name is Miss Grief, not as she in fact presented herself Miss Crief, he later discovers that her name was rather the more aristocratic Moncrieff. When he invites her to dine with him she accepts on the basis that, she says, she is 'old enough to be his mother' (although he knows that she is not); he says he 'can hardly call [her] "mother"' and suggests 'aunt', and thus discovers that her name is Aaronna because, she explains, 'my father was much disappointed that I was not a boy' (180). Even her Christian name, then, presents her as ambiguously gendered. Overall, 'Miss Grief' is a person who sits so problematically across identity categories, not least those which would separate 'woman' and 'writer', that no adequate name can be found for her.

This mystery surrounding Miss Grief's identity is the sensation we are left with in the last lines of the story. Here, the narrator explains why Miss Grief's manuscript is to be destroyed when he dies, without even his wife being permitted to see it; the story concludes 'For women will misunderstand each other; and, dear and precious to me as my sweet wife is, I could not bear that she or anyone should cast so much as a thought of scorn upon the memory of the writer, upon my poor dead, "unavailable", unaccepted "Miss Grief"' (191). There is a great deal to be said about this final line. Firstly, there is the implication (given in the male voice, but a voice which, we remember, approximates the 'norms of the work') that women tend to misunderstand each other, hinting at a female implied reader who might need to be warned against misunderstanding other women and in particular women writers. On a more positive note, here at the end of the story the woman writer is referred to first and foremost as 'the writer', which seems to recognize her primary identification as such. On the other hand this is also made identical with the name 'Miss Grief', which, while perhaps encouraging a final burst of sympathy for her on the part of the reader, also reasserts the name the narrator attached to her – not her real name. Finally, there are the mysterious quotation marks around the word 'unavailable' (a word which does not appear anywhere else in the story). Is this how he imagines she would have described herself? As unavailable for what? Perhaps sexual unavailability is implied? The use of quotation marks puts another layer of distance between the narrator and Miss Grief – indeed, between the reader and this persistently 'unavailable' mysterious character. It is thus difficult even to offer provisional readings of this word, punctuated thus, beyond the observation that it compounds Miss Grief, the character's, and 'Miss Grief', the story's, mystery. While this, I suggest, protects the woman writer from being forced, conceptually, into categories which cannot, it would seem, easily accommodate the identity position 'woman writer', it also problematically risks effacing her identity in the process, leave her as insubstantial and incomprehensible to the reader as she is to the narrator himself.

Women writers writing male narrators

If the women writers in these stories are in some way mysterious to the male writers who come into contact with them (and if, as in the case of 'The Fifth Edition', they are sometimes unaware even of the extent of their ignorance, this only compounds the sense of their lack of penetration), the reverse is most certainly not the case, in any of the stories. We have seen, for example, how Miss Suttaby offers an interpretation of one of Leyden's pretentiously opaque comments which gives the empty utterance a substance it previously lacked. The narrator of 'Miss Grief' describes the woman writer's level of insight about as strongly as is imaginable when describing his responses to the way Miss Grief interprets his own work:

> For she had understood me – understood me almost better than I had understood myself. It seemed to me that while I had laboured to interpret, partially, a psychological riddle, she, coming after, had comprehended its bearings better than I had, though confining herself strictly to my own words and emphasis.
>
> (Woolson 1993: 170)

The mutual implication of these characters, alluded to earlier, is here driven home in her almost psychic ability to understand his writing; we are reminded that both are writers, workers with words, and here this identity position is to the fore – it is what they share.

Lady Tal is the least promising of all three women writers and her eventual giving-up of novel-writing reminds us that, while she has a passing enthusiasm for this pursuit, she has contemplated 'a great many things' (Lee 1993: 245), a great many occupations and indeed marital outcomes. And yet, Lady Tal not only also demonstrates the capacity to understand the male writer even beyond the bounds of his own understanding, as in the other two stories, but she makes the most emphatic gesture of intervention in the male writer's work. At the end of 'Lady Tal', Tal reads the new story that Marion is outlining even more perceptively than he does himself. Here, with Tal having given up her novel-writing, we discover that Marion is himself planning to write a story which, as Tal discerns, is based on their own encounter. She suggests that his story (and thus the story of 'Lady Tal') conclude in a modern marriage of the kind advocated by many New Women – clearly not only an aesthetic suggestion but also a real proposal to Marion himself. Thus Tal's final gesture is an attempt to assert herself; having submitted to his suggestions about her novel (though ultimately with no productive outcome) she makes this final assertion of her identity as writer of stories. She offers an alternative ending to his story about her, and thereby aims to write her own life. And the ambiguous ending leaves the reader not knowing whether Marion pursues this suggestion in his novel or in his life.

This final observation, that Tal makes the gesture of 'writing' her own life after having failed conspicuously to write a novel, returns us to the question, or perhaps the problem, of the autobiographical ph/fallacy, which we have already come across in relation to 'The Fifth Edition'. While Lee differs from the character of Lady Tal in numerous fundamental ways, 'Lady Tal' is on one level a story *à clef* featuring Henry James as Jervase Marion and Tal as a version of Lee; Lee knew James very well and admired his work greatly, controversially dedicating her first novel to him. This issue is also relevant to 'Miss Grief', also frequently read as a story *à clef* offering an imagined meeting between Woolson herself and, again, Henry James (such a meeting was yet to take place).[8] And we have already noted the tendency (in, for example, Showalter's introduction to her collection) to read 'The Fifth Edition' as an expression of Wotton's frustration at her own impoverishment and lack of success. But these more or less autobiographical readings, problematic though they doubtless are in terms of textual evidence as well as gender politics, do at least have the effect of, ultimately, strengthening the authority of the female voices in these texts. Thus, for example, a reading which identifies Woolson with Miss Grief offers a literal understanding of the suggestion that she, Miss Grief, had understood the narrator 'better than [he] had understood [himself]' (Woolson 1993: 170), because it is she, Woolson, who has written him, in the guise of Miss Grief. In all these cases the proximity between the story and the author's life reminds us that even the male narrators or focalizers are themselves written by women; the ultimate control lies in a place designated female.

It is true that the most emphatic gesture of a woman (re)writing a man appears in a text which, returning to DeKoven's terminology, is not 'female signed'; that is, Lee's. This is in large part, of course, to do with the nature of the relationship between the two characters in 'Lady Tal' – the power dynamic as outlined earlier which is almost an inversion of that found in Wotton and Woolson's stories. But the evasion of gender categories by Lee, at least in her choice of pseudonym, in itself reinforces both the significance of gender (why otherwise would Violet Paget choose to 'disguise' hers?) and its instability in relation to the identity position 'woman writer'.

The question that remains, then, is where the balance of power lies in this tangle of voices. How distinctly are we to hear our authors' voices? How closely are they aligned with their ('unavailable' female writer) characters? These are, of course, some of the fundamental questions of literary criticism, despite the death of the author, yet ultimately undecidable ones. To be clear: obviously the question of the relative proximity between author, narrator and characters is not solely relevant to stories such as these. But in these particular instances, the proximity between author, character and indeed narrator or focalizer *specifically* in their shared status as *writers* teasingly foregrounds the fraught nature of this relationship. By inviting the reader to raise this question which can never be satisfactorily answered – is Miss Grief a version of Constance Fenimore Woolson? – and in particular by opting for a narrative from the point of view of someone else, a male writer, these authors generate narratives which parade their own vanishing points. The strategic use of the male voice serves to amplify women writers' critique of dominant discourses around the female writer at a time when this figure was, as we have seen, under attack; but also, and perhaps problematically, keeps the woman writer's identity always just out of sight.

Notes

1. The term 'focalization' is taken from Gèrard Genette (1980: 189–94). Gerald Prince summarizes the term: 'The perspective in terms of which the narrated situations and events are presented; the perceptual or conceptual position in

terms of which they are rendered (Genette). [...] FOCALIZATION– "who sees" or, more generally, "who perceived (and conceives)" – should be distinguished from VOICE ("who speaks," "who tells," "who narrates")' (2003: 31–2).

2. See for example George Egerton's 'A Lost Masterpiece' (1894), Ella D'Arcy's 'The Pleasure Pilgrim' (1895) and Ada Leverson's 'Suggestion' (1895), all published in *The Yellow Book* and discussed by Ledger in 'Wilde Women'; other examples include Mona Caird's 'The Yellow Drawing Room' (1892), Sarah Grand's 'The Undefinable' (1894) and George Egerton's 'A Nocturne' (1897).

3. For more on the female 'surplus' and women's work, see Zakreski (2006).

4. For more on the New Woman, see Ledger (1997), Richardson (2002), Richardson and Willis (2001) and Heilmann (2000).

5. There are a number of other short stories of the period featuring women writers; see for example 'The Spell of the White Elf' (1893) and 'A Nocturne' (1897) by the celebrated New Woman writer George Egerton. However, in neither story are both the male and female central characters writers, as they are in the three stories under discussion here.

6. Precisely this situation also occurs in Lady Tal, despite the very different characterization and relationship between the characters in that story (Lee 1993: 235–6).

7. See Zakreski for a discussion of the distinction between socially acceptable 'women who write' and socially dubious 'women who turn authors', and related terminology including 'authoress' (2006: 102–3).

8. For detailed readings of both texts as stories *à clef* featuring the authors as the female protagonists and versions of Henry James as the male, as well as the limits of such readings, see Colby (2003: 193–99) on Lee and Boyd (2004: 190–98) on Woolson.

Works Cited

Booth, Wayne (1996) 'Distance and Point of View: an Essay in Classification', in Michael J. Hoffman and Patrick D. Murphy (eds), *Essentials of the Theory of Fiction* (London: Leicester University Press), pp. 116–33.

Boyd, Ann E. (2004) *Writing for Immortality: Women Writers and the Emergence of High Literary Culture in America* (Baltimore: Johns Hopkins University Press).

Caird, Mona (1892) 'The Yellow Drawing Room', in *A Romance of the Moors* (Leipzig: Heinemann and Balestier).

Colby, Vineta (2003) *Vernon Lee: a Literary Biography* (Charlottesville: University of Virginia Press).

D'Arcy, Ella (1895) 'The Pleasure Pilgrim', *The Yellow Book*, V: 34–67.

DeKoven, Marianne (1991) *Rich and Strange: Gender, History, Modernism* (Princeton, NJ: Princeton University Press).

Egerton, George (2006) 'The Spell of the White Elf', in Sally Ledger (ed.), *Keynotes and Discords* (London: Continuum), pp. 25–31.

—— (1894) 'A Lost Masterpiece', *The Yellow Book*, I: 186–96.

—— (2002) 'A Nocturne', in Angelique Richardson (ed.), *Women Who Did: Stories by Men and Women, 1890-1914* (London: Penguin), pp. 187–96.

Genette, Gèrard (1980) *Narrative Discourse: an Essay in Method*, trans. Jane E. (Ithaca: Cornell University Press).

Grand, Sarah (1894) 'The Undefinable', *Cosmopolitan*, 17: 745–57.

Harland, Henry (ed.) (1895) *The Yellow Book V.*

Heilmann, Ann (2000) *New Woman Fiction: Women Writing First-Wave Feminism* (Basingstoke and London: Palgrave).

Hunter, Adrian (2007) *The Cambridge Introduction to the Short Story in English* (Cambridge: Cambridge University Press).

Jacobus, Mary (1981) 'Review of *The Madwoman in the Attic* and *Shakespeare's Sisters*', *Signs*, 6/3: 517–23.

Ledger, Sally (1997) *The New Woman: Fiction and Feminism at the Fin-de-Siècle* (Manchester: Manchester University Press).

—— (2007) 'Wilde Women and *The Yellow Book*: the Sexual Politics of Aestheticism and Decadence', in *English Literature in Transition, 1880–1920*, 50/1: 5–26.

Lee, Vernon (1993) 'Lady Tal', in Elaine Showalter (ed.), *Daughters of Decadence: Women Writers of the Fin de Siècle* (London: Virago), pp. 192–261.

Leverson, Ada (1895) 'Suggestion', *The Yellow Book*, V: 249–57.

Prince, Gerald (2003) *Dictionary of Narratology*, rev. edn. (Lincoln and London: University of Nebraska Press).

Pykett, Lynn (2000) 'Portraits of the Artist as a Young Woman: Representations of the Female Artist in the Women's Writing of the 1890s', in Nicola Thompson (ed.), *Victorian Women Novelists and the Woman Question* (Cambridge: Cambridge University Press), pp. 135–50.

Richardson, Angelique (2002) 'Introduction', in *Women Who Did: Stories by Men and Women, 1890–1914* (London: Penguin), pp. xxxi–lxxxi.

—— and Chris Willis (eds) (2001) *The New Woman in Fiction and in Fact* (Basingstoke and New York: Palgrave).

Showalter, Elaine (1993) 'Introduction', in Elaine Showalter (ed.), *Daughters of Decadence: Women Writers of the Fin de Siècle* (London: Virago), pp. vii–xx.

Wilde, Oscar (2002) 'The Sphinx without a Secret', in Angelique Richardson (ed.), *Women Who Did: Stories by Men and Women, 1890–1914* (London: Penguin), pp. 3–8.

Woolson, Constance Fenimore (1993) 'Miss Grief', in Elaine Showalter (ed.), *Daughters of Decadence: Women Writers of the Fin de Siècle* (London: Virago), pp. 165–91.

Wotton, Mabel (1993) 'The Fifth Edition', in Elaine Showalter (ed.), *Daughters of Decadence: Women Writers of the Fin de Siècle* (London: Virago), pp. 139–64.

Zakresksi, Patricia (2006) *Representing Female Artistic Labour: 1848-1890: Refining Work for the Middle-Class Woman* (Aldershot: Ashgate).

Part II
Resisting and Embracing the Other via the Abject Entity

3

'These heavy sands are language tide and wind have silted here'[1]: Tidal Voicing and the Poetics of Home in James Joyce's *Ulysses*

Sanja Bahun

Introduction

Half-awake, Molly Bloom, the female protagonist and the vocalizer of the concluding chapter of James Joyce's *Ulysses* (1922), marks the time of her husband's belated return home: 'wait theres Georges church bells wait 3 quarters the hour 1 wait 2 oclock well thats a nice hour of the night for him to be coming home [...]' (1993: 722). At this point, the chronotopic line of *Ulysses* closes, or rather, folds upon itself. The reader is enclosed in a temporality that both the Gilbert and the Linati schemata designate as time-out-of-time (the Linati schema signals it by the lemniscate, sign of infinity) and a discursive and spatial organization unlike anything that preceded it in the novel: Molly's womb. It is in this turbulent, bloody space, both private and infused with history, that the homeward journey finishes; and it is with the lengthy appropriation of a female voice that Joyce closes his novel.

This appropriation has excited, occasionally unnerved, scholars for decades. Molly's interior monologue, noticeably contrasting the male voices–perspectives that focalize *Ulysses*, has been hailed as a true *écriture féminine*, but the positioning of the monologue as a coda, or even a postscript, to the novel, and the reductive vision of femininity it seems to advance have troubled many.[2] Joyce himself repeatedly suggested that this cross-gender performance should be understood as 'the *clou* of the book'; that Molly's monologue provides 'the indispensable countersign to Bloom's passport to eternity' (1975: 285, 278). Noticeably, however, the 'Penelope' chapter both authorizes and counteracts the male protagonists' melancholic meanderings and their protracted return home: it provides an ambivalent response to the personal and

57

group losses that orchestrate the narrative. How are we, then, to interpret this voicing, which, even in the novel that is all comprised of divergent discursive styles, appears to institute a radically different relation to and vision of the material world?

I am intrigued by what scholars often fail to notice: namely, the specificity and materiality of Molly's discourse as presented above. 'Penelope' is as replete with temporal and spatial indicators relating to the Dublin of June 1904 as 'Ithaca', the fact-superannuated chapter that precedes it. More importantly for my purposes in this chapter, these details invoke, in closure, all the loss- and home-related motifs that have shaped the narrative: these range from the invocation of the spaces of nation and colony, the Home Rule Bill, and young man's self-imposed exile to the image of wives and children pleading with drunken fathers to come home and the refashioning of Irish girls as 'homemade beauties' (Joyce 1993: 713). This marked address to (real and imagined) home-space has prompted the following investigation in the political and aesthetic implications of Joyce's cross-gender performance in *Ulysses*. What is, I ask herein, the relationship between the use of differently gendered voices, the issues of narration, eternal and finite, and the material questions of home and nationhood?

Ulysses as Ithaca constructed upon 'the incertitude of the void'

Like many narratives, Joyce's *Ulysses* is structured as a homeward journey. In contrast to its eighteenth and nineteenth-century predecessors – or the *Odyssey* for that matter – *Ulysses* stages *nostos* as an impossible search. Here the hero's homecoming becomes problematic because home itself has been revealed as a relative and provisional site for our nostalgia in a self-grounding world, a nostalgia that is importantly, if delusionally, historical: Ithaca, Zion, 'true' Ireland. In Joyce's novel home appears as an affect-suffused site whose radical insubstantiality precludes both the possibility of return and that of establishing a new home: the human home, indeed the whole microcosm and macrocosm, is 'ineluctably constructed upon the incertitude of the void', the *Nostos* trio of chapters suggests (Joyce 1993: 650).

Ulysses deploys a multiplicity of voices, mostly male, to complete, correct and contradict each other on this impossible homecoming journey. Two dominate: the voice of Leopold Bloom, a middle-aged advertising agent, and that of Stephen Dedalus, a young aspiring writer. For one of them, at least, home has a provisional site: 7 Eccles Street. Yet, this home is constructed upon lack, as our entry into the evocative world of objects in the Bloom household forcefully posits. It is from the cleavage under Molly's pillow where she hurriedly stows Boylan's letter that the reader first learns about the nature of this lack: most notably, the Blooms' long-lasting problems with the conjugal desire-flow.[3] To gauge, or negotiate, this home is the major task of Leopold Bloom's mental work on 16 July 1904. In contrast, Stephen Dedalus's meandering is governed by his affective processing of the status of being away from home, now (a self-imposed 'banishment from home'; Joyce 1993: 203) and in the past (that fresh Parisian morning when he received the telegram reading 'Mother dying come home'; 42). Exteriorized in Stephen's residence-problem, this affective work is narratively articulated through a series of substitute-homes that he contemplates and rejects one by one – the tower-communion with Mulligan, Aunt Sara's house, return to his family-home, the Bloom household – and some alternative home-sites that he temporary inhabits (the cerebral home of the library and the erotic home of the brothel). Yet it is noticeable that, as we progress through the unnumbered, untitled chapters of *Ulysses*, the space of 'home' both expands and contracts: from the Martello tower, through the township of Dublin, Ireland ('the Irishman's house', we are informed, 'is his coffin'; 106), to the whole of macrocosm (the stars of 'Ithaca'), and back, pointedly equivalent, to the microcosm of a bed (the unspecifiable locus of Molly's desire). *En route* we also move from the direct representation to the overdetermination of 'home'. We eventually identify the impossibility to return home, or anchor oneself, as the very form of the novel: through its stylistic exercises, competing narrative voices, and free-floating islands of reference, the narration, we realize, simultaneously illuminates and obscures the fictional data, rendering them both '*diaphane*' (transparent) and '*adiaphane*' (opaque) (37). The main consequence of this deliberate avoidance to establish a semantic home is the dissemination, or flight, of meaning. The latter institutes Joyce's ethic poetics: that of sustaining a melancholic relationship towards one's home-space.[4]

Whereas the questions of home and homecoming organize the text structurally and thematically, its affective content is shaped by a sense of loss. Both male protagonists are engaged in thwarted mourning (emblematically, both are clothed in 'cheap dusty mourning'), which extends to their status as nation-subjects: the heroes of Joyce's 'epic of two races' are an Irish and a Jew/Irish/Hungarian who share a problematic attitude towards their points of provenance.[5] A complex network of narrative signals links the heroes' origin-anxiety to the questions of nationhood and loss. Two of these pointers are particularly deserving of critical attention due to their position as inaugural figurative moves for each protagonist and his search for home. The first appears in the opening chapter, 'Telemachus', in the image of an old woman bringing milk to the inhabitants of the Martello tower. Her arrival is expressly linked to Stephen's morose, guilt-ridden, invocation of his deceased mother, and thus the milk-woman materializes as a stand-in for the lost mother, loss of mother tongue (Gaelic), and, by extension, loss of motherland. She stands in clumsily, for the milk-woman herself does not know Gaelic; still she uncannily commands the scene, 'old and secret', somewhat ashamed of her own presence, of her own 'old shrunken paps' and 'uneager hand' accepting a florin, as a traditional and also traditionally modernist symbol of Ireland – a circumstance to which I will return soon (Joyce 1993: 14, 15). The other signal directing the reader's attention to the site of a specific nation-loss is waved in 'Calypso', the first chapter focusing on Leopold Bloom. There we become privy to Bloom's favourite breakfast, the grilled mutton kidneys (53, 57, 63). This breakfast preference is overdetermined: as the Bible exegesis specifies, and Bloom's own commentary in 'Ithaca' confirms, burned kidneys were a prominent consecrational offering in ancient Jewish rites.[6] Once introduced, this association of specific nationhood and melancholic incorporation is maintained through diverse word-inflections of 'burnt kidney' in *Ulysses*; the subsequently introduced image of pork kidney (pork being tref, i.e., not-kosher, food) will specify the nature of Bloom's loss as the loss of Jewish faith and the mythically conceived loss of race. The scenes with the milk-woman and Bloom's breakfast thus correlate language, nation, sacrifice and nourishment with the formation of complex social identities. And they prompt each protagonist on a voyage homeward.

Thereafter, the narrative material of *Ulysses* is focused through two melancholic searches, occasionally overlapping and finally intersecting: a search for the lost Father and that for the lost Son. The anxiety of patrilineage being the most visible narrative marker of both historical loss and search for home in the novel, the polyphonic organization of the text privileges male perspectives. It is indicative, though, that this male voicing of male searches and male homeward journeys ends in, or is responded by, a female voice. Juxtaposed with the beginning of the book, which is marked by Stephen's unsuccessful attempts to ventriloquize his mother's dying voice, this closing appropriation of female voice sheds a retrospective light on all those incidental female voices that have been appropriated earlier in the novel. Among those, the reader now remembers Bloom's daughter, Milly, and her teenage chirruping, briskly apologizing to her 'Papli' for writing in haste (Joyce 1993: 63–4); the verbal strategizing of Bloom's pen-lover Martha in a letter where the 'other world' and 'other word' conflate in fabrication of intimate realities (74–5); Josie Powell/Breen's conversing, with her 'womaneyes [...] melancholily' (150), and, vocally, in Bloom's hallucinations (421–7); the vocalizations of Miss Dunne, Miss Douce, the Dedalus sisters, Cissy Caffrey, and manifold female voices that introject in the male streams of consciousness in 'Circe'; and, most extensively, Gerty MacDowell's voice, in part inextricable from the ladies magazines rhetoric and partly challenging this very socio-linguistic code (333–51).

Scholars such as Frances Restuccia (1989) and Suzette A. Henke (1990) have linked the proliferation of styles and gender perspectives in *Ulysses* to Joyce's strategy of questioning the authority of the patriarchal system of values (and the author himself). Focusing on Joyce's deployment of female voices in marginal asides, Heather Cook Callow argues that Joyce uses these 'initially discredited and later vindicated female voices' to challenge 'the consensus of male Dublin opinion' and the related vision of the world (1992: 161). What is of particular interest to me is that each female voice also comments, directly or indirectly, on the notion of home. While Gerty phantasizes of 'a nice snug and cosy little homely house' (Joyce 1993: 337), what terrifies Bloom in Milly's letter is the actual ease of separation from home, once a girl is emancipated by work: learning the photographer's trade, Milly has just celebrated 'her first birthday away from home' (64). Yet Martha's titillating chastizing demands a confession: 'Are you not happy in your home you poor little naughty boy?' (75; this chiding line continues to haunt Bloom during the narrative day, changing the referential scope of 'home' in his mind from the site of sexual gratification, through the concept of family, to the township of Dublin, to Ireland). And Molly is problematically confined 'at home' for the duration of the narrative. If women in *Ulysses* seem particularly competent in (and thus less troubled by) the meaning of home, they are also symbolically reduced to home-space.

Certainly, the interlocking of home and the female is problematic. Yet, this gendering of home and homeward journeys as female and male, respectively, should also be read, perhaps primarily, in the context of the historical specificities and cultural imaginary of the year 1904, when *Ulysses* is set, and the years that saw the production of the novel. Still feeling the belated effects of the Great Famine, the failed Fennians' rising, the land reform of Davitt and Parnell, the latter's sentimental rise to and fall from power (all meticulously invoked during the 'Bloomsday'), Ireland of 1904 polarized, along the denominational lines, around the question of the Home Rule Parliament. This issue would galvanize the history of the next two decades: the 1916 Easter Rising ('the homerule sun rising up from the northwest in a laneway behind the bank of Ireland', Bloom mentally stages the rising in a chronotopic prolepsis; Joyce 1993: 55), the war of independence, the establishment of the Irish Free State and the civil war. In early 1900s, the corroboration of national identity, then, took form of a nostalgic study of 'Irish Ireland', an important aspect of which was symbolic gendering: to counter the masculinism of English colonial discourse, the writers of Irish Literary renaissance and the general populace recoursed to the traditional allegorization of Irish nation as a mysterious poor old woman, a wise motherly feminine, while simultaneously mounting a masculinist rhetoric that invoked the 'fathers' of the series of uprisings.

These efforts to re-forge the national identity as either female or male rested upon sentimental invocation of a heroic past, for which Joyce harboured little sympathy and much irony. Siting himself in the liminal space of 'neither-Irish-nor-Englishness', and thereby positioning himself both within and outside the dynamics described above, Joyce was able to rely on both, an intimate knowledge and an exotopic surplus of vision of his 'home'. Characteristic in this respect is the milk-woman episode in *Ulysses* glossed above. The episode, while duly fulfilling all the traditional fabulatory moves (sudden appearance of an old woman, her mysterious air, nourishment or liquid she provisions, old age wisdom), opens a search for home rather than confirms its presence. Ambiguous and compulsively probed by the characters *as they engage in it*, the incident is eventually annulled by its own self-reflexivity. Home, Joyce knew too well, is a construct, a board for our miscellaneous phantasies; we become aware of 'home' only when we feel we are bereft of it. And, even though 'home' abides in the realm of the imaginary, it is only through an emphatic symbolic action, including symbolic gendering, that we make sense of it. Customarily, then, we infuse 'home' with a gendered symbolic repository: Father-figures and the myth of Mother.

Male voicing: home as father–mother

In the 'Hades' chapter Joyce takes Bloom past Charles Stewart Parnell's grave. Walking unheeded along Parnell's grove, Bloom overhears the following conversation:

> –Some say he is not in that grave at all. That the coffin was filled with stones. That one day he will come again.

Hynes shook his head.

–Parnell will never come again, he said. He's there, all that was mortal of him. Peace to his ashes.

(Joyce 1993: 108)

Joyce perceived Parnell's death as Ireland's betrayal of its most important leader. He writes in the emotive closure of his 1912 essay 'The Shade of Parnell': 'In his last proud appeal to his people [Parnell] implored his fellow-countrymen not to throw him to the English wolves howling around him'. 'It redounds to the honour of his fellow-countrymen', Joyce continues, 'that they did not fail that desperate appeal. They did not throw him to the English wolves; they tore him apart themselves' (2000: 196).[7] But Joyce does not expound on the legend of Parnell's death and return in 'Hades'. Rather, he lets Bloom reclaim the discursive space with his reflections on the double loss he himself suffered on the paternal line – his father's suicide and his son's premature death – and what could or could not have been done to prevent these events. Against the backdrop of Parnell's grave, Bloom's ruminations powerfully correlate the questions of fatherhood, nation and betrayal. Here and elsewhere in the novel, patricide appears as the horrifying prerequisite of personal and general history-as-a-nightmare. Such a thought necessitates a rapture of symbolic codes: ruled by 'the law of falling bodies' (Joyce 1993: 69), the poison found on the table next to the father's bed (73) and the army recruitment poster (69) morph into an audio-pun on the march-cadence of the troops – 'Table: able, bed : ed' – earlier in the novel (70). The theme of the lost son both reinforces and expands this framework, blending the melancholic motivic line with patrilineage anxiety: 'I, too, lost of my race', Bloom reflects, 'No son. Rudy. Too late now. Or if not? If not? If still?' (273). In the 'Circe' chapter this anxiety culminates in a string of hallucinatory projections. Bloom imagines himself as a hyperbolically procreative father and a (powerful but benevolent) father of the nation – successor to Parnell or the 'king of Jews'.[8] In order to resume any of these progenitor-leader roles in phantasy, he also has to set up a phantasmatic place of origin, a home, amenable to the father narrative. This is why historical and topographical leaps mark Bloom's hallucinations in 'Circe': contemporary Ireland and various charged moments in its history, mythic Zion, imaginary Hungary, ancient Greece, and other chronotopic points serve as home-boards for Bloom's phantasms.

   A similar processing of patrilineage gives tenor to that other male voice that dominates the narration of *Ulysses*. Vocalizing an identifiable kind of intellectual nausea and dissatisfaction with the normative ways of mourning, Stephen–Hamlet spends most of 16 June 1904 negotiating the questions of heirs and heritage and his phantasmatic and real progenitors (including Shakespeare as a literary father). The image of death by drowning and the Shakespearean phrase 'full fathom five thy father lies' (Joyce 1993: 4, 21, 49) follow Stephen in his wanderings, associating his search for alternative mourning with Shakespeare's ludic exploration of the loss of the father-king in *The Tempest*. Joyce's dissemination of Shakespeare's alliterate phrase throughout Stephen's voicing adequately marks the conflation of political and personal losses in *Ulysses* (see Bahun 2004). As Seamus Deane argues, one such merger of the private and the political crisis of patrilineage also gives shape to the textual whirlpools of 'Scylla and Charybdis': it conjoins personal narration with the history of Catholicism (Church), literature (Culture) and Ireland (State) through the notion of a betrayal of the presupposed original purity/unity, in turn leading to Stephen's ingenious circumvention of patrilineage in his theory about Shakespeare's *Hamlet*.[9] But the latter theory, one should add, is also the site where a complementary anxiety becomes audible: the *Hamlet*-theory effectively fuses two parental losses/homicides (patricide and matricide) into one melancholic conglomerate.

For 'overdetermination is the rule' in *Ulysses*: Stephen actually mourns his mother while searching for the father.[10] Stephen's obsessive discursive circling around his mother's dead body reminds one of Julia Kristeva's claim that the very possibility of concatenating signifiers is dependent upon a successful mourning of an 'archaic and indispensable object – mother' (1989: 40). Stephen announces himself as a melancholic subject *par excellence*: throughout the novel he is haunted by the image of his mother's 'wasted body' emanating 'an odor of wax and rosewood', of 'wetted ashes', and by the denial, or betrayal, of her last wish (Joyce 1993: 5). Unsuccessfully 'shielding the gaping wounds' (8), Stephen tries to master expression (and he continues doing so for the next 50 pages). Meanwhile the ghost of his mother traverses, imperceptibly, into history and myth, and it transmogrifies in the sea that the Greek-passionate Mulligan hails as the 'great sweet mother' (5), the ultimate home for a Homeric hero. This 'wine-dark sea' (Mulligan, 5) procreates but its form is tomb-like: it is the mother's womb but also 'the dead sea [...] the grey sunken cunt of the world' (Bloom, 59), one that houses a 'rotting liver' (Stephen, 6). Wrapped in this ambiguity, the sea-womb thereby functions as the cavity at the heart of female gendered home; and as the Irishman's 'coffin' (106).

This maternal cavity, I notice, is exteriorized, even visualized, in language. As befitting the text in which the ultimate loss, one that lies beneath and is reactivated by all other losses, is that of mother(land), the prose of *Ulysses* always verges on the symbolic collapse. Reliant on an obsessive exploration of the onomatopoeic materiality and rhythmic potential of words, the language of *Ulysses* proceeds as it halts, approximating in this stalled movement the symptomatology of melancholia that the text ascribes to its male protagonists. The social-morphological inflection of words reflects the transformations of the melancholic self in history as it moves through maternal and paternal losses. One example of such linguistic processing sees Stephen's 'unspeeched' mouth (47) conflate the ill-fated 'blue French telegram' (42) with the dispersed Jews' lament for their homeland ('Remembering thee, O Sion'; 44) and the site-specific game of othering and violence ('I zmellz de bloodz odz an Iridzman'; 45). Issuing forth from a Freudian linguistic formula for mastering loss – '*Fort-Da*', or, in Joyce's English, 'Peekaboo. I see you' – the invoked 'galleys of Lochlanns' further confirm that this male melancholic processing is underpinned by a history of invasion and the loss of an actual language, Gaelic (45).[11] For a moment, this historical vicissitude reverts the melancholic prose to the discourse of patrilineage anxiety, to the memory of death by drowning and Thomas Aquinas's 'morose delectation' (45, 47). But the text eventually collapses, with a 'roaring wayawayawayawayawayaway', in the 'oomb, allwombing tomb' (47) – the locus of '*amor matris*', whose double determination Stephen repeatedly acknowledges (28, 199).

The crises of matrilineage and patrilineage therefore meet in language. Their intersection emerges as a knot that chiasmatically relates the two 'races' whose epic the novel is: Bloom's renounced Jewishness dominantly finds expression in patrilineage anxiety and Stephen's renounced Irish Catholicism is coded as his matrilineal heritage.[12] It is entrusted to the seemingly objective, gender-neutral, voice of 'Ithaca' to indicate that the two losses, of the father and of the mother, are one and the same: that Leopold Bloom suppressed 'a statement explanatory of his absence on the occasion of the interment of Mrs Mary Dedalus (born Goulding), 26 June 1903, vigil of the anniversary of the decease of Rudolph Bloom (born Virag)' (Joyce 1993: 648). Yet, even this disclosure is neither final nor fully effective. Not incidentally, the structure of 'Ithaca' is a *faltering* catechism.[13] A profusion of highly specified questions, the answers that provide information but repeatedly prove insufficient, and the preposterously detailed description of the contents of the Bloom household, all point to the general inadequacy of the symbolic tools – figures, classifications, logical operations, and language itself. This is so because catechism as a discursive genre operates only when the authority of the primal mover (God the

Father) is unquestionable, that is, when one's point of provenance is instantly recognizable. In the atmosphere where the father is disputed, or absent, and the existence of home is doubted, catechism fails. This is also why Joyce's modern Odyssey does not actually end with the father–son reunion at home; the reunion of the father [Bloom] and the son [Stephen] equilibrates between tragic failure and comic success.

The locus of *amor matris*, 'the only true thing in life' (Joyce 1993: 199), home is also, perhaps expectedly, the site of a new language. Signalling the end of logical narrative exploration (and the rational, male, symbol-driven type of discourse), the 'Ithaca' section closes with a narrative aperture: 'Where?' (689). This questing question is followed by an unusually large square dot, characteristic of the end of a logic syllogism.[14] The irony of this closure lies in its very inconclusiveness: there *is* something after this reinforced dot. What ensues purports to tell us 'where', that is, to address a few issues that the novel has asked us to ponder (home, loss, nation) by delineating a kind of primary space, a space where, one hopes, words might generate newly meaningful content. If one wishes to enter the space of home, the novel suggests, one must attempt to speak through the mother's voice – or at least the voice that would conclusively challenge the normative symbolic concatenation to the varieties of which we have been exposed before. The 'where' thus leads into a different type of discursive and spatial organization, whose rhythm, indecisiveness, and apparent unfinalizability preclude logic and visual recognition. Aspiring to spring from, and replicate, the bodily inwardness, this is both a space and a discourse. The last faltering description we get of it in male voice is the reiterated designation of a woman's rump as 'plump mellow yellow smellow melons' (686).

Tides: female voicing

The function of Molly's monologue, I said, is that of response. The 'Penelope' chapter responds to all prior spatio-temporal and linguistic figurations of loss, nation and home, as well as to the two dominant male voices, by an affirmative female voice and a verbiage that apparently connotes life, plentitude, fullness, unity, creation – in a word, the primordial home. At first sight Molly's nocturnal ruminations may appear to be modelled upon a tidal movement, the clash of waves (eight of them, we surmise), reminiscent of the sea and heat of Gibraltar where she grew up:

> [...] I thought it was going to get like Gibraltar my goodness the heat there before the levanter came on black as night and the glare of the

rock standing up in it like a big giant compared with their 3 Rock mountain they think is so great with the red sentries here and there the poplars and they all whitehot and the smell of the rainwater in those tanks watching the sun all the time weltering down on you faded all that [...][15]

(Joyce 1993: 706)

Scholars customarily emphasize the current-like quality of this home-voicing – the character of Molly's utterance as formless and fluid, as 'language at its loosest and most flowing' (Gottfried 1980: 35), and the property of Molly's thoughts to 'move like the tide – flowing forward, breaking, rolling back upon one another' (Henke 1978: 235). While Joyce himself associated the 'Penelope' chapter and the character of Molly Bloom with the earth and earth-goddesses rather than any kind of liquids, Molly's words have customarily inspired scholars to compare them to 'refreshing, life-giving waters' (Blamires 1966: 246), an 'unimpeded current' (Bolt 1981: 145), and 'the swell of some profound sea' (Wilson 1961: 164).[16] Of course, such formal reduction of femininity to the metaphoric incantation of either the mother-earth or 'life-giving waters' does little to absolve Joyce – or his critics – from the charge of indulging in feminine stereotypes.[17] But the fluidity of Molly's discourse has proven to be more than an impression of male critics, since it has been linked, by both male and female scholars, and after Kristeva, Hélène Cixous and Luce Irigaray, to the particular way in which a woman may write, or think, through semantic accretion, flows and overflows, resistant to the inherited, symbolic order supported syntax. Feminist critics still habitually contraposition the fluid rhythm of Molly's prose to the laws and rules of a hegemonic, male discursive world (see French 1976: 245; generally: Callow 1992) – that is, the world of Stephen Dedalus and Leopold Bloom.

To corroborate their designation of Molly's voicing in terms of fluids and flows critics usually highlight the absence of punctuation, the run-on sentences and the infrequency of capital letters or other signals of syntactic hierarchy – a feature that apparently overrides, or at least challenges, the normative syntactic rules. Anthony Burgess and Derek Attridge respectively argue, I think correctly, that this crucial piece of evidence becomes flawed as soon as we try imaginatively to fill in the missing punctuation and typographical absences, or read the text as an example of casual speech marked in advance for logical stress, as an actress acting out the paragraph quoted above might do.[18] (Needless to say, it is precisely to such detective-hermeneutic reading, or recovery of lost signs, that the text invites us.) Once punctuated and typographically corrected, Molly's sentences appear short and pointed, and the chapter as a whole strikes one as less syntactically deviant than almost any other section of *Ulysses*, and certainly more specific than the 'Proteus' chapter, narrated by Stephen, where the language tides are metatextually brought into play.

I bring together the 'Proteus' and 'Penelope' chapters since both are exemplary of the effort to capture in language the flow of associations and the transformations of mental energy as it moves from topic to topic. Joyce himself might have wished us to compare, in particular, these two chapters, since he described the technique of the first as 'monologue (male)' and that of the second as 'monologue (female)' (The Gilbert Schema, Joyce 1993: 734–5). The juxtaposition is indeed instructive. It suggests, first, that, if we wish to pursue the interpretation of Molly's monologue as a sample of a quintessentially feminine language (if such existed), we should either re-think the properties we associate with 'women's language' or reassess the conclusions that Joyce might have reached in his possible hypothesizing on female language and female mind. As I have demonstrated above, it is Stephen's voice that is 'tidal' and self-consciously so: it infringes the rules of syntax, repeatedly breaking concatenation; it flows and rolls back upon itself in painful, obsessive repetition, forcefully vocalizing fractured personal and general histories. In contrast, Molly's discourse, or the 'female voicing', is explicit, specific, if one wishes, 'earthy'; paradoxically, it always knows 'where to stop' when the vast content of past history and present worry assails one (728). Tellingly, it is Molly who successfully brings to a halt her recollections of Rudy with 'Im not going to think myself into the glooms' (ibid.). More pointedly, I would add, the juxtaposition of Stephen's narration in 'Proteus' and Molly's interior monologue in 'Penelope' tells us that we should critically rethink our gender assumptions about language, and the very habit to divide human voicing into female and male.

This is not to suggest that Joyce did not genuinely attempt to appropriate a female voice, or even a multiplicity of them. After all, we have the unsettling evidence of Joyce's mimicking, or, as some might argue, abusing, the voice audible in the letters of his own wife, Nora Barnacle, as well as those by other female family members.[19] While Joyce certainly learned a trick or two from Nora's letters, it is noticeable that this association actually does not corroborate but challenges the understanding of Molly's speech as an unmediated voicing of an exclusively 'female' interiority. Rather, it relegates the whole issue to the level of graphic presentation and letter-writing – where, indeed, Joyce seems to have had some gender prejudgments. To include this aspect in our reading of the text means to activate some uncomfortable questions about the cleavages between the assumed immediacy of rendition of Molly's thoughts, the symbolic, or emblematic, value we ascribe to the subject constituted through this language (Molly), and the uniquely 'written' existence of the text, which, as Attridge reminds us, also mimics the letter writing of some male family members.[20]

Taking this complex status of the chapter into account, it is fair to say that Molly's words relay not so much an exclusively female stream of consciousness as some indomitable life-force that counters various kinds of death-bringing hegemonies (including linguistic ones), a force which the text happens to code, but playfully so, female. 'Penelope' simply reaffirms – insofar as *'clou'* (Joyce 1975: 285) is also a reaffirmation, or a nail on the play of meaning – the link between language, creativity and home/nation loss, through a discourse of the one around whom the whole narration revolves and who, for that very reason, is destined constantly to evade us in Joyce's textual politics. As such, the last section of *Ulysses* presents us with the culmination of the struggle between the author and the material in search of home-anchorage to which *Ulysses* has accustomed us, but now with an added gender dimension that seems to be inalienable from this creative struggle. Evocatively, Molly-text challenges her author, 'Jamesy': 'I dont like books with a Molly in them' (Joyce 1993: 719, 707). Hence I should like to correct myself: the nature of the 'Penelope' chapter is rather that of the final rejoinder than of a response.

Where does this reassessment of Molly's monologue leave us with respect to the questions of nation, home and loss thereof? Refreshingly, Molly's monologue passes over mothers, fathers, nations and personal and group losses with competence; it does not obscure them but re-lodges them in their proper temporalities and sites (for example, when Molly reflects on the loss of her child; Joyce 1993: 728). Singularly, Molly's reminiscing honors each place, nation and ethnic subject, on its own terms: Gibraltar, Spain, Italy, North Africa, Ireland, and even the sculpture of an Indian god in a local museum. In line with the affirmative tenor of Molly's speech (the word 'yes' both opens and closes this chapter), the nation-politics of this chapter is both inclusive and appreciative of differences. It also offers some alternatives to the nationalist politics of the day, and adumbrates Virginia Woolf's better known association of femininity and pacifism in 'Three Guineas' a decade later. 'I dont care what anybody says', Molly retorts to an imagined opponent, 'itd be much better for the world to be governed by the women in it you wouldnt see women going and killing one another and slaughtering when do you ever see women rolling around drunk like they do or gambling every penny they have and losing it on horses yes because a woman whatever she does she knows where to stop' (Joyce 1993: 727–8). The last turn in Molly's associations reminds one that the monologue is also the narration of insomnia, of some 'waking women' (see, generally, Brivic 1995), and thus also a kind of silent vigil that assures that the world does not destroy itself, or implode unto itself.

Yet, if Molly stands in for an eternally affirmative, fertile, maternal home, as it has been entertained above, her final, and most important, voicing seems also to present her as an unstable signifier. Certainly, a come-back to this 'female' home (gestured not so much through language as by the material actions – Molly's menstruating, for example) could be understood, following Joyce's sometimes unreliable instructions, as return to the mother, to Gea-Tellus, whose affirmative fecundity ensures the male hero's passage to eternity; and, as such, Molly's function in the narrative could be convincingly linked to the ideologically charged association between Ireland and femininity which has been discussed above. Yet, whereas these symbolic and analogical links are indeed set up in *Ulysses*, they are also dismantled, parodied, in the course of narration: Molly's words might be 'earthy' but not mystically so; her menstruating points not so much to her fertility as to the fact that, to her professed relief, she is not pregnant; and, being more cosmopolitan than any other character in the novel (while also unashamedly ignorant about the world), Molly is, at best, an unorthodox symbol of home-nation. (This, parenthetically, might precisely be the point of Joyce's incongruous association of this character with the traditional female allegory of Ireland.) The space-and-time established by the character and her voice, likewise, defies being semantically pinned down. While the entry into Molly's space, where she lays on–sits in her conjugal bed in early morning hours of 17 June 1904, tantalizingly promises intimacy, warmth, synthesis and reconciliation of the scattered spatial and temporal indicators such one might imagine at the site of some primordial unity between the subject and the object (or the mother and the child), it is impossible to clearly delineate the contours of this time–space. Molly's monologue insouciantly blends temporalities and locales, interior and exterior, minor and major, inhabited by humans, as well as animals, clouds and rocks; and yet it keeps these spaces–times unreconciled. If this is the earth, then it is, just as Joyce intimated to Harriet Weaver, the 'prehuman' and 'posthuman' earth, and, as such, unreadable for humans, and approachable only as a parody of itself (Joyce 1966: 180).

At the end of 'Penelope', then, home is as elusive and unreachable as ever. This is precisely what makes *Ulysses* a paradigmatic text of modernist 'home fiction'. The maternal home, the 'Penelope' chapter suggests, is the very place to which return is impossible. Alike, a return to a 'homeland' is impossible, Joyce knew. Politically delineated, ideologically endowed, culturally moulded and linguistically shaped, it is only our projected desire that forms our 'homeland'. But the following is more important still: the self-exiled Joyce intuited that, precisely out of this severance, out of this inaccessibility, great art may emerge.

Notes

1. Joyce (1993: 44).
2. See, influentially, Cixous (1974 and 1981: 255). For the critique, see Scott (1984: 203; 206–207).
3. These problems range from adultery to having refrained from complete intercourse for – the inexorable catechism of 'Ithaca' specifies – '10 years, 5 months and 18 days' (Joyce 1993: 687).
4. The majority of the sociological, psychoanalytic and clinical discussions of mourning and melancholia define the conditions as a normative and a pathological response to grief, respectively. This common distinction is based on (sometimes simplified) reading of Sigmund Freud's 'Mourning and Melancholia' (1917), the essay whose discursive space opens with the following suggestion: mourning and melancholia have the same causes (loss of a cherished person, object or concept) and they entail similar symptoms (dejection, inhibition of the capacity to love, cessation of interest in the outer world, and others), but the two responses to loss differ in the structure of the relationship established between the subject and the lost 'Other' – whereas melancholia 'pathologically' preserves the lost object in the mourner's ego, mourning, a 'normative' grief-experience, dispels it. While he never returned to the question of mourning, Freud later revalued melancholia as an essential formative experience. In my forthcoming book (2013) I have suggested a reassessment of the concepts of mourning and melancholia and of the ways in which they are used in literary criticism, and proposed an understanding of melancholia/mourning as a bifacial dynamic whose common features are the ideal or real object-loss and the discord felt in language and personal and group self-fashioning. See Bahun (2013).
5. See Joyce (1993: 18); Joyce (1975: 271). Both Bloom and Stephen are dressed in black on 16 June 1904. Stephen is still a few days away from when he will be expected to wear gray, and Bloom wears black because he is attending Paddy Dignam's funeral.
6. Gifford and Seidman (1989: 70, n. 1). Bloom refers to his breakfast as a 'burnt offering' (Joyce 1993: 680).
7. On Joyce's politics, see Nolan (1994); on Parnell, see Lyons (1977).
8. On the father in *Ulysses*, see Rabaté (1987); Restuccia (1989).

9. Stephen's theory is based on the idea that one may become one's own pro-genitor through ghosting, and is, as argued by Deane, the expression of his urge to present himself as self-begotten (1990: 47–8).
10. In any given symptom, 'the overdetermination is the rule', claims Freud (1963: 77).
11. The 'Lochlanns' is a Gaelic word for Scandinavia/Scandinavians. The reference here is to the Norwegian Viking invasion of Ireland in 795 AD, and, possibly, also, to the establishment of the Viking settlement called Dubhlinn (Dublin) in 841 AD.
12. Noteworthy, what Bloom's father denounced when giving-up his Jewishness was the status conferred on him by his matrilineal descent, the legacy of 'mamma, poor mamma' (Joyce 1993: 107).
13. Heather Cook Callow praises the impersonal dispenser of information in 'Ithaca' for contradicting the fictional facts previously established by male voices (158–9). I find the chapter intriguing precisely because it is neither objective nor comprehensive; nor, for that matter, gender-neutral.
14. This full dot stands for 'Q. E. D.' (*quod erat demonstrandum*), the linguistic formula signifying the completion of a logical proposition. *Ulysses* opens with the terms of a syllogism (S-M-P). Cf. Gifford and Seidman (1980: 12 and 606).
15. This excerpt is taken from the middle section. Generally running without syntactic or graphic markers, 'Penelope' has seven breaks that may or may not indicate paragraphs; the middle one is marked by a full-stop. The Rosenbach MS shows that Joyce first included full-stops at the end of each block, but later removed them.
16. See the Gilbert Schema (Joyce 1993: 735). In his letter to Budgen, Joyce indicated that Molly's Ithacan name is 'Gea-Tellus' (1975: 285). Some of these descriptions have also been invoked by Attridge (1989: 543–4).
17. Ellmann (1968: 78). On Joyce's limited view of women, see Brivic (1995: 2–5).
18. Attridge (1989: 545); Burgess (1973: 59). Here one may recall Angelina Ball's memorable performance in Sean Walsh's *Bloom* (2003).
19. On the correspondences between Nora's letter-writing, the letters of Joyce's mother, and 'Penelope' see Scott (1984: 70–1). Nora never read *Ulysses*.
20. Attridge (1989: 551, n. 13). On *Ulysses*, and, specifically, Molly's monologue, as a 'written' text, see, influentially, Derrida.

Works Cited

Attridge, David (1989) 'Molly's Flow: the Writing of 'Penelope' and the Question of Women's Language', *Modern Fiction Studies*, 35/3: 543–65.
Bahun, Sanja (2004) '"Full Fathom Five Thy Father Lies": Freud, Modernists, and History', *Exit 9*, VI, 3–20.
—— (2013) *Modernism and Melancholia: Writing as Countermourning* (Oxford: Oxford University Press).
Blamires, Harry (1966) *The Bloomsday Book: a Guide through Joyce's* Ulysses (London: Methuen).
Bolt, Sydney (1981) *A Preface to James Joyce* (Harlow: Longman).
Brivic, Sheldon (1995) *Joyce's Waking Women: a Feminist Introduction to* Finnegans Wake (Madison: The University of Wisconsin Press).

Burgess, Anthony (1973) *Joysprick: an Introduction to the Language of James Joyce* (London: André Deutsch).

Cixous, Hélène (1974) *Prénoms de personne* (Paris: Seuil).

—— (1981) 'The Laugh of the Medusa', in E. Marks and I. de Courtivron (eds), *New French Feminisms: an Anthology* (Brighton: Harvester), pp. 245–64.

Callow, Heather Cook (1992) 'Joyce's Female Voices in *Ulysses*', *The Journal of Narrative Technique*, 22/3: 151–63.

Deane, Seamus (1990) 'Joyce the Irishman', in D. Attridge (ed.), *The Cambridge Companion to James Joyce* (Cambridge: Cambridge University Press), pp. 31–53.

Derrida, Jacques (1988) '*Ulysses* Gramophone: Hear say yes in Joyce', in Bernard Benstock (ed.), *James Joyce: the Augmented Ninth* (Syracuse: Syracuse University Press).

Ellmann, Mary (1968) *Thinking about Women* (New York: Harcourt Brace Jovanovich).

French, Marilyn (1976) *The Book as World: James Joyce's* Ulysses (Urbana: University of Illinois Press).

Freud, Sigmund (1963[1905;1901]) *Dora: Fragment of an Analysis of a Case of Hysteria* (New York: Collier Books).

Gifford, Don and R. J. Seidman (eds) (1989) Ulysses *Annotated: Notes for James Joyce's* Ulysses (Berkeley: University of California Press).

Gottfried, Roy K. (1980) *The Art of Joyce's Syntax in* Ulysses (London: Macmillan).

Henke, Suzette (1978) *Joyce's Moraculous Sindbook: a Study of* Ulysses (Columbus: Ohio State University Press).

—— (1990) *James Joyce and the Politics of Desire* (New York: Routledge).

Joyce, James (1966[1957]) *Letters, Vol. 1*, ed. Stuart Gilbert (New York: Viking).

—— (1975) Richard Ellmann (ed.) *Selected Letters of James Joyce* (New York: Viking Press).

—— (1993[1922]) *Ulysses* (Oxford: Oxford University Press).

—— (2000) 'The Shade of Parnell' (1912), in *Occasional, Critical, and Political Writing* (Oxford: Oxford University Press), pp. 191–6.

Kristeva, Julia (1989) *Black Sun: Depression and Melancholia*, trans. Leon S. Roudiez (New York: Columbia University Press).

Lyons, F.S.L. (1977) *Charles Stewart Parnell* (Oxford: Oxford University Press).

Nolan, Emer (1994) *James Joyce and Nationalism* (New York: Routledge).

Rabaté, Jean-Michel (1987) 'Fathers, Dead or Alive, in *Ulysses*', in Harold Bloom (ed.), *James Joyce's* Ulysses (New York: Chelsea), pp. 81–98.

Restuccia, F.L. (1989) *Joyce and the Law of the Father* (New Haven: Yale University Press).

Scott, Bonnie K. (1984) *Joyce and Feminism* (Bloomington: Indiana University Press).

Wilson, Edmund (1961[1931]) *Axel's Castle: a Study in the Imaginative Literature of 1870–1930* (Glasgow: Collins Fontana).

4

What Happens When a Transvestite Gynaecologist Usurps the Narrator?: Cross-Gendered Ventriloquism in Djuna Barnes's *Nightwood*

Sarah Hayden

Introduction

The story of Djuna Barnes's 1936 novel, *Nightwood*, is ostensibly concerned with the ecstasies and torments endured by three individuals, each consumed by their fascination with an enigmatic young American woman named Robin Vote. It is also the story of the infamously verbose quack gynaecologist Doctor Matthew Dante O'Connor who narrates much of the novel. The intricately entangled trio consists of the Baron Felix Volkbein, who marries Robin; Nora Flood, who loves her best; and Jenny Petherbridge, who appropriates this love of Robin. For them, the doctor is both confessor and interpreter; repeatedly called upon to mould words around Robin's uncompromising silence. Matthew is compelled to enunciate, for his less self-aware companions, the narrative of their thwarted love.

Damned and blessed in equal parts by the preface bestowed upon it by its eminent but infamously over-enthusiastic editor, T.S. Eliot, the clandestine orientation of *Nightwood*'s dialectic of desire was initially coded *sub-rosa*. Rediscovered and exultantly championed in the latter decades of the twentieth century by second-wave feminist scholars re-gendering modernisms, analysis of *Nightwood*'s undisguised depictions of lesbian relationships have for too long distracted the critical gaze from other, more fertile, domains of inquiry. Classed as an autobiographical queer modernist Baedeker, it is read as a guidebook to continental Sapphic subcultures of the interwar period. Suffering a fate which all too commonly befalls those female modernists latterly 'reclaimed' for scholarship, and much less often afflicts their male modernist peers, many contemporary readers are preoccupied with speculating on the autobiographical origins of the novel's characters and imagery. In her authoritative *Improper Modernism: Djuna Barnes's Bewildering Corpus* (2009), Daniela Caselli convincingly articulates the failings of such biographical readings (33). Citing Barnes's own 'stubborn determination to discourage biographical readings of her oeuvre' (121), Caselli resists the pervasive suggestion that this exquisitely dense novel was intended only to deliver a rather facile lesson on the particular perils of lesbianism. Even if we accept that Barnes took her former lover Thelma Wood as the germ for her construction of the character of Robin Vote, and that Matthew's characterization owes some element of its fantastic skeleton to a real-life character Dan Mahoney, the 'claim that *Nightwood* should be perceived as the tortured and muted expression on a lesbian relationship is critically misleading' (Chisholm 1997: 176).

In this chapter, I argue that *Nightwood* is a novel of lesbian desire only insofar as it constitutes the most explicit aspect of a much braver and more interesting project. *Nightwood* extrudes its treatise on subversive sexualities through an infinitely more sophisticated consideration of the potential capacities and exigencies of speaking in a cross-gendered voice. At the crux of this project lies a phenomenon of vocal slippage; the temporary accession of narrational responsibility from a third-person omniscient figure to a character within the novel. The patriarchal privileges conferred upon Matthew by his unlicensed gynaecological (and quasi-psychoanalytic) practice are constantly undermined and ultimately undone by his professionally incongruous deployment of a cross-gendered voice inherently resistant to, and rupturing of, the very masculinist, medical authority he illegitimately invokes. Reading *Nightwood* as an ideologically and artistically radical disquisition on voice and expression in a matrix of performative gender and problematized sex, I propose to investigate what happens when a transvestite gynaecologist usurps the narrator. Taking Judith Butler's work on drag and performed gender as a starting point, I will engage with her adaptation of Julia Kristeva's concept of the abject and theses of melancholic gender and identity as performance. Considering Matthew's cross-gendered speech in light of aspirations advanced by Hélène Cixous's 'The Laugh of the Medusa' (1976) and Luce Irigaray's *This Sex Which Is Not One* (1977), I will explore its relationship with that fugitive field of *écriture féminine*. At the end of the novel, Matthew revokes his narrational role, and prematurely quits the diegesis while Robin walks into the wild, surrenders her human voice and with it, arguably, her humanity. Reading these exits as key, attending to the silences, departures and degradations of the final two chapters, I will attempt to discover why the author designated this potently poly-valent though biologically male voice to tell her story.

Matthew

Just as, in the first chapter, Felix finds that entertainments at the home of Count Altamonte have been hijacked by 'an Irishman [Matthew O'Connor] from the Barbary Coast' (Barnes 1963: 29), so *Nightwood*'s readers are abandoned, for much of this novel, by the omniscient narrator who opens and closes the book. We are left instead to encounter the story as mediated by 'a great liar, but a valuable liar' (50), 'doctor Matthew-Mighty-grain-of-salt Dante O'Connor' (118).

My focus, then, is on the figure of Doctor. For Judith Lee, he is a problematized and rupturing 'representation of the Word' (1991: 216). In the character of Matthew, the novel's preoccupation with identity is crystallized. His body and occupation identify him as male while his language (and, occasionally, his attire) is female. Invoked to illuminate the opaque mysteries of human desire, inveigled into the role of *ersatz* omniscient narrator, the doctor proffers verbose and florid insights into every male and female character. Medium, interpreter, decoder of silence and stuttering, he allows them to speak through his problematically sexed and gendered body. Suspended in a web of tongue-tied lovers, he alone desires no Other; lamenting instead a female self that could have been. Channelled through Matthew's mouth and the incessant, compulsive, catachresis it articulates, the familiar conventions of the novel form 'plot, character, setting, theme [...] are dramatically mediated in the play of language' (Singer 1984: 67). His is a lyrically charged, often impossibly prescient performance of cross-gendered ventriloquism.

Matthew's polymorphous identity renders him capable of inhabiting and understanding myriad other minds, other 'positions' of class, race and gender, allowing him to play the role of enabling, facilitating analyst. Although Susan Gal, via Foucault, posits silence as the essential quality of the psychoanalyst, 'the silent listener who judges and who thereby exerts power over the one who speaks' (Foucault 1979) (1995: 171), Matthew is anything but silent. Rather, in the variant of talking therapy he so exuberantly practises, it is he, as the unorthodox self-appointing psychoanalyst to Felix, Nora and, through them, Robin, who is required to speak. The doctor lends form and coherence to characters whose own outcast status is foregrounded through his identification with them. Having already side-lined the rather less insightful perceptions of the putatively omniscient narrator, he then activates a second level of ventriloquism. Matthew gives us impossibly astute, accurate accounts of Robin's internal machinations, artfully explains Nora's psychic pain to herself, and belies a compassionate comprehension of Felix's angst-ridden attachment to his artificial, noble heritage.

At times, Matthew's parody of Freudian analysis veers towards the prophetic. While counselling Nora in Chapter 3, 'Watchman, What of the Night?', he predicts her fate in the entanglement with surety: 'in the end you'll all be locked together, like the poor beasts that get their antlers mixed and are found dead that way, their heads fattened with a knowledge of each other they never wanted, having had to contemplate each other, head-on and eye to eye, until death' (Barnes 1963: 145).[1] As Ed Madden (2006) observes, this presence within the doctor of preternatural ability arising out of disability has led many critics, since and including Eliot, to propose Matthew as a Tiresian figure. Anatomically male, but verbally constructed and sometimes visually coded as female, his interstitial status grants him compensatory Tiresian powers of insight. In this chapter, I hope to develop Madden's proposition towards an understanding of the nature and significance of Matthew's eventual, catastrophic renunciation of speech for silence.

Abjection

The abject is defined by Kristeva as 'what disturbs identity, system, order' (1982: 4). It is 'what does not respect borders, positions, rules. The in-between, the ambiguous, the composite' (4) is the human reaction to the threatened breakdown in meaning which occurs at the blurring of the boundaries between subject and object. Writing out of earlier feminist critiques of the constricting conflation of femininity and maternity within the phallocentric universe, Kristeva locates the origin of abjection at the point of separation from the mother; the me and (m)other. 'The abject confronts us' Kristeva writes 'within our personal archaeology, with our earliest attempts to release the hold of maternal entity even before existing outside of her, thanks to the autonomy of language' (13). Butler's reimagining of abjection moves the focus from the mother's body (and the terror-response ascribed to it by Simone de Beauvoir) to articulate the abjection of the body whose gender fails or refuses to inhabit a single position within the binary imposed by society. As Butler claims, 'Discrete genders are part of what "humanizes" individuals with[in] contemporary culture; indeed, we regularly punish those who fail to do their gender right' (1990: 139). In Sandy Stone's *Posttransexual Manifesto*, we read of the 'occulting' of the transgendered body for its refusal to submit to what she calls 'the binary phallocratic founding myth by which Western bodies and subjects are authorized' so that 'only one body per gendered subject is "right"' (1991: 298). The doctor's body – sexed male but gendered female – is abjected by the storyworld chiefly because it is just such an ideologically intersexed, intergendered body. Valorizing liminality, Matthew embodies and frequently enunciates a heroic but ultimately untenable stand against the hegemonic imperative to designate clear and absolute borders between false polarities.

Matthew's gender identity, that of the biologically male *mère-manqué(e)*, is yet empowered by his male appendage, which he calls 'Tiny O'Toole' (Barnes 1963: 188). Although he conceives of himself as female, he maintains the anatomical singularity which guarantees him phallocratic privilege. The phallus which belies the fiction of his maternal fantasies is a distressing rebuke to his self-construction. Pitiably figured as 'like a ruined bird' (188), it cannot be ignored. As he maintains the essential endowment of his masculinity, his geographical and professional mobility are unhindered; his appearance is not usually legibly other. Yet, at every juncture and in every conversation, he undermines and deplores his given gender.

Various critics have addressed the manner in which Barnes constructs the doctor as both male and female, most notably Frann Michel, who argues 'that the doctor speaks indicates his masculinity; how he speaks calls this into question' (1989: 41). While Cixous maintains that we continually fluctuate between gender roles, in *Nightwood* this fluid fluctuation is rendered an overt act of gender bi-location. Relating his horror at witnessing Jenny's seduction of Robin, Matthew claims 'It was more than a boy like me (who am the last woman left in this world, though I am the bearded lady) could bear' (Barnes 1963: 145). Matthew is simultaneously a signifier for the most patriarchal of manly professions – the gynaecologist and Freudian analyst – and the man in drag who mourns the woman he could have been. Although repeatedly referred to thereafter as 'Doctor', Matthew is first introduced with wryly framing punctuation and coyly ambiguous phrasing as 'a middle-aged "medical student" [...] whose interest in gynaecology had driven him half around the world' (29). None of the identities to which he lays claim – man, mother, doctor, therapist – go uncontested.

Thus, though no biological ambiguity is in evidence, his is a culturally unintelligible body. Within Butler's model, this gendered pluralism, making it illegible, marks Matthew's body as irrevocably abject. Of course, the historic association of the abject with the maternal female makes the doctor's preoccupation with motherhood particularly interesting. The feminine identity whose foreclosed potentiality he mourns is neither vamp nor virgin, but rather that of a ferociously fecund mother. Matthew's prohibited yearning for a forbidden femininity is compounded and complicated by his particular predilection for maternity; that most reviled and feared capacity of female embodiment. His fantasy is doubly transgressive, his cross-gendered voice made doubly subversive. Innumerable references to himself as 'the good woman in the shoe' (Barnes 1963: 134) or 'the Old Woman who lives in the closet' (196) realize their full potency in the context of his core ambition: 'no matter what I may be doing, in my heart is the wish for children and knitting. God, I never asked better than to boil some good man's potatoes and toss up a child for him every nine months by the calendar' (132). The doctor's apparent desire for and appropriation of feminine identity is anything but archetypal. As Jane Marcus has elegantly expressed it, his gender fantasy is 'a gynologos, not a cliterologos' (1991: 230).

Butler convincingly argues that the cultural construction of gender as dyadic produces an oppressive identity regime, and results in the abjection and effective vomiting of such ambiguously gendered abjected bodies out of a nauseated binary-biased society. In her 1986 essay, Butler posits that 'insofar as social existence requires an unambiguous gender affinity, it is not possible to exist in a socially meaningful sense outside of established norms' (41). Harnessing his abjection then, Barnes gives *Nightwood* to the doctor because he alone – simultaneously straddling and outside of every social category – can tell the story of 'the young, the drug addict, the profligate, the drunken' (Barnes 1963: 137). He speaks for and about those degenerates, deviants and other outsiders, hostages to their 'individual misery' (Eliot 1963: 6), the cohort amongst whom Barnes numbered herself.

Nightwood's gendered performances

My second proposition is that *Nightwood* can be read as a novel that is broadly preoccupied with identity and specifically gender as performance. *Nightwood* is a novel about questioning gender as a weighty costume we unthinkingly put on, and call nature, without thinking to consider an alternative; and it is about all that we lose by limiting ourselves to unitary identity. It overflows with images of imposture, artifice and falsehood. We read in the opening pages of Felix's fascination with the 'splendid and reeking falsification' (Barnes 1963: 25) of the circus, signalling perhaps to our fascination with the equally splendid and reeking falsification of the text. As readers, we are beset by slippage and blurring. Like anxiously improvising actors, characters grasp for props to ornament their appropriated and artificially constructed identities. Robin seeks out the antique brocaded dresses of a distant age (66). Felix inherits a fabricated family heritage. Jenny the cuckoo-interloper purloins 'the most passionate love she knew, Nora's for Robin' (103). *Nightwood* continually denies the comforting fictions of essentiality and naturalness. As Alan Singer claims, '[b]oth image and character, traditionally presented as transcendent, are here contingent and mutable' (1984: 81).[2]

Granted a knowledge which grants him enhanced, though tortured understanding, Matthew alone perceives and comprehends the ubiquity of this 'mighty uncertainty!' which adumbrates human perception (Barnes 1963: 135), proclaiming:

> Do things look in the ten or twelve of noon as they look in the dark? Is the hand, the face, the foot, the same face and hand and foot seen by the sun? For now the hand lies in a shadow, its beauties and its deformities are in a smoke – there is a sickle of doubt across the cheek bone thrown by the hat's brim, so there is half a face to be peered back into speculation.
>
> (Barnes 1963: 125)

As Susana S. Martins observes, in 'the case of gender identity categories, Freudian discourse (variously related, revised, parodied, or contested) permeates Barnes's novel' (1999: 110). Accordingly, and encouraged by the doctor's own Freudian discourses, Butler's thesis of melancholy gender can be applied to Matthew's frequent locutions of gender grief. Butler contends that 'the positions of "masculine" and "feminine," [...] are established in part through prohibitions which demand the loss of certain sexual attachments, and demand as well that those losses not be around, and not be achieved' (1997: 168). To be man, then, one must renounce – that is internalize and close off – all that is feminine and, accordingly, the man as sexual object. Rather than renouncing his femininity and desire for the male body, Matthew instead exteriorizes these prohibited aspects of his psyche. Intensely aware of this lost potential in the form of another gender, Matthew constantly refers to himself as female. He does so 15 times in a novel just 239 pages long, referring to himself as a 'bride' (Barnes 1963: 53), a 'girl' (109, 111, 131), 'the Old Woman' (196) and a 'lady' (145, 214). This gender-troubling dialogue is most startling for being so intensely self-conscious and so frequently appealing for readerly complicity[3]: 'am I to blame if I've turned up this time as I shouldn't have been, when it was a high soprano I wanted, and deep corn curls to my bum, with a womb as big as a king's kettle, and a bosom as high as the bowsprit of a fishing schooner?' (132).

Whereas this mourning process is not ordinarily visible or even tangible, in the doctor we witness an individual who not only acknowledges, but actively grieves for the femininity which has been socially foreclosed to him and for the freedom to engage in homosexual activity.[4] Compounding his revolt against society's gender injunctions, he vocalizes his homosexual desire. He is observed '[s]tanding small and insubordinate sometimes crying to' a male passerby's 'departing shadow: "Aren't you the beauty!"' (Barnes 1963: 49), compares Paris's multi-ethnic male population to '*mortadellas* slung on a table' (136) and proclaims: 'I haunt the *pissoirs* as naturally as Highland Mary her cows down by the Dee' (132).

For Butler, 'when a man drags up' he '"becomes" a woman [...] so that he can act out the psychically unacknowledged desire for the same-sex love object' (Lloyd 2007: 86). In 'Watchman, What of the Night?', Nora – herself extremely uncomfortable in her sex-gender role – calls to his dilapidated lodgings to find Matthew *en flagrante* with an image of his alternative self. Rouged and bewigged, in 'a narrow iron bed, with its heavy and dirty linen sheets, lay the doctor in a woman's flannel night gown' (Barnes 1963: 116). His drag performance (intended, Barnes implies, for the gaze of an absent or tardy another) is suspended when Nora's arrival induces the doctor to resume his pseudo-psychoanalytic function. This scene, which lies at the material and conceptual core of the novel, invokes the Red Riding Hood story to unsettling effect.

Within Butler's theory of performative gender, 'femininity is an ideal which everyone always and only "imitates". Thus, drag imitates the imitative structure of gender, revealing gender itself to be an imitation' (1997: 176). Marjorie Garber writes that 'when Nora intrudes upon Doctor O'Connor' in drag [...] 'she is "dismayed" at first, because what she witnesses is not a revelation but a recognition' of the performative nature of gender identity (1992: 386). The source of this dismay, I contend, leads us back to Butler's essential premise: that drag succeeds in unsettling our culturally constructed belief in gender as absolute and assigned. Nora is merely experiencing the shock of recognizing another who is playing at 'being a woman' (Butler 1993: 126).

Furthermore, Matthew, as the wolf in bed with grandmother, serves as an over-determined symbol for all of the performances which proliferate in the text. Thus, he leads us to re-examine Robin's performance of a primeval 'bestial' 'natural' feminine, 'like a painting by the *douanier* Rousseau' (Barnes 1963: 56) and reminds us of Frau Mann's arch refusal to verify Count Onatorio's aristocratic credentials. Disdaining to make a definitive statement, she only amplifies his anxiety, teasing, 'Am I what I say? Are you? Is the doctor?' (43).[5] Similarly engaged, Djuna Barnes repeatedly demolishes the notion of stable identity categories. Sandra Gilbert argues that after the Great War, the author's male modernist counterparts used transvestite tropes in a contrary and conservative attempt to re-establish control, 'seeking reassurance in what they hope is the reality behind appearances' (1980: 416). Against James Joyce, D.H. Lawrence and T.S. Eliot, Gilbert positions three female modernists who employ tropes of transvestism to wholly different effect. Alongside Virginia Woolf and H.D., Djuna Barnes was acutely conscious that, as Garber offers, 'one of the most consistent and effective functions of the transvestite in culture is to indicate the place of what [she calls] "category crisis," disrupting and calling attention to cultural, social, or aesthetic dissonances' (1992: 16).

The spectacle of Matthew's transvestism, his 'gun-metal cheeks and chin', 'heavily rouged' and 'painted face' (Barnes 1963: 117), draws his cross-gendered voice to the surface of the text; it inscribes the hybrid problematic of this cross-gendered voice on the surface of his body. As though in illustration of this interplay of gendered contradiction, the narrator's description of his resonant oratorical style, 'he got his audience by the simple device of pronouncing at the top of his voice', is immediately followed by the complicating parenthetical qualification that 'at such moments as irritable and possessive as a maddened woman's' (31). Like his body, his voice is distinctly coded as cross-gendered.

Écriture féminine

The third strand of this reading of *Nightwood*'s ventriloquy proposes that it is a visionary prototype of *écriture féminine*. The peculiar density of Matthew's speech – its superfluity of images and overwhelming fog of contingency which pervades its every instance – makes it a volatile, *scriptable* text. In 'The Laugh of the Medusa' Cixous posits an alternative model of bisexuality as an essential quality of the producer of *écriture féminine*, invoking a subject no longer 'enclosed in the false theater of phallocentric representationalism which has founded his/her erotic universe' (1976: 884). Matthew's exile from this false theatre grants him the further evolutionary compensation of speaking a *langue féminine*. Admitting 'I have a narrative, but you will be put to it to find it' (Barnes 1963: 141), his is a language 'in which [he] goes off in all directions and in which [Nora] is unable to discern the coherence of any meaning' (Irigaray 1985: 29). Frequently compelled to reassure his listeners, 'Don't get restless – I'm coming back to my point' (Barnes 1963: 144), his '[c]ontradictory words seem a little crazy to the logic of reason, and inaudible for him who listens with ready-made grids, a code prepared in advance' (Irigaray 1985: 29).

The doctor, as the speaking counterpart to Robin's mute somnambulist, is Cixous's 'break[er] of automatism', the 'peripheral figur[e] that no authority can ever subjugate' (1976: 883). In *Nightwood*, Barnes's genius for surreal imagistic proliferation – multiplicity constantly deferring meaning – acts upon the reader with near-hypnotic effect.[6] Even within the context of high modernist fiction, *Nightwood* appears audaciously opaque. Teeming with unmoored polyglot references, a motley assembly of 'St. John Chrysotum' (Barnes 1963: 138), 'the Lily of Killarney' and 'Prester Matthew' (139), 'Donne' and 'Montaigne' (140) is invoked within the space of three pages) and underwired by a Rabelaisian trellis of bestial and corporeal imagery, it remains at all times slippery and malleable.

Notwithstanding Eliot and Coleman's anxious snippings and sculptings of the manuscript, Barnes still succeeded, as per Cixous's exhortations in writing her body (Cixous 1976: 886) and those of multiple others into *Nightwood*. Flouting 'every possible taboo from the excretory to the sexual' (Marcus 1991: 235) strange and estranged human bodies – abjected, forbidden and grotesque flesh – people this novel. Shot through with an unblushing physicality, the transgressive impact of this poetic of embodiment is enhanced and amplified by the privileging of the voice of a cross-gendered transvestite. One of the doctor's more curious rhetorical quirks is his tendency to conflate the psychical and the physical (Martins: 1999: 111). In his prolix diagnosis of the pathology in Nora's relationship with Robin, he attempts to outdo the former's professions of misery with a fanciful composite of physio-psychological complaints: 'A broken heart have you! I have falling arches, flying dandruff, a floating kidney, shattered nerves *and* a broken heart!' (Barnes 1963: 218). Matthew's emotional landscape is inextricably mapped onto a peculiar topology of embodied existence. His construction of cross-gendered identity has heightened his awareness of the body as assigned; a given capable of infringing upon and existing in dynamic, often contested relation to, a misaligned psyche. For Matthew, who 'turned up this time' as he 'shouldn't have been' (132) in an incongruously male body, all psychic experience is correlative to bodily being.

Robin's Silence

Matthew's assumption of the role of cross-gendered ventriloquist arises from his imbricated status in relation to the three concepts discussed above, namely: abjection, performativity and *écriture féminine*. Before advancing to propose an analysis of his subsequent relinquishment of this role, it is necessary to consider the countering valency of Robin's silence. As Frann Michel writes, 'whereas [Matthew] is located as a presence [...] she is located as an absence' (1989: 41). Robin is described upon her first introduction as 'beast turning human' (Barnes 1963: 59). Her silence is 'preverbal, prerational, almost prehuman' (Lee 1991: 215). Like Matthew, she straddles categories, living 'in two worlds – meet of child and desperado' (Barnes 1963: 56); she is immensely powerful but apparently without conscious agency. Having first encountered her lying in an insensible swoon, 'surrounded by a confusion or potted plants, exotic palms and cut flowers, faintly oversung by the notes of unseen birds' (55), Felix's second meeting with Robin takes the form of a walk in the equally artificially 'natural' surroundings of the *Jardins du Luxembourg* (64). Even transposed from the verdant exoticism of their first meeting, 'she yet carried the quality of the "way back" as animals do' (64). Entranced by a quality he tragically misinterprets, Felix 'felt he could talk to her, tell her anything, though she herself was so silent' (64). Robin's allure emanates from a virgin blankness, a childish lack of definition onto which each of her lovers serially projects their own painfully self-aware personae. As Nora later discovers, Robin is silent because she is unconscious of herself as a being amongst others; selfless because, as the doctor explains, 'she can't do anything in relation to any one but herself' (207). Unmoored by memory, because she is without a sense of time past, without guilt. Without the need to articulate herself – that essential compulsion of selfhood – she is untroubled by any yearning for the communion of communication with an Other.

At the end of Chapter 2, Robin abandons her son and husband, never to contact them again. Some months later, she returns to the Parisian quarter: 'When she was seen again in the quarter, it was with Nora Flood. She did not explain where she had been, she was unable or unwilling to give an account of herself' (76). Instead, she leaves it to the doctor to construct even her internal narrative. Her silence is a surrender that Robin Lakoff terms the expropriation of 'a quintessentially human property: the ability to name and define self and environment' (1995: 33). As the animal-like and silent counterweight to the perhaps excessively human and lalomanic Matthew, Robin approaches the '*weltlos*' position

Martin Heidegger assigns to the animal while Matthew reveals himself as compulsively and conspicuously '*weltbildend*' (1995: 160).

Along with frequent animal allusions, references to sleepwalking abound. Christened 'La Somnambule' in the title of Chapter 2, Robin is not held to account for her promiscuous night-walking. Her sleep, like her animalistic lack of consciousness, and consequent position outside of language, protects her from self-knowledge. In a particularly poignant passage (Barnes 1963: 20), Nora confesses attempting to force Robin from this extra-linguistic state into the symbolic realm (Michel 1989: 45). The incident is related in terms evocative of the mishandling of an exotic, unknowable, animal. After months of enduring Robin's absences and infidelities, Nora shakes her errant lover awake and violently demands of Robin that she verbalize; that she put words on her absences: 'No rot had touched her until then, and there before my eyes I saw her corrupt all at once and withering, because I had struck her sleep away, and I went mad' (Barnes 1963: 206). Robin becomes an agent in social discourse and responsible for her behaviour only if or when she wakes from her preconscious 'animal' state. Threatened at this juncture by the presentiment of her fall, Robin elects to maintain her silence by tenaciously resisting the linguistic impetus to name herself, fleeing instead into the arms of her next lover-victim.

The Doctor's disintegration and the aftermath

In the penultimate chapter, the self-professed priest, doctor and prophet begs to be released from the narrator's role and surrenders his voice. In conversation with Nora, he abruptly stands up, in 'confused and unhappy silence' (Barnes 1963: 223) and simply walks out. Matthew, our one-time erudite narrator, screams and collapses into sobbing laughter; he pleads: 'Now that you have all heard what you wanted to hear, can't you let me loose now, let me go?' (233). Appropriately, this collapse is experienced as a physical, visceral disintegration of his hyper-embodied persona: 'He came down upon the table with all his weight, his arms spread, his head between them, his eyes wide open and crying, staring along the table where the ash blew and fluttered with his gasping breath' (233).

Matthew's hysterical deliquescence is self-diagnosed as the inevitable consequence of the emotional-linguistic excrescence he has been forced, through his monologic parables, to absorb, digest and reformulate: 'What do they all come to me for? Why do they all tell me everything then expect it to lie hushed in me, like a rabbit gone home to die?' (228). His empathy exhausted, the doctor can no longer 'see or hear anything but his own heart' (228–9). As he attempts to leave, his parting words frame a last prophecy: 'Now, he said, the end – mark my words – now nothing, but wrath and weeping' (233).

The wrath and weeping Matthew predicts close the final chapter and, indeed, the novel. His exuberant cross-gendered voice has been extinguished; replaced by the monadic voice – less troubled and less troubling – of the third-person narrator. Voiced by the reinstated omniscient narrator and ominously entitled 'The Possessed', this mercifully brief coda stands apart, signalling Matthew's absence with its every short, sequentially ordered sentence. Previously, the doctor, in prescient fulfillment of Cixous's imprecations, blew up the Law in language – but this Law is definitively restored in the last chapter. With the doctor's departure, the novel, which heretofore appeared always oblique, suddenly seems to right itself. 'The Possessed' gives us Barnes without the doctor: *Nightwood* in a more linear, (Cixous might say phallogocentric) novelistic mode. As Donna Gerstenberger describes it, 'Only the narrator's voice is heard in 'The Possessed' and this voice is straightforward and declarative' (1989: 137). By allowing us this glimpse (chapter-to-chapter) of the chasm between these two ways of writing, Barnes demonstrates her own gymnastic abilities – the straddling of phallocratic and feminine writing positions. Yet, rather than functioning solely as a virtuoso exercise in stylistic agility, 'The Possessed' crystallizes the matrix of meaning within which Robin as the eternal feminine in 'boys trousers' (Barnes 1963: 237) and the gender-riddling Matthew are suspended.

The barking woman

Arriving with Jenny in New York, Robin is depicted as a restive presence: both haunted and haunting. Her 'motive power [...] crippled' (Barnes 1963: 234), she wanders in disengaged catatonia from city to country. Abandoning Jenny to hysterics of distraught incomprehension in a darkened hotel-room, Robin is drawn, inexorably and unconsciously, towards 'Nora's part of the country' (236). Sleeping at times in the woods, at others in the equally unpopulated pews of an abandoned chapel, Robin's trajectory traces spiralling ley-lines of oblique arrival at her former lover's homeplace. Recalling Matthew's prophesy, she is awakened one night by the barking of Nora's dog. This sound acts with similar effect upon her former lover; Nora finds herself compelled to walk, blindly and shaking to the same chapel.

The description of the scene Nora witnesses closes the novel. Even the supposedly omniscient narrator can only stand and stare; the precise nature of what passes between Robin and her animal interlocutor goes unanalysed. Having already induced the dog's 'quivering', 'whimpering' retreat into 'the farthest corner' of the chapel, Robin then lowers her head, drags 'her forelocks in the dust, [and...] struck against his side' (238). This act of imponderable aggression causes the inconsolable creature to howl and bite at her whereupon she falls to her knees beside him and then 'She began to bark also, crawling after him – barking in a fit of laughter, obscene and touching' (ibid.). *Nightwood* ends in this description of languageless cross-species reflection: 'she, grinning and crying with him; crying in shorter and shorter spaces, moving head to head, until she gave up, lying out, her hands beside her, her face turned and weeping; and the dog too gave up then, and lay down, his eyes bloodshot, his head flat along her knees' (239).

In spite of the jarring conclusion it purposes, the significance of this dog has been critically overlooked. Long associated with the literary representation of precarious, interstitial, positions, the domestic dog is resistant to categorization as fully either beast or human (Serpell 1995: 254; Williams: 2007: 93). Its oscillating status fits it for its customary role as symbol of the borderland. Charting the centuries-long swing of the 'dog' signifier between the antithetical positions of 'man's proverbial best friend' and 'heretical hell-hound', Ben Ramm makes explicit this connection with the borderland of the Kristevan abject (2005: 49).

Drawing on this tradition of canine symbolism, I would like to read the encounter between Robin and her erstwhile lover's pet as an externalization of Robin's extra-linguistic alienation and concordant abjection from society. Ramm analyses the employment of the figure of the dog within medieval texts to signal 'a crisis of meaning' in language (2005: 50). He suggests that this trope derives from the canine's peculiar placement as an intimate, integrated, interpolator of human society which is, paradoxically, denied the most potent signifier of human identity: language itself (51).[7] The uncanny mechanism by which the dog is frequently anthropomorphized and read as though possessed of human qualities makes it, he argues, 'in some senses akin to an automaton, able to produce a semblance of participation in human exchanges, but nothing beyond that' (ibid.). The dog embodies Robin's marginal status as animalistic human; capable of, but resistant to, language. Trembling, rearing, mouth agape, the creature is transfixed by the spectacle of Robin sliding unchecked to join him – in kinetic mimesis of her descent into animalistic wordlessness – on the floor before the altar (Barnes 1963: 236–9).[8] Just as the passive 'sign of the dog', being deprived of linguistic agency, is determined as a vessel for externally attributed meaning' (Ramm 2005: 51), Robin, too, is ascribed meaning and motivation by those around her, most expertly and catastrophically, by Matthew. Indeed, it is Robin's wordlessly destructive trajectory from Felix to Nora and then Jenny, which he synopsizes as 'Love falling buttered side down, fate falling arse up!' that occasions Matthew's ultimately annihilative attempt to 'tell the story of the world to the world!' (Barnes 1963: 238).

Robin's silence and her unconscious acquiescence of the expropriated narration, which strives to frame and explain her, make the canine an apt final companion. Reminiscent of Jacques Derrida's location of the source of nature's sadness, not in *Sprachlösigkeit* – the inability to speak – but, rather, in the animal's 'inability to name itself' (Derrida 2008: 19–20), neither Robin nor the dog who witnesses her eventual 'turning beast' name themselves. Located on the borders of the symbolic, neither can conceive of themselves in relation to another. As Matthew explains, '[Robin] herself is the only "position"' (Barnes 1963: 207). Functioning analogously to Matthew's transvestism, which externalized his cross-gendered duality, Nora's dog makes visible Robin's extralinguistic abjection. Passive and bereft of agency, they are equally open to external interpretation and narration.

The final appalling pairing of woman and dog takes place in a wordless location beyond the frontier of the novel's capacity for making meaning. In a modernist extension of medieval tropes of canine category crisis, the barking woman stands as brute and brutal speechless symbol for the surrender of speech to silence. Robin's renunciation of language culminates in her degeneration into animality. Her non-signifying, hollow, howling mourns the cessation of Matthew's valiant, endlessly meaning-deferring catachresis. Notwithstanding the fact that he has already abandoned *Nightwood* to its appalling dénouement, with the apparition of the barking woman, the doctor enjoys a retroactive redemption *in absentia*.

Conclusion

In Matthew, Barnes created an *ür*-narrator, a demiurgic, cross-gendered, decoder and eloquent historian of human affections. Matthew usurps the narrator in a grand, desperate attempt to push the narration of a novel to the deepest layer of subcutaneous, sympathetic, storytelling. Where the initial narrator reports events and explains behaviour, the doctor illuminates the human condition. Transcending, in hyperaware lucidity, all constricting categories of belonging and identity, his cross-gendered sensibility is uniquely calibrated to channel the frequencies of the abjected bodies of the underworld. Superseding the omniscience of the original narrator, he comprehends the most perverse contortions born of love and desire. Beyond perceptive, his insights are prophetic; his analogies as luridly coloured as they are devastating. His cross-gendered voice swoops in extraordinary figures of understanding and linguistic mastery, falling silent before the novel's end. However, the ephemeral transitory nature of Matthew's cross-gendered narration does not negate its happening. Although ultimately revealed as unsustainable, the transgressive usurpation of narration by a being 'indefinitely other in her[him]self' (Irigaray 1985: 29) still transmits a powerful, subversive charge. The significance of Matthew's exit/failure calls to be reappraised in light of the much greater horror – the spectre of a barking woman – which follows in its wake.

Readdressing the concepts of voice-activating abjection and *écriture féminine*, I have shown that, having created the doctor as a ludicrously wise and articulate intergendered, intersexed being, Barnes 'defrocks' him because his fluid hybridity – engendered in and through his cross-gendered voice – is impossible. This is not to say that it is unimaginable, or, rather, that it does not warrant imagining. Cixous and Irigaray conceived of their *écriture féminine* as a utopian ideal that must, nevertheless, be theorized, described and dreamt. Matthew is called forth to speak, performs his piece with devastating aplomb, but is silenced at the end because he too is a utopian impossibility. Crucially, his eventual exit does not obliterate the trace of his temporary empowerment. Leaving us with a brutal dystopian reflection on the renunciation of speech – of silence and barking – Barnes retroactively elevates Matthew's valiant championing of an exquisite, multiplicitous and unfettered cross-gendered language. By granting and revoking Matthew's extraordinary though ephemeral vocal powers – giving him the cross-gendered voice of a transvestite gynaecologist – she rehearses modernism's paradoxically verbose expression of the crisis of faith in language. Through Matthew's vocal performance of cross-gendered abjection, Djuna Barnes explores her evanescent belief in the liberating potential of giving voice to a third sex; she voices the promise of making an escape from the bounds of gender conventions.

Notes

1. Matthew's predictions that Felix will one day find consolation in alcohol (Barnes: 1963: 36, 41), are also fulfilled: 'I said you would come to it' (172).
2. Against this, Charles Baxter suggests that *Nightwood* is 'suffocated by its own remoteness' (1974: 1176); that it bears witness to 'the dangers and consequences of "fine writing"' (1176). His reading suggests that *Nightwood* functions metatextually to chart the crisis of modernism (1187).
3. See Madden (2008: 194).
4. Eliot saw fit to excise from the novel a scene depicting the doctor arraigned in court for his homosexual activity. For a comprehensive analysis of Eliot's editing of such material out of the novel, see Gilmore (2009).
5. Barnes's commitment to problematizing notions of essential and 'natural' gender identity prefigures her investigation of it in *Nightwood* and functions as a remarkably prescient preface to the consanguineous efforts of twentieth century feminism and Barthes's theories of cultural myths. In 1922, she wrote an essay for *Vanity Fair* entitled 'Against Nature' which contested the hegemony of the putatively natural, and its particularly pernicious deployment against women. As early as 1929, the psychoanalyst Joan Rivière published an article entitled 'Womanliness as Masquerade' in which she expressed an impressively prescient interpretation of gender attribution. She writes: 'The reader may now ask how I define womanliness or where I draw the line between genuine womanliness and the "masquerade". My suggestion is not, however, that there is any such difference; whether radical or superficial. They are the same thing' (3).
6. Cixous asserts that 'only the poets – not the novelists, allies of representationalism' (1976: 879) could aspire to *écriture féminine*. But *Nightwood* calls to be read with the readerly attention appropriate to poetry, albeit swollen to novelistic proportions.
7. See Haraway (2003) for a comprehensive analysis of the dynamic of this integration/co-evolution.
8. In attempting to understand the profoundly unsettling charge of this canine–human interface, I am drawn again to *The Animal That Therefore I am*, in which Derrida considers the significance of clothing in preventing 'the single, incomparable and original experience of the impropriety that would come from appearing in truth naked, in front of the insistent gaze of the animal, a visionary or extra-lucid blind one' (2008: 4). Reading 'The Possessed' Robin's abandonment of language – a still more potent and primal signifier of humanity – can be considered as equivalent to the shedding of the Derridean dressing gown which produces the unsettling encounter he calls '*animalséance*'.

Works Cited

Barnes, Djuna (1922) 'Against Nature: in Which Everything that Is Young, Inadequate and Tiresome is Included in the Term Natural', *Vanity Fair*, 18: 60.
—— (1963[1936]) *Nightwood* (London: Faber).
Baxter, Charles (1974) 'A Self-Consuming Light: *Nightwood* and the Crisis of Modernism', *Journal of Modern Literature*, 3/5: 1175–87.

Butler, Judith (1986) 'Sex and Gender in Simone de Beauvoir's *Second Sex*', *Yale French Studies*, 72: 35–49.

—— (1990) *Gender Trouble* (New York: Routledge).

—— (1993) *Bodies That Matter: on the Discursive Limits of 'Sex'* (New York and London: Routledge).

—— (1997) *The Psychic Life of Power: Theories in Subjection* (Stanford: Stanford University Press).

Caselli, Daniela (2009) *Improper Modernism: Djuna Barnes's Bewildering Corpus* (Farnham: Ashgate).

Chisholm, Dianne (1997) 'Obscene Modernism: Eros Noir and the Profane Illumination of Djuna Barnes', *American Literature*, 69/1: 167–206.

Cixous, Hélène (1976) 'The Laugh of the Medusa', trans. Keith Cohen and Paula Cohen, *Signs*, 1: 875–93.

Derrida, Jacques (2008) *The Animal That Therefore I am*, trans. David Wills (New York: Fordham University Press).

Eliot, T.S. (1963 [1937]) 'Introduction', in *Nightwood* (London: Faber).

Gal, Susan (1995) 'Language, Gender, and Power: an Anthropological Review', in K. Hall and M. Bucholtz (eds), *Gender Articulated: Language and the Socially Constructed Self* (New York: Routledge), pp. 169–82.

Garber, Marjorie (1992) *Vested Interests: Cross-Dressing and Cultural Anxiety* (New York: Routledge).

Gerstenberger, Donna (1989) 'The Radical Narrative of Djuna Barnes's Nightwood', in E.G. Friedman, and M. Fuchs (eds), *Breaking the Sequence: Women's Experimental Fiction* (Princeton: Princeton University Press).

Gilmore, Leigh (2009) 'Obscenity, Modernity, Identity: Legalizing *The Well of Loneliness* and *Nightwood*', *Journal of the History of Sexuality*, 4/4: 603–24.

Gilbert, Sandra M. (1980) 'Costumes of the Mind: Transvestism as Metaphor in Modern Literature', *Critical Inquiry*, 7/2: 391–417.

Haraway, Donna (2003) *The Companion Species Manifesto: Dogs, People, and Significant Otherness* (Chicago: Prickly Paradigm Press).

Heidegger, Martin (1995[1983]) *The Fundamental Concepts of Metaphysics: World, Finitude, Solitude*, trans. William McNeill and Nicholas Walker (Bloomington: Indiana University Press).

Irigaray, Luce (1985[1977]) *This Sex Which Is Not One*, trans. Catherine Porter (New York: Cornell University Press).

Kristeva, Julia (1982) *Powers of Horror: an Essay on Abjection*, trans. Leon S. Roudiez (New York: Columbia University Press).

Lakoff, Robin T (1995) 'Cries and Whispers: the Shattering of the Silence', in K. Hall and M. Bucholtz (eds), *Gender Articulated: Language and the Socially Constructed Self* (New York: Routledge), pp. 23–50.

Lee, Judith (1991) '*Nightwood*: The Sweetest Lie', in M.L. Broe (ed.), *Silence and Power: a Reevaluation of Djuna Barnes* (Carbondale: Southern Illinois University Press), pp. 207–20.

Lloyd, Moya (2007) *Judith Butler: from Norms to Politics* (Cambridge: Polity).

Madden, Ed (2008) *Tiresian Poetics: Modernism, Sexuality, Voice 1888–2001* (Madison, NJ: Fairleigh Dickinson University Press).

Marcus, Jane (1991) 'Laughing at Leviticus: *Nightwood* as Women's Circus Epic', in M.L. Broe (ed.), *Silence and Power: a Reevaluation of Djuna Barnes* (Southern Illinois University Press), pp. 221–51.

Martins, Susana S. (1999) 'Gender Trouble and Lesbian Desire in Djuna Barnes's *Nightwood*', *Frontiers: a Journal of Women Studies*, 20/3: 108–26.

Michel, Frann (1989) 'Displacing Castration: *Nightwood, Ladies Almanack* and Feminine Writing', *Contemporary Literature*, 30/1: 33–58.

Ramm, Ben (2005) 'Barking Up the Wrong Tree? The Significance of the Chienet in Old French Romance', *Parergon*, 22/1: 47–69.

Rivière, Joan (1929) 'Womanliness as Masquerade', *International Journal of Psychoanalysis*, 10: 303–13.

Serpell, James (1995) *The Domestic Dog* (Cambridge: Cambridge University Press).

Stone, Sandy (1991) 'The Empire Strikes Back: a Posttranssexual Manifesto', in J. Epstein and K. Staub (eds), *Bodyguards: The Cultural Politics of Gender Ambiguity* (New York and London: Routledge), pp. 208–304.

Williams, David (2007) 'Inappropriate/d Others or, The Difficulty of Being a Dog', *The Drama Review: TDR*, 51/1: 92–118.

5
'Her speech a purely buccal phenomenon': Voice as a Lost Object in Samuel Beckett's Works

Rina Kim

Introduction

From the 1980s onwards, voice, or more precisely the ambiguity and paradox of voice, started to be included in the theoretical agendas of various fields including literature, film, philosophy and psychoanalysis, most notably by Steven Connor, Mladen Dolar and Adriana Cavarero, whose works were inspired by Kaja Silverman, Guy Rosolato and Michel Chion. As Norie Neumark points out, critics began to recognize the importance of 'the in-between, uncanny, and hinging qualities of the voice' (2010: xvii). This 'ambiguous ontology' of the 'status of the voice as "between the two"' placed 'at the juncture of the subject and the Other' can first be explained by the very characteristic of the voice which is located 'at the intersection of body and language' (Dolar 2006: 102). Following Roland Barthes's term 'grain of the voice', Neumark and Cavarero emphasize the voice as 'aesthetically bearing the marks of the body' (Newmark 2010: xvii, xvi), which comes from 'the vibration of a throat of flesh' and bone (Cavarero 2005: 6). This phenomenon of the voice 'bearing the marks of the body' is only too familiar to readers of Samuel Beckett. Indeed, his short prose piece 'L'image'/'The Image' (1959) opens with a powerful image of voice as mud: 'The tongue gets clogged with mud only one remedy then pull it in and suck it swallow the mud or spit' (1995: 165). Mud, in Beckett's earlier short prose piece, 'The Expelled' (1946), appears as a material in which the male narrator buries his memories 'until they sink forever in the mud' (1995: 47). In 'The Image', then, mud as a metaphor of voice and the repressed memories literally clogs the tongue of the narrator, causing one of the typical hysterical symptoms, aphonia, 'a sudden inability to use one's voice' (Dolar 2006: 41), as we see he 'take[s] a mouthful' of it rather than spitting it out (Beckett 1995: 165). What is intriguing is Beckett's experiment with voice as an object that is poured out from the female subject in his later play *Not I* (1972). If the male narrator of 'The Image' exhibits, as Anthony Cordingley states, the voice 'in the head during the act of rapid, silent reading',[1] in other words, if Beckett in 'The Image' employs the narrative voice of language as written and to be read, in *Not I* he vocalizes 'the buzzing [...] in the ears [...] in the skull' (Beckett 1990: 378), borrowing the female hysteric voice.

This chapter will investigate Beckett's use of the gendered Other in vocalizing emotions. Mouth can only express her fear by employing the third-person narrative, vehemently refusing to inscribe herself as the speaking subject, and locating the voice between the subject and the Other. As mentioned in the Introduction to this collection, Beckett claimed that he actually heard Mouth's story and thereby disowned or distanced himself from this voice, and in the play itself Mouth also disowns the voice and narrates the story insisting it was 'not her voice at all' (Beckett 1990: 379). This chapter will further argue that Beckett, having studied psychoanalytic theories in depth while undertaking psychotherapy sessions with Wilfred Bion at the Tavistock Clinic in London from early 1934 to late 1935, uses such knowledge in exploring the self and the role of the Other, the psychic representations of the people significant to the subject, in the development of the self.[2] More specifically, I will show that Beckett's artistic urge to create the cross-gendered voice in *Not I* is closely related to the maternal voice as a lost object, causing symptoms of melancholia and paranoia to the male narrators in Beckett's earlier fiction.

A purely buccal phenomenon

Beckett's intention to explore the aspect of Mouth's voice that is located at the intersection of body and language is clearly indicated in his 1972 letter to the American director Alan Schneider who was working on the play:

> If I made a distinction it can only have been between mind & voice, not between mouth & voice. Her speech a purely buccal phenomenon without mental control or understanding, only half heard. Function running away with organ.
>
> (Cited in Harmon 1998: 283)

As the words 'organ' and 'buccal' – which means relating to the cheeks or the mouth cavity – suggest, Beckett catalogues the voice with the body rather than the 'mind' – 'just the mouth ... lips ... cheeks ... jaws ... never– ... what?.. tongue?.. yes ... lips ... cheeks ... jaws ... tongue' (Beckett 1990: 380) as Mouth anatomizes the entire vocal apparatus where the voice comes from. Indeed, a similar kind of Cartesian split is often found in Beckett's earlier fiction, as exemplified in Malone's affirmation, 'My body does not yet make up its mind' (Beckett 1958: 198) in *Malone meurt/Malone Dies* (1951/1956). However, if Malone seems to suggest the Cartesian supremacy of mind over flesh, in *Not I*, as Beckett's comments cited above indicate, he portrays the mind's inability to understand the bodily symptoms and feelings, the very existence of the unconscious that also dictates the body. Encountering such 'buccal phenomenon without mental control', the hysteric often projects his/ her own confused feelings onto someone else. As Juliet Mitchell states, it is 'because of the hysteric's need to transmit unbearable feelings on to someone else that his hysteria cannot be manifested if he is on his own' (1997: 205). Mouth, too, claims that she is hearing someone else's voice while also expressing that she cannot control her 'sudden urge to ... tell' (Beckett 1990: 382):

> ... stream of words ... in her ear ... practically in her ear ... not catching the half ... not the quarter ... no idea what she's saying ... imagine!.. no idea what she's saying!.. and can't stop ... no stopping it ...
>
> (Beckett 1990: 380)

According to Dolar, at the bottom of such hysteric symptoms and the 'widespread experience of psychosis based on "hearing voices"' is 'the problem of the mother's voice, the first representation of the dimension of the other', which also results in the 'ambiguous ontology' of the status of the voice as between the subject and the other without belonging to either (2006: 40–1, 103).

Following Rosolato, in her seminal study of filmic voice *The Acoustic Mirror: the Female Voice in Psychoanalysis and Cinema* (1988), Silverman elaborates the function of the maternal voice that 'plays a major role in the infant's perceptual development' as the first object which 'provides the first axis of Otherness' (80, 86). What is presupposed in this statement is that the infant has not yet formed a sense of the self or the Other. The process of developing the self, according to Julia Kristeva, is achieved by way of abjecting the Other, the object which is first identified and eventually distinguished and separated from the subject's own self. As Silverman explains, Rosolato characterizes the maternal voice as a 'lost object', and puts it in the category of the Lacanian *'objet petit a'* (85). Central to Silverman's study is the ongoing relationship between the male subject, the maternal voice as a lost object and artistic creation – the representation of the maternal voice that 'grows out of a powerful cultural fantasy' (72). Silverman argues that where 'the child "finds" its "own" voice by introjecting the mother's voice, the male subject subsequently "refines" his "own" voice by projecting onto the mother's voice all that is unassimilable to the paternal position', making the mother's voice the 'abject' (81). The maternal voice as a lost object is culturally recuperated in classic cinema, with the image that is 'charged with either intensely positive or intensely negative affect'; Rosolato, for example, associates 'the "pleasurable milieu" of the maternal voice' with 'the first model of auditory pleasure' – as *objet petit a* that is longed for – whereas Chion regards it with the 'terror of an "umbilical night"' (72) – the abject that must be 'jettisoned' (95).

Even though Silverman's book does not directly refer to Melanie Klein, Silverman's ideas, which are developed from Rosolato and Chion's views of the 'profoundly ambivalent nature of the fantasy' (72) of the maternal voice and Kristeva's concept of the abject, are remarkably similar to Klein's theory in which such mixed feelings of love and hatred towards the first love-object give rise to pathological disorders such as paranoia, mania and melancholia. In Klein, for instance, the mother's breast which is the infant's first love-object is installed as polarized objects: as a 'good object' when the infant is satisfied by feeding, and as a 'bad' one when its desire is frustrated. In the infant's fantasy splitting the first love-object into good and bad objects is one of the earliest defence mechanisms against the loss of it in order to preserve at least the good part. Furthermore 'a conception of extremely bad and *extremely perfect* objects' contributes to form the super-ego, that is exacting and divine on the one hand, and severe and relentless persecutory on the other (Klein 1988: 268, Klein's italics). The infant's defence mechanisms against the loss of its first love-object, the mother's breast, are comparable to the adult's reaction to their loss of the loved one, and moreover, are 'revived whenever grief is experienced in later life' (344). For Klein, 'reparation' is a process of recalling the lost object, which is damaged in one's fantasy, and restoring it as a good object through increasing love and regaining trust in the lost object by evoking happy experiences. Notably, as Klein explains in 'Infantile Anxiety-Situations Reflected in a Work of Art and in the Creative Impulse' (1988[1929]), reparation is the strongest element of the constructive and creative urges just as Silverman's theory.

Voice as a lost object in Beckett's fiction: a Kleinian approach

As I have argued elsewhere, Beckett was familiar with not only the Kleinian ideas above but also other key Kleinian concepts such as infantile sadism, rage, guilt, introjection and projection via his study of Karin Stephen's *Psychoanalysis and Medicine* (1933), the first book summarized in his 'Psychology Notes'.[3] My previous study has provided empirical links between the 'Psychology Notes' and Klein's theory, and offered a Kleinian reading of Beckett's later drama such as *Footfalls* (1975) and *Rockaby* (1980), in which he recuperates the female subject that has been damaged and silenced in his early fiction as a good object through a process that is comparable to Klein's reparation.[4] For C.J. Ackerley and S.E. Gontarski, Beckett's application of Kleinian ideas to his works can be traced much earlier. In *The Grove Companion to Samuel Beckett*, they claim that Beckett's *Quatre nouvelles/Four Novellas* (1946)[5] 'respond to Kleinian readings that equate the text and the mother's body, although SB [Samuel Beckett]'s fixation was more upon the womb than the breast' (Ackerley and Gontarski 2004: 299). All four stories share the same structure of male narrators obsessively repeating the story of setting off on a journey after having been expelled from his family house or a refuge. Even if, due to the nature of the book, Ackerley and Gontarski do not offer a detailed Kleinian reading *of Novellas*, they comment that *Premier amour/First Love* (1946/1973), the first story of *Four Novellas* 'defines love in psychoanalytical terms deriving from Melanie Klein, that between the child and the breast, as conducive to the first awareness of otherness' (2004: 197), as the telling title of the story suggests. While Beckett indeed uses the womb metaphor extensively in his oeuvre as well as in *First Love*,[6] it can be argued that in the short story the male narrator's first recognition and separation with the female Other is through an auditory experience. This section is going to offer a Klenian reading of *First Love* and *From an Abandoned Work* (1954–5) evidenced by his 'Psychology Notes', especially focusing on the maternal voice as a lost object and the traumatic memory of the severance with the mother.

In this regard, Beckett's transcriptions of Otto Rank's *The Trauma of Birth* (1929), which views the severance from the mother's womb as the prototype of all later anxieties, provide a helpful way of tracing his investigation into psychoanalytic ideas in relation to the mother's womb. Beckett, for example, notes, 'Just as all anxiety goes back to anxiety at birth (dyspnoea), so every pleasure has as its final aim the reestablishment of the primal intrauterine pleasure' (TCD MS

10971/8/34, cited in Feldman 2006: 107), which echoes the ambivalent views of the maternal voice by Rosolato and Chion – as the first model of auditory pleasure and the terror of the 'uterine darkness' (Chion 1999: 61). Chion's explanation about the infant's unpleasant auditory experience is worthy of attention:

> In the beginning, in the uterine darkness, was the voice, the Mother's voice. For the child once born, the mother is more an olfactory and vocal continuum than an image. Her voice originates in all points of space, while her form enters and leaves the visual field. We can imagine the voice of the Mother weaving around the child a network of connections it's tempting to call the *umbilical web*. A rather horrifying expression to be sure, in its evocation of spiders – and in fact, this original vocal connection will remain ambivalent.
>
> (Chion 1999: 61, Chion's italics)

Chion not only extends the infant's perceptual development to the intrauterine moment, but also argues that the maternal voice 'could imaginarily take up the role of an umbilical cord, as a nurturing connection, allowing no chance of autonomy to the subject trapped in umbilical web' (62). What Chion describes here is strikingly similar to Beckett's memories of 'being in his mother's womb at a dinner party', where 'he could remember the voices talking' (cited in Knowlson and Knowlson 2006: 151). Beckett's own account of the memory that he claimed to recall during one of the therapy sessions is as follows:

> I used to lie down on the couch and try to go back in my past. I think it probably did help. I think it helped me perhaps to control the panic. I certainly came up with some extraordinary memories of being in the womb. Intrauterine memories. I remember feeling trapped, of being imprisoned and unable to escape, of crying to be let out but no one could hear, no one was listening. I remember being in pain but being unable to do anything about it.
>
> (Cited in Knowlson 1996: 171)

While these extraordinary memories were likely to be triggered by his study of *The Trauma of Birth*, what is notable is that these are specifically described as auditory – 'the voices talking' that he overheard in his mother's womb and his 'crying to be let out'. Beckett's such unusual memories and psychoanalytic knowledge feed into *First Love*. In *First Love* the old narrator talks of his young self when he was 'about twenty-five at the time of [his] marriage' (Beckett 1995: 25). Having been evicted from his father's house after his death, and 'having nowhere to go' (30), the narrator settles on a bench on the bank of the canal, where he meets his first love Lulu who later on offers him a room, a womb-like shelter, one of the metaphors Beckett often uses in his work, as clearly signified in his 'Psychology Notes': '(as <u>room</u> for <u>womb</u> or for <u>woman</u>)' (TCD MS 10971/8/12, Beckett's emphasis).[7] Significantly, the narrator describes how he first recognizes Lulu from her voice rather than her image when she says 'Shove up' to him while he is resting on 'the bench' (Beckett 1995: 30). What follows next is his description of overhearing her singing 'some old folk songs' next to him sitting on the bench, 'so disjointedly, skipping from one to another and finishing none' (ibid.). He further remarks, 'The voice, though out of tune, was not unpleasant' (ibid.). Here Beckett characteristically uses a double negative construction for expressing a positive, in this case Lulu's 'pleasurable' voice as Rosolato would put it.

The male narrator's initial reaction to this encounter with his first love-object is bewilderment; he is confused by his 'feeling which gradually assumed, to [his] dismay, the dread name of love' (33). In portraying the narrator's ambivalent state after his first attempt to leave Lulu by 'abandon[ing] the bench' (ibid.), Beckett employs Rank's theory about the weaning process, which functions as 'a second trauma' after the primal trauma of birth: 'The temporary (or, after weaning, the complete) substitution of a finger for the mother's breast shows [...] the child's first attempt to replace the mother's body by its own ("identification"), or by a part of its own.' (Rank 1929: 21, 18) The narrator says 'I found myself inscribing the letters of Lulu in an old heifer pat', 'tracing her name in old cowshit', and 'with my devil's finger into the bargain, which I then sucked' (Beckett 1995: 34). The allusion to weaning becomes apparent when examining 'The End', the last of *Four Novellas*, in which the male narrator after having been expelled from home just like the narrator in *First Love*, 'trie[s] to suck [...] milk' from the surrogate of the mother's breast, a cow's 'udder' which 'was covered with dung' (Beckett 1995: 90).

Such ambivalent feelings towards the male narrator's first love-object – his identification with her and excrement – is expressed not only using Rank's theory of weaning, but also Klein's concept of the depressive state, melancholia. As I have demonstrated elsewhere, Beckett knew Klein's theory that accounts for the significant relation between the weaning process and melancholia as he aptly puts it in his 'Psychology Notes': 'a baby denied the breast at 2 months might reasonably become a melancholic' (TCD MS10971/8, cited in Kim 2010: 5). According to Klein, the very early psychic and emotional development of the infant and the experience of the loss of the first love-object continuously affect the adult's psychic processes. The most critical period in this sense is the weaning period. Klein claims that the infant's depressive feelings reach 'a climax just before, during and after weaning' (1988: 345) when the baby experiences the impending loss of the breasts. As Klein explains, one of the main causes of melancholia is the infant's mixed feelings towards the love-object. On the one hand, the baby mourns for the mother's breast and all that the breast and the milk represent in its mind, namely, love, goodness and security. All this goodness is felt by the baby to be lost, and are lost as a consequence of its rage, 'own uncontrollable greedy and destructive phantasies and impulses against [its] mother's breasts' (345) – the infantile sadism which Klein believes as instinctual. On the other hand, distress about the impending loss further increases the persecutory fear of the bad object which gives rise to feelings of guilt as well as the fear of losing the good object, all of which constitute the depressive position. The infant's first experience of loss is, thus, not only a gradual process as it repeats the loss of its first object, the mother's breast, over and over during the weaning period, but also creates the overriding problem, a problem with which, in Klein's theory, the infant and later the adult have to cope; the infant's rage mixed with the original love towards the first love-object produces melancholia and paranoia.

The process that is comparable to the Kleinian gradual weaning process is depicted in lengthy detail in *First Love* when the narrator repeats the separation with Lulu. Just as her song has initially served as the first object, when he decides to leave her first time, he says 'before going, to be on the safe side, I asked her to sing me a song' (Beckett 1995: 36).[8] Once again, the mother's breast is replaced by Lulu's song, and with this song the narrator practises his weaning. He leaves her and walks until the song becomes 'fainter and fainter' and does not reach him anymore, then he retraces his steps until he hears 'the sound emerged so softly from the silence' (37). He repeats this leaving and returning to the bench until 'the voice ceased at last' (ibid.). The first severance, however, is not successful, and he eventually moves in her house and settles in her room, until he leaves her again on the moment of her giving birth – the birth which is seen as that of his own, to 'be "properly born" a second time' as Phil Baker's helpful study *Beckett and the Mythology of Psychoanalysis* shows (1997: 82). This time, the narrator begins 'playing with the cries' of her during her labour, 'in the same way' as he 'had played with the song, on, back, on, back' (Beckett 1995: 45). However, unlike the first soft sound with which the narrator joyfully plays a game, the cries are extremely disturbing. He says, 'Precautions would have been superfluous, there was no competing with those cries' (ibid.). Then the cries 'pursued [him] down', and continues to haunt him as the story is concluded with his confession: 'For years I thought they [the cries] would cease. Now I don't think so any more.' (45) As such, in *First Love* Beckett vividly depicts the symptoms of hearing cries, the maternal voice as a lost object which resembles what Chion calls umbilical web. For Klein, this kind of haunting voice of the first love-object is an indication of the unsuccessful work of mourning in contrast to the successful one which aims to establish a healthy relationship with the lost psychic other within the ego; a failure to restore the lost object as a good object produces symptoms like paranoia and melancholia. In the closing scene of *First Love*, by providing the compelling image of the weaning process that is mixed with the primal trauma of birth which also alludes to the narrator's own, Beckett shows the traumatic effect of the severance with the mother's womb that continues to affect one's psychic world. As the ceaseless cries imply, Lulu's cries haunt him despite his wish 'all that matters is that it [the cry] should cease' (Beckett 1995: 45). However, not realizing that he has lost something important, the male narrator displays the symptoms of melancholia and paranoia, troubled by the lost object, the maternal cries.

   In Beckett's short story, *From an Abandoned Work* in which the male narrator painfully describes his moment of departure from home, the 'cries' is more specifically linked to his mother's cries he hears when he sets off his journey, leaving his mother behind: 'Then I raised my eyes and saw my mother still in the window waving [...] in sad helpless love, and I heard faintly her cries [...] and my mother white and so thin I could see past her [...] into the dark of the room', that echoes the womb (1995: 156). The narrative is governed by his 'most savage rage' and 'violence' that he claims to be 'suddenly rising' from unknown sources: 'Now why this sudden rage I really don't know, these sudden rages, they made my life a misery. Many other things too did this, my sore throat for example' (157). However, his rages are clearly traced to his separation from his mother. A close reading of the text reveals that his 'savage rages' and 'violence', provoked while watching the 'white horse', are impelled by the association between the word white and his mother. In spite of his denial, 'the white horse and then the rage, no connexion I suppose' (158), the narrator hints at the connection later on: 'the white horse and white mother in the window, please read again my descriptions of these', jokingly pre-empting a psychoanalytic reading of the association (160–1). While the Kleinian concepts of destructive fantasies and rages against the mother in experiencing the separation from her are evident, when describing the moment of departure the male narrator, without consciously being aware of the origin that causes such emotions, which is a typical feature of melancholia, turns his aggression and rage inward: 'There was a time I tried to get relief by beating my head against something.' (157) As his claim, 'I have never known what is to be without a sore throat, but the rages were the worst', suggests, his rages are not efficiently verbalized but converted into physical violence either towards himself or 'all moving thing, getting in [his] path' (155). On another occasion, he more specifically damages his mother in fantasy as he feels he has killed his mother: 'My father, did I kill him too as well as my mother, perhaps in a way I did' (159).

As the next section will show, Beckett knew the significance of 'talking cure', the importance of verbalizing a traumatic experience with abreacting the affect, in other words by discharging the emotional energy associated with a trauma that has been repressed. As Sigmund Freud famously said, 'Recollecting without affect almost invariably produces no result' (Breuer and Freud 1991: 57). Yet, in *From an Abandoned Work* Beckett does not allow his melancholic male narrator to disclose such repressed elements nor his feelings verbally abreacted. Instead, the male narrator, now 'old and weak' (Beckett 1995: 158), can only repeat the same story of the departure from home:

> [...] again again, and the feet going nowhere only somehow home, in the morning out from home and in the evening back home again, and the sound of my voice all day long muttering the same old things [...]. All this talking, very low and hoarse, no wonder I had a sore throat. Perhaps I should mention here that I never talked to anyone.
>
> (Beckett 1995: 159)

In contrast to his 'very low and hoarse' voice that is murmured to himself, in *Not I* we hear the female voice outpouring repressed energy. While the male narrator seems to feel the need of blowing off steam as he tells us 'these flashes, or gushes, vent the pent, that was one of those things I used to say, over and over' (158), this act delivered without affect cannot be therapeutic especially when he is not even consciously aware of his loss. Even if the male narrator claims that he did not talk to anyone, we see that at least his story is narrated in the story.

His mother's story, however, is silenced: 'My mother was the same, never talked [...] Sometimes she cried out on me, or implored, but never long, just a few', or other times, she was 'talking to herself' or 'reciting her hymns' (159).

Before moving to the next section, it is important to note that in spite of the haunting nature, the female voice, as well as her story, is silenced in *First Love* and *From an Abandoned Work* by the male narrators. Beckett in these stories can be seen as participating in what Adrianna Cavarero claims 'the most famous stereotype of western culture' exemplified by the Sirens in Homer's *Odyssey*: 'Feminized from the start, the vocal aspect of speech and, furthermore, of song appears together as antagonistic elements in a rational, masculine sphere that centers itself, instead, on the semantic. To put it formulaically: woman sings, man thinks.' (2005:5–6) Just as the Siren's 'speech' was not taken into account in the 'western imaginary', embodying the 'irresistible voice that is almost like an animal cry', 'a vocal expression that is "different" from the humanized sphere of the *phone semantike*' (Cavarero 2005: 102), the content of Lulu's song is completely muted. The narrator claims, 'It had something to do with lemon trees, or orange trees, I forgot, that is all I remember, [...] I have retained nothing, not a word, not a note' (Beckett 1995: 37). Arguably, in *Not I* what is at stake is to reconstruct the female subject that has been silenced and expelled by the male subject in his earlier fiction like *First Love* and *From an Abandoned Work*. By borrowing the hysterical voice of the woman who has been repressed, Beckett also seems to express his own experience of alienation represented in his account of the intrauterine memories, his sense of loss, and his emotion that has not been abreacted. In this sense, Kristeva's reading of *First Love* and *Not I* in her essay 'The Father, Love, and Banishment' (1980) is telling as she suggests that Mouth is closely linked to the male subject (hinting at Beckett) and indicates that the male narrator in *First Love* takes up Mouth's position. Kristeva claims, 'Faithful to his paternal love, he has become an old lady (*Not I*)' (152). Thus, the final section is going to show Beckett's use of hysteria in exploring the phenomenon of hearing voice and his need of cross-gendered voice in *Not I*.

Hysteria and the vocal Medusa in *Not I*

When examining Beckett's 'Psychology Notes', his understanding of the link between the hysterical symptoms and the traumatic severance with the mother's womb becomes apparent. What is most notable is Beckett's summary of Josef Breuer's case study of Anna O. from Rank's book, which opens with her case. Beckett's own transcriptions, however, begin from page 48 from 'Neurotic Reproduction' the fourth chapter of Rank's book: 'Anxiety of child left alone in dark room due to his unconscious being reminded (*er-innert*) of intrauterine situation, terminated by frightening severance from mother' (cited in Knowlson 1996: 172, Beckett's italics). Beckett perhaps felt that this particular aspect of the chapter more directly speaks to his own intrauterine memories than the other chapters. Following this, Beckett notes that anxiety neurosis such as 'feminine anaesthesia (vaginismus)' rests on the same primal fixation on 'the mother's genitals (dangerous *vagina dentata*)' (Rank 1929: 49, Rank's italics).[9] For Rank, the 'physical symptoms of *hysteria* not only in their manifest forms but also in their deepest unconscious content, show various directly physical reproductions of birth' (ibid.). The case is recorded by Beckett: 'hysterical *paralysis*, of which, for example, the inhibited function of walking or moving is nothing other than the physically materialized agoraphobia, while the immobility brings to realization at the same time the pleasurable primal situation, with the dread or horror of being freed therefrom' (Rank 1929: 49–50, *Rank's italics*). After transcribing three more items up until page 79, in the middle of summarizing the fifth chapter 'Symbolic Adaptation', Beckett goes back to the very beginning of Rank's book, and transcribes Anna O.'s case:

> Freud has occasionally remarked that Psychoanalysis was really invented by the first patient whom Breuer treated in the year 1881, and whose case (Anna O—) was published many years later (1895) in the *Studien über Hysterie*. The young girl who understood only English in her nervous states, called the soothing hypnotic speeches to her doctor the *talking cure*, or jokingly referred to them as *chimney sweeping*.
>
> (Rank 1929: 1, Rank's italics)

Whatever made him go back to the first page of Rank's book, it is significant to note that Beckett was exposed to the theory of hysteria which views it as a consequence of not merely repudiated sexual desire as Freud mainly focuses, but also the traumatic severance with the mother's womb. Most importantly, the Freudian or rather Anna O.'s 'invented form of a talking cure' as a therapeutic process that 'only uses the voice' (Chion 1999: 1) as a vehicle of psychoanalysis employs the fascinating image of the voice as an object that clogs the throat and that needs to be cleared away just as Beckett's mud in 'The Image' and the voice that is spewed out in *Not I*.

Beckett's transcriptions from Rank's *The Trauma of Birth* point to one of the central aspects of *Not I* in terms of his use of the female hysteric voice presented with the striking visual image of Mouth, the rapid movement of her lips, teeth and tongue that recalls the 'dangerous *vagina dentata*'. Despite the rather obvious element of the male castration fear projected onto the image of Mouth, what is also equally important is the quality of 'vocal Medusa' (Kahane 1995: x), like the abject entity that simultaneously haunts and attracts the subject. In her book *Passions of the Voice: Hysteria, Narrative, and the Figure of the Speaking Woman, 1850–1915*, Claire Kahane, using Klein's theory of oral rage as 'the strongest factor in repression and its symptomatic consequences' (1995: xii), explains that because 'the voice was itself construed as a fetishistic object of presence and power, the woman with a potent voice figured a kind of vocal Medusa both fascinating and fearsome, arousing apprehension in the very narrative voice that imagined her' (x). As Beckett's notes above suggest, the *vagina dentata* is the reminder of the 'pleasurable primal situation' – intrauterine – and the 'dread or horror' of the severance from it as well as the manifestation of one's own aggression and rage that are projected onto the mother.

According to Klein, as Beckett also remarks in his 'Psychology Notes',[10] the infant's own rage and anger derived from the frustration and forcible separation from the mother are projected onto the bad mother, or as Klein puts it, bad objects. This not only makes the infant conceive of the bad objects as actually dangerous persecutors who will devour it (i.e., the oral incorporation) but also results in its fear of retaliation from the bad objects as well as the sense of guilt. The fear of internalized persecutors that cannot be overcome by projection forms the basis of paranoia. Through the ambivalent portrait of Mouth as the dangerous vocal Medusa (i.e., as the source of the voice) and the victim of the paranoiac fear of hearing a voice, Beckett in *Not I* presents the ambiguous ontology of the status of the voice as between the subject and the Other, and shows how the maternal voice as the abject entity plays a key role in the infant's psychic development. The maternal voice is the first object of identification, of love, and of rage, 'the most ambivalently constructed other, who bears at the same time the traces of self' (Kahane 1995: 36).

In his fascinating study *Dumbstruck: a Cultural History of Ventriloquism* (2000), Steven Connor, employing the Kleinian concept of bad objects, further unveils the ambiguous ontology of the voice. As noted in the Introduction to this collection, when the infant cries for hunger, just as it projects its own frustration and anger onto the bad breast that fails to satisfy its desire, it projects its aggression onto the voice as well: 'the voice is not something other than the breast, which cannot satisfy precisely because it is other than the breast, but is the breast gone bad, the breast that refuses to feed, the breast that screams instead of yielding pleasure' (Connor 2000: 31). Therefore, the 'bad voice is the infant's own voice which has been violently estranged from it', projected onto the Other, and conceived as the Other (32). Mouth claims, 'that time she cried ... the one time she could remember ... since she was a baby ... must have cried as a baby [...] just the birth cry' (Beckett 1990: 380). All of this indicates why it was so vital for Beckett to make Mouth's story begin with the traumatic experience of birth, 'out into this world' – the earlier manuscript reads 'birth ... into the world ... this world' (UoR MS 1227/7/12/1, cited in Pountney 1988: 254). Mouth also offers frequent references to finding 'herself in the dark' (Beckett 1990: 377), echoing the uterine darkness. According to Chion, the 'voice is inscribed in the umbilical rupture', when the 'act of "closing off" at birth' by 'the cutting of the umbilicus' correlates 'strongly with the attention paid to the opening of the mouth and the uttering of the first cry' (1999: 61), making the moment of birth all the more traumatic and ambivalent as well as an auditory experience. Little does the infant know that the unpleasant cries are its own.

Conversion-hysteria and logorrhea

Mouth's denial of the ownership of her own voice that is fittingly described by Beckett as 'a purely buccal phenomenon without mental control' and her inability to understand her feelings can be explained using the concept of conversion-hysteria, exemplified in her claim 'feeling was coming back ... imagine!.. feeling coming back!', but she had 'no idea what she was saying!.. till she began trying to ... delude herself ... it was not hers at all ... not her voice at all' (Beckett 1990: 379–8). From Ernest Jones's *Treatment of the Neuroses* (1920) Beckett extensively summarized many different types of hysteria including conversion-hysteria that he entirely transcribed: 'an afferent impulse which is inhibited from finding its normal expression, corresponding to an emotional manifestation, flows along other neural paths, producing motor effects appropriate to the latter' (Jones 1920: 120, see TCD MS 10971/8/22). In other words, the conversion symptoms are derived from the lack of the conscious understanding of feelings that are transferred to the bodily symptoms. What is most interesting is his own typed comment next to the transcription of conversion-hysteria: in

French, he typed a phrase meaning the constipated are wandering around,[11] and thus Beckett here amusingly offers his own example of conversion-hysteria that is also resonant with the etiology of hysteria – the 'wandering womb'.

Beckett uses this metaphor of constipation in order to represent the male narrator's repression in *First Love*: 'One day, on my return from stool, I found my room locked and my belongings in a heap before the door. This will give you some idea how constipated I was, at this juncture' (Beckett 1995: 28). In the following sentence the narrator does not forget to diagnose his own symptoms as anxiety neurosis: 'It was, I am now convinced, anxiety constipation [...] What can that have been but constipation? Or am I confusing it with diarrhoea [sic]? It's all muddle in my head [...] the different varieties of motion' (ibid.). Here, the narrator is so repressed that he cannot even produce 'motor effects appropriate' to his 'emotional manifestation'. In contrast, in *All That Fall* (1956) Maddy Rooney's 'explosive constipation' (cited in Ben-Zvi 1990, 7) in Beckett's own words is diagnosed by herself as 'hysterical' (Beckett 1990: 174). Whereas Mrs Rooney, as Beckett commented, is 'terribly constipated; she has all these feelings, and wants to explode, to release them, but she can't' (cited in Ben-Zvi 1990, 7), in *Not I* the suppressed female hysteric explodes, the quality which is often described by critics as logorrhea, the linguistic symptom that is translated into the motor sphere. In feeling 'sudden urge to ... tell', Mouth rushes out to the 'nearest lavatory' and 'start[s] pouring it out ... steady stream ... mad stuff' (Beckett 1990: 382).

Significantly, in Beckett's first novel, *Dream of Fair to Middling Women* (1932), the male narrator uses the same word 'logorrhœa' to describe the speech of Smeraldina-Rima – a reminiscence of the author's cousin and first love, Peggy Sinclair: 'ropes and ropes of logorrhœa streaming out in a gush' (Beckett 1996: 14). Typically, as in Beckett's other early fiction, Smeraldina's voice is muted by the male narrator, who depicts the spectacle as simply 'extremely amusing', without informing us of 'the words flooding and streaming out' (14). It is also important to note that as his biographer Anthony Cronin remarks, Beckett's 'moral torment' from which he suffered until late in life is closely linked to the hostile 'portrait' of women such as Smeraldina (1997: 578). An example can be found immediately after the logorrhea passage when the male protagonist Belacqua senses that he has lost her: 'that raised the hopes of Belacqua until she made it clear [...] that she did not mean all what he had hoped rather she might' (Beckett 1996: 14–15). The narrator then verbally assaults her body: 'Because her body was all wrong [...]. Poppata, big breech, Botticelli thighs, knock-knees, ankles all fat nodules, wobbly, mammose, slobbery-blubbery, bubbubbubbub, the real button-bursting Weib, ripe'[12] (15). Born of this sense of guilt, in *Not I* Beckett attempts to reconstruct the female subject that has been damaged and silenced in his early creation. Underneath Mouth's urge to purge the voice she hears in the brain, there is the author's urge to recuperate the previously muted female voice by borrowing Smeraldina's ropes of logorrhea with outpouring energy that is combined with explosive emotions such as hysterical laughter and screams.[13]

Conclusion

As Hélène Cixous claims in 'Difficult Joys', theatre gives people an easier access to emotions by taking other person's position: 'They appear, although they say "I", as "she" or "he", but not "me" – which is the reason why, I feel, some people write for theatre, because they can be extremely violent and at the same time, not very violent' (1990: 21). While here Cixous talks about violence, her point can be equally applied to Beckett who borrows the female hysteric voice to express his emotion in *Not I*. Taking up the female position also seems to offer Beckett the opportunity to understand his own significant others and to move away from the focus on the self and from the burden of 'searching for the non-pronounial' that avoids the subject pronoun 'I' as in his fiction.[14] Remarkably, what is described in *Not I* is the experience of marginality and 'suffering' by woman who confronts a difficulty in articulating her own sense of alienation in a public space like a 'busy shopping centre' and 'court' (Beckett 1990: 377, 379, 381).[15]

Beckett's borrowing of the cross-gendered voice in *Not I* then needs to be seen as more than a simple appropriation, which exploits a culturally gendered form of the hysterical vocal Medusa.[16] If Beckett makes Mouth refuse to be inscribed as a speaking subject, he also does not allow her to be a mere object of fear or desire of the male subject. The female voice that is recuperated in *Not I* is the abject entity, bearing not only the trace of the female characters who have been expelled and whose stories are not sufficiently told in Beckett's early fiction, but also the fantasy of the maternal voice that Beckett claimed to hear. At the heart of hysteria, as Dolar claims, there is also the fantasy of overhearing 'the mysterious sound-object, which is the paramount sign' of 'an excess' in the Other, and the infant's inability to understand the Other (2006: 134). The mysterious sound-object the infant hears is also its own unpleasant voice that is projected onto the (m)other, just like the endless cries the male narrator of *First Love* hears. The inclusion of the figure Auditor in *Not I* is particularly significant in terms of rewriting the representation of the internalized mother. While Beckett's own intrauterine memories are linked to him being in pain as 'no one could hear, no one was listening', it is noteworthy that the main sources of inspiration for *Not I* shows that the genesis of the Auditor is the maternal figure awaiting her child, who 'was in a position of intense listening' (Brater 1987: 24), even though Beckett's stage direction states that the sex of the Auditor is '*undeterminable*' (Beckett 1990: 376). Echoing the mother's 'sad helpless love' (Beckett 1995: 156) in *From an Abandoned Work*, the Auditor's 'gesture of helpless compassion' (Beckett 1990: 375), which is made four times when Mouth vehemently denies herself as a subject of her voice, seeks to help Mouth understand the voice as her own.

According to Dolar, the 'voice is always understood *nachträglich* [belatedly], subsequently, retroactively, and the timeloop of the primal fantasy is precisely the gap between hearing and making sense of what we hear, accounting for it' (2006: 136). And the problem is that 'the moment for a proper understanding never arrives; it is as if it were infinitely deferred' (ibid.). Beckett also knew this too well, as he noted from Jones's *Treatment of the Neuroses*: 'The hysteric is always out of date in his emotional reactions' (TCD MS 10971/8/21, cited in Kim 2010: 151). Borrowing the hysteric's ability to pour out words that have been suppressed, Beckett displays his own deferred emotional reactions to the separation from the mother using the womb motif, or rather his own fantasy of the maternal voice that is represented in his early fiction, as well as offering a fascinating study of the voice as the lost object and the abject. The voice we hear in *Not I* is 'not her voice at all' as Mouth claims, but the author's own, but notably that is the voice muted in his earlier fiction. Yet, if Mouth speaks for Beckett, we also see Beckett speaking for the woman lost.

Notes

1. See Cordingley (2008).
2. As Matthew Feldman shows, Beckett took 'some 20,000 words of typewritten notes' on nine psychoanalytic texts (2006: 2).
3. See Kim (2010: 6–12).
4. Indeed, the maternal voice that is recuperated in *Rockaby* can be seen as the 'sonorous envelope', which encloses the infant and offers it what Rosolato calls the 'pleasurable milieu' (Silverman 1988: 72). For example, as the title of the play suggests, the rhythmical rocking and the soothing narration resembles a lullaby, evoking auditory pleasure. Due to the limited space, this chapter will mainly focus on the examples of negative affect in Beckett's works.

5. These are the years when *Four Novellas* were written in French, not the years of publication. By *Four Novellas*, I mean the short stories, 'L'Expulsé'/'The Expelled', 'Le Calmant'/'The Calmative', 'La Fin'/'The End' and *Premier amour/First Love*.
6. See Kim (2010: 69–73).
7. See Kim (2010: 70) for the detailed discussion on this association of the room for womb in Beckett's French fiction.
8. This example is also often seen as the narrator playing the Freudian game of *Fort-Da* as a kind of mastery over a painful loss. See Connor (1988: 9–10).
9. See TCD MS 10971/8/34 for Beckett's own transcriptions of Rank's text in this section.
10. See Kim (2010: 111) for details.
11. See TCD MS 10971/8/22.
12. The same description is also used in his first published novel, *More Pricks Than Kicks* (1993[1934]: 189–90).
13. Similarly, Mrs Rooney in *All That Fall 'laughs wildly'*, and in *Play* (1962) W2's *'wild low laughter'* is also noticeable (Beckett 1990: 177, 317).
14. Lawrence Shainberg states, Beckett 'tried to describe the work he wanted to do now. It has to do with a fugitive 'I' [or perhaps he meant 'eye']. It's an embarrassment of pronouns. I'm searching for the non-pronounial' (Shainberg 1987: 134).
15. See Sherzer (1992) for more discussion of the female experience of marginality in *Not I*.
16. Shane Weller claims that Beckett 'appears to adopt precisely that "old view"' of seeing 'an hysterical derangement' as 'specifically feminine' (2008: 35, 37).

Works Cited

Ackerley, C.J. and S.E. Gontarski (2004) *The Grove Companion to Samuel Beckett* (New York: Grove Press).
Baker, Phil (1997) *Beckett and the Mythology of Psychoanalysis* (London: MacMillan).
Beckett, Samuel (1958) *Three Novels: Molloy, Malone Dies, The Unnamable* (New York: Grove Press).
—— (1990[1986]) *The Complete Dramatic Works* (London: Faber and Faber).
—— (1993[1934]) *More Pricks Than Kicks* (London: Calder Publications).
—— (1995) *The Complete Short Prose 1929–1989*, ed. S.E. Gontarski (New York: Grove Press).
—— (1996) *Dream of Fair to Middling Women* (London: John Calder).
—— 'Psychology Notes', Trinity College Dublin, MS 10967.
—— 'Untitled original manuscript of *Not I*', University of Reading, MS 1227/7/12/1.
Ben-Zvi, Linda (1990) 'Billie Whitelaw – Interviewed by Linda Ben-Zvi', in L. Ben-Zvi (ed.), *Women in Beckett: Performance and Critical Perspectives* (Urbana: University of Illinois Press), pp. 3–10.
Brater, Enoch (1987) *Beyond Minimalism: Beckett's Late Style in the Theatre* (New York: Oxford University Press).
Breuer, Josef and Sigmund Freud (1991) *Studies on Hysteria: the Penguin Freud Library, Vol. 3*, ed. James Strachey (London: Penguin Books).

Cavarero, Adriana (2005) *For More Than One Voice: toward a Philosophy of Vocal Expression* (Stanford: Stanford University Press).

Chion, Michel (1999) *The Voice in Cinema*, trans. Claudia Gorbman (New York: Columbia University Press).

Cixous, Hélène (1990) 'Difficult Joys', in Helen Wilcox et al. (eds), *The Body and the Text: Hélène Cixous, Reading and Teaching* (New York: Harvester Wheatsheaf), pp. 5–30.

Cordingley, Anthony (2006) 'The Reading Eye from *Scriptura Continua* to Modernism: Orality and Punctuation between Beckett's *L'image* and *Comment c'est/How It is*', *Journal of the Short Story in English*, 47, http://jsse.revues.org/index800.html [accessed 20 January 2012].

Connor, Steven (1988) *Samuel Beckett: Repetition, Theory, and Text* (Oxford: Basil Blackwell).

—— (2000) *Dumbstruck: a Cultural History of Ventriloquism* (Oxford: Oxford University Press).

Cronin, Anthony (1997) *Samuel Beckett: the Last Modernist* (London: Harper Collins).

Dolar, Mladen (2006) *A Voice and Nothing More* (Cambridge, Mass.: MIT Press).

Feldman, Matthew (2006) *Beckett's Books: a Cultural History of Samuel Beckett's 'Interwar Notes'* (London: Continuum).

Harmon, Maurice (ed.) (1998) *No Author Better Served: the Correspondence of Samuel Beckett and Alan Schneider* (Cambridge: Harvard University Press).

Jones, Ernest (1920) *The Treatment of the Neuroses* (London: Baillière, Tindall and Cox).

Kahane, Claire (1995) *Passions of the Voice: Hysteria, Narrative and the Figure of the Speaking Woman, 1850–1915* (Baltimore and London: Johns Hopkins University Press).

Kim, Rina (2010) *Women and Ireland as Beckett's Lost Others: Beyond Mourning and Melancholia* (Basingstoke: Palgrave Macmillan).

Klein, Melanie (1988) *Love, Guilt and Reparation and Other Works 1921–1945* (London: Virago Press).

Knowlson, James (1996) *Damned to Fame: the Life of Samuel Beckett* (New York: Simon & Schuster).

—— and Elizabeth Knowlson (eds) (2006) *Beckett Remembering Remembering Beckett: a Centenary Celebration* (New York: Arcade Publishing).

Kristeva, Julia (1980) *Desire in Language: a Semiotic Approach to Literature and Art*, ed. Leon S. Roudiez, trans. Thomas Gora, Alice Jardine and Leon S. Roudiez (Oxford: Blackwell).

Mitchell, Juliet (2000) *Mad Men and Medusas* (London: Penguin).

Neumark, Norie, Ross Gibson, and Theo van Leeuwen (eds) (2010) *Voice: Vocal Aesthetics in Digital Arts and Media* (Cambridge, Mass.: MIT Press).

Pountney, Rosemary (1988) *Theatre of Shadows: Samuel Beckett's Drama 1956–1976* (Gerrards Cross: Colin Smythe).

Rank, Otto (1929) *The Trauma of Birth* (London: Kegan Paul, Trench, Trubner & Co., Ltd.).

Shainberg, Lawrence (1987) 'Exorcising Beckett', *The Paris Review*, 104: 100–36.

Sherzer, Dina (1990) 'Portrait of a Woman: the Experience of Marginality in *Not I*', in L. Ben-Zvi (ed.), *Women in Beckett: Performance and Critical Perspectives* (Urbana: University of Illinois Press), pp. 202–7.

Silverman, Kaja (1988) *The Acoustic Mirror: the Female Voice in Psychoanalysis and Cinema* (Bloomington: Indiana University Press).

Stephen, Karin (1933) *Psychoanalysis and Medicine: a Study of the Wish to Fall Ill* (Cambridge: Cambridge University Press).

Weller, Shane (2008) '"Some Experience of the Schizoid Voice": Samuel Beckett and the Language of Derangement', *Forum for Modern Language Studies*, 45/1: 32–50.

Whitelaw, Billie (1995) *...Who He?* (London: Hodder and Stoughton).

6
The Engendered and Dis-engendered Other in Iris Murdoch's Early Fiction

Miles Leeson

Outside of the developing community of Iris Murdoch scholars it is rare for those with a passing interest in her work to question her relationship with gender in fiction and the underlying sexual conflict. Murdoch's work is often viewed as exclusively concerned with moral realism. It is only in recent years that the dearth of criticism connecting Murdoch's fiction with the themes of gender and power relations has begun to be rectified. Tammy Grimshaw's work *Sexuality, Gender and Power in Iris Murdoch's Fiction* (2005) has invigorated scholarship in this area and, along with Deborah Johnson's *Iris Murdoch* (1987), is the only critical text commenting directly upon sexuality and gender in Murdoch's oeuvre. Previously, the oft-repeated critical method was to consider Murdoch's theoretical writing on the novel and then apply the template she provides to her own fiction. Although this offers some insight into Murdoch's work, it in no way allows for the large variety of readings that her novels warrant; it also debases her philosophy and theory to an extent as it fails to attend to (a very Murdochian concept) the contradictions and self-division within her work. This chapter will investigate the reasons behind Murdoch's conflicting relationship with gender in her early fiction. I shall be discussing *The Bell* (1958) and *A Severed Head* (1961) at some length as these provide clear examples of Murdoch's relationship with gender narratives and I will also be giving space to *An Unofficial Rose* (1962). Naturally, there are many other novels that contain clear thoughts on the engendered and dis-engendered 'Other', but these three novels seem to me most complementary and well-developed. Although each novel to be discussed approaches the nature of 'the voice' (sometimes fixed, occasionally disembodied) in a variety of ways – there is, for example the existential male voice that Murdoch develops in her essay 'The Novelist as Metaphysician' (1950), the voice of the enchanter and the liberated feminine voice to name but three – parallels can be drawn across her work and particularly in her cross-gendering of both the narrative voice and that of a specific character. This must be seen as both a literary technique and a philosophical statement of belief concerning social constructions of gender. A reader of Murdoch's fiction must always keep in mind that her use of the male narrative voice does not imply omniscience or omnipotence. As attentive readers, we must mediate between the various positions that she outlines in her fiction: both truth and reality are behind the layers of narration and we must stumble through them toward the Platonic reality she wishes us to grasp.

A distinguishing feature of Murdoch's work is the reliance (indeed, over-reliance) on first-person narrative by a morally-degenerate, or at least egotistical male who is also the protagonist. The narration of some of her early works such as *Under the Net* (1954), *A Severed Head* and *The Italian Girl* (1964) de-centres the feminine perspective. Murdoch is obviously aware of what she is doing:

> I'm not interested in the 'woman's world' or the assertion of a 'female viewpoint'. This is often rather an artificial idea and can in fact injure the promotion of equal rights. We want to join the human race, not invent a new separatism.
>
> (Cited in Dooley 2003: 63)

If we refer to an interview from just a year later, 1978, Murdoch expands on this theme, and gives a more nuanced appraisal of her fiction:

> About writing as a man, this is instinctive. I mean I think I identify more with my male characters than my female characters. I write through the consciousness of women in those stories which have different narrators, so I write as a woman also in those kind of stories as well as men; but I suppose it's a kind of comment on the unliberated role of women [...] I think I want to write about things on the whole where it doesn't matter whether you're male or female, in which case you'd better be a male, because a male represents ordinary human beings, unfortunately as things stand at the moment, whereas a woman is always a woman! In fact of course I'm very interested in problems about the liberation of women, particularly, for instance, in so far as these concern education. I'm interested in them both as a citizen and as a free writer, so they do come in to some extent. [...] It's a freer world that you are in as a man than a woman.
>
> (Chevalier 1978, cited in Dooley 2003: 82)

This may appear odd if one agrees with the assessment of early Murdoch critics who claimed Murdoch as the heir-apparent of women writers such as Elizabeth Bowen and Virginia Woolf, but perhaps the reason for her need to simultaneously critique the male gaze and the power relations inherently given by the 'omniscient' narrative voice, is largely due to her personal life, university education, and her previous relationships. Women often undermine such sustaining fictions as male sexual dominance and fictional patriarchy, while Murdoch simultaneously dis-engenders the male voice through a range of techniques that I will discuss. Although there is not the space or scope to go into detail here it is worth noting that her relationships with figures of power, most notably Elias Canetti and Raymond Queneau, heavily influenced her decisions concerning narrative form.[1] Both men were major influences on her early life, with Canetti being a sporadic lover and controlling 'enchanter' figure in the late 1940s and early 1950s. Murdoch mentions that her early life at home was like being 'in a perfect trinity of love' (which posits her as a potential messiah figure) although after the death of her father it lacked a core element (Conradi 2001: 24). Peter Conradi argues that the overriding male narrative voice that seemingly dis-engenders Murdoch's central female characters is directly related to her own submissive personality:

> Canetti, in one of his 'transformations', touches all her male enchanter figures, from *A Severed Head* and *The Unicorn* to *The Sea, The Sea*. He would sometimes proudly claim to be her discoverer. If he helped 'make' her a writer, it was not quite in the manner that he assumed: an *argument* with him is latent throughout.
>
> (Conradi 2001: 35)

However, it is not only the vaunted position that Murdoch gives to the male voice within the narration but also to the liberated feminine that is of interest. The tensions and ambiguities arise in her novels as she seeks to consciously place conflicting voices within her text for narrative effect. Far from creating a fiction of freedom 'a novel must be a house fit for free characters to live in' (Murdoch 1999: 286); there is, for Murdoch, a personal need to re-create the Other as mysterious, saint-like and uncanny. It is my contention that the engendering and dis-engendering within Murdoch's fiction is inextricably linked to her moral vision. Although Murdoch states that she herself requires fictional freedom it is clear that in her early work, the primary focus of this chapter, is an underlying exploration of the use of voices, both narrative and character-centred, that works in two ways: as an unsettling mix of traditional reassertion of value and as a comedic destruction of first-person male narrative. In *A Severed Head* for example, an intricate comedy detailing the loves and disasters of a group of friends and relations in west London (where a great deal of Murdoch's fiction takes place), the primary purpose of the narrative is the deconstruction of Freudian thought through both the comedy and the use of the uncanny against itself. Further, it is conversely unsettling as the dis-engendered Other (both in the character of Honor Klein, the female character who primarily catalyzes the breakdown of 'normal' sexual behaviour amongst the other players, and classic psychoanalytic thought itself) becomes both the joke of the novel and our lasting memory of it. The language employed by Murdoch is the key to exploring her ideas relating not only to sexuality, and the vain pursuit of personal sexual greed, but also to gender difference. Martin Lynch-Gibbon, the protagonist and centre of the intricate web of desire, is emasculated first by his wife and subsequently by Honor: a name given to her by Martin as he sees her as more than female, nearer a 'god'. Her incestuous relationship with her brother, who is involved with Martin's wife, is the crucial point at which the web disintergrates. The cross-gendering of 'Honor' – in stark contrast to ultra-feminine Georgie, Martin's mistress – is a comment not only about traditional power structures but also Murdoch's attitude towards gender stereotypes. The danger is twofold; that an 'unliberated woman' cannot have any access to formal modes of power, and the 'liberated woman' must give up her femininity to gain mastery over her life. For Murdoch her art appears to mirror her earlier experiences of close relationships. The dis-engendering that occurs in this novel is pivotal to understanding all of Murdoch's works as it is here that the reader explicitly experiences the dangerous relationship of voice to physicality: she promotes her enchanter figures as dis-engendered in order to make them both uncanny – for both the reader and the other related characters – and hugely unpredictable. Without a fixed gender type they are able to inhabit both male and female personas and by doing so direct the course of action that others may take.

In *The Bell* it is the central conflict between male heterosexual and homosexual voices that requires our attention although these voices are understood via the appropriation of biblical texts through which they are filtered, and the reader must determine whether these intertexts are being mis-read or not. The novel revolves around an enclosed Benedictine community at Imber Abbey and a separate ancestral home, Imber Court, that lies in the abbey grounds and acts as a half-way house for those who wish to escape the world. Imber Court is led by two males,

James Tayper-Pace (conservative heterosexual) and Michael Mead (liberal closeted homosexual) and it is their leadership, as opposed to the female headship of the Abbess, who drives the moral centre of the novel. A three-way dialogue concerning the development of the community evolves and the reader is left in no doubt that the novel leads us toward the soothing disembodied voice of the Abbess who advises and cajoles the community into remaining together. That the community disbands at the close of the book is uplifting as all must now make individual choices made not by a single communal voice (James and Michael are not attuned to the needs of others and disagree on what should constitute a workable rule of life) but by an internal personal one.

Murdoch has stated that *The Bell* is 'essentially a study of two types of moral and religious attitude' (Barrows 1961: 498), and this is exemplified by the two sermons in the novel. Michael Mead, the vaguely chaste homosexual character, favours salvation through self-exploration, which is rather odd as his individual issue is precisely his unacknowledged sexuality, whereas James Tayper-Pace preaches about unquestioning allegiance to the word of the Bible. James, however, is able to address his listeners from a position of, we are led to believe, purity of inexperience. He preaches that we have no need to examine or calculate; attitudes and practices are either sanctioned or forbidden by divine wisdom. Murdoch opposes these two positions as both are examples of false vision; both Michael and James fail to pay attention to the rest of the community. Wisdom needs to come from within hence her use of the disembodied voice of the Abbess that echoes from behind the grill. The engendered voice – the voice that is seen *and* heard – can never be attuned to the needs of the Other as this must come from within and be gender neutral; Murdoch is hinting at the omniscience of a deity that is shown in the raising of the bell from the bottom of the lake.

In James's view the universality of God's judgements demonstrates that perfection resides objectively in the Hegelian world of spirit. James argues that by exploring subjectivity, like Michael, we only distort the simple rules governing human behaviour. Michael replies in his sermon that:

> We must not, for instance, perform an act because abstractly it seems to be a good act [...] self-knowledge will lead us to avoid occasions of temptation rather than to rely on naked strength to overcome them.
> (Murdoch 1958: 203–4)

Of course, this is not to say that either of these positions is, according to Murdoch, correct. We should mediate between the two of them, she insists, in order to create an idea of perfection suitable for understanding the attention the self must pay to the other, while also allowing for some setting of boundaries. This is the point Murdoch wishes us to grasp: the narrative voice is not the only arbiter of either truth or reality. Although traditional religious views have some grounding in reality, to 'attend' properly to the individual one must listen to his voice. This is best shown in the pulling of the ancient bell from the lake midway through the book; inscribed on its surface (in Latin) is 'I am the Voice of love. My name is Gabriel' (182). That this bell is said to ring in the depths is a sure sign that any internal voice must be bent to the will of an 'Other' in order for any personal development. For both Michael and James the failure to recognize the voice of the other is central. James, when he discovers Michael's latent sexuality, and his past sexual history, asks him to leave the community. Michael's refusal to do so precipitates the breakdown of communication between the two. Why must this be so? It is clear from their reactions to each other's sermons that neither has listened. James views Michael as emasculated as his sexuality is at odds with the moral basis of the community. Michael's actions rob him of his privacy and ultimately of his standing that represents masculinity to the rest of the group. Murdoch has feminized Michael's actions from the beginning of the novel and he is now shorn of any traditional male attributes. That Murdoch consciously creates them at disparate sexual orientations is no accident: they fail in love for one another and, hence, the community fails. The mediating and female voice of the Abbess is, by design, in a position of power and influence, and, notably, is also disembodied. Her voice must be in direct contrast to those of Michael and James because it needs to remove itself completely from any notion of physical attachment. Although we are told it is the Abbess who speaks she cannot be seen because to embody a voice is to humanize it. Murdoch believes that only an ego-less, gender-neutral voice may speak of both truth and love.

The feminine disembodied voice becomes the voice of benign omniscience and as such is crucial to reassessing Murdoch's feminist credentials. Although Murdoch often places male narrators at the centre of the text, narrative power can reside with a female. I disagree with Elizabeth Dipple when she states that:

> [Regarding] the frequent presence of a male first-person narrator, and the absence of a corresponding female voice [...] it is unprofitable to conjecture *why* Murdoch does it (because all the first-person narration

takes place through corrupted male psyches, is this a thinly veiled indication that men are more likely to be debased than women?) especially since she has said she is more comfortable there.

(Dipple 1982: 88)

There are several female characters who act as a counter-points to the Abbess: Honor Klein in *A Severed Head*, Hannah in *The Unicorn* (1963), Emma Sands in *An Unofficial Rose* and several others. Murdoch is interested in the discerning reader who will notice and attend to these feminine voices of reflection.

Deborah Johnson states that the story of the main character Dora's progression through *The Bell* is of primary importance as she remains, at the end of the novel, with the most potential to move forward with her life: in this context then *The Bell* may well be a feminist, as well as moral fiction.[2] Johnson's argument is that a sustained focus on Dora is crucial if we are to decipher Murdoch's fictional intent: that the feminine perspective must be central in order for a double-voiced discourse to come to the fore. It is all too easy to focus exclusively on Michael and James and negate the influence of Dora.

So it can be argued that the novel is engaging not only in reassessing the nature of the engendered female voice positively but also the homosexual voice. I agree with Elaine Showalter and believe that Murdoch's rationale is in disembodying both the voice – of the physical bell as it rings in the lake and the voice of the Abbess – and that it is not chaos that descends out of the silence of the empty space but clarity.[3] Johnson also usefully explains that any female subtext can illuminate the story as it provides a refocused narrative that not only distracts us from the dis-engendering of Michael but develops the exploration of isolation felt by both Dora and Catherine Fawley, a resident of Imber Court who wishes to enter the Abbey as a postulant (Murdoch 1956: 54).

Murdoch's thesis containing her views on fiction and fictional dialogue is contained in 'Against Dryness', an essay from 1961. She posits that to have a better form of fiction one must return to nineteenth-century realism for guidance. In the essay Murdoch engages in her foremost attack upon behaviourism for its view that 'the inner life is identifiable as existing only through the application to it of public concepts, concepts which can only be constructed on the basis of overt behaviour' (1999: 288). She argues here for a shift in focus toward the inner moral life of the individual, one which must allow for the ostracized voice to be heard, and goes on to lament that 'we no longer use a spread-out substantial picture of the manifold virtues of man and society. We no longer see man against a background of values, of realities, which transcend him' (290). It is useful to view these statements, within her fictional representation of homosexuality for example, by understanding that moral dilemmas were especially prevalent for the homosexual in the 1950s as their sexuality was, as in the case of Michael Mead, constrained by moral and social dilemmas. She depicts Michael as struggling in private with his sexuality while trying to maintain a public image of moral worthiness. As a leader of the community at Imber Court it is crucial that he maintains the illusion of his supposed heterosexuality in order to prevent any collapse of his public standing within the group. He believes that he will only be judged on his public behaviour. In addition to this, Michael has to contend with his past, embodied in Nick Fawley (the ostracized embittered young man and brother of Catherine for whom he feels a 'Byronic passion' (101)), a former pupil he taught and with whom he had his first sexual encounter. Michael also kisses the teenager Toby Gashe. Both of these incidents, Michael believes, could lead to his social downfall. Michael's failure to master his inner life, as discussed above, and come to terms with his homosexuality ultimately result in his moral failure to acknowledge Nick with 'attention'; a factor which Murdoch suggests may be largely responsible for Nick's suicide.

In *The Bell* Murdoch represents the homosexual subject's attempt to suppress knowledge, and therefore the affects of power, related to his sexuality. She describes the manner in which autonomous inner linguistic and moral processes affect the subject and emphasizes the importance of seeking the truth in these processes. Murdoch's use of the homosexual voice is crucial as it not only provides a counterpoint to James's traditional male position but also Michael's failure to acknowledge it as central to his identity and inner dialogue. As this interior voice has been silenced for so long it is unsurprising that allowing it to speak its name causes insurmountable difficulties for the community. Murdoch's strategy in using this device is to challenge not only the preconceptions of her audience but to place male-centric homosexuality as equal in stature to the heterosexual male voice: both are equally to blame for the destruction of Imber Court. Finally, she depicts the moral failures of the individual that spring from solipsism and egoism, in addition to portraying the effect on the homosexual of the community's failure to see him truthfully and lovingly. In *A Severed Head* Murdoch changes the scenario dramatically and focuses on normative sexual relations and the darkest taboo of desire.

A Severed Head is set in Murdoch's London of the early 1960s. The beautiful Antonia Lynch-Gibbon and the 'radiant' (Murdoch 1961: 24) Palmer Anderson, a psychiatrist, need Martin Lynch-Gibbon's (our narrator) acquiescence, or rather his complete capitulation, to make their adulterous love known so they may live together. Martin, although also involved in an extra-marital affair with the young lecturer Georgie Hands, remains the source of authority for them – they need his permission as Palmer and Antonia wish to formalize their relationship – even though they wish to debase him to the level of a child; the irony being of course that he has wronged Antonia equally by sleeping with Georgie, except that Antonia is unaware of it. Life requires structure, discipline and organization; unable to supply themselves with these things, Antonia and Palmer look to Martin to provide for them – naturally they become offended when Martin's secret lover is announced. As Antonia and Palmer lack the specific principles that derive from their own inner convictions, Antonia is positively revivified by Martin's disclosure. If we envision this situation in Freudian terms, which Murdoch wishes us to do, albeit with a sense of humour given the movement of the narrative, the impulses deriving from the brute authority of (laughably as a psychiatrist) Palmer's id clashes with his moral code and the superego assumes control. In satisfying his own psycho-rational needs, however, Palmer violates Martin's freedom to act or to choose as he talks Martin into his scheme. Palmer and Antonia now become parental figures for Martin and, due to a lack of courage he begins to see them as such. Underlying all this is, obviously, a satirical but accurate version of Freud's evolutionary mechanism. Absent from Palmer's understanding of the individual are the accidental, the contingent, and an awareness of the human personality – what Simone Weil would note as a lack of attention to the Other – which underlines the comedic element of the novel, and is its moral core. Palmer overlooks the equal validity of these other points of view and the countless ways in which people confront the world. Consequently, he cannot understand Martin's deviation from the emotional needs of his own underdeveloped relationship with Antonia. Murdoch believes that rather than functioning as the mechanical constituents of a depersonalized social network, we are virtually involved in each other's lives; everyone in the novel is in some way unsettled by the decision of Antonia and Palmer to live together. Martin, so forceful and domineering in his relationship with Georgie, is unable to verbally impose himself onto those his own age. He is dis-engendered by Antonia and Palmer who include him in their relationship out of a perverse sense of responsibility. Martin however, gives in to their demands:

> It was important to them that I let them off morally, that I should spare them the necessity of being ruthless. But if I had power, I was already surrendering it. It was already too late for violence. I was indeed facing something big and formidably well organised. Palmer seemed to ignore me. 'You see', he said, 'it is not at all our idea that you should leave us. In a strange and wonderful way we can't do without you. We shall hold onto you, we shall look after you. You'll see.
>
> (Murdoch 1964: 29)

This lack of a Platonic unselfment and the ignorance of the Other in preference to selfhood are at the root of the characters' strife but also the dramatic element of the novel. The effect of Martin's dis-engendered voice, along with his voice as narrator, is key here as Honor Klein, the anthropologist academic, and instigator of the sexual merry-go-round, disrupts Martin's stereotypical engendered voice and discourse, specifically by providing him with the evidence of Palmer's incestuous behaviour in her bedroom that enables Martin to reassert his dominance, and causes all of the characters, except herself, to reassess their outer relationships and inner lives. The argument between the symbolic, which can be seen as both action and physical reality, and the imaginary is at the centre of *A Severed Head*. Martin's ego is negated when he realizes that both his mistress and his wife have been unfaithful to him but he is reinvigorated in his self-belief when he discovers Honor in bed with her brother Palmer who has seduced his wife. Honor plans this scenario in order for Martin to be shocked out of his depression and, through his action, disband the web of deceit. These events provoke him into a clearer understanding of the other as the sense of self is formed in the process of expelling the other and through this Martin is able to reassert himself as the dominant male force. Honor, as the enchanter figure and de-feminized other, does not need to stand in his way as she is an outsider to domestic events. By revealing this process of realization Murdoch not only critiques Freudian psychoanalysis but also promotes attention to the other as central to understanding our true selves; a transcendence through fiction.

Martin has to realize his own predilection for sexual violence – against Georgie in order to prevent her from becoming involved with his brother Alexander – along with his use of intimidation and fear, prevents him from recognizing the reality of others. He needs to decide whether his ego leads him or whether he has control of his own will.

His predilection for sexual violence enhances his fear of castration – which comes through his infantalization at the hands of Antonia and Palmer – and his repentance over such violence reflects a marked change in the narrative toward a more honest assessment of his inner life. A.S. Byatt and Dipple both label Martin as the protagonist,[4] but it is more useful to see him, as I believe Murdoch does, as a narrative device with which to expose the ultimate indestructibility of the true protagonist Honor Klein. She becomes an anti-hero and remains static throughout the novel; if she were to develop some form of self-knowledge and vision of others then perhaps this stasis would not pervade either her or the novel. This provides the critic with a firm footing for discussing Honor's use of language when she strikes the pose of enchanter, goddess and master of all. In this scene Klein is in the process of emasculating Martin:

> I began to stare at the sword and to want very much to get hold of it. Honor was holding it in a possessive predatory way, her two hands on the scabbard like a large animal holding down a small one [...] I said, 'Is the sword yours?' and as I spoke I put my hand on the end of the scabbard. She stared a little and said, 'Yes. It's a Japanese Samurai sword, a very fine one. I used to have a great interest in Japan. I worked there for a time.' She drew the sword away again [...] I wanted her to know that I was present. I said, 'May I see the sword?'
>
> (Murdoch 1961: 95–6)

This small section of the novel is rife with dark comedy and dis-engendering: we can see it unfolding before us. The phallic symbolism on display is, as always with Murdoch, no accident. That Honor has control of the male symbol dis-engenders Martin who must ask permission to touch it. The reader is doubly amused; first by the obvious Freudian tropes and secondly by the deconstruction of them as we realize that it is the individual that is being enchanted – it is not a universal. As this narration is performed by one of Murdoch's disembodied males we must consider that this scene is not here by mere chance. Murdoch is calling into question this 'Other' as an omnipotent male by her diminishing of Martin; how can one male be so demoted but not a virtual male? The web of intrigue surrounding the sexual activity on display is mirrored and expanded upon by the questioning and destruction of traditional roles of both genders. Let us discuss Honor a little more.

Byatt links Honor with a 'vaster and vaguer and more general truth who combines in human form [...] respect for the individual [...] and that love we have discussed in terms of *The Bell*, and which is both inevitable and truth-seeking' (1965: 118). The reading of the novel that I wish to explore positions Honor as the embodiment of the darker side of Freudian psychoanalysis (and the issues that this provides for the gendering of others). However, this is diffused somewhat by the comedic value of the text and Honor's role as the equal of the male characters. The sexual relationships of the major characters are (necessarily for the narrative to work) certainly immoral and occasionally illegal.

If we examine Murdoch's use of Freud and sexuality it becomes clear that it is symbolic of the power struggle which pervades the novel and the development of the narrative. The totemic icon around which the narrative develops is Honor. Her voice, demonic though it may be, is crucial to the development of plot as she exhibits within her female frame – although this is certainly not a traditional femininity that the reader is faced with – an omniscient male voice that neither Martin nor Palmer possess. Both of the men are reliant on the other in their pursuit of Antonia; Honor, as the totemic icon that embraces both genders simultaneously, is reliant on no-one. Her incestuous relationship with Palmer is shown as merely an extension of her existence outside of morality. When we first encounter her Martin refers to her as a 'headless sack' (Murdoch 1961: 55) and this dis-engendering is central as without her the male characters have nothing to align themselves to, or react against, and the novel would fall apart. She is, of course, the collector of severed head(s) of the title, the uncanny enchantress figure who, once revealed in her nakedness, is to some extent demystified. As a professional anthropologist she is only too aware of the history of 'savage' tribes collecting severed heads as trophies to prove their own worth in their communities, the joke being that even within polite society in London primal lusts and urges are never far from the surface. She styles herself as 'a severed head such as primitive tribes and alchemists used to use. And who knows but that long acquaintance with a severed head may not lead to strange knowledge' (182). The unravelling of this 'strange knowledge' hinges on this moment in the novel.

The novel continually evokes the image of the uncanny severed head. It is used to good comedic effect but it also reflects Freud's original discussion which places the uncanny notion of a severed head at the heart of what can be thought to be peculiar and at times nauseatingly disconcerting.[5] The relevance of this has for both the disembodied and dis-engendered voice is clear: if one's head is removed the voice is physically silenced but the narrative effect is increased as the voice appears to emanate from the very epicentre of the character. Martin refers to Honor as a 'headless sack' and this may not only refer to her lack of emotion but to her dis-engendering as a woman that Murdoch consciously creates to aid the development of the narrative. This also relates to Honor as a totemic icon for all other characters: she must be dis-engendered so that she may stand outside the primary narrative as an enchanter figure, controlling the actions of Palmer and Martin. Martin's voice as narrator is changed by Honor and this stylistic device emphasizes his inner development. Without a head one is removed of part of one's humanity; this shapeless thing in Martin's car, this 'sack' is dis-engendered to such an extent that its physical self is rendered as both uncanny and dangerously unpredictable.

In Freudian terms the severing of the head primarily denotes castration and in this respect is a short-hand term for the disempowerment Martin feels when Palmer seduces Antonia.[6] Martin's position is first usurped and then his mind is ruled by his body (and low eros) when he decides to become attached to Honor, although this desire is developed more out of fear than out of (true) sexual wanting. This use of philosophy by Murdoch is vital to her use of gender differentiation in the novel and, moreover, her use of dialogue to exemplify it. According to Jacques Lacan, the subject is himself an object of the symbolic and a distinction must be drawn between what belongs in experience to the symbolic and what belongs to the imaginary (2007: 10).

Murdoch plays on the reader's discomfort with this imagery of incest to form the basis of the novel's uncanniness and comedic value, both coming from the inability of anyone but Honor (however falsely) to control his environment, but at the expense of a deeper awareness or development of the self. Martin's (and Murdoch's) strange obsession with incest goes together well with his other fixation of being 'mothered' first by Antonia and secondly by Honor. Martin notes how Antonia resembles his mother, how he married her because she reminded him of his mother, and is sometimes mistaken for his mother as well as mothering him. Honor also resembles the fearsome matriarch and this creates three types of mother-obsession which add to the comedic structure and call into question the process that Martin goes through in the novel; from assuming the archetypal sexual male, through a dismembering of his masculinity, to a more rounded understanding of his gender he comes to a realization of his own failings. Honor is also the forbidden, what Lacan calls 'the thing' (2007: 34) which must not be touched – the forbidden object of incestuous desire, the phallic mother (enhanced by her use of the sword in Chapter 13). Here Lacan veers away from Freud and represents his own take – namely that of the cannibalistic fantasies of devouring, and being devoured by the mother. There is a nostalgic yearning to return to the mother's womb, even if the mother no longer exists. Honor fills these roles both for Martin and for Palmer, the uncanniness and comedy emanating from Palmer's role as a psychoanalyst and Martin's supposed mastery of his inner self. Although it is Palmer who initially is incestuous, Martin is merely acting an immoral rather than illegal role.

It is easy to see why the novel was adapted for the stage given its small set of characters and limited number of locations.[7] The characters are overtly restrained by Murdoch's set roles and narrative form and crystalize the criticism she offers in her essay 'Against Dryness'. She employs this narrative technique as it is perfectly suitable for her early novels and, although she has been accused of double standards, the novels work as fiction because of this. It is also fair to say that Murdoch's final work, *An Unofficial Rose*, not only confirms the previous arguments relating to her fiction but also develops these through a close relationship between two females; a narrative device employed for the first time in Murdoch's oeuvre. Although it is not specifically stated that the two are lovers it is not made clear that they are reliant on each other for company either.

What then of Murdoch's place as an author concerned with gender division, sexuality and feminist thinking? Her biographer Peter Conradi emphasizes the notion that Murdoch's 'best work came out of the struggle, discontinuity and self-division' and it is obvious that her work is 'plagued by contradiction and her best fiction reflects it' (2001: 553). This is a fair assessment but I would add that as her discussion of the 'Other', be it gendered or dis-engendered, is concerned with 'attending' to them correctly, it may be prudent to revisit our previous assumptions concerning her fiction and delve a little deeper. Perhaps by subjecting her work to different critical techniques and theories we will uncover a new Murdoch. Murdoch's cross-gendered voice is then central as it illuminates the philosophical stance behind her fiction. By dis-engendering the male narrative voice, and several male characters, Murdoch points us toward her understanding of a Platonic reality (that the individual is in a constant struggle to see the world, and others as they truly are) and how we must act if we are to develop a moral inner life that may be expressed in outward action. The purpose of allowing the feminine voice to be disembodied relates specifically to traditional gender division as the feminine is required to act as exterior, omniscient and remote from the stuff of real life: by doing so it can affect those who, like the prisoners in the platonic cave, grope toward the light of knowledge and self-realization. The reassessment of Murodch's work in a new critical light is crucial if we wish to expose new layers of understanding of her novels.

Notes

1. Textual and background information can be found in Peter Conradi's excellent *Iris Murdoch: a Life* along with works by her husband John Bayley and her ex-pupil A.N. Wilson.
2. See Johnson (1987).
3. See Showalter (1982: 34).
4. See Byatt (1965: 118) and Dipple (1982: 76).
5. See Freud (1987: 225–76).
6. See Freud (1974: 273–6).
7. See Murdoch and Priestley (1964) A *Severed Head: a Play in Three Acts* (London: Chatto and Windus).

Works Cited

Byatt, Antonia S. (1965) *Degrees of Freedom: the Novels of Iris Murdoch* (London: Chatto and Windus).

Chevalier, Jean-Louis (ed.) (1978) *Rencontres avec Irish Murdoch*. Centre de Recherches de Littérature et Linguistique des Pays de Langue Anglaise, Université de Caen (Presses Universitaire de Caen, France).

Conradi, Peter J. (1986) *The Saint and the Artist* (London: Harper Collins).

—— (2001) *Iris Murdoch: a Life* (London: Harper Collins).

Dipple, Elizabeth (1982) *Iris Murdoch: Work for the Spirit* (London: Methuen).

Dooley, Gillian (ed.) (2003) *From a Tiny Corner in the House of Fiction: Conversations with Iris Murdoch* (Columbia S.C.: University of South Carolina Press).

Freud, Sigmund (1974) *The Standard Edition of the Complete Psychological Works of Sigmund Freud*, trans. James Strachey (London: The Hogarth Press).

—— (1987) *The Origins of Religion: the Penguin Freud Library, Vol. 13*, trans. James Strachey (London: Penguin).

Grimshaw, Tammy (2005) *Sexuality, Gender and Power in Iris Murdoch's Fiction* (Cranbury NJ: Associated University Presses).

Johnson, Deborah (1987) *Iris Murdoch* (Brighton: Harvester Press).

Lacan, Jacques (2007) *Ecrits: the First Complete Edition in English*, trans. Bruce Fink (New York: W.W. Norton and Co Ltd.).

Murdoch, Iris (1958) *The Bell* (London: Chatto and Windus).

—— (1961) *A Severed Head* (London: Chatto and Windus).

—— (1997) *Existentialists and Mystics*, ed. Peter Conradi (London: Chatto and Windus).

—— (1999) 'Against Dryness', in Peter Conradi (ed.), *Existentialists and Mystics* (London: Penguin), pp. 287–97.

—— and J.B. Priestley (1964) *A Severed Head: a Play in Three Acts* (London: Chatto and Windus).

Showalter, Elaine (1982) 'Feminist Criticism in the Wilderness', in Elizabeth Abel (ed.), *Writing and Sexual Difference* (Brighton: Harvester Press), pp. 9–36.

Weil, Simone (1952) *The Need for Roots* (London: Routledge and Kegan Paul Ltd.).

Part III
Gender as Performance and the Vocalization of Transgendered Bodies

7
'His almost vanished voice': Gendering and Transgendering Bodily Signification and the Voice in Angela Carter's *The Passion of New Eve*

Claire Westall

Introduction

Angela Carter is widely recognized for her repeated and probing engagement with the complexities of subject formation, sex, gender, female sexuality, sexual violence and gendered performance. As Joseph Bristow and Trev Broughton suggest, her work anticipated many of the feminist concerns of the 1990s as well as the formation and fashionability of gender and queer studies (1997: 14). It also substantially preceded transgender studies and interest in transsexual and transvestite figures as potentially disruptive, as established by Sandy Stone (1991), Marjorie Garber (1992) and the canonical writings of Judith Butler (1990, 1993, and 2004). Readings of Carter based on Butler's conception of 'gender-as-performance' are now prevalent and substantially aided the feminist claims for her significant place in debates about postwar writing, post-modern fiction and deconstructions of sex and gender binaries, not to mention discussions of embodiment, myth, spectacle, theatricality, the carnivalesque and much more. Importantly, the influence of Butler has led to Carter's representations of the female body, the inscriptive power of normative discourses, and the freedom-orientated potential of chaotic or unsettling forms of physical display being thoroughly investigated, resulting in particularly profitable studies of Carter's key fictional works. In *The Infernal Desires of Angela Carter* (1997) Bristow and Broughton identify this 'after-the-fact "Butlerification" of Carter's writing' (1997: 19) and several of their contributors re-examine Carter through alternative, or reconsidered, lines of feminist theorization: Paulina Palmer redeploys

Luce Irigaray; Clare Hanson mobilizes Foucauldian thinking; and Elisabeth Mahoney supplements Butler's conception of fantasy with Julia Kristeva and a strong psychoanalytical reading. The 'Butlerification' process has also been questioned by Joanne Trevenna who argues that Carter's fiction needs to be (re)positioned as closer to Simone de Beauvoir's earlier view of 'gender acquisition' encapsulated by the famous dictum 'one is not born, but rather becomes, a woman' (Trevenna 2002: 268–9) and that this is especially true of *The Passion of New Eve* (1977) as it tells of Evelyn's transformation into Eve. Exploring this sense of becoming, Heather L. Johnson contends that the novel's narrative style anticipates and overlaps with non-fictional transgender autobiographies which narrate their own bodies and selves (1997: 166–83). Yet the 'Butlerification' process, which includes Johnson, and critical responses to it have largely minimized the importance of the voice in Carter's writing and, in contrast, this chapter will prioritize the voice in a re-reading of *The Passion of New Eve*.

First published in 1977, *The Passion of New Eve* is narrated by Eve/lyn in the first-person, primarily in the past tense, and recounts the journey of Evelyn to Eve.[1] Initially, Evelyn, an ex-public school Englishman, travels to New York for academic work only to find a dangerous dystopian city rife with interpersonal and political warfare based on the categories of race (akin to an exaggerated Black Power movement) and sex (as in militant feminism). Carter has said that she was drawing on her experience of dissent and disorder in the USA in 1969 (Kenyon 1992: 31), and the novel is clearly an example of her aggressive response to the essentializing tropes of the Women's Movement of that time. In New York, Evelyn indulges his penchant for sexual dominance in the 'domestic brothel' (Carter 2009: 25) he enjoys (but grows to disdain) with Leilah, a young black exotic dancer he abandons after her disastrous abortion. Next, in the Californian desert, Evelyn is captured by the militant women and taken to the subterranean city of Beulah where he is castrated by the 'Holy Mother' and transformed into a new Eve.[2] When Eve escapes she becomes one of the enslaved and brutalized wives of Zero and eventually flees from Zero with Tristessa, the former Hollywood starlet exposed as a transvestite. Following the death of Tristessa, Eve meets Leilah again, now revealed as the daughter of the Mother whose real name is Lilith, and she helps Eve to leave America for home. Where Carter described her work as 'black comedy' (Kenyon 1992: 31), Lorna Sage's sense of it as both 'raw and savage' (1994: 36) seems more apt. And while the novel shares much in common with Carter's preceding text *The Infernal Desire Machines of Doctor Hoffman*

(1972), David Punter is right to state that it marks Carter's move from sexuality to the deconstruction of gender (1984: 209–10), because she is relentless in unpacking the commodification of femininity, the mythologizing of woman and the restrictions of (hegemonic/hetero-sexual) masculinity as she creates transgender bodies and voices.

This chapter will examine Carter's use of the voice in the novel – as narrative voice and as character speech – and its crucial relation to the destabilization of sex and gender in a re-reading of *The Passion of New Eve*. This is not a rejection of the usefulness of Butler's theories of per-formativity for an analysis of this text, but rather an effort to refocus attention on the voice and Carter's use of it when creating challenging speaking subjects and bodies. The chapter examines the manner in which the mouth is used as a site of consummation and inarticulacy (i.e. lacking voice); how masculine and feminine voices are offered to the reader through an always already transgendered narrative voice; the significance attached to the vocalization of extreme versions of masculinity and femininity; and the potential filled doubling, perhaps even indeterminacy, of the voices of Tristessa and Eve/lyn. The chapter revisits key critical readings of the narrative voice offered by Alison Lee and David Punter and deploys Michel Chion's conception of the acousmatic power of the voice, particularly the voice of the mother. It posits that what has been lost through the Butlerized concern with the body is the weight Carter gives to the voice and acts of vocalization, to the relationship between the voice and speech in both its assertive and self-representing abilities and in its weakened and whispering proximity to silence, and the complexity and potentiality granted to trans-vocalization, that is, the ability to speak across or from a position beyond the heteronormative and hierarchized binaries of sex and gender.

Mouths as non-vocal consuming sites

Amongst a layering of interwoven connections, the opening two chapters of the novel draw attention to important images of consum-ing mouths that are linked to masculine pleasure and fear, and this imagery is reused later to portray Tristessa's feminine vulnerability. Notably, Evelyn's last night in London revolves around the act of fel-latio he received from a nameless, and tearful, female in a cinema as he looked on at the 'beautiful' (Carter 2009: 1) figure of Tristessa, the MGM star and 'spectacle [...] of suffering' (4) he has desired since boyhood. The act of fellatio represents female sexual service which, in this scene, is tied to a young woman's emotional uncertainty, concern at separation, and inability to speak (even afterwards) beyond the utterance of a single word – 'Evelyn' (5). The nameless female mouth is reduced to 'hesitancy' (5), inarticulacy and sexual consumption, while Evelyn consumes another aggrandized female icon made for and sold to the heterosexual male gaze, but it also announces the identity of the male subject in a clichéd reduction of 'woman' that the text clearly refutes through the use of ironic and revelatory narrative distance. Nevertheless, later, as Tristessa is revealed as biologically male, it is her mouth that is an 'open wound' (125), marking her feminine passivity, and when 'blood was caked at the corners' (126) her mouth becomes the transposed site of sexual assault. In these moments the mouth is marked as the silent site of violation on bodies that appear feminine and perform femininity as they take (or swallow) the will of the men around them.

In contrast, Eve/lyn's explanation of arrival in New York describes how in America 'Mouth is King' (6) because consumption – as ingestion, sexual appetite and death – is dominant, masculinized and monarchical, the leading authority in a land that, as Lucie Armitt argues, closely mirrors Baudrillard's reading of America as the epitome of postmodernism's simulacra (see Armitt 1996). The mouths Evelyn initially sees are threatening visions of grotesque horror encapsulated by a disgusting and obese squatting gnome and large devouring black rats eating 'comestibles' (6) and these images of oral consumption are linked to the dangerous excess of the city. New York is supposedly the city of 'visible reason' (12) aligned with masculine strength, temporality and rationality but 'the age of reason is over' (9) and it is the city's gothic, lurid and carnivalized 'terror' (11) that attracts Evelyn. He repeatedly exhibits a desire to consume the capital of consumption and simultaneously to be consumed by it. This is mapped onto his first intoxicating encounter with Leilah, 'the night's gift [...], the city's gift' to him (21), as his sexualized gazing flaneurism absorbs her just as he fears that she, the unknown stranger, will erase or extinguish him. However, Evelyn's fear of the female mouth is most obviously captured by the red insignia of the militant women, 'bared teeth in the female circle' (9) that represents *vagina dentata* and reworks feminine silence into a threatening, potentially castrating abyss that is later vocalized in the womb of the Mother. In each of these scenarios, Carter identifies the mouth as the body's opening, as a transitory zone or space that is vulnerable to intrusion, often fails to articulate a sense of self or protest, but is also the void into which men like Evelyn fear they will fall. Critically, this use of the mouth, as the silent marker of the voice's potential, sits, in the novel, alongside a series of complicated versions of active voices.

Masculinities, masculine voices and male readers

> As a male reader, I find myself the victim of illusions. Although I am aware that Carter is a woman, and although that extra-textual consciousness is incarnated within the text in her obvious proximity to Leilah/Lilith, I nonetheless find that the first-person narrative of Evelyn/Eve appears to me throughout, no matter what the overt sex of the new Messiah at the time, as a masculine narrative. When Evelyn becomes Eve, my experience is of viewing a masquerade; I read Eve still through the male consciousness (Evelyn's) of what he has become. [...] I too am forced [...] to respond as a male to the residual male in Eve. Perhaps this is a recourse against humiliation, a refusal of the childed quality of masculinity [...].
>
> (Punter 1984: 218)

In his well-known 1984 article 'Angela Carter: Supersessions of the Masculine' and his subsequent study *Hidden Script: Writing the Unconscious* (1985), Punter emphasizes Carter's gothic interests, her repeated use of mirrors and gazing, and their intersection with fragmented identities. He argues that in *New Eve* there is kind of 'supersession' of a specific and sometimes exaggerated version of hegemonic masculinity and male sexuality. He sees Carter as undercutting the 'historical system of masculine competitive individualism' (217) which underpins the USA, and capitalist consumption, and any notion of evolution/progression as determined by the strength of masculinity-in-action (represented by Zero). Like numerous commentators, Punter recognizes that the Evelyn's views as contained in the early phase of the novel are exploded by Carter's deconstruction of the patriarchal dominance of women but, as quoted above, he reads the novel as a 'masculine narrative'. Further, Punter's identification of himself as a 'male reader' is similar to Nicole Ward Jouve's description of her 15-year-old son's reaction to the novel as defeating 'every pornographic expectation from its male readers' (1994: 143) and Jouve's subsequent view that Carter's play with expectations was in some ways 'geared to a male readership' (148). Both reactions indicate that Carter's text issues a set of challenges directed towards the straight male reader's very stability as a subject. This idea is developed by Paul Magrs who argues that Carter's fiction rarely focuses on heterosexual men, but that when they are portrayed it is usually as 'men in flux' (1997: 193) whose 'male egos' have been put under 'transformative' (184) pressure by 'reconstructed women' (185). Drawing on Carter's own explanation of how men only need to 'find out what is going on' when they realize they are not 'natural', Magrs reads Evelyn as one such figure of transformed maleness whose very survival is enabled by an ability to change, adapt and self question – an ability not possessed by Zero, or numerous other men who stand as 'Executioners' and 'Seducers' in Carter's work (187–9). Magrs claims that via Eve/lyn's narrative 'Carter outs the self-consciousness [Evelyn] has tried to keep hidden' (189), prompting male readers to be attentive to the enactment of heterosexual masculinity being rendered visible. Because, as Mother states; 'To be a *man* is not a given condition but a continuous effort' (Carter 2009: 60).

Perhaps more crucially for this discussion, Punter sees Carter as having accomplished a literary crossing of gender to create Evelyn in a way that has made his masculine position, identity and voice believable for the male reader throughout – even if its dominance fades. That is, he perceives a 'masculine narrative' continuity that stretches from Evelyn's understanding of himself as 'perfectly normal' in his 'tying a girl to a bed' (5), instantly imaging Leilah's legs as 'clasped around [his] neck' (15) and delivering 'punishment' (23) to her when he sees fit, through the castration, rape and enduring humiliation that causes Eve to gain 'knowledge' of herself 'as a former violator' (98), to the closing scenes in which Eve/lyn narrates a second rebirth. There seems to me to be both a critical problem and potential within Punter's analysis. Problematically, his position appears to be premised on the idea of Evelyn as an originary male voice and body. However, this is distinctly not the case. Eve/lyn, the narrator, is from the outset in a woman's body (sexed as female), has been 'fitted' with a uterus (5) and is thereby always-already transformed and transgendered. There is never an exclusively male voice or sex only a remembered, reoccupied and reanimated version of male storytelling emerging from a hybridized and disruptive voice. As Eve/lyn says: 'I only mimicked what I had been; I did not become it' (129). This complicates the gender crossing that Punter highlights because Carter's literary crossing moves first through Eve/lyn, as transgendered vocalizer, to Evelyn, Eve or any of the other characters. Usefully, Alison Lee portrays Eve/lyn as 'both the I and not-I narrator' (1996: 93) where the I is actually a narrative voice juggling an uncertain and uneven coexistence of gender positions which the masculine or feminine voice of the I (at any particular time) exists within. In terms of potentiality, Punter's sense of the 'masculine residual' can be read through Raymond

Williams's terminology to allow for a more dynamic, shifting and 'emergent' voice that has not yet relinquished the masculine learning curve of its past but is not masculine in and of itself.[3] Lee insightfully posits that while there is a journey and movement within the plot there is 'no marked change of "voice" between the parts of the novel' (1996: 93). The word 'marked' is the key here – there is a change, the masculine mode of articulation provided by Evelyn diminishes, and the feminine vocalization of Eve rises, but both are always held, and are deployed, alongside one another, within Eve/lyn's narrative voice. This is why, in singular moments of action or commentary, Eve/lyn's voice draws together masculine and feminine modes of expression. For example, according to Johnson, Eve/lyn's account of a near-death sexual assault by Zero quickly shifts from a masculine form of heroic stoicism supposedly set to protect the other women to a feminized exclamation of honesty – 'Not I'm lying [...] I cried because of the pain' (Carter 2009: 104) – required by a new body-based knowledge of female hurt (Johnson 1997: 174). And such movements across, between and beyond gendered articulation are further complicated towards the close of the novel, as explored below.

There are two other moments in which a 'residual' reading of male voices may be useful. First, as Evelyn travels into the in-between space of the desert, he stops at a village in Colorado where the 'old men in broad-brimmed hats heckled the [TV] screen in eroded voices' (36). Wanting the blacks bombed but watching 'armed tussles' as 'entertainment' they are heard 'clicking their tongues between their teeth' (ibid.). Lacking urgency, articulation and power, these male voices are the residual elements of an old, white, heteronormative patriarchy in retreat but still present – eroded but not yet erased. Second, and again in the desert, Eve and Tristessa encounter the Colonel whose 'masked voice' (149) speaks in 'clipped consonants, breaks sometimes, on a squeak' and rises 'an octave in outrage' while his troops possess 'sweet, shrill voices' (151). His presence, and the resultant killing of Tristessa by his men, violently reminds Eve of the lingering force of masculine military control and its accompanying vocal power which lasts almost until the textual end.

The novel also provides one key example of the destruction of a male voice – the voice of bestial instruction and control that belongs to Zero and stands for all that is worst about patriarchal oppression and sexual violence. He is a version of hyper-heterosexual-masculinity – always unbalanced, as indicated by his wooden leg – who has given up scribal forms because he was 'disgusted with words' and 'almost abandoned verbalization' (82). Rendering him an absolute gendered other beyond comprehension or communicative link, Carter gives Zero a voice of animalistic baying, of non-linguistic vocal expression which he imposes on his wives, including Eve:

> He would bark, or grunt, or squeak, or mew at us because he only used the language of the animals towards his wives unless there was a very exceptional emergency and we had to answer in kind. If he did not like the tone of your response, he would savage the offender unmercifully with his bullwhip. So our first words every morning were spoken in a language we ourselves could not understand; but he could. Or so he claimed [...].
>
> (Carter 2009: 93)

Zero ensures that the bodies and voices of his wives are disconnected from their own understanding of themselves, so that only he can gain access to meaning or action. It is only when Zero discovers the hide out of Tristessa, whom he believes cursed him and stole his 'virility', that he speaks in 'plain English' about the 'The Witches' liar' (106). Here Carter is presenting a voice of hyper-heterosexual-masculinity that can still draw upon the language of Standard English for its dominating strength if chosen and this pushes Eve to see that she must 'atone for the sins of [her] first sex vis-à-vis [her] second sex' (104) because her former male identity and behaviour existed on a continuum that ends with Zero. It is only Zero's final destruction that eliminates his reductive voice of masculine terror – a voice that is only exceeded in its gendered force by the figure of 'Holy Mother'.

Female articulation and the acousmatic power of the voice

> a sonorous, dark voice intoned: EXCEPT A MAN DIE AND BE BORN AGAIN HE MAY NOT ENTER THE KINGDOM OF HEAVEN [...] A woman's voice said: NOW YOU ARE AT THE PLACE OF BIRTH [...] and other women's voices took up the refrain [...] I realised the warm, red place in which I lay was a simulacrum of the womb [...].
>
> (Carter 2009: 48–9)

Eve/lyn's narrative contains two dominant modes of feminized articulation that are distinct from the reduction of femininity to silence but do juxtapose silence or silencing with the impact of vocal resonance. On one hand, Carter animates female voices in restrictive masculinized environments as tied to heterosexual binds in which their articulatory abilities are obscured, suppressed or mocked by their male counterparts. On the other hand, Carter's depiction of Beulah mobilizes the female voice, particularly the voice of the Mother, as an acousmatic force of subject creation which begins with Evelyn's experience in his womb-like cell, cited above, and is extended in his violent encounters with the castrating Mother. Together, these approaches are indicative of Carter's ambition to move past the singularly gendered voice as dominant authority, suggested in the destruction of Zero, as Patriarch, and the de-acousmatization of the Mother as matriarch.

As Lee notes, Leilah has no direct speech in New York (1996: 245) and when Eve/lyn recaptures Evelyn's impression of Leilah her voice is reported as 'so high it seemed to operate at a different frequency from the sounds of the everyday world' – making it both aloof and other worldly – and 'it penetrated [Evelyn's] brain like a fine wire' (Carter 2009: 15) – painfully piercing the skull of supposed reason and reasonableness. Her singing, barely audible, was 'more like a demented bird than a woman (15) and her repeated 'ripple of laughter' (17) and 'patois' are 'infinitely strange' and incomprehensible to Evelyn (22). Evelyn's view of the gendered otherness of Leilah is attached to the incommunicability of her sounds – as both inhuman and insane – as her voice is obviously feminized, racialized and patronized, but this is undercut by Eve/lyn's critical distance and Leilah's later transformation into Lilith, whom Eve encounters as calm and eloquent, with a 'dark voice' (170) that matches a voice from the Beulah cell, quoted above. Echoing this sense of the female voice as reduced and estranged, Eve's encounter with Zero's harem draws attention to how 'Thin, sharp, female voices babbled' (82) in their own sleeping space yet 'perpetual whispering' was also required because 'if Zero did not hear them it was as if they had not spoken' (84), that is, they could not be punished. In *Gender Variation in Voice Quality* Monique Biemans explains how with 'a whispery voice the muscles are tense [and the] middle portion of the vocal cords is tightly closed' (2000: 24). This is certainly reflected in the tense voices, bodies and lives of Zero's wives who attempt to control their voices based on a predetermined system of socio-cultural expectation. As she is acculturized into this world of female submission, Eve could not trust to a 'normal speaking voice' (Carter 2009: 84) that might be still marked by a masculine form of confidence, self-articulation or volume despite the 'softer' and 'more musical' (70) note her voice has taken since the castration.

In contrast, the female voice is entirely dominant within the all-female 'underground town' (43) of Beulah. It replaces the 'perfect silence' (38) of the desert in which Evelyn experienced his voice, his laughter, as a 'parody' that became 'silent' (38) and when Evelyn becomes a 'prisoner' (42) his voice punctures the 'inhuman silence' (48) of his womb-like cell. Having travelled 'towards the source', the 'inwards part of the earth (36) and found himself in a round, darkened uterine-like room, Evelyn is subject to an invisible 'loudspeaker' (50) that pumps in 'unknown female voice[s]' (47) and reveals surveillance via 'ironic laughter' (48) before his castration and the instructional and indoctrinatory pressures of such voices becomes incessant after his sex-change surgery. As indicated in the above citation, individual and collective female voices announce Evelyn's arrival at the site of rebirth in a language of god-like declaration (marked in full capitals) and go onto announce in mythic, symbolic and encoded terms how an ascension into the female form is to be desired, how masculine time will be replaced with feminine space to create an eternity, and how Oedipus wrongly 'wanted to live backwards' (50) by attempting to move forwards into a linear future and should instead have sought a return to the space of the mother's womb. These unseen voices speak on behalf of the Mother, act themselves as engendering mothering voices, perhaps mothering daughters, and carry a power that was mostly clearly explained by Chion's use of 'acousmatic' and 'acousemêtre' in *The Voice in Cinema*. Developing Paul Shaffer's rediscovery of the arcane word acousmastic, meaning a sound heard without a seen origin or cause, Chion explains that an acousemêtre, an acousmatic being (1999: 21), possesses 'ubiquity, panopticism, omniscience, and omnipotence' (24) – powers clearly exerted by Carter's each unseen female voice as they reshape Evelyn's psyche. However, when the voice is made visible and embodied the acousemêtre undergoes a process of de-acousmatization that decreases and eventually erases their power (27). Chion also extends Denis Vasse's *The Umbilicus and the Voice* – which posits that 'contact with the mother becomes mediated by the voice', creating an 'umbilical web' meaning that 'the voice is inscribed in the umbilical rupture' of birth (61) – and contends that the voice 'could imaginatively take up the role of the umbilical cord [...] allowing no chance of autonomy to the subject' (62). This psychoanalytical approach to the voice is critical for a reading of Carter's portrayal of the Mother as Carter attempts to recapture all that is most pressing about the male psyche and its fear of the devouring and castrating mother. Before she is seen, the 'Holy Mother', also called 'The Great Parricide' and 'Grand Emasculator' (Carter 2009: 46), is known to control all that is Beulah and to embody its matriarchal hope for an all-female future that is represented by the public display of a 'broken column' – a 'stone cock with testicles' (44) with the top broken off. Importantly, Holy Mother is 'the destination of all men' and their 'home' (55). As Evelyn stands before her, however, she is also a 'scared monster' of many breasts and 'self-fulfilling fertility' (56) who has made 'symbolism a concrete fact' by becoming the embodiment of all matriarchal myths – drawing together the force/legacies of 'Kali Maria Aphrodite [and] Jocasta' (59) and claiming that 'the garden of Eden' lies 'between [her] thighs' (60). Even before any physical attack, the reality that Mother was never a 'refuge for a full grown man' (57) is made obvious to Evelyn and her announcement of herself as 'the wound that does not heal' (61) catches her vision of herself in/on all female bodies. Yet as he stands face-to-face with Mother her imposing body is linked to her overwhelming voice, the enormity of its declarations and their impact on Evelyn and then Eve.

'Her voice was like an orchestra composed entirely of cellos, sonorosity made speech' (57) and 'went down a scale of brooding tenderness' to inform Evelyn that he was 'lost in the world' (60). It has its own 'coming and goings' too, as the 'storm' (61) of motherhood and femininity rages against Evelyn and Mother rapes him as part of her plan to secure his seed for his own fertilization (as Eve). Thereafter Evelyn looks up and Eve/lyn recaptures his view:

> Mother; but too much mother, a femaleness too vast, too gross for my imagination to contain, a voice whose rumbling basso-profundo set up vibrations inside my head as if every tiny hair in the vestibule of my ear had turned into a tuning-fork. [...] the voice like an army with banners [...].
>
> (Carter 2009: 63)

While the body of the Mother strikes fear into Evelyn and ensures that she is larger and more forceful than he can comprehend, her voice carries her mark of authority and is the height of a musical crescendo that is supported by a hi-fi that pushes out the celebratory sounds of a choir, and is accompanied by the 'prodigality of decibels' (63) created by the union of the other female voices. More significantly, the voice of the Mother has consequential reverberations in Evelyn's ear and mind – deep, powerful, even militaristic in their strength – which makes it feel, as in Chion's analysis, inescapable. And when Evelyn is returned to the Mother her 'reassuring baritone' (67) only precedes the act of castration that creates Eve, a 'playboy centrefold' in appearance who makes 'the cock in [her] head [...] twitch' (71). Although this moment of castrating force appears to be the height of Mother's power, her visibility and the embodiment of her voice and articulation of feminine strength mark the beginning of the de-acousmatization of the female voice. For once she has been made material, and once the anonymity of the voices from the cell has been lost, Mother's voice recedes and the female voice no longer possesses the acousmatic powers Chion named. In fact, Mother's plan to impregnate Eve (with Evelyn) fails because Eve escapes. At the close of the novel, Mother is a withered old woman living in a cave and about to die as Carter seemingly rejects the matriarchal omni-figure of Mother, whom Eve labels 'a figure of speech' (180), in favour of mothering and a second rebirth that moves beyond a restrictive matriarchy order.

Throughout the sex change imprisonment, Evelyn and then Eve struggle to find and/or use their own voice/s. As a captive, Evelyn 'cannot shout because the sand had got into [his] throat' (47) and only 'gagged and choked' when he tried to scream (60). When Eve awakens to see herself as female she lets out a 'scream' (65) as a jolt of recognition but immediately becomes 'speechless' at the 'injustice of it all' (70) and on looking at 'where [her] cock used to be' Eve registers only 'a voice, an insistent absence, like a noisy silence' (71). Through these articulations of silence as an inability to use the voice and speak Carter is opening up the space provided by the amalgamation of the masculine and feminine in 'the place where contrarieties exist together' (45) and the potentiality of this trans-vocalization is presented through the paralleling of Tristessa and Eve/lyn.

Trans-vocalization and a second rebirth

> Masculine and feminine are correlatives which involve one another. I am sure of that – the quality and its negation are locked in necessity. But what the nature of masculine and the nature of feminine might be [...] I do not know. Though I have been both man and woman, still I do not know the answer to these questions.
>
> (Carter 2009: 146)

Carter's fiction often depicts doubles, pairs or twinned characters as a means of exposing gendered performativity and moments of individualized difference and repetitive revelation in a Butleresque fashion, as Trevenna points out (2002: 269). The dialectical, as well as sexual, connection between Tristessa, the male-to-female transvestite, and Eve/lyn, the male-to-female transsexual, as 'twins [...] outside history'

(Cater 2009: 122) is an important example of Carter's investment in the transgendered body as 'a battlefield' of signification (Elliott 2010: 3) that precedes many of the debates and tensions within and between transgender, queer and feminist groups.[4] Notably, if one were to view Tristessa's 'passing' as a silent figure of womanhood through Janice Raymond's infamously 'transphobic' (ibid. 18) work *Transsexual Empire* (1979), written at a similar time, Tristessa may appear to reinforce a restricting, heteronormative and masculine view of femininity as something worthy of aspirational mimicry. Indeed, such thinking – namely, that transvestite performances may adhere to rather than challenge gender stereotypes – stands against Butler but has been seen in debates between some 'trans' groups, as Patricia Elliot explains. Johnson's analysis of the novel draws out a similar point of tension. She claims that the transsexual is privileged over the transvestite as Tristessa's story is absorbed within Eve/lyn's narration, and that within this narrative absorption Tristessa is the mediating body used to stand between Evelyn and Eve and act as 'the figure onto which Eve(lyn) projects her own anxiety about her sexual status' (1997: 175). Johnson's reading seems entirely fair, especially as she recognizes the transformative potential of Eve/lyn's narration, but all of the characters exist within Eve/lyn's narrative voice and are all sites of projection for Eve/lyn's self exploration and development. What is purposefully distinct in the relational pairing and parallelism Carter uses to unite Tristessa and Eve/lyn is the continuous exposure of masculine and feminine as uncertain 'correlatives', as cited above, that is, part of a grammar in which two distinct bodies represent (or mark) a collectivity of what might be called 'both-ness' that is negotiated through their Tiresias-like qualities. While this sense of both-ness is maintained through Eve/lyn primarily, by drawing attention to the voice and articulation of Tristessa, it is easier to see how Carter establishes a voice for Tristessa that is 'almost vanished' (Carter 2009: 147) but not entirely lost, the way this forms part of Eve/lyn's narrative voice and efforts to speak of physical experiences, and the way that Carter uses these voices to repeatedly shift into, out of, and across gendered idioms and discursive registers to clear a new articulatory space, a trans-vocal space, that is made ready through Eve/lyn's second and final rebirth.

When Tristessa finally appears in person, that is off-screen, her voice, seemingly found for the first time, is repeatedly described in terms of fading, as if vocalization and speech have been made almost impossible by years of (imagined) celluloid silence. When she is discovered in her own waxwork 'HALL OF THE IMMORTALS' by Zero (120), she projects a calm voice of feminine composure – greeting the intruders as 'visitors' (121) – in an effort to maintain the gendered illusion. 'Her voice is soft and a little faded, as if it has been locked away in scented cachets in her throat all these years' (ibid.). It seems to Eve/lyn that her voice had previously existed (perhaps more as potential) but had been 'locked' away, trapped, paralysed in the distinguished elegance of her throat until required for quiet acts of defiance for self-preservation. In the 'dreadful wedding scene' (130) that follows Tristessa's exposure as biologically male, Eve and Tristessa are forcibly paired – where 'both here the bride, both the groom' (132) – and are made to consummate their union by Zero and his wives in an act that Sarah Gamble contends is akin to a 'mutual rape' that exposes the extreme 'biological essentialism represented by Zero and Mother' (1997: 125). As Betty, one of Zero's wives, sucks Tristessa's penis into an erect state, Tristessa cries out, vocalizing her resistance, surprise and violation. Thereafter she becomes 'perfectly silent' (Carter 2009: 133), refusing to represent herself to her enemies, until she speaks to Eve claiming to have believed she was 'immune to rape' in 'that rustling whisper, [with] the dead leaves of his voice' (134). Although Tristessa verbally protests against Zero's subsequent anal rape of Eve and then directly requests that Eve set them both free from Zero, Carter's text insists repeatedly that Tristessa's voice is almost lost but still speaks in an 'unused voice of a revenant' (135) as if her voice emerges from a body that is not alive, that is inanimate or dead, as if it is her voice, rather than her body that is significant for self-articulation. This persistence of the voice, even as it fades, reoccurs in the desert after Tristessa and Eve's consensual consummation. In the post-coital struggle to survive, 'the slow death of the desert was already at work in [Tristessa's] voice', and 'His voice had almost vanished in his parched throat' (147). In these moments, Carter juxtaposes the desert's spacialization of silence with a fading of the voice that seeks to represent itself as contradictory both-ness, whose past can only be told as an entry into the visual but whose present is the vocalization that Eve receives and Eve/lyn keeps alive or reanimates through the act of narration. In short, Carter's text has crossed into a doubly gendered imaginative zone, creating an echo chamber of transgendered voices (with one existing within another) which refuses to silence these voices or their potential reverberations even as the silencing of speech through Eve/lyn's final journey is explored.

Eve/lyn's discovery of female sexual pleasure through Eve's body is presented as a desire to become part of Tristessa through the return of images of consumption – 'Eat me. Consume me, annihilate me' (145).

However, what seems like explicit re-gendering as feminine submission and relinquishment of self – 'I lost my body in his' (ibid.) – is complicated by the combinatory force of their mutual enjoyment, their duality of meaning and Eve/lyn's sense of the limitations of speech for bodily acts and moments of embodied transcendence:

> Speech evades language. How can I find the words the equivalent of this mute speech of flesh as we folded ourselves within a single self in the desert [...]? [T]he point of orgasm [...] require[s] another language, not speech, a notation far less imprecise than speech [...].
> (Carter 2009: 144–5)

Speech, understood as direct, spoken, out-loud verbalization seems to fail Eve but Eve/lyn's narration is the very act of vocalization that renders silence communicative as speech and silence are joined together through the narrative voice – and, indeed, speech and silence do collectively constitute the voice as mute potential and active vocalizing force. This sense of a dialectic of active and passive, of opposing aspects of a whole vocal ability can be directly connected to Eve/lyn's insistence on the combinatory and interlinked significance of his/her own identity and that of Tristessa with statements such as 'He, she, neither will do' (140) because 'we are Tiresias' (143). As suggested in this section's opening quotation, Carter's text holds on to a self-reflexive narrative uncertainty or bewilderment about gender demarcation as the narrative voice articulates its own indeterminacy and refuses to categorize, analyse or diagnose itself beyond a sense of both-ness, rejecting any notion of an answer being found in sex (as sexed bodies) because Eve/lyn has already experienced both.

This rejection of sex is important to a reading of the close of the novel because Eve rejects her former penis, shown to her in a refrigerated box by Lilith, and the possibility of a return to biological manhood. This rejection is most usefully read as a rejection of the past in its entirety and specifically Evelyn's representative heteronormative masculinity. It is not, however, a rejection of home, as Eve is taken by Lilith to the edge of America in order to return to England. At this point, Eve/lyn undergoes a second rebirth that Carter uses to open a space for the availability of a future and future-self built on but never reducible to its masculine and feminine pasts. Travelling through caves and towards contact with mother (formerly Mother) – now old, frail, and with a comforting, 'triumphant voice' (186) that indicated she would die – Eve/lyn is journeying to an end that is also a beginning. Yet in contrast to his first rebirth in Beulah mother is not the matriarchal oppressor and castrator; there is no severance from her body, no point of rupture or trauma to be worked through. There is only the vast expanse of the natural water-scape (the Atlantic) – 'Ocean, ocean, mother of mysteries, bear me to the place of birth' (187) which places Eve/lyn at the edge of the borderless space of potentiality that is fully fluid, uncertain, and not yet shaped or defined. This is reminiscent of Chion's analysis, but the lack of trauma is critical here as there is no more violence to be had. This closing request, articulated in a voice that carries both genders and has narrated experiences of itself in differently sexed bodies, is Carter's opening out of gender through a transgendered vocalization of future potentiality.

Notes

1. Throughout this discussion Eve/lyn shall be used to identify the narrative voice which conveys what happened to Evelyn, after his transformation, Eve. Eve/lyn is used to indicate that the narrative voice is transgendered and draws upon the gendered views, idioms and knowledge gained from the experiences of Evelyn and Eve.
2. While beyond the limitations of this discussion, Carter's mobilization of such sci-fi motifs, plots moves and surrealist landscapes mean that the novel can be read alongside, but also against, other feminist science fiction works.
3. In *Marxism and Literature* Raymond Williams uses emergent, dominant and residual to explain the simultaneously existing of fading, dominant and new cultural formations and I am suggesting that a parallel case can be made in relation to gender within the novel, and within Eve/lyn's narrative voice.
4. For a full, robust and eloquent theoretical exploration of these debates, tensions and ways of working through such problematics see Patricia Elliot's book *Debates in Transgender, Queer and Feminist Theory*. It should be noted that Carter does not attempt to solve any tensions arising from different transgendered labels or identities.

Works Cited

Armitt, Lucie (1996) *Theorising the Fantastic* (London: St Martin's Press).
Biemans, Monique (2000) *Gender Variation in Voice Quality* (Utrecht: Netherland Graduate School of Linguistics).
Butler, Judith (1990) *Gender Trouble: Feminism and the Subversion of Identity* (New York: Routledge).
—— (1993) *Bodies That Matter: on the Discursive Limits of 'Sex'* (New York: Routledge).
—— (2004) *Undoing Gender* (New York: Routledge).
Carter, Angela (1982[1972]) *The Infernal Desire Machines of Doctor Hoffman* (London: Penguin).
—— (2009[1977]) *The Passion of New Eve* (London: Virago).

Chion, Michel (1999) *The Voice in Cinema*, trans. Claudia Gorbman (New York: Columbia University Press).

Elliot, Patricia (2010) *Debates in Transgender, Queer, and Feminist Theory: Contested Sites* (Surrey: Ashgate).

Gamble, Sarah (1997) *Angela Carter: Writing from the Front Line* (Edinburgh: Edinburgh University Press).

Garber, Marjorie (1992) *Vested Interests: Cross-Dressing and Cultural Anxiety* (New York: Routledge).

Hanson, Clare (1997) '"The red dawn breaking over Clapham": Carter and the Limits of Artifice', in Joseph Bristow and Trev Broughton (eds), *The Infernal Desires of Angela Carter: Fiction, Femininity, Feminism* (Harlow: Addison Wesley Longman), pp. 59–72.

Johnson, Heather L. (1997) 'Unexpected Geometries: Transgressive Symbolism and the Transsexual Subject in Angela Carter's *The Passion of New Eve*', in Joseph Bristow and Trev Broughton (eds), *The Infernal Desires of Angela Carter: Fiction, Femininity, Feminism* (Harlow: Addison Wesley Longman), pp. 166–83.

Jouve, Nicole Ward (1994) 'Mother is a Figure of Speech', in Lorna Sage (ed.), *Flesh and the Mirror: Essays on the Art of Angela Carter* (London: Virago).

Kenyon, Olga (1992) 'Angela Carter', in *The Writer's Imagination: Interviews with Major International Women Novelists* (Bradford: University of Bradford), pp. 23–33.

Lee, Alison (1996) 'Angela Carter's New Eve/lyn: De/Engendering Narrative', in Kathy Mezei (ed.), *Ambiguous Discourse: Feminist Narratology and British Women Writers* (Chapel Hill: University of North Carolina Press), pp. 238–49.

Magrs, Paul (1997) 'Boys Keep Swinging: Angela Carter and the Subject of Men', in Joseph Bristow and Trev Broughton (eds), *The Infernal Desires of Angela Carter: Fiction, Femininity, Feminism* (Harlow: Addison Wesley Longman), pp. 184–97.

Mahoney, Elisabeth (1997) 'But Elsewhere?: The Future of Fantasy in *Heroes and Villains*', in Joseph Bristow and Trev Broughton (eds), *The Infernal Desires of Angela Carter: Fiction, Femininity, Feminism* (Harlow: Addison Wesley Longman), pp. 73–87.

Palmer, Paulina (1997) 'Gender as Performance in the Fiction of Angela Carter and Margaret Atwood', in Joseph Bristow and Trev Broughton (eds), *The Infernal Desires of Angela Carter: Fiction, Femininity, Feminism* (Harlow: Addison Wesley Longman), pp. 24–41.

Punter, David (1984) 'Angela Carter: Supersessions of the Masculine', *Critique*, 25/4: 209–22.

—— (1985) *Hidden Script: Writing the Unconscious* (London: Routledge & Keegan Paul).

Raymond, Janice (1979) The *Transsexual Empire: the Making of the She-Male* (Boston: Beacon Press).

Sage, Lorna (1994) *Angela Carter* (Plymouth: Northcote House Publishers).

Stone, Sandy (1991) 'The Empire Strikes Back: a Posttranssexual Manifesto', in Julia Epstein and Kristina Straud (eds), *Body Guards: The Cultural Politics of Gender Ambiguity* (New York: Routledge), pp. 208–304.

Trevenna, Joanne (2002) 'Gender as Performance: Questioning the "Butlerification" of Angela Carter's Fiction', *Journal of Gender Studies*, 11/3: 267–77.

Williams, Raymond (1977) *Marxism and Literature* (Oxford: Oxford University Press).

8

No Man's Land: the Transgendered Voice in Jeffrey Eugenides's *Middlesex* and Rose Tremain's *Sacred Country*

David Brauner

> The bells of the church were pealing like mad, pealing for this joining of the two sides – woman and man. I thought, they're ringing like they ring at the end of all the wars. They think all the soldiers have come home. They don't know I'm still out there in the mud, in no-man's-land.
>
> (Tremain 1992: 168)

> This was part of being sophisticated, too. You drank cheap Liebfraumilch in plastic cups, calling it cock-tails, and carved off chunks of Cheddar cheese with a Swiss army knife [...]. We headed back out across the no-man's-land, while Scheer directed me to open the wine and serve him snacks. I was now his page. He had me put in the Mabel Mercer tape and then enlightened me about her meticulous phrasing.
>
> (Eugenides 2003: 455)

Fiction has always been a site of metaphorical intersexuality, in the sense of male authors ventriloquizing female characters and, less commonly, female authors appropriating male voices. From the inception of the novel in English, male authors were drawn towards female protagonists, who were also often narrators of their own stories. Among the earliest English novelists, Daniel Defoe in *Moll Flanders* (1722) and *Roxana* (1724) and Samuel Richardson in *Pamela* (1740) and *Clarissa* (1748), wrote in the first-person in the guise of their eponymous heroines, while Aphra Behn took on a male voice in *Loveletters Between a Nobleman and His Sister* (1684). Although the prefaces to these novels take great pains to establish the authenticity of the narratives that follow, they do not engage specifically with the question of gendered discourse. In the nineteenth century, many of the most eminent English female novelists, including the Brontë sisters and Mary Ann Evans, crossed gender in another sense, publishing under male pseudonyms, and, in the case of George Eliot, arguably adopting a self-consciously masculinist rhetoric. Novels such as Wilkie Collins's *The Woman in White* (1860), M.E. Braddon's *Lady Audley's Secret* (1862) and George Gissing's *The Odd Women* (1893) depicted female protagonists who, in different ways, radically challenged conventional constructions of gender.

In the twentieth century, more literal cases of intersexuality occasionally manifested themselves, but they tended to be confined either to the mythological realm (as in Virginia Woolf's *Orlando* (1928)), to feminist science fiction, such as Ursula LeGuin's *The Left Hand of Darkness* (1969), Marge Piercy's *Woman on the Edge of Time* (1976), and Angela Carter's *The Passion of New Eve* (1977), or to grotesque surrealism, as in Philip Roth's *The Breast* (1972) and Will Self's *Cock and Bull* (1992). It was not until the final decade of the twentieth century and the first of the twenty-first that realistic representations of the intersexual and transsexual subject were published in English.

Rose Tremain's *Sacred Country* (1992) was her seventh work of fiction. She is best known for two historical novels set in the seventeenth century – *Restoration* (1989), which was shortlisted for the Booker Prize, and *Music and Silence* (1999), which won the Whitbread Novel of the Year – and for *The Road Home* (2008), a novel dealing with immigrant life in contemporary London, which won the Orange Prize. *Sacred Country* received generally favourable reviews and won the James Tait Black Memorial Prize for fiction and the Prix Femina Etranger. Published in 2002, a decade after *Sacred Country*, *Middlesex* was Jeffrey Eugenides's second novel, following the critical and commercial success of its predecessor, *The Virgin Suicides* (1998) (augmented by the film adaptation with which the director Sofia Coppola made her name). *Middlesex* won the Pulitzer Prize for Fiction in 2003, firmly establishing Eugenides as one of the most ambitious and accomplished American novelists of his generation.

Both novelists had already demonstrated a predilection for unorthodox first-person narratives. Tremain's previous narrators included an 87-year-old retired butler in *Sadler's Birthday* (1976) and an unnamed 13-year-old boy in *The Way I Found Her* (1997), while *The Virgin Suicides* is narrated in the first-person plural, by a group of unnamed adolescent boys. Moreover, it is clear that Tremain's decision to tell the story of a transsexual girl and Eugenides's that of a hormonally male intersexual brought up as a girl derived as much from the rhetorical possibilities offered by such unusual subjects, as from the intrinsic interest of their particular conditions. Tremain has acknowledged in interviews that she is drawn to 'people who are not valued or are marginalized' because they are 'more likely to have a unique and original perspective on life', a 'voice [...] from the wings' (Menagaldo 1998: 107). Eugenides, similarly, confesses that he 'like[s] impossible voices [...] the ability of novels to be told by voices that you don't encounter every day' (van Moorhem 2003: 3). In particular, he liked the idea of an intersexual protagonist, as 'a novelist has to have a hermaphroditic imagination, since you should be able to go into the heads of men and women if you want to write books' (2–3). For Eugenides and Tremain, then, the transgendered narrator is primarily a vehicle for a narrative journey into uncharted territory, an opportunity to develop a voice that is beyond the bounds of ordinary human experience and at the same time more representative of that experience than any conventional, single-sexed narrator could be, by virtue of being able, as Cal puts it, 'to see not with the monovision of one sex but in the stereoscope of both' (Eugenides 2003: 269).

Following the highly influential work of theorists such as Judith Butler, a large corpus of work has developed over the last two decades on 'the body' in literature. Although Butler herself insists that material bodies are constituted discursively, or, as she puts it, performatively, she, in common with many other feminist and queer theorists, tends to focus on the representation of physical characteristics of the body, rather than discussing the rhetorical mechanism – the voice – that articulates these characteristics. Most of the critical work published on *Sacred Country* and *Middlesex* is very much in this tradition, being concerned primarily with the representation of the transgendered body in these texts.[1] In this chapter, I want to redress this imbalance by tracing some of the ways in which the transgendered voice is identified, and the transgendered identity voiced, in *Middlesex* and *Sacred Country*.

In *Gender Trouble*, Judith Butler poses the question: 'Are there ever humans who are not, as it were, always already gendered?' (2006: 151). On the face of it, *Middlesex* and *Sacred Country* offer different answers to this question. The protagonist of Tremain's novel is born Mary Ward but has an epiphany, aged six, that she is in fact a he, a conviction that grows stronger as she gets older, so that at the end of the novel she lives as a man named Martin Ward. Calliope Stephanides, the narrator of Eugenides's novel, is brought up as a girl but develops male secondary sexual characteristics in adolescence and finishes the novel as a man named Cal in a heterosexual relationship. Mary/Martin is a female-to-male transsexual who undergoes hormonal treatment and surgery to reverse her gender assignment, whereas Callie/Cal is a hormonally and biologically male 'pseudo-hermaphrodite' who refuses to submit to surgery that would have enabled him to live as a woman. They might both reasonably be referred to under the rubric of transgender, according to Judith Butler's definition: 'Transgender refers to those persons who cross-identify or who live as another gender, but who may or may not have undergone hormonal treatments or sex reassignment operations' (2006: 6). Moreover, as Butler points out, 'Although intersex and transsex [identities] might sometimes seem [...] at odds with one another, the first opposing unwanted surgery, the second sometimes calling for elective surgery, it is most important to see that both challenge the principle that a natural dimorphism should be established at all costs' (ibid.). The principle of 'natural dimorphism' is indeed challenged in both novels, since Mary/Martin, as the recipient of a double mastectomy and hysterectomy, but not phalloconstructive surgery, remains anatomically anomalous, neither conventionally female nor conventionally male, as does Callie/Cal, who retains the ambiguous genitalia with which he was born. More central to the concerns of Tremain and Eugenides, however, as novelists rather than sociologists or surgeons, is what we might call the principle of natural divocalism.

Both authors were clearly anxious about adopting what Eugenides calls a 'hermaphroditic voice'. Although Eugenides attempts to naturalize his narrative strategy, posing the comical, rhetorical question: 'Why is a hermaphrodite not the narrator of every novel?' (Weich 2002: 1), he also concedes that he struggled for a long time (the novel took ten years to write) to find a narrative voice that could 'render the experience of a teenage girl and an adult man, or an adult male-identified hermaphrodite' (Bedell 2002: 2). The novel began life as the fictionalized autobiography of a hermaphrodite, but Eugenides wanted to extend its parameters, 'making the book turn into a family saga [...] as opposed to constructing the book as merely the story of a hermaphrodite' (van Moorhem 2003: 1). The word 'merely' here implies that Eugenides felt uneasy about the reception of a book with an intersexual protagonist and narrator and indeed in his interview with fellow contemporary American novelist Jonathan Safran Foer, Foer observes that he was 'surprised [...] how little of the book is "about" Cal' (2002: 4). Although Eugenides claims to believe that 'there's not an innate difference between the way women and men write' (Foer 2002: 8), he also acknowledges that 'the voice's gender' was a 'problem', since he was uncertain as to whether 'the voice [should] sound like a woman writing or a man writing' (van Moorhem 2002: 2). Ultimately, Eugenides explains, he 'just let the voice be either masculine or hermaphroditic, whatever it was' (ibid.), but this sounds less like a solution to the problem than a dismissal of it, the apposition of 'masculine', 'hermaphroditic' and 'whatever', like the slippage between 'teenage girl', 'adult man' and 'adult male-identified hermaphrodite' in the quotation above, suggesting an unresolved anxiety about the variety of subject positions that the narrative voice occupies. From this perspective, the evolution of the book – from the first-person confessional account of the life of an intersexual, to a comic epic that utilizes the third-person as well as the first to trace the progress of a genetic mutation to its 'final inheritor' (Winfrey 2002: 2) who turns out to be a self-styled 'pseudo-hermaphrodite' – seems like an attempt, conscious or otherwise, to shift the emphasis away from Cal/Callie's psychosexual conflict and to divert attention from questions of narrative authenticity.[2]

Like Eugenides, Tremain incorporates an omniscient, third-person authorial perspective alongside the first-person account of her protagonist. In fact, the novel employs a tripartite narrative structure (the third narrator being Estelle, Mary's mentally unstable mother), the rationale for which, Tremain explains, was the need to 'find a form' that would do justice to the 'complexity not just of Mary's life but of all the things surrounding Mary' (Menegaldo 1998: 116). Like the word 'merely' with which Eugenides qualifies his reference to Cal's fictional autobiography, Tremain's use of 'just' implies that Mary's life is not, in itself, of sufficient interest to justify devoting the whole novel to it. It is also clear, once again, that Tremain's desire to tell a number of stories alongside Mary's (Mary's life, like Callie's, takes up less than a third of the novel) is connected to the formal problem posed by the transgendered voice. Whereas Eugenides actually gave the manuscript of *Middlesex* to his wife and 'a few other women' so that they could 'tell me what I'd done wrong' (Foer 2002: 8), Tremain wondered, after the publication of *Sacred Country* 'if the women readers would say, "yes, it's fine" and the male readers would say, "no, you've got this wrong, and you've got that wrong"' (Menegaldo 1998: 112).

The first words addressed to Mary Ward by her father, the saturnine Sonny (an ironic homophone for 'sunny') – 'Shut you up, girl!' (Tremain 1992: 5) – dramatize powerfully the connection between voice and gender identity in the novel. Although her father's injunction is delivered in the context of a minute's silence for the death of King

George that he insists the family observes, the violence of his diction, coupled with the generic term, 'girl', resonates powerfully in the context of the novel as a whole. Later in the novel, Estelle, Mary's mother, recalls how, when she was pregnant with Mary, Sonny used to press 'his damaged ear on my belly', intoning 'Pray it's a boy. Pray and pray' (45). Estelle's revelation attests to Sonny's misogyny, which manifests itself more disturbingly later in the novel when he assaults his daughter, grabbing her by the neck and choking her (a physical analogue to his verbal stifling of Mary), tearing off the bandages with which she has been secretly binding her breasts, throwing her to the ground, kicking her in the thigh and calling her 'an abomination' (118). Just as significant, however, is the reference to Sonny's deformed ear. It is, on the literal level, the result of a war injury, but metaphorically it seems to be associated with – perhaps even, in some supernatural sense, to precipitate – Mary's gender dysphoria. Indeed, most of the central characters in the novel seem to be disabled or disfigured, either physically or mentally. In addition to her father's ear and her mother's mental illness (Estelle moves in and out of an asylum throughout the novel), Mary's grandfather, Cord, with whom she lives for some years, suffers from a mysterious palsy that paralyses one side of his face. The other family at the centre of the novel – the Loomises – are similarly afflicted: Walter Loomis, who longs to escape from the family butcher business and become a country and western singer, has severe gingivitis; his father, Ernie, dies after inadvertently hacking off two of his fingers with his butcher's cleaver, and his uncle, Pete, develops a cancerous growth on his nose. Finally, Mary herself is myopic – a condition which, before it is diagnosed and treated, makes it appear to her that '[p]eople would separate and become two of themselves' (13), an optical illusion that mirrors her internal bifurcation.

All these maladies correspond, symbolically, not just with Mary's psychic wounds but also with the injuries she inflicts on the body from which she feels so profoundly alienated. Long before she uses bandages to hem in her breasts, Mary chafes so violently at her smock dress that she draws blood from her chest – which anticipates the blood that seeps from her wounds after her double mastectomy later in the novel. However, Mary's greatest source of discomfort (a discomfort so acute as to render it a disability) is neither the constraints of her female clothing nor her short-sightedness, but her difficulty in articulating her deepest feelings. In this sense, Sonny's silencing of his daughter at the start of the novel is the symbolic act that deprives her of a voice for the rest of the novel.

There are two episodes in the novel that dramatize this aporia particularly powerfully. The first occurs when Mary, as a young schoolgirl, is asked by her teacher, Miss McRae, to bring to class something precious to her. Whereas her classmates bring in toys or other family possessions, Mary takes in baby Pearl, the illegitimate daughter of a young woman who has befriended her.[3] When asked whether Pearl is her 'precious thing' (17), Mary simply nods; when invited to explain to the class why Pearl is precious to her, instead of replying, Mary announces that she was originally 'going to bring this locket with some of my grandmother's hair in it' (ibid.). Pressed further, Mary simply asserts that 'Some things are [precious]', adding 'But you can't say it properly' (ibid.). Miss McRae waits for 'a bit' but then realizes that Mary 'couldn't say anything more' (ibid.). Meanwhile, Mary feels that her face is 'boiling red' and fears that she might 'explode and see my insides splatter out all over my desk' (ibid.). Mary's visceral response here – her fear that she will be literally eviscerated, turned inside out by the intensity of her emotions – might at first appear to lack an objective correlative. Why does Mary's attachment to Pearl – and her inability to verbalize it – cause her such agony? The answer to this question lies in the second episode in which Mary is overwhelmed by her feelings for Pearl and by her failure to express them.

Visiting Mary as she is convalescing from her double mastectomy, Pearl tells her old friend that she is engaged to be married to Timmy, Mary's brother. Prior to this revelation, Mary had 'deluded [her]self that [her] life as Martin, holding Pearl in [her] arms, was going to come one day' (311). When Mary learns of Pearl's engagement, she expresses her resentment – her furious sense of betrayal – by hurling objects at her (ibid.). Then she assaults Pearl, pinning her wrists down and kissing her repeatedly (ibid.). Throughout, the only words Mary utters echo those addressed to her by her father at the start of the novel: 'I told her to shut up' (ibid.). Afterwards, when she attempts to apologize, Mary explicitly invokes the incident when she had taken the infant Pearl into school, telling her 'You're my precious thing', but Pearl packs her things and leaves, repeating 'I am not a *thing*!' (312). Mary affects bewilderment at Pearl's objection to being objectified ('Thing. Person. Beloved. What matters is that she was precious to me' (ibid.)), but there is an ironic correspondence between the way in which Sonny habitually refuses to acknowledge Mary's autonomy and the dehumanizing label Mary attaches to Pearl. Seen in this light, Pearl becomes an externalization of Mary's own self. In other words, the inexpressible passion and confusion of Mary's feelings for Pearl are a projection of the intense ambivalence with which she regards herself.

Just as she had been in Miss McRae's classroom, Mary finds herself overcome with emotion, struck dumb. Even as she is bearing down on Pearl, aware of her 'wounds tearing and starting to bleed', Mary thinks to herself: 'mouths are wounds worse than these, the pain of what mouths say is worse' (311). Although the second half of this clause seems to refer to the pain inflicted by the revelation of Pearl's engagement, the first part hints at the existential anguish that Mary associates with the act of speech. For Mary, it is not just Pearl's mouth that wounds with its words, it is her own mouth, with its lack of words, and when she presses her mouth to Pearl's the symbolic connection between the two is literalized. Mary's mouth is a wound worse than those caused by her sex-change surgery because the latter will heal, the fleshly pain fade, leaving only scars, whereas the former will always be a source of metaphysical pain, a gash that will never close, a constant reminder of the failure of language to offer a means for her to express herself.

At one point Mary reflects on the fact that she cannot use her mouth to exercise the most basic function – to say who she is: 'I had never ever in sixteen years dared to give the literal answer [to the question 'Who am I?]' because I was afraid to be loathed' (129). Yet there is no literal answer that will do justice to the complexity of her identity, no words available that will adequately answer the apparently straightforward question. For all her naive conviction as a child that she is a boy mistaken by others for a girl, when confronted by the physical changes of adolescence she begins to realize how intractable her gender identity is. Prior to her sex-change surgery and hormonal treatment, the first psychiatrist she sees, Dr Beales, warns her:

> You will never be a man [...] a true biological male [...] You will [...] be able to pass as a man in ninety-nine per cent of social situations. But you will not be a man. Nor will you any longer *be* a woman.
>
> (Tremain 1992: 203)

This is the no-man's-land described, symbolically, in the first epigraph to this essay, a state for which there is no scientific or social designation. Dr Beales defines Mary's status negatively – she will neither be a man nor a woman – but he cannot say what she *will* be. As she gets older, Mary begins increasingly to conceive of herself as occupying not so much a liminal space as two spaces simultaneously; as being a self split into two subject positions. When she writes a letter to the agony aunt of a feminist journal (with whom she has her first sexual relationship), she signs it 'Divided, Devon', explaining that her 'body is a woman's' but in her 'mind' she is 'male' (199–200) and after her surgery she often draws a distinction between her past and present selves ('I thought, Mary would cry now, but I refuse to' (289)). Even at the end of the novel, when Mary has apparently achieved an equilibrium of sorts, her language reveals unresolved internal tensions: 'Days unfold. Martin lives them [...] I am him and he is me and that's all. That's enough' (353). Paradoxically, the diction that Martin uses to assert reconciliation between his two selves only serves to emphasize the continuing disjunction between them: referring to himself in both the first and third-person and using his male name as the subject of the verb 'live', implies that the first-person pronoun 'I' is still identified in his head as Mary and that the subject called 'Martin' is still partly alienated from that original 'I'. Like Dr Sterns, Mary's second psychiatrist, who tells her that 'your two selves will be better integrated' (260) after her surgery, and Pearl, for whom the 'old Mary [...] was still visible' while the 'new Martin [...] stood to one side, waiting' (272), Mary/Martin cannot fully reconcile his/her two selves. Although Pearl's vision of Martin waiting implies that he will eventually displace Mary, this never really happens, partly because Mary decides not to proceed with the final stage of her reconstructive surgery (the phalloplasty) and partly because both 'selves' will always co-exist, even if, as Dr Sterns believes, they will become '*better* integrated' (my italics).

This unresolved tension between the two (gendered) aspects of Mary's self manifests itself not just in Mary's self-representation as a split self, but also in the splitting of her own narrative voice, between chapters attributed to 'Mary' and 'Martin'. The novel is divided into four parts, each of which is split into numbered and dated chapters (from 'Chapter One, 1952' through to 'Chapter Twenty, 1980'), which consist of subsections bearing either the name of their narrators, or a thematic title for those narrated by the third-person voice. Out of a total of 58 subsections, 12 are narrated by Mary, two by Martin. The name-change occurs, logically enough in one sense, after Mary has undergone a hysterectomy. However, in another sense the change is both belated and misleading: belated because Mary renames herself Martin at the age of 11, 18 years prior to the surgery; misleading because the change of attribution implies a definitive transition, a sudden shift of identity from Mary to Martin, whereas the post-operative identity of Martin is a work-in-progress, a self that is constantly being renegotiated, and that, rather than erasing Mary, is superimposed on her, in the same way that Cal, in *Middlesex*, even after he begins living his life as a man, feels 'Callie [rising] up inside [him]' at times, like a spirit possessing his body, 'her girlish walk tak[ing] over' (Eugenides 2003: 41–2). When Mary fantasizes about 'the future of Martin Ward', she tries to cement her elective change of name by writing out the 'new name hundreds of times in different writing' (Tremain 1992: 55). In practice, she cannot simply write herself into a new gender: the repetition and variation of this ritual imply a restless dissatisfaction that anticipates the disillusionment she experiences after her mastectomy, when she decides that her 'whole life has been absurd' (309).

Spending Christmas with Cord in the winter of 1963, the 17-year-old Mary, already addressed as Martin by her grandfather, rejects his theory that everything in nature is divided into binary categories:

> He said [...] everything important in life was dual, like being and not being, male and female, and that there was no country in between. I [...] thought, Cord is wrong, there is a country in between, a country that no one sees, and I am in it.
>
> (Tremain 1992: 148)

The 'country in between' that Mary inhabits is the sacred country of the novel's title (which also punningly refers to the holy grail of country music to which the other protagonist, Walter Loomis, dedicates himself). It is not just invisible, as Mary notes here, but also unspeakable. Like Cord's mysterious palsy, for which there was, according to the doctors, 'no specific name' (148), Mary's condition cannot be formally diagnosed. There is no term to describe who Mary is, no linguistic space that corresponds to the existential limbo that Mary inhabits, no voice that can be both male and female, or neither.

Just as Mary chooses a spatial metaphor to describe her ambiguous gender position, so Eugenides takes as the title of his novel the name of the house in which Cal grows up (as Callie), Middlesex, to symbolize the in-betweenness of his protagonist's gender identity.[4] This concept of a middle position between the two normative gender categories, like the 'no-man's-land' of the second epigraph of this essay (the other key spatial metaphor that Eugenides invokes to refer to Cal's indeterminate gender) has become hotly disputed territory. Eugenides himself has commented that the novel argues for a 'middle place' '[b]etween the alternatives of nurture and nature', a 'third gender' that 'represents a certain flexibility in the notion of gender itself' (Eugenides 2003: 5). Francisco Collado-Rodriguez likewise perceives a 'third space' delineated in the novel in which 'intersex identities can coexist' (2006: 386), while Zachary Sifuentes suggests that the term '*queer heterosexuality* may be the only available means to capture rhetorically the difficult paradox of his body' (2006: 156, Sifuentes's italics). Other critics have criticized what they see as the novel's reification of heteronormative orthodoxy: Anne Koch-Rein argues that rather than representing the realities of the intersexual body, the novel retreats into euphemism, 'titillat[ing]' its readers with 'floral and metaphoric descriptions of [Cal's] "crocus"' (2005: 249), while in Rachel Carroll's view *Middlesex* is 'a nominally transgressive narrative' that ultimately 'remain[s] captive to normative discourses' (2010: 188). Debra Shostak steers a middle course, suggesting that Cal is 'driven to erase the in-between position that he unmistakably inhabits and to accept the terms of identification that promise to make him a subject' (2008: 405) and that the 'conundrum of Cal's sex forces Eugenides into a binary model' (410) that 'does not support a position of betweenness' (411). For Shostak, however, this is not a failure on the part of the author, but rather the inevitable result of the gendered limitations of language itself: 'the conservatism lies not in the messenger but in the materials with which he can work' (410). Shostak is right to suggest that there is a tension in the novel between the coercive forces of what she calls 'social discourse' (410) and 'the need to devise figures of the newly thinkable with which to rescue the hermaphrodite from the position of the strange' (391). Rather than being 'driven' and 'force[d]', respectively, to reinstate the conventional gender categories they have sought to disrupt, however, it seems to me that Cal and Eugenides recalibrate the parameters of social discourse by repositioning the hermaphrodite as quintessentially human, rather than a 'strange' deviation from the human.

At one point in the first section of the novel, which deals with the migration of Cal's grandparents from Greece to America, and the transformation of their relationship from that of brother and sister to husband and wife, Cal delivers a lengthy eulogy to Smyrna, 'a city that was no place exactly, that was part of no country because it was all countries' (Eugenides 2003: 54). Like Middlesex, Smyrna here seems to me to function as a metaphor for the hermaphrodite: just as the Greek port paradoxically partakes of all countries, cutting across national borders, precisely because it is 'part of no country', so Cal is universally human because he belongs properly to neither sex, his ambiguous gender identity blurring the ordinary distinctions between male and female. As Eugenides has made clear, his intention was 'not to tell the story of a freak or someone unlike the rest of us', but to explore the predicament of an intersexual character 'as a correlative for the sexual confusion and confusion of identity that everyone goes through in adolescence' (Weich 2002: 8). As Cal himself puts it, overstating the case provocatively: 'My change from girl to boy was far less dramatic than the distance anybody travels from infancy to adulthood' (Eugenides 2003: 520). Elsewhere, Cal suggests that his story can be seen as a micro-cosmic version of a larger, historical trend, his 'medical story' being 'only a reflection of what was happening psychologically' during the 1970s, when '[w]omen were becoming more like men and men were becoming more like women' and 'it seemed that sexual difference might pass away' (478). The movement here from the physical (Cal's 'medical story') to the metaphysical (the *Zeitgeist* of the 1970s) is symptomatic of the movement in the novel from the notion of gender identity as some-thing that is embodied to something that is voiced. In other words, this universalizing impulse – the desire 'not to make something mundane strange, but rather, something that is somewhat freaky more normal' (Bedell 2002: 2), as Eugenides puts it – manifests itself, in *Middlesex* as in *Sacred Country*, primarily not in the representation of the gendered body but in the articulation of a transgendered voice.

From the outset, Cal's gender dysphoria is implicitly connected both to his fluency and to the sound of his voice. Of his first sexual experi-ence (kissing the girl next door, Clementine Stark), Cal notes that he 'was aware that there was something improper about my feelings [...] but I wouldn't have been able to articulate it' (Eugenides 2003: 265). As I have pointed out elsewhere, it is important to be aware that Cal is likely to be reinterpreting his earlier experiences in the light of his later choice of gender role, so the judgement of impropriety may be retro-spective.[5] Similarly, when he complains that he has 'never had the right words to describe [his] life' (217) it might seem at least partly ironic in the context of a six-hundred-page novel notable for the verbal facility, indeed flamboyance, of its narrator. However, Cal is not necessarily being disingenuous in either case: the challenge of putting into words his anomalous subjectivity is real. If Dr Luce, the celebrated sexologist to whom Cal is referred when his male secondary sexual characteristics manifest themselves in puberty, is correct to suggest that 'Children learn to speak Male or Female the way they learn to speak English or French' (411), then Cal's acquisition of this language must have been disrupted by his indeterminate gender. Certainly, this view is consistent with the adult (male-identified) Cal's remark that whenever his earlier (female-identified) incarnation, Calliope, 'surfaces', 'she does so like a childhood speech impediment' (41). On the other hand, Luce is hardly an authority in the novel: in spite of 'register[ing]' Cal's 'tenor voice' (408), and establishing that he is hormonally male, he allows his own prejudices (confirmed by Calliope, in the mistaken belief that giving Luce the answers he wants will persuade him to leave her alone) to cloud his judgement and recommends to Cal's parents that he should have 'corrective surgery' to allow her to continue her life as a female.

In fact, Cal's voice is both a signifier of gender dysphoria and the means by which he locates and articulates a gender position that is not 'strange'. During puberty, Cal's voice undergoes a 'slow descent', which results in '[s]ales ladies look[ing] past [him] for the woman who had asked for help' (303). Not only do others fail to recognize the source of this voice, but Cal struggles to reconcile himself to the 'strange [...] Eartha Kitt voice that came out of [his] mouth' (326). The passive construction here implies that to Cal his own voice seems disembodied – to arise unbidden from somewhere outside himself. In spite of this sense of self-alienation, however, Cal continues to gender his voice as female – the sales ladies expect to find a mature woman behind the adolescent girl, and Cal invokes a female singer (albeit one renowned for her deep vocals), rather than a man. A mature female voice issuing from the frame of a pubescent boy, identified at this stage in the narrative as a girl, inevitably calls to mind Shakespeare, but it also echoes an earlier moment in the novel, when Cal explains that the genetic connection between himself and his grandmother (with the Shakespearean name) allows him to ventriloquize her, 'so that when I speak, Desdemona speaks' (38). Just as the novel itself is split into two sections, one dealing with Desdemona and her husband/brother Lefty, so Cal's narrative voice itself is split: between a first-person account of his own story and an account of his grandparents' and parents' experiences that, though technically also in the first-person, reads more like an omniscient third-person narrative; and between the female-identified and male-identified years of his life; between Calliope and Cal.

At one point in Lorrie Moore's novel *Who Will Run the Frog Hospital?*, the protagonist, Berie Carr, recalls how, as a child, she 'tried hard to split my voice [...] to splinter my throat into harmonies' (Moore 1995: 5). Dreaming of being 'able to people myself, unleash the crowd in my voice box, give birth', Berie finds instead that her efforts lead only to 'much coughing, wheezing, and [...] hoarseness' (ibid.). What eludes Berie becomes Cal's gift and his curse: his is the 'impossible' narrative voice *par excellence*. In this context, there is another passage, near the end of the novel, which demands to be read allegorically. Reunited with his brother for the first time since he fled Dr Luce's custody, and began to inhabit a male role, Cal is at first uncertain of how to approach a relationship that is at once familiar and strange, before deciding that when '[c]onfronted with the impossible, there was no option but to treat it as normal' (Eugenides 2003: 516). Lacking 'an upper register, so to speak' in which to converse, the brothers confine themselves to 'the middle range of our shared experience' (ibid.). Here, implicitly, is the manifesto for *Middlesex*: rather than straining for an upper register – trying to find a new language to describe the strangeness of the hermaphrodite – Eugenides treats the impossible as though it were normal, finding a 'middle range' that rejects the binary opposition of male/female in favour of the 'shared experience' that is Cal's life.

In the letter that she writes to her parents explaining her flight, Callie states unequivocally 'I am not a girl. I'm a boy' (439, Eugenides's emphasis) and indeed when she first begins to live her life as a male, she marvels at how easy it is to 'defect to the other side' (442). When he returns home at the end of the novel, however, Cal has clearly renounced the either/or paradigm of conventional gender classification and embraced a 'both/and' view, expressed movingly in a brief exchange that forms part of the final conversation of the book, between Cal and an aged, bed-bound Desdemona:

> 'You're a boy now, Calliope?'
> 'More or less.'
>
> (Eugenides 2003: 526)

Just as, earlier in the novel, when she is penetrated by the brother of her best friend, Callie 'clearly understood that I wasn't a girl but something in between' (375), so here Cal recognizes, through the equivocal nature of his response to his grandmother's question, that he will always inhabit a middle ground, a no-man's-land that paradoxically is also an everyman's and everywoman's, since gender is always, as theorists such as Judith Butler remind us, something that is 'more or less', a relative, contingent process rather than a fixed identity.

In spite of the affinities I have emphasized, *Sacred Country* and *Middlesex* offer contrasting reading experiences: Tremain's novel ends with Mary in exile, with no partner and estranged from her family, and is rather downbeat in tone, albeit laced with characteristic dry humour; *Middlesex* is an exuberant, predominantly comic epic that ends with Cal returning home, reconciled to his family, and with the prospect of a relationship with a woman who seems to have accepted him. Judith Butler has argued that 'the transsexual desire to become a man or woman [...] can be a desire for transformation itself, a pursuit of identity as a transformative exercise, an example of desire itself as a transformative activity' (2004: 8). This seems to me a dubious theory to apply to actual transsexuals but it describes accurately something that *Middlesex* and *Sacred Country* share, namely the compelling dramatization of their protagonists' transformative desires, both literally as transgendered subjects, and metaphorically, as individuals whose 'pursuit of identity as a transformative exercise', and struggle to articulate that pursuit, make them surrogates for the novelists themselves.

Notes

1. Very little has been published on *Sacred Country*: the only previous detailed criticism of the novel I am aware of are two pieces by Pia Brinzeu, one a book chapter comparing the novel with the Romanian novelist Mircea Cărtărescu's *Travesti* (1994), in which Brinzeu argues that for Mary '[t]he confusion of transsexualism' is 'a form of spatial transcendence equivalent to transmigration and exile' (2000: 134), the other an article which reads the novel in terms of narratological theory and which does use the term 'transsexual voice' (Brinzeu 2004: 115). Of the critics who have written on *Middlesex*, Anne Koch-Rein analyses the novel from the perspective of Queer and Disability Studies, alleging that its 'mild transgendered sensitivities' are compromised by a prevailing 'naturalized heterosexuality' (2005: 250), Zachary Sifuentes adopts a more sympathetic Queer Studies approach, focusing on what he calls 'the queer body' in the novel, Kenneth Womack and Amy Mallory-Kani offer an 'adaptionist' reading of the novel that emphasizes the 'biological forces' at work in *Middlesex* (2007: 161), Debra Shostak is interested in Eugenides' 'construction of an identity [...] for the anomalous body' (2008: 384).
2. The medical term for the condition that Cal has is 5-alpha-reductase deficiency, in which, as Amy Bloom explains in her book *Normal* 'apparently female children masculinize during puberty' (2003: 134).
3. Pearl's name may allude to that of her namesake, the daughter of Hester Prynne in Nathaniel Hawthorne's *The Scarlet Letter* (1850), who is similarly illegitimate and similarly striking in appearance.
4. The house is notionally named Middlesex because it is on Middlesex Boulevard, but its allegorical status is clear not just by virtue of its name but also because of its paradoxical properties: it is, for example, 'futuristic and outdated at the same time' (Eugenides 2003: 258).
5. See Brauner (2010: 91–3).

Works Cited

Bedell, Geraldine (2002) 'He's not like other girls' (interview with Jeffrey Eugenides), *The Observer*, Sunday 6 October, p. 2, http//:www.guardian.co.uk/books/2002/oct/06/fiction.impacprize/print [accessed 20 January 2012].
Bloom, Amy (2003) *Normal: Transsexual CEOs, Crossdressing Cops and Hermaphrodites with Attitude* (London: Bloomsbury).

Brauner, David (2010) *Contemporary American Fiction* (Edinburgh: Edinburgh University Press).

Brinzeu, Pia (2000) *Corridors of Mirrors: the Spirit of European Contemporary British and Romanian Fiction* (Lanham, Maryland: Maryland University Press).

—— (2004) 'Narratology Revivified: Androgynous and Transsexual Voices', *British and American Studies*, 10: 115–25.

Butler, Judith (1993) *Bodies That Matter: on the Discursive Limits of Sex* (London: Routledge).

—— (2004) *Undoing Gender* (London: Routledge).

—— (2006) *Gender Trouble: Feminism and the Subversion of Identity* (London: Routledge).

Carroll, Rachel (2010) 'Retrospective Sex: Rewriting Intersexuality in Jeffrey Eugenides' *Middlesex*', *Journal of American Studies*, 44/1: 187–201.

Collado-Rodriguez, Francisco (2006) 'Of Self and Country: U.S. Politics, Cultural Hybridity, and Ambivalent Identity in Jeffrey Eugenides' *Middlesex*', *International Fiction Review*, 33/1–2: 71–83.

Eugenides, Jeffrey (2003[2002]) *Middlesex* (London: Bloomsbury).

Foer, Jonathan Safran (2002) 'Jeffrey Eugenides' (interview with Jeffrey Eugenides), *BOMB* 81 (Fall), p. 9, http://bombsite.com/issues/81/articles/2519 [accessed 20 January 2012].

Koch-Rein, Anne (2005) 'Intersexuality – In the "I" of the Norm?': Queer field notes from Eugenides' *Middlesex*', in Yekani Haschemi and Beatrice Michaelis (eds), *Quer Durch Die Geistewissenschaften* (Berlin: Querverlag), pp. 238–52.

Menegaldo, Gilles (1998) 'On Art and Life' (interview with Rose Tremain), *sources* (Easter): 101–19, http://www.paradigme.com/sources/SOURCES-PDF/Pages%20de%20Sources04-3-1.pdf [accessed 20 January 2012].

Moore, Lorrie (1995[1994]) *Who Will Run the Frog Hospital?* (London: Faber and Faber).

Moorhem, van Bran (2003) 'Bran van Moorhem interviews Jeffrey Eugenides' (interview with Jeffrey Eugenides), *3am Magazine*, p. 7, http://www.3ammagazine.com/litarchives/2003/sep/interview_jeffrey_eugenides.html [accessed 20 January 2012].

Shostak, Debra (2008) '"Theory Uncompromised by Practicality": Hybridity in Jeffrey Eugenides' *Middlesex*', *Contemporary Literature*, 49/3: 383–412.

Sifuentes, Zachary (2006) 'Strange Anatomy, Strange Sexuality: the Queer Body in Jeffrey Eugenides' *Middlesex*', in Richard Fantina and Thomas Calvin (eds), *Straight Writ Queer: Non-Normative Expressions of Heterosexuality in Literature* (Jefferson, NC: McFarland), pp. 145–57.

Tremain, Rose (1992) *Sacred Country* (London: Sinclair-Stevenson).

Weich, Dave (2002) 'Jeffrey Eugenides Has It Both Ways' (interview with Jeffrey Eugenides), Powells.com, p.10, http://www.powells.com/authors/eugenides.html [accessed 20 January 2012].

Winfrey, Oprah (2007) 'A Conversation with *Middlesex* Author Jeffrey Eugenides' (interview with Jeffrey Eugenides), *Oprah's Book Club*, June 5, p. 4, http://www.oprah.com/oprahsbookclub/A-Conversation-with-Middlesex-Author-Jeffrey-Eugenides [accessed 20 January 2012].

Womack, Kenneth and Amy Mallori-Kani (2007) '"Why don't you just leave it up to nature?": An Adaptionist Reading of the Novels of Jeffrey Eugenides', *Mosaic* 40/3: 157–73.

9
Transvestic Voices and Gendered Performance in Patrick McCabe's *Breakfast on Pluto*

Claire Nally

Who or *what* are you?' (McCabe 1998: 193) is one of the most definitive statements from Patrick McCabe's *Breakfast on Pluto*, which presents the transgendered subject as a significatory body who not only interrogates the nature of sexuality but the very stability of gendered identity. This chapter focuses on the effect of fragmentation and postmodern style in McCabe's novel: given the variety of competing voices in the text as well as the frequently fanciful and downright duplicitous narration which is a hallmark of *Breakfast on Pluto*, what emerges is a polyvocal text which provides incisive commentary on the instability of gendered personae, and the ideological discourses which inform them. As a peripatetic figure, Patrick 'Pussy' Braden, the protagonist, transgresses sexual borders through female impersonation, and this is specifically enacted in the stylistic form of the novel and in everyday life, underscoring the multivalent theatricality of his/her identity. Narrated in the first-person, with shifts to omniscient narration via self-consciously fictional scenes embedded in the text, as well as sections of dreamy prose inserted at the request of Terence, Pussy's psychiatrist, the elaborate and exuberantly verbose story of Pussy is presented as fluid, multiple and unstable, in 'feminine' voices which disrupt the dominant ideology of Ireland in the 1960s and 1970s even while it conforms to various stereotypes of femininity. The issue of border crossing is seen as intensely traumatic in the novel. McCabe's Preface identifies '1922; a geographical border drawn by a drunken man, every bit as tremulous and deceptive as the one which borders life and death' (x). The arbitrary nature of the border between the North and the South is obvious and clearly delineated here, relating as it does to Braden's own negotiation of gender categories: 'Dysfunctional double-bind of border-fever, mapping out the universe into which Mr. Patrick Braden, now some years later found himself tumbled' (x).

In the preface to the novel, McCabe declares that Braden is a 'fragile, flamboyant self-styled emissary' (xi) who embodies the outsider in modern Irish culture. As a 'fucking queer' (106) in the fictional border town of Tyreelin, who declares politics are 'of no consequence' (20); a 'Blahdy bog Arab' (87) and cross-dressing prostitute in London, who is accused of planting an IRA bomb in a soldier's bar; and finally as an abandoned child, supposedly the offspring of the local priest and his young housekeeper, Braden is quiet clearly the representative of the marginal, the dysfunctional and the tragic. The employment of the transvestic voice in Irish literature to figure the excluded elements of society is not a new phenomenon. In Neil Jordan's *The Crying Game* (1992), Dil's persona has secured much critical debate for its presentation and impersonation of the feminine (see Cullingford 2001: 60–2). As far back as 1922, James Joyce offered the world Leopold Bloom's cross-dressing fantasies in the 'Circe' episode of *Ulysses* (1922). While rather neatly coinciding with the decriminalization of homosexuality in Ireland in 1993, *The Crying Game* is often lauded as a film which presents alternative sexualities and the possibility of a queer space. It also, however, as Lance Pettitt has highlighted 'continues to manifest male anxieties about women, as well as offering fun to gay men' (1997: 256).[1] Emerging from this critical position, I seek to approach McCabe's text by concentrating on Braden's appropriation of the feminine voice. The notion of the 'transvestic voice', as elucidated by Elizabeth Harvey, addresses how the 'author' and gendered narrative voice interrelate, and more specifically how biologically male characters can articulate themselves as feminine, often invoking cultural stereotypes as well as complicated strategies with reference to gendered characteristics (1992: 32). In short, the 'transvestic voice' invokes how the 'gap between the male voice and the female voice [...] has much to say about cultural constructions of gender' (ibid.).

One of the significant features of McCabe's preface to the novel is the way in which the authorial voice seeks to impose a sense of unity and declared intention on an emphatically multivalent text, by stabilizing one reading over another. The preface declares that Braden-as-transvestite signifies 'those first few steps which may end unease and see us there; home, belonging, and at peace' (McCabe 1998: xi), essentially securing a radical and sexually accommodating agenda for the novel, especially relevant given the fact that the novel's year of publication shares a historical moment with the Good Friday Agreement (1998). McCabe comments upon the fictional Tyreelin, highlighting the violent trauma implicit in border locations: 'cattle and bombs and butter and guns seem to travel with dizzying and bewildering rapidity' (ix). Negotiating the border of both gender and geography is clearly a major operation in the text itself. Jason Buchanan has suggested that 'By inserting his own voice into the narrative, McCabe's prelude frames his text as an alternative history that truthfully represents the violent tradition of the Troubles but still retains a space for forgiveness' (2008: 69). However, the text is potentially far more complex. In his discussion of paratextual material (those things which hover on the borderlands of a text, such as prefaces, introductory material, footnotes etc.), Gèrard Genette has remarked 'we see the preface, like all other overly obvious paratextual elements, carefully avoided as much as possible by those authors who are most closely associated with classical dignity and/or realistic transparency' (1997: 293). 'Truthful' representation is less of an issue, as Buchanan confirms by suggesting McCabe's preface 'blurs the lines between critic, reader and author' (2008: 69). McCabe's pose here represents, not authenticity, but a fictive and self-conscious-insertion:

> [T]he prefatorial malaise, whether it proceeds from a sincere modesty or from unavowed disdain, turns into a kind of generic hyper-consciousness. No one writes a preface without experiencing the more or less inhibiting feeling that what's most obvious about the whole business is that he is engaged in writing a preface.
>
> (Genette 1997: 275).

This self-conscious authorial voice thereby has much to align it with the text proper. We may note how much of Braden's text is ironic and self-aware: s/he suggests of his/her early letters to his/her father that s/he was 'Quite the prolific author' (McCabe 1998: 30), signalling how far the text and the protagonist are acutely self-aware of themselves. Likewise, in his/her discussion of his/her mother's apparel for housekeeping at the presbytery, s/he states 'one had no difficulty whatsoever in acquiring a washed-out, pale blue housecoat with a ringpull zip', which carries a footnote exclaiming 'Not entirely unlike my own!' (24). The use of the footnote itself registers how pointedly we are dealing with a self-referential text. Like McCabe's aforementioned testimony for Ireland: 'home, belonging and at peace', Braden's own paratextual irruption in the footnote reveals his/her search for 'home' and 'belonging' through identification with the mother, neatly combining the objectives of 'author' and the 'character'. Through this conflation, McCabe seeks to disavow the potentially errant aspects of his text (the representation of stereotypical femininity through Braden's transvestic voice), and impose a neat unity on the text. Genette argues that prefaces to novellas, essays and poems often seek to reject multiplicity: 'One theme of value-enhancement which, for an obvious reason, is characteristic of the prefaces to collections (of poems, novellas, essays) consists of showing the unity – formal, or, more often, thematic– of what is likely to seem *a priori* a factitious and contingent jumble of things' (1997: 201). In simple terms, McCabe's novel (itself a jumble of Braden's diaries, essays, thought processes and fictions highly suited to this form of paratext) is denied competing voices, but instead represents accommodation and unity – something that would have seemed imperative at the time of the Good Friday Agreement. In its bid to suggest Braden is a voice from the margins, the preface closes down any other interpretive gesture. Peter Mahon's claim that 'McCabe's text proposes an alternative to phallic authoritarianism and sameness' through the transvestite (2007: 453), is thereby negotiable: on the surface, Braden is indeed a resistant figure who challenges the stereotypical ideas of Irish masculinity in 1970s Ireland. But at the same time, s/he also occupies exceptionally conventional notions of femininity which are directly attributable to patriarchal influence.

In the light of this discussion, the text is most usefully situated as a postmodern enterprise. Indeed, the nostalgia for stability, rootedness and unity which the prefatorial voice invokes is displaced by the novel itself. Clare Wallace identifies McCabe's fiction as marked by 'narratives which are fragmentary, repetitive and often disjointed. A "cut-up" style, which clearly owes much to cinematic techniques', which McCabe himself identified with the postmodern (2004: 145). If this is the case, despite McCabe's own declared appeal for unity, several other emerging voices are present in the text, rendering the text multi-voiced or heteroglossic, as Mikhail Bakhtin explained. Apart from the dominant ideology, there are conflicting species of meaning and interpretation which unfold through the linguistic identity of the text:

> Language is heteroglot from top to bottom: it represents the co-existence of socio-ideological contradictions between the present and the past, between different socio-ideological groups in the present, between tendencies, schools, circles and so forth.
>
> (Bakhtin 1981: 291)

Furthermore, as Bakhtin perceptibly remarked, 'The novel can be defined as a diversity of social speech types (sometimes even diversity of languages) and a diversity of individual voices, artistically organised'

(1981: 262). One such voice was that of the Irish woman. Indeed, in terms of the Irish Free State, Éamon de Valera's address to the nation in 1943 (which was to influence a generation in terms of its perceived 'normative' values regarding gender and social hierarchy), we can see how that voice was marginalized and over-sentimentalized: '[Ireland as] a land whose countryside would be bright with cosy homesteads [...] with the romping of sturdy children, the contests of athletic youths and the laughter of comely maidens, whose firesides would be forums for the wisdom of serene old age' (De Valera 1943). To signify women as bearers of children, as managers of hearth and home, is a highly conservative vision which was to influence the Irish state's notion of idealized womanhood for decades to come. If the South can be seen as policing ideas of housewifery and normative femininity down to the 1980s and even today (when abortion laws still need to be liberalized), the North was subject to debate surrounding gay rights, with the Democratic Unionist Party's Ian Paisley uniting with the Free Presbyterian Church in the late 1970s to support the status of homosexual intercourse as a criminally actionable offence, otherwise known as the 'Save Ulster from Sodomy' campaign (Ferriter 2009: 475–6). Due to such historical events, the varying composition of feminine and queer voices within Patrick 'Pussy' Braden are perhaps the most pertinent for analysis.

As a transvestite, one of Braden's major poses is signified through the feminine voice, a concept first theorized by Robin Lakoff. Characteristics frequently attributed to a feminine language include the following: empty adjectives such as 'divine', 'charming' and 'cute'; specific colour adjectives such as 'mauve', 'lavender' or 'beige'; and euphemisms (Lakoff 2004: 78, 15, 52). Braden's texts are littered with the phraseology and linguistic register of how women are popularly imagined to behave: 'I beamed, utterly consumed by the proud, exquisite, giddy tremor of a girl who knows she's loved' (McCabe 1998: 51). The convention of the romance narrative, with the verbose excesses ('utterly consumed', 'proud, exquisite, giddy'), alongside the appeal to emotionalism, suggest the trope of femininity, which is further confirmed in the clear infantalization of Braden's voice when s/he occupies the feminine role: the references to 'huggy-warm' (67), 'yummy' and 'clothesies' (68), 'tootle' (69) and 'Mr Nicey' (69) are childish euphemisms employed as a distancing effect in an otherwise extremely traumatic situation (s/he is being strangled by Mr Silky String). However, such lexical choices are deliberately purposeful. Not only does it register Braden's increasing pathological obsession with his/her mother and her absence in his/her life, it also denotes the influence of a patriarchal vision of womanhood: the female as a child to be petted and indulged but never really taken seriously. This pattern continues in several instances from Braden's love life. For example, Braden asks his/her lover, the double-dealing politician Eamon Faircroft (aka Dummy Teat), the measure of his affection in the following terms: '"Do you love me, Dummy?" I simpered and would those peepers answer "Yes!"' (37) The overt sentimentality, emotional dependency and need for a classic romance narrative are obvious in such a statement, and especially in its linguistic register ('simpered', 'peepers'). Braden later remarks, 'One minute I'm there black and broody as ever a woman could be, pulling away from him and going: "Oh, get your hands off me! You'll never understand!" and the next I'm gone all woozy, like never until the end of time will I leave this lovely man' (42). The irrationality of Braden's behaviour ('as ever a woman could be') simultaneously proposes a misogynistic gesture and defeats it. If women are coded throughout history and literature as irrational, then the statement 'black and broody as ever a woman could be' reinforces this. But the fact that Braden-the-transvestite is making such statements is on another level, suggesting the nature of gender as performative, in Judith Butler's designation of the term in *Gender Trouble* (1990). If a biological male can inhabit the feminine role, and indeed voice, the nature of essential gendered characteristics are completely undone. Others, including Luce Irigaray (1985: 76) and Simone de Beauvoir ('One is not born, but rather becomes, a woman' 1997: 295) have in different ways articulated the notion that femininity is a performance rather than correlated with biology. However, with specific reference to the transvestic articulation, the problem is decidedly more complex. Carole-Anne Tyler's *Female Impersonation* (2003) explores the debate with critical lucidity, suggesting that social constructionism is at the root of such performance: 'catching gender in the act, as an act, so as to demonstrate there is no natural, essential, biological basis to gender or to heterosexuality' (89).

This problematization of gender stereotypes is highly laudable, and something to which I shall return later. However, the mimicry of femininity invoked by the transvestic persona has often received much censure from the gay community itself. As Tyler claims 'denigration of drag queens in gay culture may be a rejection of the heterosexist stereotype of the female invert, who is contrasted with the "real thing", the gay-identified masculine man, but it also may be a misogynistic rejection of the feminine' (2003: 92). Leo Bersani adds:

A certain type of homosexual camp speaks the truth of that femininity as mindless, asexual, and hysterically bitchy, thereby provoking, it would seem to me, a violently antimimetic reaction in any female spectator. The gay male bitch desublimates and desexualises a type of femininity glamorized by movie stars, whom he then lovingly assassinates with his style, even though the campy parodist may himself by quite stimulated by the hateful impulses inevitably included in his performance.

(Bersani 1987: 208, cited in Tyler 2003: 92–3)

The misogynistic association between women and the 'bitchy' or 'catty' feminine role is perhaps the most troubling aspect of this statement, but it is one with which Braden is identified during the course of the novel. During his/her relationship with Dummy Teat, as the 'other woman', Braden plays up to this paradigm of femininity:

He was a lovely companion, no matter what lies they told about him in the papers! And I'll tell you something else – no matter what they'd been through or whatever terrible things she had said about me or our relationship, I never heard him once speak ill of his wife. Not that I wouldn't have welcomed the odd 'old cow!' or 'jealous bitch!', to tell you the truth! But it was never forthcoming [...] If I was married to someone and *they* went off with somebody, I wouldn't just shout a few words of abuse. I'd make their lives miserable, if you want to know the truth! Everywhere they went, they'd find me there – and not the nice, well-groomed, soft-spoken version either. The wicked, cat-hissing one, more like, harridan of all harridans who would think absolutely nothing at all of tearing your clothes or cutting your face with a few well-aimed scratches of her polished nails.

(McCabe 1998: 42–3)

Again, the lexical choice involved in Braden's transvestic voice is important to note. The description invokes a very specific type of feminine violence (tearing clothes and scratching the face with fingernails) and his/her identification of the politician's wife as an 'old cow' is gender specific, and links with a set of androcentric and linguistic patterns designed to identify a woman's unattractiveness to men (Mills 1995: 87). Equally, Braden's reference to the 'harridan' is significant, as the word relates to how women are censured for 'having opinions and voicing them' (ibid.), and while originating in Old French for 'Broken-down horse, nag' (*haridelle*), it entered the English language in the late seventeenth century to mean 'broken-down woman, old whore' (Heller, Humez and Dror 1984: 86). Both instances of insult denote the patriarchal formations implicit in language which are designed to subjugate women. While Braden's (comic and transvestic) identification with these terms complicates the notion of biologism, at no point in the novel does such an empathy result in an obvious critique of the system of patriarchy itself.

This trajectory is also developed in the way in which Braden conducts his/her liaisons. At the very end of the novel, Braden speculates on his/her fantasy-relationship with Dr Terence (the analyst in the psychiatric unit where Braden eventually ends up), and expresses a sincere longing to bear his/her lover's children:

> [...] to wake up in the hospital all around me, exhausted after my ordeal maybe, but with a bloom like roses in my cheeks, as I stroke his soft and tender head, my little baby, watching them as they beam with pride, in their eye perhaps a tear or two – who cares! – hardly able to speak as they wipe it away and say 'He's ours!'
>
> (McCabe 1998: 199)

As the final statement of the novel, Braden's ardent wish suggests McCabe's discussion of 'home [...] belonging and [...] peace' (xi) in the Preface, especially so given the context of the Good Friday Agreement and the Northern Irish Peace Process. Despite this, it also represents a very complex schema in terms of gendered representation. An illustrative point is during Braden's fantasy of gender realignment in Chapter 11. Here s/he states:

> I wanted at least ten of a family. I know some women nowadays would say 'Pussy Braden! You're out of your mind! You are out of your fucking tiny mind! Do you know, do you for one second knows, what it would be like looking after that number of people?' To which I could only say that I do and probably if the truth be told, probably know it a lot more than feminists or anyone else who might hold those views.
>
> (McCabe 1998: 40)

On the one hand, Braden is clearly articulating the notion that a biological male can appropriate the traditionally 'feminine' desire for children and motherhood. On the other hand, his/her evaluation of the 'feminist' warrants close analysis. In terms of representation, to speak *for* a woman as an inescapably biological male is ultimately fraught with difficulty. Tyler draws on the theoretical position of Gayatri Spivak and the subaltern, which articulates the problem of *depiction* (speaking about) and *delegation* (speaking for or instead of) (2003: 148; see also Spivak 1988: 274–80). To claim to have access to a privileged knowledge base ('[I] know a lot more than feminists or anyone else') re-enacts a patriarchal logic rather than any especially resistant gesture:

> [Male] contributions seek to determine – to describe and prescribe – what a woman/feminist wants and then to demonstrate that the man in question has the right stuff [...] Once again men have arrogated to themselves the power to know and fulfil a woman's wishes, and in doing so, they remain caught in a masculine imaginary.
>
> (Tyler 2003: 148)

So far from Braden's transvestic voice providing a space for alterity and the negotiation of gender roles, it actually parades them and subtly legitimates them. Nowhere is this more obvious than in Braden's ecstatic vision of what home life should be. In Braden's fantasy of his/her childhood with 'Patrick' the father and 'Eily Mammy', 'Daddy' comes in from work to the smell of Apple cakes baked by Eily's fair hands, and the conversation runs that 'Mammy' is loved because she bakes 'bread' and 'buns', 'scrubs the floor' and loves her son (McCabe 1998: 110). 'Eily Mammy' is essentially appraised for her cooking skills, her cleaning ability and her maternal duty. While cooking and cleaning also suggest her role as the errant priest's housekeeper, it is clear that Braden's dreams coincide more with De Valera's vision of Irish home life than with any radical agenda. In one of his/her reveries regarding Dr Terence, Braden effusively describes their 'Christmas' together:

> [...] we kissed and I made us some lovely hot cocoa which we had with plum pudding [...] The fact is he stayed for one whole week and we loved one another like any man and woman should. I lay there in his arms and Perry Como sang 'Have Yourself a Merry Little Christmas'. It was so funny because I had a strip of silver tinsel around my neck like a necklace and Terence kept calling me his 'Christmas angel'.
>
> (McCabe 1998: 97)

As with the aforementioned fantasy, the overarching principle of hetero-normativity organizes the scene here. Braden, in the 'feminine' role, is the caregiver ('hot cocoa' and 'plum pudding'), while the reference to him/her as a 'Christmas angel' invokes a version of the nineteenth-century ideal: the Angel in the House. The hint at sexual congress merely replicates heteronormal values ('we loved one another like any man and woman should'): while we are aware that Braden is biologically a man, the (sexual) passivity with which s/he approaches his/her feminine role does not particularly confound gender norms. Equally, there is no 'revelation' of the biological male (as in *The Crying Game* or *Pink Flamingos*, 1972, dir. John Waters) which may complicate our reading. In one sociological study of transgendered behaviour (including pre- and post-op transsexuals, cross-dressers, transvestism, drag queens, gays, lesbians, bisexuals and straights) Janice Raymond suggests that transgression of boundaries can often masquerade conformity to heteronormativity, with many biological males posing as 'ultra-feminine women': '[it is] a repackaging of the old gender roles [...] While transgenderists break through the semblance of masculinity, they don't break through its political reality, that is, its power' (1996: 216–18).

In many instances, careful studies of literary transgender performance need to underscore that the 'transvestite' is not always the transgressive or radical icon she may appear. For instance, a significant proportion of transvestite men identify as heterosexual (unlike Braden), and many have seemingly 'normal' family lives (see Ackroyd 1979: 14). One of the few instances which confounds the passive/active, feminine/masculine binary opposition is Braden's relationship with Louise. In the main, Braden's relationships are with men, but s/he also begins a sexual liaison with Louise, the 'darling landlady' with whom Braden lives during his/her affair with 'Uncle Bertie' (McCabe 1998: 91, 78). She is conventionally presented, insofar as she is the 'harridan' Braden spoke of earlier in the text, earning his/her censure for loudly identifying his/her failure to shut doors or tidy up after himself/herself (91). However, s/he also expresses a common bond of loss: 'With her it was her son, with me a mother – it was the same thing all in all' (91). Her son Shaunie was run over by a bus in 1961, and as their intimacy progresses, Braden poses as Shaunie: 'with the shorts and the Shaunie suit and everything [...] after a while I got more than accustomed to the little grey jacket and the short trousers' (92). Sitting on her knee, he would exclaim 'Mammy' with the same intonation as the dead child – 'she asked me to call her "Mammy" which, apparently, because of his dad being Irish, was exactly the way Shaunie pronounced it' (92). Alongside the transvestic voice (being Braden's most frequent incarnation) there is another, altogether more complex articulation. The way in which this sexual performance defeats our usual categories of gender and sexuality is confirmed when Bertie walks in while Braden is sucking Louise's breast and addressing her as 'Mammy': 'It's not fair! [...] He's my girlfriend, you fucking old cow! Mine! [...] He's not a schoolboy! He's my girl and you have no right to be doing this to him' (93). Perversely, the complete erasure of stable gender categories becomes obvious at the level of pronouns. The transvestite homosexual male posing as a male child in a relationship with a heterosexual woman clear confounds all classifications or stable gender categories. The relationship with Louise also marks Braden's further progression into a very macabre pathology eventually resulting in his/her nervous breakdown. Louise dresses up as Braden's own mother (who apparently bore an uncanny likeness to Mitzi Gaynor in *South Pacific*, 1958) and sings 'I'm gonna wash that man right outa my hair!' (115). She then asks Braden – 'Please stay for breakfast' (115). The vocalization of this one word ('breakfast') in fact marks a pattern inhabiting the significant events in the novel: the preparation of breakfast which is the central part of Braden's conception in the presbytery; the repeated iteration of the Don Partridge song 'Breakfast on Pluto' (1969) which Braden references as a distancing technique every time s/he experiences particularly shocking or psychically traumatic periods of his/her life. Indeed, John Bolton notes how Braden is compelled 'to travel to Pluto in order to find a habitable and welcoming space' (2010: 155). It is also the *articulation* of longing and desire for which Braden castigates himself/herself rather than any sexual transgression: 'Why had I to go and do a stupid thing like *blab* it all to Louise instead of keeping it to myself' (McCabe 1998: 112, my italics). The boundary between public and private narration, fantasy and reality, has been transgressed through the spoken word, and ultimately results in psychic collapse.

More overtly, of course, the vocalization of this word *breakfast* confronts Braden's abandonment by his/her mother, and his/her own dispossessed childhood (see Jeffers 2002: 169 for further discussion of the word's multiplicity in the text). Indeed, the failure of the mother figure (Mother Ireland and the Mother Church, as much as 'Eily Bergin') to care for her sons is notable in Braden's description of Christmas in the Braden house.[2] While being 'suitably drunk', 'Whiskers Braden' exclaims to her various brood of unwanted and unloved children: 'Quit youser fucking fighting! [...] Come on over here and pull this fucking cracker till we get this fucking Christmas finished with!' (9). At a later date, Braden speculates 'All you ever gave me, all you ever handed down was the smell of piss and clothes nobody ever bothered to wash! Thanks a bunch! Thanks a whole fucking pile, Whiskers!' (60). Far from being a model of Irish familial devotion as outlined by De Valera in his St. Patrick's Day Broadcast, the Braden clan are dysfunctional, poor and unhappy.

Clearly this is an implicit critique by McCabe on a certain strain of Irish nationalist social mores.[3] De Valera is something of a ghostly voice in the text, a critical point given his role in the Constitution of Ireland (1937), which declared the Republic's *de facto* right to govern the North (effectively alienating many Northern Unionists from the debate).[4]

A number of critics have noted McCabe's investment in popular culture (British and American) signifies the emergence of the media's voice in Ireland. John Kenny observes that 'McCabe is of that generation of Irish writers that had cinema, television and singles records as pervasive cultural influences, and he loves the schlock and schmaltz of even the poorer manifestations of consumerist culture' (1998: 428). Bolton has similarly remarked that McCabe's coming of age represents the transitional period in Ireland where Irish cultural nationalism came into conflict with the imported culture of television, film and pop music. Bolton highlights that this was 'a younger generation attracted to cultural offerings from abroad, particularly those that contained a transgressive sexuality and diversity' (2010: 167). *Breakfast on Pluto* is heavily inflected with such polyvocal pastiche as related to Braden's transvestic persona. Following Dummy Teat's death, Braden and Charlie visit Dublin for a shopping spree:

> [M]y arms I filled with Max Factor, Johnson's Baby Oil, Blinkers Eyeshadow, Oil of Olay, Silvikrin Alpine Herb Shampoo, Eau de toilette, body moisturizers, body washes, cleansing milks, St Laurent Eye and Lip make-up, Noxema Skin Cream and Cover Girl Professional Mascara. Not to mention clothes! Knitted tops in white, purple, lavender, blazing orange, satin-stripe velveteen pants, turtleneck leotards, flouncing skirts, ribbed stretch-nylon tights.
>
> (McCabe 1998: 35–6)

This is a crucial scene in terms of Braden's construction of himself as a woman, and the ideological implications behind this: 'When women go shopping for clothes and cosmetics, they make decisions about how to feminize themselves' (Talbot 2010: 138). Alongside various references to brand names and commodities – 'so each night, jangly-bangly, whiff of No. 5 [...] in knee boots she'd come tripping, Aubrey-bob lacquered in place' (McCabe 1998: 131, see also 32 and 156) – we may note how much Braden's visual construction of femininity is conceived through the language of fashion and celebrity lifestyle magazines. She/he reads '*Weekend* magazine' (64), '*Modern Screen*' (12), '*Loving, True Confessions*' (40) and more generally 'a yummy stack of magazines and I'll be happy, as once more I go leafing through the pages of *New Faces of the Fifties,*

Screen Parade, gaily mingling with the stars of long ago' (1). The magazine industry is of course of one the most obvious ways in which femininity is socially constructed and delineated by commercial forces:

> [C]onventional kinds of feminine appearance are shaped by the mass media, fashion and related industries. Being feminine involves, among other things, a particular mode of consumption. A conventionally gendered appearance requires a good deal of grooming and, especially for women, beauty work. A feminine identity has to be worked at [...] Femininity is articulated in and through commercial and mass-media discourses, especially in the magazine industry and in the fashion industries of clothing and cosmetics.
>
> (Talbot 2010: 137–8)

The irruption of references in the novel to iconic women (Mitzi Gaynor, Audrey Hepburn among others) and magazine culture which operates to support these signify a very predictable type of femininity. We might note that Braden's persistent verbalization of fashionable identity as filtered through such discourses relate to prescribed types of gendered behaviour. What is radical about such references is less to do with Braden's transvestite persona, and more related to his/her 'queer' sexuality. As Susannah Bowyer notes in her theory of the 'gay brand':

> At the end of the twentieth century, a stereotype of a gay Other that I call the gay brand was uniquely placed for manipulation as an icon of postmodern, globalized national identity in that it combines some of the key cultural themes of postmodernity [...] Camp's ironic commentary, its fascination with artifice, surface appearance and the stylization of life echo key cultural themes identified with the 'aestheticization of everyday life' (Featherstone 1995: 73) – the celebration of transgression, the project of turning everyday life into a work of art, the playful experimentation with fashion.
>
> (Bowyer 2010: 804–5)

In terms of reading the transvestic voice, the context of the emergent globalized Ireland which so pervasively influences Braden, positioned alongside a 'gay' aesthetic and directly against the nationalist vision of old Ireland as propounded by De Valera, does far more to challenge stereotypical behaviour than his/her cross-dressing as such. This is clearly the case in terms of Braden's approach to the Irish/Northern Irish political milieu.

While Braden declares a distinct lack of interest in Irish politics, this reflects his/her status as an unreliable narrator, as it becomes progressively more obvious as the novel proceeds that s/he is heavily implicated in a revolutionary agenda. Several instances of sectarian murder are narrated in a different voice, which is marked by its cool pragmatism and self-assurance: 'Laurence, being Down's syndrome, couldn't pronounce his words right – which was why I called him Laurence Lebrity. No matter how hard he tried he just couldn't get it right, the name of his favourite programme – *Celebrity Squares*' (McCabe 1998: 46). Narrating Laurence's murder, purely on the basis that he was a Catholic, the section concludes: 'I think *it was* the first Down's syndrome boy *shot* in the Northern Ireland war. The first in Tyreelin anyway.' (47, my italics) In considering this completely different narrative style (which may or may not be Braden's) we may especially note the passive voice: by controlling the focus of attention, and thereby who commits the atrocity, such a voice can deftly avoid any blame, and that is certainly the case here, the effect being to legitimize border violence. This aspect of the narrative supports the notion that Braden is significantly more complicit in physical force politics than s/he would otherwise admit. While Jennifer M. Jeffers posits that Braden in fact may be a member of the IRA disguised as a transvestite prostitute, '[for] who would imagine a male transvestite as a member of the IRA?' (2010: 171), I suspect attention to the murder scene here may imply a form of 'double-dealing' akin to 'Dummy Teat's' (McCabe 1998: 33). For how does the narrative voice here have privileged access to such information unless s/he was present at the scene? The complexity of the voices in *Breakfast on Pluto* becomes still further enmeshed when we consider this voice, the pragmatic political commentator, also narrates the bomb-campaign of a unit with a member called 'Faigs' (138), ostensibly because of his accent when requesting cigarettes, but also a derogatory term for a homosexual ('fag'). Similarly, another member of the gang, 'Big Pat' (139) bears the same given name as Patrick 'Pussy' Braden. As Jeffers remarks, 'There is a "queer" element in this short chapter' (2010: 174), marked by the following sentence: 'Faigs chuckled as he winked at the *femme deshabilleé* on the cover [of *True Detective* magazine] and grabbed his friend between the legs' (McCabe 1998: 139). Jeffers speculates Braden may plant a coded reference to homosexuality in his/her narrative fantasy, or 'indicating that there are homosexuals working for the IRA' (2010: 174). In any event, the reader is pressed into the same question as Dr Terrence in reading Braden's literary works: 'Did you imagine all this, Patrick? Or were you actually at some point involved with these bombers?' (McCabe 1998: 137). Braden's disavowal in response to the question is therefore interesting:

> I ought to have played him along a little – it would have been fun just teasing him! Instead of saying, all coyly like I did: 'Oh, Terence! Don't start pretending my writing skills are that good!'
>   But you could still see him looking at me – *Pussy! Mad Bomber! Could it be true?*
>
> (McCabe 1998: 137)

Clearly this denial of physical force action is no denial at all: it merely offers more possibilities. Is Patrick no good at writing because s/he can't *hide* his/her political involvement through his/her multiple-voiced narrative, or because his/her fictions are revealed *as* fictions? Following the IRA bomb in Hammersmith, Braden admits to the police force that s/he planted the bomb, and identifies himself/herself as *'Paddy* Pussy' (145). By Chapter 40, however, the questions re-emerge: 'What if the callow, fair-skinned youth (David Cassidy – we love you!) was, in fact, as he insisted, nothing more than a drifting transvestite prostitute from the backwoods of Ireland, in search of nothing more than a good time and a reasonable living on the streets of London?' (149). The descriptive but determinedly aloof narration here has Braden's exuberant voice disrupting proceedings in parenthesis: '(David Cassidy – we love you!)' which implies how far the transvestite persona can indeed disorder the text and any assumptions a reader may make.

This point is finalized following Braden's collapse in the prison cell. S/he fantastically speculates on his/her role as the 'wrong-to-right avenger' (154) who would return to Tyreelin and banish 'stench' or the corruption and degradation of his/her home town on the border. In formulaic and highly poeticized language, a voice in 'husky tones' declares (with Whiskers Braden as witness):

> To the town of her birth she now returns, to visit every hill and dale, there her mark to leave, not one eye its sight which does not retain to say: 'I do not see her!' for such will not be possible whilst amongst you now she walks, she who thenceforth shall be called – *The Lurex Avenger!* She who shall be named Stench-Banisher, Perfume Bringer, Flower-Scatterer, Ender of Darkness, she who shall wrench this place and the people from the shadows into light!
>
> (McCabe 1998: 155)

The lexical choices here are parodic, reminiscent of nationalist narratives such as W.B. Yeats's *Cathleen Ní Houlihan* (1902) and those heroines of Irish legend who mysteriously enter a town or village in order to free the people from the tyrannous yoke of English colonial rule. Here, however, Braden figures as an antidote to this very form of nationalist narrative: the 'Lurex Avenger' comes to save the Irish from themselves, by bringing an iconic possession of 'gay branding', of consumerism and modernity which is, of course, the fragrance of Chanel which has featured throughout the novel as one of Braden's prized possessions and signifiers of his/her feminine persona. This gesture towards moderni-zing the Irish nation is confirmed in Chapter 44, where 'The Nolan Family at No. 39' puzzlingly detect the scent of Chanel No. 19:

> If mum didn't know better she'd say to the kids: 'Have you been meddling around in my bedroom upstairs? Stealing my Chanel No. 19?' But she didn't, of course – mainly because she didn't possess any. Wouldn't be caught dead wearing it, in fact! 'Oh God no!', she often said. 'In fact I rarely wear perfume of any kind!'
>
> (McCabe 1998: 156)

Speaking here is 'The Lurex Avenger', Braden's alter-ego, whose voice simultaneously offers a critique of Irish nationalist models of femininity and modesty (the vanity of cosmetic adornment was often derided by twentieth-century nationalists as a foreign vice), and intersperses his/ her own version of a 'gay brand' femininity in the text. While this is quite far from being a radical presentation of femininity, it is nonethe-less a counter to the insular and closed society which De Valera and permutations of Irish nationalism popularly advocated. With reference to the modern commodity, to European values of fashion and appear-ance, Braden's 'Lurex Avenger' offers a neat conflation with many of McCabe's own declared values of the worthy aspects of modern 'non-Irish' culture.

In conclusion, McCabe's text is a highly sophisticated account of the way in which narrative and indeed authorial voices can offer different and frequently contradictory ideologies within one narrative. *Breakfast on Pluto* presents the transgendered subject as a complex sign who simultaneously troubles and conforms to patterns of gendered behav-iour. McCabe himself is seen, through the prefatorial voice, to articulate a very specific agenda for the novel, but arguably, the voices within the text itself confound any univocal reading. As a peripatetic figure, Patrick 'Pussy' Braden transgresses notions of a unitary identity, and this is specifically enacted in the stylistic form of the novel as well as in everyday life. While flirting with paradigms of essentialist femininity and occasional misogyny, Braden's transvestic voice also disrupts the dominant nationalist ideology of Ireland in the 1960s and 1970s.

Notes

1. See also Cleary (1996: 257–67) for discussion of the 'conventional' nature of the film.
2. For the trope of Mother Ireland in McCabe's fiction more generally, see Ellen McWilliams (2010).
3. See for instance, Article 41.1.1. of the Constitution of Ireland (1937) which declares 'The State recognizes the Family as the natural primary and fundamental unit group of Society, and as a moral institution possessing inalienable and imprescriptible rights, antecedent and superior to all positive law.' Indeed, de Valera's rustic vision of Ireland from his Radio Broadcast (1943) romanticizes the reality of hardship and struggle which many rural communities experienced: he saw Ireland as 'the home of a people who valued material wealth only as a basis for right living, of a people who, satisfied with frugal comfort, devoted their leisure to the things of the spirit.' See Tom Herron (2000: 175) for further details.

Works Cited

Ackroyd, Peter (1979) *Transvestism and Drag: the History of an Obsession* (London: Simon and Schuster).

Bakhtin, M.M. (1981) *The Dialogic Imagination: Four Essays*, trans. Caryl Emerson and Michael Holoquist (Austin: University of Texas Press).

Bolton, Jonathan (2010) *'Blighted Beginnings': Coming of Age in Independent Ireland* (Lewisberg: Bucknell University Press).

Bowyer, Susannah (2010) 'Queer Patriots: Sexuality and the Character of National Identity in Ireland', *Cultural Studies*, 24/6: 801–20.

Butler, Judith (2006[1990]) *Gender Trouble* (London: Routledge).

Buchanan, Jason (2008) '"The First Few Steps": Gender and Forgiveness in Patrick McCabe's *Breakfast on Pluto*', in Marti D. Lee and Ed Madden (eds), *Irish Studies: Geographies and Genders* (Newcastle: Cambridge Scholars), pp. 69–76.

Cleary, Joe (1996) '"Fork-Tongued on the Border Bit": Partition and the Politics of Form in Contemporary Narratives of the Northern Irish Conflict', *South Atlantic Quarterly*, 95/1: 227–76.

Cullingford, Elizabeth (2001) *Ireland's Others: Gender and Ethnicity in Irish Literature and Popular Culture* (Cork: Cork University Press).

De Beauvoir, Simone (1997[1949]) *The Second Sex* (London: Vintage).

De Valera, Éamon (1943) 'St Patrick's Day Radio Broadcast', *Radio Éireann*, 17 March.

Ferriter, Diamaid (2009) *Occasions of Sin: Sex and Society in Modern Ireland* (London: Profile Books).

Genette, Gèrard (1997) *Paratexts: Thresholds of Interpretation*, trans. Jane E. Lewin (Cambridge: Cambridge University Press).

Heller, Louis G., Alexander Humez and Melcah Dror (1984) *The Private Lives of English Words* (London: Routledge).

Harvey, Elizabeth D. (1992) *Ventriloquized Voices: Feminist Theory and English Renaissance Texts* (London: Routledge).

Herron, Tom (2000) 'ContamiNation: Patrick McCabe and Colm Tóibín's Pathographies of the Republic', in Liam Harte and Michael Parker (eds), *Contemporary Irish Fiction: Themes, Tropes, Theories* (Basingstoke: Macmillan).

Irigaray, Luce (1985[1977]) *This Sex Which Is Not One*, trans. Catherine Porter with Carolyn Burke (Ithaca: Cornell University Press).

Jeffers, Jennifer M. (2002) *The Irish Novel at the End of the Twentieth Century* (Basingstoke: Palgrave Macmillan).

Kenny, John (1998) 'Irish Writing and Writers: Some Recent Irish Writing' (Review), *Studies: an Irish Quarterly Review*, 87/348: 422–30.

Lakoff, Robin (2004[1975]) *Language and Woman's Place: Text and Commentaries* (ed.) Mary Bucholtz (New York: Oxford University Press).

McCabe, Patrick (1998) *Breakfast on Pluto* (London: Harper Perennial).

McWilliams, Ellen (2010) 'Madness and Mother Ireland in the Fiction of Patrick McCabe', *Irish Studies Review*, 18/4: 391–400.

Mahon, Peter (2007) 'Lacanian "Pussy": towards a Psychoanalytic Reading of Pat McCabe's *Breakfast on Pluto*', *Irish University Review*, 37/2: 441–71.

Mills, Sara (1995) *Feminist Stylistics* (London: Routledge).

Pettitt, Lance (1997) 'Pigs and Provos, Prostitutes and Prejudice: Gay Representation in Irish Film, 1984–1995', in Éibhear Walshe (ed.), *Sex, Nation and Dissent in Irish* Writing (Cork: Cork University Press), pp. 252–84.

Raymond, Janice (1996) 'The Politics of Transgenderism', in Richard Ekins and Dave King (eds), *Blending Genders: Social Aspects of Cross-Dressing and Sex Changing* (London: Routledge), pp. 215–23.

Spivak, Gayatri Chaktavorty (1988), 'Can the Subaltern Speak?', in Cary Nelson and Lawrence Grossberg (eds), *Marxism and the Interpretation of Culture* (Urbana: University of Illinois Press), pp. 271–313.

Talbot, Mary (2010[1998]) *Language and Gender* (Cambridge: Polity Press).

Tyler, Carole-Anne (2003) *Female Impersonation* (London: Routledge).

Wallace, Clare (2004) 'Patrick McCabe: Transgression and Dysfunctional Irelands', in Neil Sammells (ed.), *Beyond Borders: IASIL Essays on Modern Irish Writing* (Bath: Sulis Press), pp. 143–56.

Part IV
Authority and Anxieties of Appropriation in Historical Narratives

10

Authenticity, Authority and the Author: the Sugared Voice of the Neo-Victorian Prostitute in *The Crimson Petal and the White*

Mark Llewellyn

> Post-Modernism encouraged me to assert my freedom
> to do whatever I pleased. I was The Author; I was in
> charge. The reader must be reminded that this story
> was an artificial construct. Text must be playful, must
> discard the shackles of bogus mimesis, must define
> itself against the pointless inhibitions of the 19th
> century bourgeois novel.
>
> – Michel Faber, 'Eccentricity and
> Authenticity: Fact into Fiction' (2003: 102)

The genre of neo-Victorianism – contemporary novels set in the
nineteenth century with a distinctive metafictional element to their
portrayal of the historical as literature – relies upon a variety of textual
and narratological motifs and tricks in order to play at convincing its
readers of the authenticity and authority surrounding the fiction they
are reading.[1] Such encounters between fabrication and fiction and the
factual performativity implied by the assumption of an 'historical' voice
regularly move towards varying degrees of mimicry, pastiche or ventriloquism, even when grounded in the postmodernism referenced by this
opening quotation from Michel Faber. In writing *about* the Victorians,
the contemporary novelist frequently seeks to present writing *like* the
Victorians. There is an ambivalence here concerning both the mission
and the method. One of the most frequently cited neo-Victorian novels
that provides this kind of knowing assumption of ventriloquism is
A.S. Byatt's Booker Prize winning *Possession: a Romance* (1990). In that
novel, Byatt generates pastiche texts for her fictional Victorian poets,
Randolph Henry Ash and Christabel LaMotte. In the case of the former,

Byatt's mimicry of the dramatic monologue (an appropriate taking on of other voices) and the different styles employed by the Victorian poet Robert Browning, among others, serves as a potential example of how such ventriloquism allows for a cross-gendered performance. As an illustration of both sides of a poetic dyad inside the text, Byatt's mimicry must demonstrate a convincing marker of difference: between the two poetic voices of Ash and LaMotte but also between the narrative of the contemporary literary critics and its play with academic-speaking and postmodern *langue*. That Byatt's example is based in an awareness of the 'authentic' style she seeks to ape in her Victorian characters is very clear, and thus foregrounds the sense in which contemporary readers need to be aware of and have a reading knowledge within the 'original' voices re-imagined in and through her characters. In placing the emphasis on reading and interpretation, Byatt's text foreshadows what has become something of a trend in more recent neo-Victorianism, particularly since the turn of the millennium. This strand locates its experience and development of neo-Victorian literary techniques within an increased emphasis on the relationship between the writer and the reader, both in terms of the contemporary author and reader, and the pseudo-Victorian realist narrator and reader embodied through the text itself. At the core of this construction is often the issue of a cross-gendered voice and its impact on questions of authority, authenticity and authorship. Blurring notions of time and narrative construction, the cross-gendered voice in neo-Victorian fiction also seeks to reclaim a gendered experience of historicity in ways that play with identity politics and authorial control. Much of this strand of neo-Victorian writing has sought to re-imagine female experience of gender identity and sexuality in the nineteenth century with the novels of Sarah Waters serving as a prominent example.

Within the context of neo-Victorianism such cross-gendering in the line of narrative voice or omniscient perspective raises significant critical and cultural questions. For if cross-gendering can represent imaginative capacity and understanding towards the 'Other' of the historical narrative, then it nevertheless simultaneously invokes perspectives that are inherently caught between the authenticity of past voices and the authority of contemporary authorship. The slipperiness here resides in the nature of the cross-gendered encounter and its implications: Is there, for example, an ethics to the use of voice in the claim to the authentic, true and previously silenced? If so, how does such voicing engage the reader (and critic) at an aesthetic level which makes such cross-gendered performativity comprehensible and realistic? Indeed, we might wonder whether such narrative play with the concept of literary voice constructs itself within the parameters of the realist mode in a self-mockery or parody that undermines the attempt at cross-gendered revelation or insight at all.

In Michel Faber's *The Crimson Petal and the White* (2002) the author plays with a series of ludic encounters with narrative space itself in order to underline the *faux* authenticity of the novel. The key to this is the presentation of an absurdly un-realistic 'voice' of the protagonist, a prostitute and aspiring writer of sadomasochistic pornography named Sugar. Faber's narrative does dual service in representing a knowing omniscient figure as our guide through late-Victorian London, a confiding and seemingly ahistoric narrator, and yet also seeking to accommodate fragments of a multiplicity of different textual encounters through which questions of gender and identity are refracted. Sometimes, these are in the first-person format of diaries or fictions-within-the-fiction, and at others more impersonalized documentations of the female body as textual figment. In such interruptions to the overt overarching realist narrative form, Faber, I would suggest, enacts a (potentially) deliberate tension between the contemporary reader's voyeuristic desire to 'know' the seedier lives of those well-known 'Other' Victorians through imitation of the female sexual subject's voice and the early twenty-first century writer's desire to subvert, re-invent and challenge the hegemonic social claims of the nineteenth-century realist mode.

This is the tension present in Faber's comments about postmodernism I have already quoted above. The statement comes from a short article in a Victorian studies journal where Faber seeks to address the inherent difficulties of writing a contemporary text that endeavours to under-mine the realist mode but which also revels in the fact that 'many readers, including historians, have found it to be a highly convincing time-travel experience' (2003: 101). In order to meet both sides of the model – to be postmodern but to be readably attractive to those wanting realism now – Faber indulges an all-knowing narrator's perspective while also slipping into character-specific forms of speaking by matching them to specific forms of writing. This is achieved through the omnis-cient narrative's portrayal of Sugar's voice through the classic technique of free indirect discourse (narrated monologue), which is in turn undermined by the direct discourse when Sugar's own pornographic, violent and debased writings are presented within the text.

Faber's novel demonstrates a simultaneous cross-gendered parody of both postmodernism and Victorianism as configured in the reader's imagination and writerly projection. What Faber's narrative highlights is an intriguing and often disturbingly unsettling slippage between voices, and readerly assumptions about the comforts to be found in omniscient narratorial structures. Sugar's pornography is blatantly not the gendered voice of the omniscient narrator, who is decidedly male and has a mimetic relationship to the Victorian patriarch or all seeing/knowing 'I' of classic realism. But neither does it successfully imitate the cross-gendering possibilities of other neo-Victorian fiction. Instead, the novelist appears to balance the narrative voice deliberately between the imitation of an historical male narrator and an ahistorical female identity straddled between realism and anachronism. This anxiety of appropriation is part of an ethical dilemma faced by those literary fiction writers who seek to utilize the neo-Victorian form in order to raise problematic questions about the nature of authenticity in historical fiction narratives, and challenge the possibility of presenting an authoritative or believable cross-gendered sense of voice from the Victorian period (see Llewellyn 2009). In some respects, Faber's novel, like that of other neo-Victorian novelists, desires to resurrect the problems of realist forms of knowledge and knowability that intrigued and inspired the Victorians themselves.

The Crimson Petal and the White is a text that, from the outset, plays deliberately with a sense of what I term 'textual sexuality'. In his two female protagonists, the prostitute Miss Sugar and Agnes Rackham, the wife of her most devoted customer William, Faber presents us with the standard female dichotomy so often disrupted in Victorian fiction itself. Importantly, both Agnes and Sugar are writers. Agnes pens a mundane spiritual diary which reveals how she mistakes her own menstruation for stigmata (the allusion to the virgin martyr St Agnes is evident, and she also thinks Sugar is an angelic form made flesh). Sugar is the author of violent, aggressive and depraved pornographic fantasies in which she has the opportunity to enact a daemonic revenge on her male clientele through variously sexualized abuse and death scenes. The dialectic between the two women, including their different functions within the text as part of the supposed Victorian virgin/whore, wife and mother/prostitute, is signalled by Faber's title and its invocation of the lines from Tennyson's poem 'The Princess: a Medley' (1847):

> Now sleeps the crimson petal, now the white;
> Nor waves the cypress in the palace walk;
> Nor winks the gold fin in the porphyry font:
> The firefly wakens: waken thou with me.
>
> Now droops the milk white peacock like a ghost,
> And like a ghost she glimmers on to me.

Now lies the Earth all Danae to the stars,
And all thy heart lies open unto me.
Now slides the silent meteor on, and leaves
A shining furrow, as thy thoughts in me.

Now folds the lily all her sweetness up,
And slips into the bosom of the lake:
So fold thyself, my dearest, thou, and slip
Into my bosom and be lost in me.

(Tennyson 1883: 225)

Tennyson's poem is about the male overthrow of a proto-feminist university community, and serves as an explicit challenge to women's right to education and, indeed, women's right to write. In the context of Faber's narrative and within the terms of what I argue in this chapter, it is also worth noting that Tennyson's poetry was frequently quoted in literature on prostitution in this period; see William Acton's *Prostitution* (1857) for numerous examples, or writings on the nocturnal visits of the Prime Minister William Gladstone to ladies of the night during which he was known to recite the Poet Laureate's verses. It is thus somewhat unavoidably ironic that Faber should adopt Tennyson's lines for his title, and thus signal the fact that his female protagonists, like the women of Tennyson's poem, remain caught within the patriarchal control of male narrative and literary structures. This creates a tension and general uneasiness about the narrative's possibility to endorse or support the position of either Agnes or Sugar. Both women are commodities in the text, a fact in Sugar's case that is signalled not only by her very name, but also by her first textual and sexual introduction into the narrative through the juxtaposition of different written forms. Text and sex are often combined in this narrative, thus adding an additional layer to the game about the author's intended readership and meaning. Just before Sugar enters the novel, her soon-to-be protector and exclusive customer, William Rackham, heir to the Rackham's perfume and soap industry, is reading a set of business notes:

Utilisable cuttings down 15% from last year. Many would not div. at the root but crumbld. 4 gross ordered from Copley. Only 60 of the 80 acres prime.

?Buy more prime from Copley. ?Rackhams good name. First gallons will tell. Drying House needs new roof – ?Saturday afternoon if workers will stretch to it. Rumour of trade union infiltraitor.

2% rise in cost of manure.

(Faber 2002: 82)

Mundane, technical, abbreviated, stunted even, and one might suggest deliberately and decidedly male (in this context because concerned with the masculine world of Victorian business) these fragmented notes are replaced on the opposite page with the details of Mrs Castaway's brothel, listed as an establishment that is 'Mid Loin (For Moderate Spenders)', in Rackham's friends' annual publication '*More Sprees in London – Hints for Men about Town, with advice for greenborns*' (83, Faber's italics). Here Rackham reads about a different kind of commodity:

> *This Good Lady's Establishment contains an Embarrassment of Pulchritude, viz, Miss Lester, Miss Howlett, and Miss Sugar. These Ladies may be found at home from the middle of the afternoon; after six o'clock they are wont to take Entertainment at 'The Fireside', an unpretentious but convivial place for Nocturnals, and will leave with any suitable Escort, at a time of mutual choosing.*
> *Miss Lester is of middling stature, with ...*
> William pursues Miss Lester no further, but proceeds directly to:
> *We can presume that 'Sugar' was not the name our third Lady bore at her christening, but it is the name under which she rejoices now, should any man wish to baptize her further. She is an eager Devotee of <u>every</u> known Pleasure. Her sole purpose is to put the demanding Connoisseur at his ease and far Exceed his expectations. She boasts tresses of fiery red which may fall to the midriff, hazel eyes of rare penetration, and (despite some angularity) a graceful enough carriage. She is especially accomplished in the Art of Conversation, and is most assuredly a fit companion for any True Gentleman. Her one shortcoming, which to some may well by a piquant virtue, is that her Bosom scarcely exceeds the size of a child's. She will ask for 15s., but will perform Marvels for a guinea.*
> (Faber 2002: 83–4, Faber's italics and emphasis)

This textual announcement of Sugar's physical desirability naturally makes up for the bad news about the '2% rise in the cost of manure' (82), one assumes. But in a way what Faber signals here is the artificiality of both textual discourses, and the deliberateness of the parallels, binaries and seemingly coincidental events of the narrative structure which follows. The masculine world of the commercial outlined in Rackham's first reading matter is in tension with the (feminine) nature of the end-product of perfumed soap; the olfactory issues of the novel have been discussed elsewhere (see Colella 2010) suffice to state here that the rising cost of manure towards the process of creating perfume highlights not only a commercial concern but a problem between the nature of meaning and representation, end product and its process. The concern is shared in the second piece of Rackham's reading in that it raises the aesthetic and the sensual portrayal of the product on offer (Sugar's services) even as it disguises beneath the euphemistic 'marvels' the true nature of the transaction. Indeed, this is a novel which layers up different forms of textuality alongside sexuality: Agnes's diary; William Rackham's account books and perfume sale adverts; Sugar's pornographic fantasies; the brothel-guide; even William's religious brother Henry's sermons. All these texts serve as diagrammatic encounters among a multitude of voices within the text. As Eckart Voigts-Virchow notes, 'Faber shares the view [...] that the European tradition of painting caters predomi-nantly to the male gaze. [...] [The novel] conflates three metaphors of ownership: books (writing, possessing, reading), images (painting, photographing, possessing, gazing), and prostitution (selecting, pos-sessing, intercourse)' (2009: 115). We soon learn that the description of Sugar's physical appearance matches her own self-textual portrayal in her fantasy revenge narrative pornography and is caught between these 'three metaphors of ownership' (ibid). Indeed, Faber returns us to the roots of the word pornography in recognizing its meaning from 'the Greek "porno graphos", meaning "writing about prostitutes"' (Ussher 1997: 184). In this case, that 'writing about' is meant to be conveyed partly through the writing of Sugar.

Despite the description of her in the brothel guidebook, in reality Sugar suffers from a skin disease related to psoriasis which causes a red-dening and flaky appearance across the epidermis. The prostitute's body is thus written over both in terms of the guidebook appearance of Sugar and other female commodities, and in the ways that her physical disease becomes a text-like figuration of her body as written upon by an author not herself. This is made clear in one of the moments where Sugar is encountered as both sexual object and writer. This is an important scene in the novel because of the conflation of authorship and prostitution, sex and text. It begins with Sugar asleep on her writing:

> Raising herself from her writing-desk, Sugar blinks, scarcely able to believe she could have fallen asleep when, only an instant before, she was so seriously pondering what word should come next. The page on which her face landed is smudged, still glistening; she stum-bles over to the bed and examines her face in the mirror. The pale flesh of her forehead is branded with tiny, incomprehensible letters in purple ink.

> (Faber 2002: 227)

Taking the materials she is in the process of completing from the manuscript over to the bed, Sugar reads the fate of her latest fictionalized victim:

> *'Please,' he begged, tugging ineffectually at the silken bonds holding him fast to the bedposts. 'Let me go! I am an important man!' – and many more such pleas. I paid no heed to him, busying myself with my whet-stone and my dagger.*
>
> *'But tell me, exalted Sir,' I said at last. 'Where is it your pleasure to have the blade enter you?'*
>
> *To this, the man gave no reply, but his face turned gastly grey.*
>
> *'The embarrassment of choices has taken your tongue,' I suggested. 'But never fear: I shall explain them all to you, and their exquisite effects ...'*
>
> (Faber 2002: 227 Faber's italics)

With the bluntness and 'get on with it' nature of much Victorian pornography, Sugar's narrative positions her client as grappling with the contradictions of a desire to be subservient to the power of the mistress while asserting his own mastery. But more important than the penetration to be enacted on the customer in the scene is the ongoing problem, for Sugar, of having found herself marked and penetrated by the inkiness of her own voice and desires:

> Sugar frowns, wrinkling the blur of backwards text on her forehead. There's something lacking here, she feels. But what? A long succession of other men, earlier on in her manuscript, have inspired her to flights of Gothic cruelty; dispatching them to their grisly fate has always been sheer pleasure. Tonight, with this latest victim, she can't summon what's needed – that vicious spark – to set her prose alight. Faced with the challenge of spilling his blood, she hears an alien voice of temptation inside her: *Oh, for God's sake, let the poor fool live.*
>
> *You're going soft*, she chides herself. *Come on, shove it in, deep into his throat, into his arse, into his guts, up to the hilt.*
>
> (Faber 2002: 227–8, Faber's italics)

There is a neatness about things here; an easiness about the possible comparisons which underline the text's artificiality: Sugar as text, the written over body, the narrative as a form of prostitution itself on the one hand, and Sugar's fantasy of aggressive reverse/revenge sexual penetration and symbolic castration of her male victim on the other.

Faber's narrative voice has warned us from the outset of the book that we should not believe what we are told:

> Watch your step. Keep your wits about you; you will need them. This city I am bringing you to is vast and intricate, and you have not been here before. You may imagine, from other stories you've read, that you know it well, but these stories flattered you, welcoming you as a friend, treating you as if you belonged. The truth is that you are an alien from another time and place altogether.
>
> (Faber 2002: 3)

The 'Watch your step' of the narrator here is later reflected in the 'three magic words' (107) uttered by Sugar to her client, thus drawing a parallel between the voice of the omniscient narrator and that of the Victorian prostitute. The 2011 BBC adaptation of Faber's novel conflates the two voices throughout, making Sugar the narrator from the outset; in a further blurring of the textual and sexual contexts I am discussing in this chapter the same adaptation makes William Rackham into an aspiring, but frustrated, writer. The parallel between Sugar and the omniscient voice is something which Faber expands upon in his subsequent short story collection *The Apple: New Crimson Petal Stories* (2006).[2] Except that the opening of the novel has, by the point Sugar states these magic words, rearticulated itself as an explicitly male discourse: 'Just three words, if spoken by the right person at the moment, are enough to make infatuation flower with marvellous speed, popping up like the nub of bright pink from an unfurling foreskin' (Faber 2002: 107). This pen(is) envy concerning authorship and narrative control is brought into a deliberate context of textual/sexual desire here, just as the 'dagger' represents both the seized penis and the seized pen, the tools of penetration and authorship combined in a supposed act of liberation for the female prostitute, except, of course, that it remains the case that Sugar's body is the one written upon. Although the novel does present us with two female writers, neither is ever able to do what the omniscient novelist can, and they are instead placed in the text for us to engage in a misogynistic mockery of their efforts. Even the giving of a textual voice to Sugar raises questions about how revisionist the text attempts to be. For the arching voice of the omniscient narrator carries resemblance to that of Victorian social reformers such as Henry Mayhew, in works such as *The Criminal Prisons of London and Scenes of Prison Life* (1862) used as a source by Sarah Waters for her neo-Victorian novel *Affinity* (1999) (see Llewellyn 2004). In his volume on prisons,

Mayhew mixes travelogue for the discerning London tourist with an anthropological and voyeuristic eye not dissimilar to Faber's omniscient narrator. Here is Mayhew's introduction to the section on Millbank Prison, the location for much of Waters's novel:

> Millbank [...] is only approached by land, in the case of the unfortunate convicts who are taken there. The visitor instinctively avoids the uninteresting route down Parliament Street, Abingdon Street, and the dreary Horseferry Road, and proceeds to the prison by water. We will suppose him to do as we did, take the boat at Hungerford Stairs, with which view, he must pass through the market of the same name, which is celebrated for its penny ices ('the best in England') [...].
>
> (Mayhew 1862: 232)

The same passage continues with allusions Hungerford Stairs' market's reputation 'for its periwinkle market' (232). The tone is present in Mayhew's other works, which mix this eye of the social reformer with the narrative detail of a realist writer. Writing in relation to prostitution in *London Labour and London Poor* (1851), Mayhew stated 'Who can tell the influence exercised on society by one single, fallen woman? Woman waylaid, tempted, deceived, becomes in turn the terrible avenger of her sex' (Ussher 1997: 112). The binary is Tennysonian; the echoes in Faber's text stark and apparent. In the case of Agnes, William Rackham's wife, even her thoughts about the differences she sees as evident in male and female writings become a kind of joke, partly because they make us reflect back on the opening of the narrative itself:

> The difference between men and women is nowhere plainer, thinks Agnes, than in the novels they write. The men always pretend they are making everything up, that all the persons in the story are mere puppets of their imagination, when Agnes knows that the novelist has invented nothing. He has merely patchworked many truths together, collecting accounts from newspapers, consulting real soldiers or fruit-sellers or convicts or dying little girls – whatever his story may require. The lady novelists are far more honest: Dear Reader, they say, This is what happened to *me*.
>
> (Faber 2002: 220–1)

Agnes's view of female literary style and its honesty or authenticity is of course a reflection on Charlotte Brontë's *Jane Eyre* (1847), a text which Faber's novel engages with at the level of the governess (Sugar) and the mad woman in the attic (Agnes herself). Sugar, on the other hand, has no desire to claim 'Reader, I married him', as Jane does, because she recognizes that such a declaration can lead only to the inarticulacy of an (St) Agnes. When Sugar finds Agnes's diaries, kept since childhood and providing the back-narrative to her present insanity, she can only be taken aback by the naivety and the inarticulate nature of Agnes's writing. She reads:

Dear Diary,
How do you do? My name is Agnes Pigott, or should I say that <u>was</u> my name, but now

Dear Diary,
I

(Faber 2002: 528, Faber's italics and emphasis)

Agnes's inability to write and to speak for much of the narrative is in contrast to Sugar's desire and action as a writer. Between them the two women do share a need to tell their own stories but are forced to do so in a language that is, for them, unutterably male and dominated by male fantasies, desires, commodification, purchases and fulfillment. Thus when Sugar, while living as governess to the Rackhams' daughter and while suspected of being an angel of mercy come to save her by Agnes, tries to find additional pages of Agnes's diary, her hand discovers instead her own pornographic manuscript. Sugar's desire to know more about Agnes through her self-representation in the diary stems from both Sugar's impulse as a writer and as a reader. Part of the need to place herself within the domestic space of the Rackham's house might be found in this quest to see the performance of middle-class marriage in order to change her own narrative constructions. Sugar's awareness of Rackham's or any of her former male client's lives outside of her brothel is presented as partly a textual disadvantage: her own growing knowledge of Rackham has earlier been fostered in the narrative through her access to the perfume catalogues and the imagined landscape of hearth and home in which such smells suffuse reality. Thus the need to read Agnes in a physical and textual sense is a driving impulse in her search for further personalized and voiced evidence of the wife. In finding her own masochistic imaginings, however, the slippage between the two texts and their exchangeability at this moment becomes symbolic of the futility of female writing as presented to us in Faber's narrative, and the possible similarities between voiceless women who serve different social functions within that virgin/whore dichotomy:

> She scrabbles under her bed once more, and what emerges is not another of Agnes's diaries, but her own novel. How her heart sinks to see it! This raggedy thing, bulging out of its stiff cardboard jacket: it's the embodiment of futility. All its crossed-out titles – *Scenes from the Streets, A Cry from the Streets, An Angry Cry from an Unmarked Grave, Women Against Men, Death in the House of Ill Repute, Who Has Now the Upper Hand?, The Phoenix, The Claws of the Phoenix, The Embrace of the Phoenix, All Ye Who Enter Here, The Wages of Sin, Comes Kiss the Mouth of Hell*, and, finally, *The Fall and Rise of Sugar* – are tainted by her own juvenile delusions.
>
> (Faber 2002: 768, Faber's italics)

It is no accident that even the latest and last title Sugar has provided for her memoir sounds more like an economic pamphlet for the commercial traveller (*The Fall and Rise of Sugar*) than the narrative of a woman's sexual revenge. It thereby takes us back to the earlier comment from the economic text concerning the rise in the price of manure by '2%'. One of the 'juvenile delusions' here must be the idea that she can actually enact any form of textual revenge on the men who purchase her body; indeed, the titles she has over time allotted to the narrative and then decided against and crossed-through are each likely to serve well as the titles for Victorian pornography of the period. Thus the revenge narrative itself represents not a gendered voice of freedom, but the inescapable fact that even her fantasies – dominated by sex, desire, bodies, lusts – are instead a re-articulation of male narrative norms, and are as stymied by inarticulacy of individual voice as the silence of Agnes's diary's 'I'. Where Agnes can only get as far as 'I', itself a mere cross or line on the page, Sugar cannot assert voice confidently enough to prevent her own crossing out of title. This is not a proto-feminist writing out of the body; this is not about a gendered performance at the textual level that can be sustained. Sugar has become her own voyeur and is led to question (or rather should be) the way in which her narrative has provided the reader of her pornographic accounts with what he most desires. The meta-textual comment here needs little explication, except to say that we too are left with the question of why we are reading this text, and what we want from it. As Charles Taylor points out in his review of the novel, 'I don't know when I have read a novel that so consciously sets out to chastise the reader for desiring the very things that led him or her to pick it up in the first place' (Taylor 2002). Desire here is textual and sexual, authorial and (in)authentic. Importantly, while Sugar's narrative performance of pornographic excess could be seen as a form of proto-feminist writing, it would be dangerous to see this as its exclusive meaning. There is a significant question here about the narrative perspective into which the readers – both the imagined reader of Sugar's pornography and the reader of Faber's novel – are placed when one considers that the very torturous nature of Sugar's account fits into the category of Victorian pornography as consumer product. Sugar's revenge may be less obvious through her writing given that it would in itself fit within the conventional marketplace of male consumers for this material in the period. Far from liberating her desires or freeing her voice from the constraints of prostitution, the narrative she seeks to embrace replaces her bodily penetration by clients with a textual prostration on their own terms. A similar point could be made about Sarah Waters's *Fingersmith* (2002) where the supposed economic and emotional freedom for the characters Sue Trinder and Maud Lilly at the novel's conclusion is found in being the lesbian authors of pornographic texts (see Llewellyn: 2007, 201–6).

What we come to recognize in Faber's text is the fact that there is a mimetic connection between Sugar's novel, Agnes's diary and Henry's sermons, alongside William's adverts (which Sugar later goes on to write for him, using her descriptive flair elsewhere deployed in her pornography) and the guide to the best brothels. All are forms of narrative that must convince within their specific contexts: the sermon must convert or redeem; the catalogues must sell stock, just like the brothel guide; Sugar's text must merge realism and Gothic excess; and Agnes's diary, most poignantly of all, must convince her that she exists. That floating 'I', a phallic statement of identity, is castrate without its referent. There might even be an argument that it is in the eradicable differences of voice, register and purpose that Faber's textual interplays re-enact new historicist dilemmas about privileging different voices and denying others. Perhaps more pertinently, however, Faber's over-construction of these reflective textualities, the voices which echo one another across the pages as we saw in the parallel between the opening introduction of text within William's business entries and Sugar's commodification in the guidebook, indicates the very fabrication of authenticity at the core of the book. As Frederick Holmes comments in writing about Byatt's *Possession*, '[t]he paradox exists in the way that such works create the illusion of immersing the reader in independently existing historical events only to undercut that experience by exposing the process of artifice through which the illusion is created' (320). The same point can be made about Faber's immersing of the reader in different voices displayed within these textual remains. We do not hear the characters speak but we see them write, and that poses a different problem. As Rackham stumbles across Sugar's narrative at the end of the novel, he reads Sugar's denunciation of what he stands for and so we read a denunciation of ourselves, and our urge to find narrative comfort in the potential of Sugar's voice, or the authentic signals of her writing:

> *How smug you are, Reader, if you are a member of the sex that boasts a scrag of gristle in your trousers! You fancy that this book will amuse you, thrill you, rescue you from the horror of boredom (the profoundest horror that your privileged sex must endure) and that, having consumed it like a sweetmeat, you will be left at liberty to carry on exactly as before! Exactly as you have done since Eve was first betrayed in the Garden! But <u>this</u> book is different, dear Reader. This book is a <u>KNIFE</u>. Keep your wits about you; you will need them!*

> (Faber 2002: 816, Faber's emphasis)

The final line again mirrors the opening of the novel itself: 'Watch your step. Keep your wits about you; you will need them.' (Faber 2002: 3) It is unclear what exactly Faber hopes to achieve through the textual engagement between his own omniscience and the weakness of Sugar. I want to propose that by this point Faber's narrative engages not only in a formulation of cross-gendering that fails but that failure itself is part of a self-mocking, ironic and ultimately camp projection of a narrative identity collapsing and fragmenting. In 'Notes on Camp' (1964), Susan Sontag comments that 'the essence of Camp is its love of the unnatural: of artifice and exaggeration' (1964: 515). In his ironic embracing of a gendered performativity (in multiple sexual and non-sexual ways) within the novel, Faber underlines the campness associated with objects, things, cosmetics and consumables that permeate his reconstruction of faux Victoriana in the novel. The elaborateness of the conceits and wordplay are overt: the prostitute is/as Sugar; the perfumery magnate addicted to various forms of filth; the angel in the house Agnes, named after a stigmata-suffering saint. These are coupled with the archness of the various voices utilized in a narrative of extremes and excess on the one hand and the mundane and the quotidian on the other. Such highs and lows of form, content, and style reinforce this sense of camp. Camp is, in Sontag's formulation, an 'art that proposes itself seriously, but cannot be taken altogether seriously because it is "too much"' (1964: 523). It is the very excessive nature of Sugar's violence in her pornographic writing, and in turn Faber's intrusive omniscient perspective, working in conjunction, that create a layering of the self-parodied voice of both Victorian prostitute and Victorian narrator/writer. Camp here might be perceived as a mode of realism inextricably and inescapably heading towards the grotesque. Sontag makes reference to the specific performative nature of sexual identity within the construction of camp aesthetics; she writes of 'camp taste' that 'draws on a mostly unacknowledged truth of taste: the most refined form of sexual attractiveness (as well as the most refined form of sexual pleasure) consists in going against the grain of one's sex' (1964: 519). Such inversion against the type Sontag suggests is itself attraction and beauty: 'What is most beautiful in virile men is something feminine; what is most beautiful in feminine women is something masculine' (ibid.). In concluding this comment, Sontag proposes that the attraction and the motivation for camp lies partly in this 'relish for the exaggeration of sexual characteristics and personality mannerisms' (ibid.).

The Crimson Petal and the White performs cross-gendering in a way that might be directly associated with this representation of campness as sexuality distorted, albeit the narrative is concerned with narratorial authority distorted at the same time. Faber's slippage between the voices of different characters, frequently represented as it is through supposed challenge to dominant modes of sexual construction and distortion of desire across perceived natural and unnatural boundaries, provides a camp 'exaggeration of sexual characteristics and personality mannerisms' by textual means. In the Gothicized and camp address to the 'dear Reader' for example, Sugar only confirms that she has fallen into the trap of 'truth' synonymous with the work of women writers in Agnes's mind, which seems like the final condemnation of her writing. But the voice which assumes authority again at this point is that of the omniscient narrator, closing off Sugar's own voice for a displaced voicing of her thoughts:

Her readers? Why, yes! She has every intention of submitting the manuscript for publication once it's finished. But who on Earth would publish it, you may protest, and who would read it? Sugar doesn't know, but she's confident it has a fighting chance. Meritless pornography gets published, and so do respectable novels politely calling for social reform [...]. Yes, there must be receptive minds out there in the world, hungry for the unprettified truth – especially in the more sophisticated and permissive future that's just around the corner. Why, she may even be able to live by her writing: A couple of hundred faithful readers would be sufficient; she's not coveting success on the scale of Rhoda Broughton's.

(Faber 2002: 229)

The slippages present in this moment serve as indications of the various points in the narrative which move between the supposition of Sugar's perspective, to the question from the narrator to the reader, to a seemingly combined perspective ('Yes, there must be [...] corner') where it is Sugar's thought that slips into omniscient comment in which we, as the 'permissive future', are implicit and implicated. As John Sutherland notes in his *Washington Post* review, 'Sugar is, it emerges, a feminist *avant la lettre*. Self-educated, she writes vengeful pornographic fantasies in which the tyrannical sex has the tables sadistically turned on it (should the woman's knife go into the heart, the bowels – or, happy thought, some more intimate area?)' (2002). Expressing an uneasiness about the suffusion of violent sex in the novel, Sutherland makes reference to the text's very excessiveness in comparison with its supposed Victorian precursors: 'page for page, it has more graphic sex than even that classic of nineteenth-century porn, *Lady Pokingham, or They all Do It*' (ibid.). But Sugar's writing is hardly *écriture féminine*; the language, narrative structures and stylistics are decidedly male. In *Feminist Stylistics*, Sara Mills argues that '[t]exts are invaded by sociocultural norms, by ideologies, by history, by economic forces, by fashions, by gender and racial stereotyping, and so on (1995: 198). That is not to say that authors have no control whatsoever about what they write, but that authors themselves are also subject to interpellation and interaction with these discursive forces' (ibid.). No attempt is made in Sugar's narrative of revenge to change the style into something that is recognizably other than the main narrative mode. The fact that Sugar's textual outbursts are surrounded by a male authored narrative in which inventiveness is often restricted to finding additional euphemistic descriptions for semen illustrates again the interconnections between the novel's exploration of female exploitation through prostitution and the text's own status as a purchased product meant to provide thrills, spills, titillation and some form of intellectual voyeurism. This is why Sutherland's articulation of a sense of unease about the over-egged nature of the sexual is in part also recognition of the attention-seeking nature of the narrative style. The cross-gendered signals provide another layer of exploitation rather than exploration. Cora Kaplan comments on the work of Byatt's pastiche in relation to Roland Barthes's ideas in *The Pleasure of the Text*, specifically 'the distinctions that Barthes draws between the bliss (*jouissance*) and the pleasure (*jouer*) of reading' (2007: 107). As Kaplan suggests, Byatt's 'bravura imitation' of the Victorian 'cool[s] down rather than warm[s] up the reading experience' (ibid.). Similarly, Faber's text, for all its voyeurism, sexual perversity and concentration on the commodification of the body through the eyes (or rather pen) of the Victorian prostitute, is about denying pleasure to the reader, removing the heights of the reading experience ironically through the elaborateness of the conceit, and the fabric of the detail. If we contrast Sutherland's discomfort (he also, rightly, complains about the length of the book as far longer than any Victorian triple-decker could get away with) with the review of James Kincaid, I think we can begin to tease out some of the complex ludic nature of Faber's playfulness. Kincaid argues, surprisingly from the perspective of a Victorianist, that:

> Slowly we find ourselves inside the heroine's head, led there by a rhetoric so skilled and daring that we hardly know it's operating. Like George Eliot, Faber teases us into making mistakes, almost forcing us to make easy judgments and indulge in stereotyping. Through nearly half of the novel his voice is omniscient, mocking the characters and us [...]. The narrator sets himself up as our guide, offering little lectures on the scenery and exploring the innermost thoughts of the characters, as if both were of equal interest and transparency. This device, so reminiscent of the great Victorian realists, allows us the space we need to exhaust our knowingness and move past satire and into that haven carved out by 19th-century agnostics: inescapable sympathy. This sympathy is neither sentimental nor observed; it is seeded and nurtured.[3]
>
> (Kincaid, 2000)

What Kincaid interprets as an emulation of (and a successful emulation of) Victorian high realist narrative style, noticeably through a gendered language of the 'seeded and nurtured', reflects rather the hollow, postmodern and inescapably aggressive in its offensiveness towards its reading public. The parallels mentioned between the opening lines of Faber's novel and the words uttered and written by Sugar do not allow the direct address to disappear but rather reinforce its inappropriateness. It also highlights the fact that the signal towards the writing of a cross-gendered perspective on the nineteenth century and its vicarious desires is a half-hearted one. Faber's text, deliberately or not, is about anything but authenticity and female authorship. One could read the echoes between Faber's narrator and Sugar as an illustration of the possibility that Sugar is herself narrator of a tale in which she appears as a character; but the contrary argument suggests that Faber's narrative is from the outset constructed on the understanding that he, the resolutely male voice of the opening taunts, is in control and that Agnes's diary and Sugar's fantasy are never more than (or meant to be more than) projections of the male (authorial) narrative voice. Faber's cross-gendering of literary voice in this book, then, is ultimately as flaky as Sugar's skin.

Notes

1. For a summary of key critical definitions of the term 'neo-Victorianism' and a rationale for the use proposed here, see 'Introduction' in Heilmann and Llewellyn (2010).
2. I discuss the 'Preface' to Faber's collection *The Apple*, where he collects letters received from readers demanding satisfaction of textual desires cut-short at the end of *The Crimson Petal and the White*, in 'Neo-Victorianism: on the Ethics and Aesthetics of Appropriation' cited above.
3. See Kincaid (2002).

Works Cited

Byatt, A.S. (1990) *Possession: a Romance* (London: Chatto and Windus).
Colella, Silvana (2010) 'Olfactory Ghosts: Michel Faber's *The Crimson Petal and the White*', in Rosario Arias and Patricia Pulham (eds), *Haunting and Spectrality in Neo-Victorian Fiction* (Basingstoke: Palgrave Macmillan), pp. 85–110.
Faber, Michel (2002) *The Crimson Petal and the White* (Edinburgh: Canongate).
—— (2006) *The Apple: New Crimson Petal Stories* (Edinburgh: Canongate).
—— (2003) 'Eccentricity into Authenticity: Fact into Fiction', *Victorians Institute Journal*, 31: 102–5.
Heilmann, Ann and Mark Llewellyn (2010) *Neo-Victorianism: the Victorians in the Twenty-First Century, 1999–2009* (Houndmills: Palgrave Macmillan).
Holmes, Frederick (1994) '*The Historical Imagination* and the Victorian Past: A.S. Byatt's *Possession*', *English Studies in Canada*, 20/3: 319–34.
Kaplan, Cora (2007) *Victoriana: Histories, Fictions, Criticisms* (Edinburgh: Edinburgh University Press).
Kincaid, James R. (2002) 'The Nanny Diaries', *New York Times*, September 15, http://www.nytimes.com/2002/09/15/books/the-nanny-diaries.html [accessed 20 January 2012].
Llewellyn, Mark (2004) '"Queer? I should say it is criminal!": Sarah Waters' *Affinity*', *Journal of Gender Studies*, 13/3: 203–14.
—— (2008) 'Breaking the Mould? Sarah Waters and the Politics of Genre', in Ann Heilmann and Mark Llewellyn (eds), *Metafiction and Metahistory in Contemporary Women's Writing* (Houndmills: Palgrave Macmillan), pp. 195–210.
—— (2009) 'Neo-Victorianism: on the Ethics and Aesthetics of Appropriation', *LIT: Literature, Interpretation, Theory*, 20/1–2: 27–44.
Mayhew, Henry (1862) *The Criminal Prisons of London and Scenes of Prison Life* (London: Griffin, Bohn and Company).

Mills, Sara (1995) *Feminist Stylistics* (London: Routledge).

Sontag, Susan (1964) 'Notes on Camp', *Partisan Review*, XXXI: 515–30.

Sutherland, John (2002) 'Making It: *The Crimson Petal and the White* by Michel Faber', *Washington Post*, September 15, http://www.washingtonpost.com/ac2/wpdyn?pagename=article&node=&contentId=A12475-2002Sep13 [accessed 20 January 2012].

Taylor, Charles (2002) 'Review of *The Crimson Petal and the White*', *Salon*, http://dir.salon.com/story/books/review/2002/10/21/faber/index.html [accessed 20 January 2012].

Tennyson, Alfred (1883) *The Works of Alfred Tennyson: Poet Laureate* (London: Kegan Paul, Trench and Co.).

Ussher, Jane M. (1997) *Fantasies of Femininity: Reframing the Boundaries of Sex* (Harmondsworth: Penguin).

Voigts-Virchow, Eckhart (2009) 'In-yer-Victorian-face: a Subcultural Hermeneutics of Neo-Victorianism', *LIT: Literature, Interpretation, Theory*, 20/1–2: 108–25.

Waters, Sarah (1999) *Affinity* (London: Virago).

—— (2002) *Fingersmith* (London: Virago).

11
'Queering' the Speaking Subject in Sarah Waters's *The Little Stranger*

Joanne Bishton

> Both work in literary studies and biography privilege
> the lives and work of middle- and upper-class women
> (and within this a select group of those who were
> cultural producers). In the new century we need more
> large-scale work to deepen and widen the analysis of
> lesbian lives.
>
> (Oram 2001: 5)

Introduction

Over the past 12 years, Sarah Waters has become established as a
popular and successful writer of mainstream lesbian fiction. Her work is
noted for its historical engagement with working-class lesbian life and,
one might argue, can be read as an attempt to validate an existence
that has consistently been written out of the pages of history. Although
same-sex relationships between women are documented, Alison Oram
is quite right when she suggests that we generally only have access to
accounts that examine and discuss the middle and upper-class affairs
of lesbian existence.[1] Part of this scarcity is caused by a lack of suitable
primary sources. For instance, Chris White's *Nineteenth-Century Writings
on Homosexuality: a Sourcebook* (1991) contains a vast array of primary
material, some now out of print, from the nineteenth and early twentieth century. Yet, on close inspection, this book gives little over 20 pages
to relationships between women; far more is given over to writings that
deal with men, the legalities and consequences of homosexuality at this
time and so forth. With obvious reasons to put forward for an apparent
lack of collatable material such as levels of education and literacy, it
seems possible to suggest that one of the reasons working-class lesbian

relationships have not had so much scholarly attention is because of such a dearth. Writers like Waters have realized this void and have consistently been attempting to plug it.

However, her most recent book *The Little Stranger* (2009) appears on the surface to veer away from this commitment: not least because her protagonist is a heterosexual male. Yet, it is the surfaces and depths that are created by this notable change that this chapter is going to consider. Whereas the narrators of Waters's previous works have always been explicitly engaged with exposing and, in a way, legitimating their gendered narratives, such as Nan's constant reference to 'pearl'[2] in *Tipping the Velvet* (1998), Dr Faraday in *The Little Stranger* adopts a masculinist perspective from the outset warranting 'that, in admiring the house, I wanted to possess a piece of it [...] like a man, I suppose, wanting a lock of hair from the head of a girl he had suddenly and blindingly become enamoured with' (Waters 2009: 3). In this regard, the apparent evolution in Waters's narrative stance might cause some to question the direction being taken. The overt lesbian voice that features so prominently in Waters's previous novels is, in part, connected to a sense of self that has championed lesbian issues vocally in interviews and is a mitigating factor in bringing the lives of marginal voices to a mainstream audience. As a response, some readers might read her newly cross-gendered voice as a sign that the working-class lesbian narrative, synonymous with Waters, has now been exhausted, that the gaps that existed in the historical reception of such lives are now filled and their existence rendered fully visible in a hetero-normative world-view. The potential for such a reaction has wide ranging implications for Waters's fiction, not least because her work queries the notion of what constitutes a lesbian text. This is because Waters's writing is inextricably bound with the body politic and aimed at popularizing what many have historically derided. It is from this point of departure that this chapter proceeds and interrogates the uncertainty and seeming instability that a male narrator brings to Waters's oeuvre.

The Little Stranger then, to coin Freud, is *unheimlich*. It appears unfamiliar to those readers of Waters's fiction who are expecting a romping lesbian romance and its story is a ghostly tale featuring the typical gothic motif of the decaying country house. Yet, to come back to the idea of surfaces and depths for a moment, it is going to become apparent that this book is not solely a tale of a murdering social climber, because, amongst the many things, it is a book that queries the notion of the 'queer'. Queer becomes a disrobed term that is exposed through the levels of artifice that encompass it. The setting of the house, the gothic excesses of the form and the role of the speaking subject all mitigate our understanding of the term queer. Thus, this chapter will argue that Waters exploits the instability that Faraday, the doctor, brings to the text. Through him, using a cross-gendered voice, Waters presents a character that is both trusted and dubious in equal measure. As such, these qualities are exposed through his dialogue, from his third-person descriptions and from his first-person narration, and consequently his narrative holds a certain duality within it. This double nature provides a schizophrenic quality necessary to explore a creative space from which Waters can engage with and redraft the concept of queer.

'Shape shifting' – as we might term such schizophrenic literary creativity – underscores aspects of the queer because there is a vacillation between dominant and submissive positions, as the term itself insinuates. Excesses here can be tempered, but such an exchange between their fluid economies means that this is only experienced as a temporary phase, rather than an altered state. In this way, we might regard the relationships between artifice and subjectivity, inanimacy and objectivity as properties that collide and collapse into one another producing a flux that signifies the liminalities of the corporeal. As a consequence, any gendered position can be regarded in this way, especially when they are viewed from a position of absence and lack. Thus masculinity can be experienced as a state of excess and femininity as a place of recession. As such, when the reader is told by Mrs Ayres that 'men acquire gallantry, as women acquire lines' (Waters 2009: 119) she is highlighting this particular point, as 'gallantry' is socially aligned with actions above and beyond personal expectations and 'lines' are evocative of the emptiness associated with female aging: a view that is proffered by a woman whose character in the book is closely aligned with her gendered and classed position in society. In light of this, I want to suggest that the liminal space between these two positions can be viewed as a queered space and furthermore, that in using a cross-gendered voice in the guise of Dr Faraday, Waters is querying the creative capacity of a subject; one that is enabled to transcend the boundaries of its position. In this regard, Waters's own lived experiences permeate the narrative and present moments of alterity within the perspective of an otherwise conservative character.

Surfaces, depths and the speaking subject

Julia Kristeva's notion of the speaking subject articulates a similar idea. For her, the speaking subject is capable of adopting a dominant position within a given context and, in so doing, is seen to be upholding a traditional, conservative and rational perspective (1980). Thus, throughout the book, Faraday moves between the rational and the irrational, constantly upholding and contesting normative positions in the same breath. His relationship with Hundreds Hall is the focus through which all of these traits are exposed to the reader. Hundreds is a country house estate in decline, following two costly world wars, and the current generation are struggling to make ends meet. Though their standing within the community is still respected, new money in the shape of the Baker-Hydes is a constant reminder of the evolution of the class system and it represents a challenge to an older way of life. In fact this threat becomes genuine when Gyp, the family dog, is destroyed after biting Baker-Hydes's child on the face following a party to show the Hall 'decked out in the style of its grander days' (79). In this way, Faraday exoticizes Hundreds as it is prepped, cleaned and trimmed for the party. Commenting on the way the place is stripped, Faraday declares '[the gardens] emerged lush and trimly textured [...] making the house look more impressive – more, I thought, as it was meant to look' (76). Yet, Faraday is also capable of romanticizing the Hall, stating, 'the thought of the Hall being opened up to strangers unsettled me slightly' (77). Here the reader is witnessing the shape-shifting abilities of Faraday as a speaking subject. He appears motivated by reason, for instance, constantly seeking a rational explanation for all the poltergeist activity, while also being concerned with providing a consistent and linear narrative throughout, reminding the reader of 'the story, as I pieced together' (210). In addition, his job as doctor enhances and privileges his relationship with the other characters in the book, as he quickly becomes seen as an able confidant and this ensures that he is a regular visitor to Hundreds Hall.

Presenting a cross-gendered narrative in this way creates a symbiotic relationship between writer and character, as they both trade qualities redolent to each; both assigned and subjective. However, I hope to show that the interface that is created by the cross-gendering process generates new reading experiences. Faraday becomes a portal through which his personality provides the disruptive elements that are needed to challenge those same social forces he is also seen to uphold. As a consequence, he becomes a site of ambiguity. For instance, following on from a particularly awkward dinner party, Faraday states, 'the house, I thought, didn't deserve their bad feeling; and neither did I' (188). Although this is only a minor remark made as Faraday was asked to leave by Roderick Ayres (the heir Faraday eventually unseats to a mental institution), it highlights Faraday's irrational and emotional side. Moreover, in emotionally aligning Faraday with the house, Waters draws attention to his artifice. This is again demonstrated when Roderick charges Faraday with the question, *'who the hell are you? You're no one!'* (199, Waters's italics). Faraday's apparent invisibility here, while symptomatic of an ailing class system, could also be an attempt by Waters to further explore the concept of indeterminacy.

Roderick Ayres presents Waters with an opportunity to explore what can be termed as notions of surfaces and depths in a way that removes certainties. For example, on the surface Faraday represents the respectability of a notable profession, but this covers the personal insecurities he harbours, as he recounts:

> [...] on the one hand I wanted desperately to live up to my own reputation for cleverness; and on the other it seemed very unfair, that that cleverness, which I had never asked for could be turned into something with which to cut me down [...].
>
> (Waters 2009: 4)

Similarly, Roderick symbolizes a certain duality, as a plane fire in the war left him physically and emotionally scarred. Outwardly he is described in reptilian terms with '[his skin] rough as crocodile in some spots, oddly smooth in others' (6). Socially he is the bastion of a fading social order, as 'master of the estate and its servants' (198) but his emotional state means that he is unable to meet the landed responsibilities handed to him, unable as it might be to accept the 'rough' with the 'smooth' and suffers for it. Within this chapter's exploration of surfaces and depths, Ayres sits firmly in the latter category because his mental illness prevents him from having an outward perspective and, as a result, he is left vulnerable. Consequently, Ayres becomes Faraday's first intended victim with him declaring that 'with Roderick's removal, it was clear to all of us that Hundreds had entered a distinct new phase' (234). With this new era begins the weakening of the family power base, seen through the eyes of Faraday, 'as though Rod had never been master of the house at all' (233). Here, the reader begins to associate the actions of the transgressor with Faraday, and the power of transgression itself comes to the surface.

Gothic influences in *The Little Stanger*

Within the Gothic genre, acts of transgression are used to reinforce social norms, to serve as warnings as to the consequences of an abandonment of moral conviction. It can be better understood if we consider Fred Botting's view on this matter. He states that:

> Not only [is transgression] a way of producing excessive emotion, a celebration of transgression for its own sake, Gothic terrors activate a sense of the unknown and project an uncontrollable and over-whelming power which threatens not only the loss of sanity, honour, property or social standing, but the very order which supports and is regulated by the coherence of those terms.
>
> (Botting 1996: 7)

Therefore, transgressive deeds in literature are acts of malevolence and threat. While the argument so far has suggested that Faraday is a trans-gressor, because he brings about threat, terror and death to the Ayres, it is also possible to suggest that Waters 'queers' this aspect through the speaking subject. As already mentioned, the duality of Faraday means that he is a site where social mores are conflated and reformed. This internal struggle allows Waters, on the one hand, to make a direct challenge to patriarchy, as a way to atone for the treatment of lesbians at the hands of the meaning-making systems of the past, while on the other hand, also bring about regenerative capacity. Waters signposts this for her readers as a 'new phase' (Waters 2009: 234), both in terms of the plot and also the literature she is now writing, which is perhaps experienced as a new generation.

With a new generation always comes the possibility of creativity and Waters shows us that queering the motives of the transgressor can sometimes bring fortune, rather than dread. In this regard, I want to touch on the work of Elizabeth Grosz and Gilles Deleuze, not neces-sarily the natural choice of theorists in relation to a discussion around the Gothic, but nevertheless, echoing the creative processes that are being explored at this juncture. Grosz tells us new bodies occur from the 'fissures between strata that allows something from them to escape' (1995: 135). The creative response is not achieved from the result of transgression, which in Gothic terms is associated with the return of the repressed and the terror exacted from the transfiguring of the mon-strous Other. Rather, it comes from the interruption of the habitual life that precedes the act. In this Grosz see a space into which the reader can realize a different subjectivity, as she says 'metamorphosing new bodies from the old through their encounter' (134). She is undoubtedly indebted to the work of Deleuze. What Grosz calls a 'stammer' (135) on the everyday, Deleuze sees as the creation of something akin to a foreign language. This chimes very well with the effect Waters has in queering the narrative voice in this way. Her playful manipulation hails the opportunity to experience a more diverse lived experience than she has previously engaged with. While she has always voiced the narratives of working-class lesbians, she may well have done so at the potential expense of excluding others. I would like to argue that, on this occasion Waters uses the cross-gendered potential of Faraday to dislodge the binary forces that hold phallocentric perspectives in place and holds the gaps apart long enough for other minority voices to populate.

Queering a sense of identity through intertexts

The sense of layering that has so far been building in this argument is, in many ways, in step with Roland Barthes's notion of 'intertexts' (1981: 39).[3] Intertexts are part of a process of rewriting, whereby they exhibit a rich fabric of cultural codes and practices that have contributed towards their existence. In this, readers recognize the loaded referents in order to read them in a new way, a creative way and possibly as a 'new phase'. For this reason and by their very nature, intertexts have the capabilities of rendering 'queer' the processes of authorship and readership, because of the mirroring, shadowing and echoing of the stories and lived experiences that have gone before and become entwined within each new reading. Coming to *The Little Stranger* can feel like meeting an old familiar. The manor house, for instance, is redolent with the themes of many early to mid-twentieth-century novels concerned with the decline of the country house. Evelyn Waugh's *Brideshead Revisited* (1945) is strikingly reworked as the character of Charles Ryder is replaced with that of Dr Faraday. Where religion is the entity that appears to sustain the Flytes at various points throughout their lives, a dark malevolence drives the Ayres beyond the brink. Thus one of the residing motifs that Waters exploits is a sense of Englishness.

Englishness has, as Christine Berberich argues, become tinged with 'nostalgia, evoking images of a traditional, tranquil, in some cases even *mythical* England' (2007: 23). Waters evokes these images for her readers by opening the narrative from a retrospective stance, 'I first saw Hundreds Hall when I was ten years old' (Waters 2009: 1), the doctor announces. 'It was summer' we are told, and the 'Ayres still had most of their money then [and] were still big people in the district' (1). The idyllic feelings of community spirit are rife in these words and a shared sense of the collective is further emphasized by the fact that Faraday and the others are attending an Empire Day celebration. Celebrations like this were used to remind people of their position within the Empire and to reinforce the principles of empire building that underpinned the British State. Although the popularity of such events was beginning to wane, this form of communal gathering survived into the 1970s (and is currently being revived) with street parties and similar events moving the emphasis from empire to other state endorsed moments of celebration, such as royal weddings. Waters uses such moments to exploit the nature of English and British nostalgia and thereby hook her readers as she encourages them to inscribe their own experiences of public celebration over the Empire Day event in a way that causes a two-way communication between the story and the reader.

Waters, like many other contemporary novelists, incorporates meticulously researched details into her work; again layering the familiarity of the text. Yet, it is possible to see that by their very nature of being intertexual they 'queer' the textual space. Whereas, it is possible to see that a lack of historical and primary sources may cause Waters's previous books to be seen in light of their instability,[4] in that their very foundation is rooted in myth, *The Little Stranger* presents a world that is both familiar and yet defamiliarizing at the same time. Familiarity in this way is inspired through the nods and winks to Englishness, even though the processes of alienation very quickly begin when identity is purposefully juxtaposed with and represented by artifact.

The oak tree, a quintessential emblem of Englishness, is presented to the reader through the symbolism of the acorn. The acorn forms part of the wall freeze that catches the attention of Faraday as a boy, but, the mightiness of this image is desecrated when he uses his pen-knife to 'prise it from its setting' (Waters 2009: 3) on the Hall wall during the Empire Day visit. A subsequent discovery by his mother sees the acorn being disposed of in the fire and this results in it being reduced to a 'blackened nub' (4). The point being that Waters overlays the image of the power and excess of the Empire, with its reliance on idealized images of rural England, with that of a deformed charred remain retrieved from 'among the clinker' (ibid.). In so doing, she displaces any feelings of nostalgia, because as the house declines and retreats into the background, where 'there was no spot, on any of the lanes in that part of Warwickshire, from which it could be glimpsed' (ibid.), the acorn remains ever present in the story, constantly fingered by Faraday in his trouser pocket. Moreover, Faraday's cross-gendered voice adds further to this noted distortion, because of the 'stammering' interface between shared existence and diversity. Therefore, what was recovered from the fire and seen as a 'queer little thing' (3) in the hand of Faraday's mother is cleansed of its aforementioned normative associations and is now able to represent a new set of perspectives while ever in the hands of Faraday.

Waters enlists the sense of crisis that goes with this period in order to add a further dimension of menace and threat. Historically, by the end of the 1940s the country house was in decline and Berberich argues that at times of crisis the beauty of the countryside becomes praiseworthy and enchanted (2007: 24). Where Stanley Earl Baldwin in 1926 might have found the 'eternal sight of England' (cited in Berberich, 2007: 24), Waters dispossesses another iconic emblem of England, the garden, to queer the process of identity. Thus the 'neat rhododendron and laurel' is over-run by self-seeding weeds and 'spreading ivy' (Waters 2009: 5). Where Faraday has to break 'free of the bushes' in order to locate the gravel path, even his car, he says, 'had to fight its way down the drive' (ibid.). Hence, the temptation for the neat lines and edges associated with managed horticulture is being returned back to their natural state and, in so doing, the emphasis is on the fuzzy boundary lines.

Readers of Gothic fiction may well recognize that Waters is flirting with the uncanny here. Botting argues that contemporary readers of the Gothic are thrilled and chilled in equal measure by the 'narrative forms and devises [that] spills over from worlds of fantasy and fiction into real and social spheres' (1996: 168). Through Botting's description of what he calls, 'postmodern gothic' (ibid.) it is possible to detect other intertextual influences. As Botting asserts:

> [...] the hybrid mixing of forms and narratives has uncanny effects, effects which make narrative play ... another duplicitous object to be expelled from proper orders of consciousness and representation.
>
> (Botting 1996: 169)

Botting's reference here to the duplicitous nature of the narrative echoes the argument that has been constructed around the speaking subject during the discussion up to this point. Such is the contradictory nature of the cross-gendered narrative, played out through an exchange between levels of respectability and indecency, that readers may begin to question the levels of trust placed in the hands of doctors. The expected professionalism that comes with this role becomes a site of contradictions, as the reader witnesses moments of conflict between the switching of duty for disgust. This tension is perhaps most notable when the male narration exposes moments of internal monologue, for instance, during the post-mortem on Mrs Ayres. The notion of rebellion is initially hinted at here, as Faraday's mind 'revolted' at the idea of allowing anyone else to intrude upon his duty of care to 'Mrs Ayres' poor marked body' (Waters 2009: 418). Further, his 'nerve' is tested once he realizes that the 'injuries were less shocking' than he had expected (419). However, during the procedure 'a darker reason for wanting to perform the post-mortem' (ibid.) himself comes to the surface. Any sense of duty is now becoming estranged and replaced with feelings of fascination, such that the 'nips and tucks [...] began, on inspection, to lose some of their horror' (ibid.). In this way, Waters is employing a typical Gothic narrative ploy, whereby examples of superficiality like this serve to highlight a greater anxiety that is present in the narratives. This fear is self-containing, in that Botting argues that 'one of the principle horrors lurking throughout Gothic fiction is the sense that there is no exit from the darkly illuminating labyrinth of language' (1996: 14). Waters's cross-gendering of language serves only to emphasize this point entirely.

Traditionally, language carries and conveys power and those who can occupy and mobilize the dominant discourse control the rest of society through their normative and hegemonizing force. This power dynamic is referenced by Waters through the observable splitting within the speaking subject, whereby feelings of power can be replaced by revulsion and fear with fascination. Thus the cutting of 'the dreadful, bloated and dark' (Waters 2009: 412) body of Mrs Ayres performs as another act of transgression that enables a discharge of emotional excess (Botting 2008: 7). As a consequence, Faraday concludes the scene by saying, 'Now, finally, the doubt was dispelled' (Waters 2009: 419). With this release and the 'restored [...] body' of Mrs Ayres, a sense of equilibrium is re-established with the narrative (ibid.). Faraday returns to his rational self and we are told that the evidence for the coroner is so 'pointed', that 'the whole process took less than thirty minutes' to conclude (ibid.). However, while 'normality' seems to prevail, there is always a sense that the perverse is lurking somewhere in the shadows. Therefore, the air of officialdom, of bureaucratic and legal power centred upon the inquest is undercut by Water's use of the phrase 'summary affair' (ibid.). The play on the word 'summary' with 'summery', as in seasonal weather, seems to enchant the whole situation and lighten, if not bypass the seriousness of the verdict of 'suicide whilst the balance of mind was disturbed' (ibid.).

Enchanting the text with a cross-gendered voice

Enchantment is a trope that warrants further investigation in relation to the way that the Ayres family is set in opposition to the world around them. From the very beginning they are bound with 'the horrified [...] signs of decay' (5) that strips away at the layers that have contributed towards its mass. This causes the reader to query the process of layering texts with historical information and readers are asked to question the validity of such facts and events that are being put before them. As we have established, Waters employs the typical gothic motif of the house in order to explore this concept. Thus, as a child Faraday remembers the house, 'its lovely ageing details: the worn red brick, the cockled window glass, the weathered sandstone edgings. They made it looked blurred and slightly uncertain – like an ice, I thought, just beginning to melt in the sun' (1). Here he is drawing a vision of a house that holds no solid shape, which is unstable and likely to dissolve in front of our eyes at any moment. Once again, the reader is reminded of the *unheimlich*, as the 'solid structure, felt precarious' (5). Freud's notion of the unhomely, where the safety of the domestic space is replaced with the prison like structure is exposed by the cross-gendered narrative voice and the reader witnesses the Ayres steady retreat from society, as 'Hundreds Hall withdrew even further from the world. The gates of the park were kept almost permanently closed' (4).

The inward-facing collapse of the Hall and its retreat from society creates a feeling of isolation for the reader. Reminiscent of other familiar texts, we are given images from Edgar Allan Poe's *Tales of the Grotesque and Arabesque* (1840), Henry James's *Turn of the Screw* (1898) and Wilkie Collins's *Woman in White* (1859). Such layering serves to add depth to *The Little Stranger*, with one tale spliced with another. But, their inclusion also acts to 'queer' the story of *The Little Stranger* even further. Their presence complicates the reader's view of Hundreds Hall and its setting. Similarly, the state of the home is further threatened and weakened by the invasion of nature, that has a strangle hold on the property, as 'ivy had spread [and the] steps leading up to the broad front door were cracked, with weeds growing lushly up through the seams' (Waters 2009: 5). Botting argues that this undermines the 'comfortable domestication' (1996: 129) of the space. Similarly, Roderick's appearance also adds weight to this notion that the house and its inhabitants are slowly being returned to nature, as when Faraday notices that Roderick's 'reptilian hand' felt 'queer against' his own (Waters 2009: 6). Summer is also aligned with Roderick as we are told he is wearing 'summer trousers' (ibid.). Waters aligns feelings of ease with the relaxed atmosphere of summer despite the other, darker and more Gothic elements that are also at play meaning that she upsets and thereby 'queers' this mood of supposed calm.

In contrast, while Emily Brontë's *Wuthering Heights* (1857) and Charlotte Brontë's *Jane Eyre* (1847) both provide additional intertexts for *The Little Stranger*, in regards of the fact that they both swap the domesticated comfort of the home into an incarcerated existence, their protagonist and antagonists are not so transferable. Waters does not convincingly present her readers with the type of hero-villain that Heathcliff and Rochester represent, though it is true that Caroline and Faraday appear to mitigate each other's inadequacies. She, on the one hand, being, '"a clever girl" – [...] noticeably plain, over-tall for a woman', he 'wanted desperately to live up to my own reputation for cleverness' (Waters 2009: 9, 4). The excesses of Caroline's 'wide hips and large bosom' (9) make up for the 'bitter little battles' (4) of Faraday's existence. Finally, where she is masculinized in appearance with, 'thickish legs and ankles [...] boyish flat sandals [...] angular jaw [...] muscular legs' (9), Faraday is emasculated through 'passionless embraces [...] mechanical detail [...] pity for the women involved' (39) in failed attempts at romance. These doublings appear throughout the text, but would not seem to provide a complete, unified whole. This is because when the two are brought together, unlike Cathy famous words to Nelly 'I am Heathcliff' (Brontë 1985: 122) Caroline is described as not feeling 'quite enough' (Waters 2009: 464) for Faraday. For these reasons, it is not to the other characters that we need to look in order to find a doubling with Faraday. Instead, we need to look outside of the text. Via a combination of the narrator and speaking subject, I want to suggest that Waters 'queers' the whole narrative process. The moments when a unified presence of author and narrator are detectable are those moments when the reader is unsettled, when the gaps occur and when the schizophrenic nature of the speaking subject becomes evident. During these moments an alternative reader response is elicited. This comes directly as a result of an additional creative capacity being provided within the textual space.

The feeling then that life is not what it seems is an enduring theme in *The Little Stranger*, and the various acts of transgression open up the voids that exist in and around such modes of thought production. In light of this, we have so far considered the influence of a cross-gendered voice on the mingling of fact and fiction in order to blur the edges of distinction between the real and the constructed, the trusted and the feared and the loss of the rational self. So far, we have come to realize how the dualities that are associated with the speaking subject interact with the world around it. Thus, Waters uses a male narrator to vocalize certain fractures that occur in the skein of society and posit alternative perspectives. These narrative excursions seem to be driving towards a complete disassembly of all that can be relied upon and taken for granted in relation to gender and identity. Thus the resulting shape shifting is, I believe, an attempt to construct something new and unfamiliar. To return to Botting again:

> Unstable, unfixed and ungrounded in any reality, truth or identity other than those that narratives provide [...] emerges a threat of sublime excess, of a new darkness of multiple and labyrinthine narratives, in which human myths again dissolve, confronted by an uncanny force beyond control.
>
> (Botting 1996: 171)

As the narrative can be the only place where reality and truth are sought by the reader, its constant re-shaping by Faraday causes narrative anxiety and it is this dissolution of the rational self that ushers in feelings of 'anarchic disintegration' (ibid.). The point perhaps needs reiterating here, that it is the stuttering that occurs between these forces that then produces the new effects: the Deleuzian foreign language. In this regard, queerness can be experienced as a continually altering state. It is transformative precisely because it is not static and has proved an efficient way of determining textual slippages via the male narrator. However, so far we have failed to address the performative aspect of queerness in relation to gender and how this may be transmitted to the reader through the narrative.[5]

Performing queerness through a cross-gendered voice

The final section will consider queerness in terms of gender and ask if and whether *The Little Stranger* can be perceived as a queer text in this way. Here I am not directly referencing Waters's own sexuality, though to be clear she firmly situates herself within a canon of lesbian writers and, as such, this alone begs us to ask what it is that constitutes a lesbian text. In addition, as this chapter has so far played with the notion that there is slippage between author and narrator via the device of the speaking subject, it is inevitable that some comparisons centred upon Waters's lesbianism will abound. In order to navigate this matter correctly, 'queerness' has thus far been argued from the perspective of its liberatory capacity. Identity, intertextuality and the Gothic all help readers enter a world that is familiar and yet strange in order to experience something new. However, using the Gothic in this way gives primacy to a heteronormative position and reads homosexuality through its absence. This chapter will now attempt to reverse this process and see if such iterations channelled through queerness can take gendered categories beyond their limitations. In this way, it is clear that the Gothic has many shared features with homosexuality, not least because they exist on the boarders of normative social propriety. Yet, they both share a desire to expose difference. To this end then, queerness becomes relevant because of its infinite meanings, from its generic sense of estrangement to its gender specificity of homosexuality. In light of this, *The Little Stranger* is 'queered' on many levels.

In the introduction to their book, *Queering the Gothic* (2009), William Hughes and Andrew Smith argue that 'it is its [the Gothic's] ability to express the power of mock, surprise and shock [which] may well hold the key to the more elusive queerness of the genre' (3). So far, we have taken many examples from *The Little Stranger* to engage with this idea. We may well argue that Waters parodies some conventional forms of Gothic horror, such as those of the successful Hammer Horrors of the 1960s and 1970s. We might also argue that Waters subverts the levels of importance that is placed upon the transgressor in conventional Gothic forms, because, as we have already discussed, she appears more concerned with the transformative processes than the act of transgression itself. However, what is apparent is that Waters is in keeping with contemporary women writers of Gothic fiction who opt for 'figures that are boundary breakers' (Wisker 2009: 126). Additionally, these figures challenge conservative notions of lesbianism too.

There are no direct references to abjection in Waters text and little evidence of direct Othering, both of which are consistent motifs engaged by contemporary women writers of queer Gothic fiction to evoke, expose and challenge normative structures, according to Gina Wisker (2009: 127). Waters does not evoke the demonizing of animals, spells or social taboos. Her text does not have a sexually driven subplot about vampires or werewolves and it does not contain any detectable elements of sexual deviancy. Wisker identifies these as the means by which contemporary women writers of queer Gothic fiction destabilize social hierarchies and gender categories (127). Moreover, Wisker argues that queer Gothic contains lesbian characters precisely for the purpose of exploding the myths associated with gender. Therefore, how is it possible to situate Waters within the auspices of queer Gothic via a cross-gendered voice?

In order to answer this question, we need to expand the term of reference and provide an alternative reading of the text from the one that has taken place so far. I am conscious of the limitations that placing someone within a given gendered category has, albeit if the author herself appears comfortable in this regard. But, neither does the following discussion intend to rule out any potential creative capacity because of this. In addition, I want to suggest that queer Gothic infers an infinity of meaning of gender, rather than the four categories that are currently applied in this regard. Layering of the text occurs, but not necessarily in a way that readers are overtly and immediately aware of because Waters plays around with the nature of sexuality through the textual space, using it to highlight the weaknesses in the dominant and the strengths in the submissive.

From the outset then, Waters complicates the space of the text in playing out the story of a heterosexual couple on the pages of a lesbian book.[6] This initially introduces a sense of queerness to the text, because of the obvious difference in sexuality between her and the male narrative voice of the doctor. Waters inevitably devolves her own sense of homosexual culture and politics into the transcript. As a consequence, within the liminal space of a queer text conformity takes on a strange guise. The heterosexual romance in the plot falters before it gets going 'Caroline having very little to say' and 'everything was "too unsettled"' (Waters 2009: 421, 422). The emphasis with the additional inverted commas is interesting here. It seems as if Waters wants her readers to realize that this whole subplot is meant to disrupt conventional readings of romance plot lines and, as such, the unsettling stands proud of the rest of the narrative. This argument gains support when we read that the doctor took it upon himself to chose Caroline's dress, flowers and gloves for their wedding day, stating 'I've been very busy, on your behalf' (444). If the mixing of gender roles was not overt enough for readers, Waters goes further when Faraday says, 'Look, I know this is flying in the face of convention, rather, but I didn't think you would mind. There hasn't been much of the conventional – well about us' (445). Here, you might argue, Waters is using a cross-gendered voice to dislodge a traditional romance and the resulting marriage, the mainstay of patriarchy, by narrating the story through a doctor who is prepared to 'fly in the face of convention' (ibid.). In other words, he deconstructs its social values and everything it stands for. Throughout this scene there is evidence of further conflation and exchange of gendered roles. Faraday is paralysed by 'panic' (449). Caroline is 'hardened' (446). Faraday 'flinched' from Caroline's expression and she softened this in response 'growing kinder' (ibid.). However, Faraday makes the most telling statement when he says 'she was like a stranger to me' (448). Here heteronormative positionalities appear to have broken down because their boundaries do not exist. In this way, they have no meaning, no point of reference, and make no sense. Waters highlights the senseless nature of specific gendered roles. Instead, what she evidences is a constant flux between male and female and a regenerative co-opting of emotional states.

Hundreds Hall presents the reader with an exploitable place for queering. Therefore, Caroline and Faraday's inability to achieve and maintain a sexual relationship can, in itself, be seen as a form of denial. Hughes and Smith argue that when orthodoxy becomes fictionalized within a queered space, it becomes subject to the same levels of deviancy used to critique the 'Other' from a heteronormative position – something they term the 'reciprocal states of queerness and non-queerness' (2009: 4). These reciprocal states demonstrate the relationship between the marginal and the mainstream and flag up the numerous slippages of the various sociopolitical identities presented within and of the novel. Recognizing this state and fluidity means that any viable alternative can become performative. In this instance, the concept of identity is presented as a choice, rather than a set of assigned codes of identification. Queering the text in this way means that self-denial can be reversed and be reinterpreted and experienced as self-fashioning (Hughes and Smith 2009: 4).

The importance of the speaking subject has remained at the heart of this discussion. Primarily, its purpose is to explore the fissures that can erupt when aspects of duality break with traditional narrative forms. These spaces are the places where reader response generates greatest capacity for meaning, which is complicated further by the redolent intertextuality that has been highlighted. While readers feel comfortable and secure in the cultural codes and references that are placed before them, they quickly become unsettled when they are compromised by the processes of 'queering'. Queering has been understood and examined in its pejorative sense and aligned with the Gothic in order to further destabilize any conventional readings of identity that readers may attempt. Subsequently, queering has also been explored in relation to sexuality and the Gothic in order to expose the limitless possibilities that can come from de-centering the hierarchical nature of heteronormativity. Furthermore, while Waters is a contemporary woman writer of Gothic fiction, she queers this generic reference, because she authors a distinctly different version. Avoiding the current trend which transforms a sexual exchange between beast and human into a 'boundary breaking' lesbian Gothic encounter, Waters shapeshifts with her cross-gendered narrative and brings a distinctly unique, ungendered, 'queered' perspective.

Notes

1. For further reading on this see Marcus (1998), Lee (1996), Sproles (2006) and Raitt (2002). While all share a common thread in their interest in two of the most prominent modern-day lesbians, Virginia Woolf and Vita Sackville-West, they also serve to demonstrate an academic dearth on working-class lesbian experience.
2. Nancy Astley often refers to her lovers as 'pearls' specifically at points of heightened sexual tension. From this, it seems plausible that Waters's over-use of the word is an attempt to assert lesbian culture into the vernacular, as 'pearl' is imbued with many lesbian cultural referents. Yet, there appears to be a direct play on the word 'pearl' too. *Pearl* was a highly successful Victorian gentleman's magazine celebrating heterosexual erotica and was first published in the late 1890s. In this regard, every time Nan utters this word during sex, she is disassociating the word from within a heterosexual narrative and claiming it as lesbian.
3. Intertextuality came to prominence with the poststructuralist movement of the 1960s. For further reading on this matter see Barthes (1981), Derrida (1967), Foucault (1986), Lévi-Strauss (2001) and Kristeva (1980).
4. For further reading on the notion of textual instabilities see Michel Foucault's 'What is an Author' (1979) and Julia Kristeva's work on the palimpsests in 'The Bounded Text' (1980).
5. Performativity was introduced into queer theory by Judith Butler who famously argued that individuals perform their gender according to the way it is culturally assigned. However, performativity is a way in which the performance can rupture the cultural codes that are in place and applied to a specific role. To be performative is to challenge the heteronormative world view. For further reading see Bulter (1990).
6. The nature of a text is a contested site. Without wanting to invoke the pathetic phallacy it seems highly relevant to an author who has so explicitly associated their sexuality with their writing, both personally and politically. While it is not being suggested that there should be any autobiographical elements to this discussion, it is not so clear cut that you can divorce a person's sexuality from their writing. To do so seems to deny a creative capacity that comes from the layering of the text that this sexuality will bring. Therefore, in response to these concerns and for the purposes of this chapter *The Little Stranger* is considered to be a lesbian text.

Works Cited

Barthes, Roland (1981) 'Theory of the Text', in Robert Young (ed.), *Untying the Text: a Post-structuralist Reader* (London: Routledge), pp. 31–49.

—— (1988) 'The Death of the Author', in David Lodge (ed.), *Modern Criticism and Theory: a Reader* (London: Longman), pp. 166–95.

Benstock, Shari (1998) *The Private Self: Theory and Practice of Women's Autobiographical Writings* (London: Routledge).

Berberich, Christine (2007) *The Image of the English Gentleman in Twentieth-Century Literature* (Hampshire: Ashgate).

Botting, Fred (1996) *Gothic: the New Critical Idiom* (New York, Canada, Oxon: Routledge).

Brontë, Charlotte (1994[1847]) *Jane Eyre* (London: Penguin).

Brontë, Emily (1985[1847]) *Wuthering Heights* (London: Penguin).

Butler, Judith (1990) *Gender Trouble* (London: Routledge).

Collins, Wilkie (2008[1859]) *The Woman in White* (Oxford: Oxford University Press).

Deleuze, Gilles (1988) *Foucault*, trans. Sean Hand (Minneapolis: University of Minnesota Press).

Derrida, Jacques (1967) *Derrida: Writing and Difference*, trans. Alan Bass (London: Routledge).

Foucault, Michel (1986[1979]) 'What is an Author', in *The Foucault Reader*, trans. and ed. P. Rabinow (London: Penguin).

Grosz, Elizabeth (1995) *Space, Time and Perversion* (New York: Routledge).

Hammer Horror, http://www.hammerfilms.com [accessed 20 January 2012].

Hughes, William and Andrew Smith (eds) (2009) *Queering the Gothic* (Manchester: Manchester University Press).

James, Henry (1898) *The Turn of The Screw* (London: Penguin).

Kristeva, Julia (1980) *Desire in Language: a Semiotic Approach to Literature and Art*, ed. Leon S. Roudiez, trans. Thomas Gora, Alice Jardine and Leon S. Roudiez (Oxford: Blackwell).

Lee, Hermione (1996) *Virginia Woolf* (London: Chatto & Windus).

Lévi-Strauss Claude (2001[1978]) *Myth and Meaning* (London: Routledge).

Marcus, Jane (1988) 'Invincible Mediocrity: the Private Selves of Public Women', in Shari Benstock (ed.), *The Private Self: Theory and Practice of Women's Autobiographical Writings* (London: Routledge), pp. 114–46.

Marcus, Sharon (2007) *Between Women: Friendship, Desire, and Marriage in Victorian England* (New Jersey: Princeton University Press).

Oram, Alison (2001) *Lesbian History: Sources on Love and Sex Between Women, 1870–1970* (Florence, KY: Routledge).

Poe, Edgar Allan (1994[1840]) *Selected Tales* (London: Penguin).

Raitt, Suzanne (2002) *Vita and Virginia: the Work and Friendship of V. Sackville-West and Virginia Woolf* (Oxford: Clarendon Press).

Roof, Judith (1994) 'Lesbian and Lyotard: Legitimation and the Politics of the Name', in L. Doan (ed.), *The Lesbian Postmodern* (New York: Columbia University Press).

Sproles, Karyn Z. (2006) *Desiring Women: the Partnership of Virginia Woolf and Vita Sackville-West* (Toronto, Buffalo and London: University of Toronto Press).

Waters, Sarah (1998) *Tipping the Velvet* (London: Virago Press).

—— (2009) *The Little Stranger* (London: Virago Press).

Waugh, Evelyn (1945) *Brideshead Revisited* (London: Penguin).

White, Chris (1999) (ed.) *Nineteenth-Century Writings on Homosexuality: a Sourcebook* (London and New York: Routledge).

Wisker, Gina (2009) 'Devouring Desires: Lesbian Gothic Horror', in William Hughes and Andrew Smith (eds), *Queering the Gothic* (Manchester: Manchester University Press), pp. 123–41.

Conclusion: Crossings and Re-crossings

Claire Westall

Voices can be loud or soft, high or low, clear or muffled, and anything in between. The voice itself offers a sense of possibility and forthcoming communication, but it is also suggestive of an always already spent force because at the very moment of sound or articulation the thought, the effort, the actions required to create the sound of the voice are almost past, they are approaching their own end. That is, the voice is suggestive of a forward moving potentiality – that even when silent it carries the potential for speech – and it is indicative of a backward orientated gesture of delay, or a time lag, because the sounds of the voice can only be received by a listener after the moment of vocalization, after a pause, after the voice has begun to work. The voice, it may be said, then, carries a sense of agency and potential and also marks the need for reception, the need for the Other to wait and then to receive, making or reconstructing meaning as they can. In a physical sense, the voice is not a single organ, and is not reducible to a single site though, as a number of authors in this collection have made clear, the mouth is crucial to the imaginative weight attached to the voice. However, the voice works via the moment of air, through tensions and vibrations, via the creation of shapes and articulatory movements and, as we have seen, it is therefore embodied in a complex and multifaceted way that links organs, breathing apparatuses and facial features.

Voice, then, comes from movements, connections, flows, a sense of fluidity and constant reshaping. Consequently, there is dynamism to its very existence. It emanates from the body but is not merely located within it, because at the point of audibility the voice is in the air, outside the body, in the world or, in a literary sense, in the world of the text. More importantly, perhaps, the voice, at this point, stands between the self and the Other, acting as a bridging, even unifying, medium that captures the effort to link the self and the Other, to communicate across the distance between the self and the Other, while also marking the fundamental gap between the self and the Other. The voice can occupy time and space in a way that is not obviously tied to a single body. It can emerge from a hidden, masked, obscured source or body as in cinematic, theatrical and narrative efforts that carry what Michel Chion calls an acousmatic force – a force derived from the absence of the voice's origin. Hence, the voice is also disembodied, a phantom of air and sound, that may invoke fear, power, omniscient sight and knowledge. It can seem ephemeral and evasive even if it is heard, and it has a multidirectional, omnipresent quality. It is this variety, variability and complexity of the voice, as an embodied object and a disembodied force, which enables diverse and probing analytical interests and readings, and demands increasing critical attention.

Notably, cross-gendered literary voices reveal to us the ambiguous ontological complexities involved in the status and use of the voice and in the ways we experience, represent and imagine the gendering of subjects. The purpose of this collection has been to open up and critically explore the ways in which literary production involves the cross-gendering of voice, and to provide a set of provocative and exciting case studies that, individually and collectively, illuminate the multiple, complicated and challenging ways in which the vocalization of gender and gender-crossing has been used by authors since the mid-nineteenth century. The historical trajectory of the collection, from the 1850s through to the present, has enabled an overarching literary transformations to be rendered visible and at the same time the chapters have demonstrated that, from the Victorian period onwards, the engagement of authors with their gendered Other has never been a matter of simple appropriation and efforts to fully embrace the Other have been problematic and anything but smooth. Most often, as the collection has shown, there is a robust and constant renegotiation, a tussle almost, between efforts to appropriate the voice of the gendered Other and contestatory pressures of resistance, opposition and disruption. Such contests occur within single texts, within the narrative voices of novels, and also within the oeuvre of particular authors as they repeatedly re-engage with their dominant socio-political and aesthetic concerns. What has become obvious is that there is never a clear, singular move across gendered positions, there are only crossings, as plurals, and re-crossings, as many gendered journeys take place in the vocalized moves back and forth between and across gendered voices, positions and identities, revealing the discursive instability upon which categories of sex and gender have been historically built. In looking to the voice, the collection has made clear the need to supplement, rather than bypass, a focus on the body and physical performativity, especially given the dominance of such modes of thinking within feminist and queer theory. Indeed, much of the work offered here is specifically concerned with the relationship between the body, gender and voice and it has sought to ensure that the voice can speak (so to speak) within this triad of inter-related connections.

This collection was premised upon an appreciation of the voice as active, as full of agency in a way that was under-valued in literary debates despite attention being given to bodies, subjects, selfhood and self-representation. We recognized that the voice and its use overtly establish efforts on the part of any vocalizer to mark themselves as present, to demonstrate their being-in-the-world, and underscore their own agency (especially when use of the voice is primarily tied to willed action). Underlying the collection was a motivating desire for the voice and the strengths of speech, as well as vocalization and articulation, to become key sites of literary, cultural, theoretical and political attention. Identifying and sustaining an examination of the voice, and related aspects of literary practice, is part of an effort to identify active, self-conscious and crafted attempts to vocalize, to bring to the literary debate the power of the voice that is being offered through a mechanism, or set of mechanisms, that make noise, that create communicative links, that may be part of a person's attempt to represent themselves within and to the world and those around them.

Clearly, as with any edited collection, the process of selection means that coverage of any large and consequential area of analysis must be, in some ways, limited and leave numerous avenues open to future lines of critical enquiry. This collection is no exception and it has, purposefully, opened the debate about the crossing of gendered voice by concentrating on Anglo-Irish-American works, particularly prose texts that are within, or exist in relation to, the key markers of what has become the literary canon although we have sought to specifically engage with the most recent debates about such works and authors. Importantly, the collection has also brought to light new readings of contemporary writers whose work has not yet received the critical weight that they deserve. We hope that the foundational groundwork laid out here will be taken up as a prompt for additional explorations of the voice in other literary modes, periods and places, and that theorization of the voice, which has, to this point, been primarily linked with the cinema and psychoanalysis, will proliferate and expand given the obvious need to continue extending our understanding of the voice, its everyday value and vulnerability, and its literary-cultural deployment and impact. Critical readings, such as those provided here, may not be understood as themselves offering 'new' voices, but by unpacking and probing the voice as it is used in literary texts and as it is cross/trans-gendered such readings shed light on the manner in which differing modes of writing do create and give voice to their characters, their aesthetic endeavours and even their political interventions. Such readings also work to build a theoretical bank of approaches and manoeuvres that establish the terrain of the voice as a pivotal medium of analytical interest. To concern ourselves with the cross-gendering of voice is to re-examine key literary and cultural mechanisms of representation and to think through how such aesthetic practices enable us to re-imagine the world around us and its literary landscape. We hope that this will be the legacy of *Cross-Gendered Literary Voices*.

Bibliography

Ackerley, C.J. and S.E. Gontarski (2004) *The Grove Companion to Samuel Beckett* (New York: Grove Press).

Ackroyd, Peter (1979) *Transvestism and Drag: the History of an Obsession* (London: Simon and Schuster).

Armitt, Lucie (1996) *Theorising the Fantastic* (London: St Martin's Press).

Attridge, David (1989) 'Molly's Flow: the Writing of 'Penelope' and the Question of Women's Language', *Modern Fiction Studies*, 35/3: 543–65.

Bahun, Sanja (2004) '"Full Fathom Five Thy Father Lies": Freud, Modernists, and History', *Exit 9*, VI, 3–20.

—— (2012, forthcoming) *Modernism and Melancholia: Writing as Countermourning*.

Baker, Phil (1997) *Beckett and the Mythology of Psychoanalysis* (London: MacMillan).

Bakhtin, M.M. (1981) *The Dialogic Imagination: Four Essays*, trans. Caryl Emerson and Michael Holoquist (Austin: University of Texas Press).

Barnes, Djuna (1922) 'Against Nature: in Which Everything that Is Young, Inadequate and Tiresome is Included in the Term Natural', *Vanity Fair*, 18: 60.

—— (1963[1936]) *Nightwood* (London: Faber).

Barta, Peter I. et al. (2001) *Carnivalizing Difference: Bakhtin and the Other* (London: Routledge).

Barthes, Roland (1981) 'Theory of the Text', in Robert Young (ed.), *Untying the Text: a Post-structuralist Reader* (London: Routledge), pp. 31–49.

—— (1988) 'The Death of The Author', in David Lodge (ed.), *Modern Criticism and Theory: a Reader* (London: Longman), pp. 166–95.

Bauer, Heike (2009) 'Theorizing Female Inversion: Sexology, Discipline and Gender at the *Fin de Siècle*', *Journal of the History of Sexuality*, 18/1: 84–102.

—— (2006) *Women and Cross Dressing* (London: Routledge).

Baxter, Charles (1974) 'A Self-Consuming Light: *Nightwood* and the Crisis of Modernism', *Journal of Modern Literature*, 3/5: 1175–87.

Beckett, Samuel (1958) *Three Novels: Molloy, Malone Dies, The Unnamable* (New York: Grove Press).

—— (1990[1986]) *The Complete Dramatic Works* (London: Faber and Faber).

—— (1993[1934]) *More Pricks Than Kicks* (London: Calder Publications).

—— (1995) *The Complete Short Prose 1929–1989*, ed. S.E. Gontarski (New York: Grove Press).

—— (1996) *Dream of Fair to Middling Women* (London: John Calder).

—— 'Psychology Notes', Trinity College Dublin, MS 10967.

—— 'Untitled original manuscript of *Not I*', University of Reading, MS 1227/7/12/1.

Bedell, Geraldine (2002) 'He's not like other girls' (interview with Jeffrey Eugenides), *The Observer*, Sunday 6 October, p. 2.

Ben-Zvi, Linda (ed.) (1990), *Women in Beckett: Performance and Critical Perspectives* (Urbana: University of Illinois Press).

Benstock, Shari (1998) *The Private Self: Theory and Practice of Women's Autobiographical Writings* (London: Routledge).

Berberich, Christine (2007) *The Image of the English Gentleman in Twentieth-Century Literature* (Hampshire: Ashgate).

Bernheimer, Charles and Claire Kahane (eds) (1990) *In Dora's Case: Freud – Hysteria – Feminism* (New York: Columbia University Press).

Biemans, Monique (2000) *Gender Variation in Voice Quality* (Utrecht: Netherland Graduate School of Linguistics).

Blamires, Harry (1966) *The Bloomsday Book: a Guide through Joyce's* Ulysses (London: Methuen).

Bloom, Amy (2003) *Normal: Transsexual CEOs, Crossdressing Cops and Hermaphrodites with Attitude* (London: Bloomsbury).

Bolt, Sydney (1981) *A Preface to James Joyce* (Harlow: Longman).

Bolton, Jonathan (2010) *'Blighted Beginnings': Coming of Age in Independent Ireland* (Lewisberg: Bucknell University Press).

Booth, Wayne (1996) 'Distance and Point of View: an Essay in Classification', in Michael J. Hoffman and Patrick D. Murphy (eds), *Essentials of the Theory of Fiction* (London: Leicester University Press), pp. 116–33.

Botting, Fred (1996) *Gothic: the New Critical Idiom* (New York, Canada, Oxon: Routledge).

Bowyer, Susannah (2010) 'Queer Patriots: Sexuality and the Character of National Identity in Ireland', *Cultural Studies*, 24/6: 801–20.

Boyd, Ann E. (2004) *Writing for Immortality: Women Writers and the Emergence of High Literary Culture in America* (Baltimore: Johns Hopkins University Press).

Brater, Enoch (1987) *Beyond Minimalism: Beckett's Late Style in the Theatre* (New York: Oxford University Press).

Brauner, David (2010) *Contemporary American Fiction* (Edinburgh: Edinburgh University Press).

Breuer, Josef and Sigmund Freud (1991) *Studies on Hysteria: the Penguin Freud Library, Vol. 3*, trans. James Strachey (London: Penguin Books).

Brinzeu, Pia (2000) *Corridors of Mirrors: the Spirit of European Contemporary British and Romanian Fiction* (Lanham, Maryland: Maryland University Press).

—— (2004) 'Narratology Revivified: Androgynous and Transsexual Voices', *British and American Studies*, 10: 115–25.

Bristow, Joseph and Trev Broughton (eds) (1997) *The Infernal Desires of Angela Carter: Fiction, Femininity, Feminism* (Harlow: Addison Wesley Longman).

Brivic, Sheldon (1995) *Joyce's Waking Women: a Feminist Introduction to* Finnegans Wake (Madison: The University of Wisconsin Press).

Brontë, Charlotte (1994[1847]) *Jane Eyre* (London: Penguin).

Brontë, Emily (1985[1847]) *Wuthering Heights* (London: Penguin).

Buchanan, Jason (2008) '"The First Few Steps": Gender and Forgiveness in Patrick McCabe's *Breakfast on Pluto*', in Marti D. Lee and Ed Madden (eds), *Irish Studies: Geographies and Genders* (Newcastle: Cambridge Scholars), pp. 69–76.

Bulman, James C (2008) *Shakespeare Re-Dressed: Cross-gender Casting in Contemporary Performance* (Madison [NJ]: Fairleigh Dickinson University Press).

Burgess, Anthony (1973) *Joysprick: an Introduction to the Language of James Joyce* (London: André Deutsch).

Butler, Judith (1986) 'Sex and Gender in Simone de Beauvoir's *Second Sex*', *Yale French Studies*, 72: 35–49.

—— (1990) 'Performative Acts and Gender Constitution: an essay in phenomenology and Feminist Theory', in Sue-Ellen Case (ed.), *Performing Feminisms: Feminist Critical Theory and Theatre* (Baltimore: Johns Hopkins University Press), pp. 270–82.

—— (1990) *Gender Trouble: Feminism and the Subversion of Identity* (New York: Routledge).

—— (1993) *Bodies That Matter: on the Discursive Limits of 'Sex'* (New York: Routledge).

—— (1997) *Excitable Speech* (New York: Routledge).

—— (1997) *The Psychic Life of Power: Theories in Subjection* (Stanford: Stanford University Press).

—— (2004) *Undoing Gender* (London: Routledge).

Byatt, A.S. (1965) *Degrees of Freedom: the Novels of Iris Murdoch* (London: Chatto and Windus).

—— (1990) *Possession: a Romance* (London: Chatto and Windus).

Caird, Mona (1892) 'The Yellow Drawing Room', in *A Romance of the Moors* (Leipzig: Heinemann and Balestier).

Callow, Heather Cook (1992) 'Joyce's Female Voices in *Ulysses*', *The Journal of Narrative Technique*, 22/3: 151–63.

Carroll, Rachel (2010) 'Retrospective Sex: Rewriting Intersexuality in Jeffrey Eugenides' *Middlesex*', *Journal of American Studies*, 44/1: 187–201.

Carter, Angela (1982[1972]) *The Infernal Desire Machines of Doctor Hoffman* (London: Penguin).

—— (2009[1977]) *The Passion of New Eve* (London: Virago).

Caselli, Daniela (2009) *Improper Modernism: Djuna Barnes's Bewildering Corpus* (Farnham: Ashgate).

Cavarero, Adriana (2005) *For More Than One Voice: toward a Philosophy of Vocal Expression* (Stanford: Stanford University Press).

Chevalier, Jean-Louis (ed.) (1978) *Rencontres avec Irish Murdoch*. Centre de Recherches de Littérature et Linguistique des Pays de Langue Anglaise, Université de Caen (Presses Universitaire de Caen, France).

Chion, Michel (1999) *The Voice in Cinema*, trans. Claudia Gorbman (New York: Columbia University Press).

Chisholm, Dianne (1997) 'Obscene Modernism: Eros Noir and the Profane Illumination of Djuna Barnes', *American Literature*, 69/1: 167–206.

Cixous, Hélène (1974) *Prénoms de personne* (Paris: Seuil).

—— (1976) 'The Laugh of the Medusa', trans. Keith Cohen and Paula Cohen, *Signs*, 1: 875–93.

—— (1990) 'Difficult Joys', in Helen Wilcox et al. (eds), *The Body and the Text: Hélène Cixous, Reading and Teaching* (New York: Harvester Wheatsheaf), pp. 5–30.

Cleary, Joe (1996) '"Fork-Tongued on the Border Bit": Partition and the Politics of Form in Contemporary Narratives of the Northern Irish Conflict', *South Atlantic Quarterly*, 95/1: 227–76.

Colby, Vineta (2003) *Vernon Lee: a Literary Biography* (Charlottesville: University of Virginia Press).

Colella, Silvana (2010) 'Oflactory Ghosts: Michel Faber's *The Crimson Petal and the White*', in Rosario Arias and Patricia Pulham (eds), *Haunting and Spectrality in Neo-Victorian Fiction* (Basingstoke: Palgrave Macmillan), pp. 85–110.

Collado-Rodriguez, Francisco (2006) 'Of Self and Country: U.S. Politics, Cultural Hybridity, and Ambivalent Identity in Jeffrey Eugenides' *Middlesex*', *International Fiction Review*, 33/1–2: 71–83.

Collins, Wilkie (1995[1866]) *Armadale*, ed. John Sutherland (London: Penguin).

—— (2008[1859]) *The Woman in White* (Oxford: Oxford University Press).

Connor, Steven (1988) *Samuel Beckett: Repetition, Theory, and Text* (Oxford: Basil Blackwell).

—— (2000) *Dumbstruck: a Cultural History of Ventriloquism* (Oxford: Oxford University Press).

Conradi, Peter J. (1986) *The Saint and the Artist* (London: Harper Collins).

—— (2001) *Iris Murdoch: a Life* (London: Harper Collins).

Cordingley, Anthony (2006) 'The Reading Eye from *Scriptura Continua* to Modernism: Orality and Punctuation between Beckett's *L'image* and *Comment c'est/How It is*', *Journal of the Short Story in English*, 47, http://jsse.revues.org/index800.html [accessed 20 January 2012].

Cronin, Anthony (1997) *Samuel Beckett: the Last Modernist* (London: Harper Collins).

Cullingford, Elizabeth (1993) *Gender and History in Yeats's Love Poetry* (New York: Cambridge University Press).

—— (2001) *Ireland's Others: Gender and Ethnicity in Irish Literature and Popular Culture* (Cork: Cork University Press).

D'Arcy, Ella (1895) 'The Pleasure Pilgrim', *The Yellow Book*, V: 34–67.

De Beauvoir, Simone (1997[1949]) *The Second Sex* (London: Vintage).

De Valera, Éamon (1943) 'St Patrick's Day Radio Broadcast', *Radio Éireann*, 17 March.

Deane, Seamus (1990) 'Joyce the Irishman', in D. Attridge (ed.), *The Cambridge Companion to James Joyce* (Cambridge: Cambridge University Press), pp. 31–53.

DeKoven, Marianne (1991) *Rich and Strange: Gender, History, Modernism* (Princeton, NJ: Princeton University Press).

Deleuze, Gilles (1988) *Foucault*, trans. Sean Hand (Minneapolis: University of Minnesota Press).

Derrida, Jacques (1967) *Derrida: Writing and Difference*, trans. Alan Bass (London: Routledge).

—— (1988) '*Ulysses* Gramophone: Hear say yes in Joyce', in Bernard Benstock (ed.), *James Joyce: the Augmented Ninth* (Syracuse: Syracuse University Press).

—— (2008) *The Animal That Therefore I am*, trans. David Wills (New York: Fordham University Press).

Dickens, Charles (1982[1857]) *Little Dorrit*, ed. Harvey Peter Sucksmith (Oxford: Oxford University Press).

—— (1999[1838]) *Oliver Twist: Or the Parish Boy's Progress*, ed. Stephen Gill (Oxford: Oxford University Press).

Dipple, Elizabeth (1982) *Iris Murdoch: Work for the Spirit* (London: Methuen).

Dolar, Mladen (2006) *A Voice and Nothing More* (Cambridge, Mass.: MIT Press).

Dooley, Gillian (ed.) (2003) *From a Tiny Corner in the House of Fiction: Conversations with Iris Murdoch* (Columbia S.C.: University of South Carolina Press).

Egerton, George (1894) 'A Lost Masterpiece', *The Yellow Book*, I: 186–96.

—— (2002) 'A Nocturne', in Angelique Richardson (ed.), *Women Who Did: Stories by Men and Women, 1890–1914* (London: Penguin), pp. 187–96.

—— (2006) 'The Spell of the White Elf', in Sally Ledger (ed.), *Keynotes and Discords* (London: Continuum), pp. 25–31.

Eliot, T.S. (1963 [1937]) 'Introduction', in *Nightwood* (London: Faber).

Elliot, Patricia (2010) *Debates in Transgender, Queer, and Feminist Theory: Contested Sites* (Surrey: Ashgate).

Ellmann, Mary (1968) *Thinking about Women* (New York: Harcourt Brace Jovanovich).

Eugenides, Jeffrey (2003[2002]) *Middlesex* (London: Bloomsbury).

Faber, Michel (2002) *The Crimson Petal and the White* (Edinburgh: Canongate).

—— (2006) *The Apple: New Crimson Petal Stories* (Edinburgh: Canongate).

—— (2003) 'Eccentricity into Authenticity: Fact into Fiction', *Victorians Institute Journal*, 31: 102–5.

Feldman, Matthew (2006) *Beckett's Books: a Cultural History of Samuel Beckett's 'Interwar Notes'* (London: Continuum).

Ferenczi, Sándor and Sigmund Freud (1992) *Correspondence: 1908–1914*, eds Eva Brabant, Ernst Falzeder and Patrizia Giampieri-Deutsch (Paris: Calmann-Lévy).

Ferriter, Diamaid (2009) *Occasions of Sin: Sex and Society in Modern Ireland* (London: Profile Books).

Foer, Jonathan Safran (2002) 'Jeffrey Eugenides' (interview with Jeffrey Eugenides), *BOMB* 81 (Fall), p. 9, http://bombsite.com/issues/81/articles/2519, [accessed 20 Jabuary 2012].

Foucault, Michel (1986[1979]) 'What is an Author', in *The Foucault Reader*, trans. and ed. P. Rabinow (London: Penguin).

French, Marilyn (1976) *The Book as World: James Joyce's* Ulysses (Urbana: University of Illinois Press).

Freud, Sigmund (1963[1905;1901]) *Dora: Fragment of an Analysis of a Case of Hysteria* (New York: Collier Books).

—— (1974) *The Standard Edition of the Complete Psychological Works of Sigmund Freud*, trans. James Strachey (London: The Hogarth Press).

—— (1976) *The Interpretation of Dreams*, trans. James Strachey (London: Vintage).

—— (1985) 'The Theme of the Three Caskets', in *Art and Literature*, trans. James Strachey (London: Penguin).

—— (1987) *The Origins of Religion: the Penguin Freud Library, Vol. 13*, trans. James Strachey (London: Penguin).

—— (2001a) *Fragment of an Analysis of a Case of Hysteria*, in *The Standard Edition of the Complete Psychological Works of Sigmund Freud, Vol. 7*, trans. James Strachey and Anna Freud (London: Vintage), pp. 1–122.

—— (2001b) 'Remembering, Repeating, Working Through', in *The Standard Edition of the Complete Psychological Works of Sigmund Freud, Vol. 12*, trans. James Strachey (London: Vintage), pp. 146–56.

—— (2001c) 'Mourning and Melancholia', in *The Standard Edition of the Complete Psychological Works of Sigmund Freud, Vol. 14*, trans. James Strachey (London: Vintage), pp. 239–58.

Gal, Susan (1995) 'Language, Gender, and Power: an Anthropological Review', in K. Hall and M. Bucholtz (eds), *Gender Articulated: Language and the Socially Constructed Self* (New York: Routledge), pp. 169–82.

Gamble, Sarah (1997) *Angela Carter: Writing from the Front Line* (Edinburgh: Edinburgh University Press).

Garber, Marjorie (1992) *Vested Interests: Cross-Dressing and Cultural Anxiety* (New York: Routledge).

Genette, Gèrard (1980) *Narrative Discourse: an Essay in Method*, trans. Jane E. (Ithaca: Cornell University Press).

—— (1997) *Paratexts: Thresholds of Interpretation*, trans. Jane E. Lewin (Cambridge: Cambridge University Press).

Gerstenberger, Donna (1989) 'The Radical Narrative of Djuna Barnes's Nightwood', in E.G. Friedman, and M. Fuchs (eds), *Breaking the Sequence: Women's Experimental Fiction* (Princeton: Princeton University Press).

Gifford, Don and R. J. Seidman (eds) (1989) Ulysses *Annotated: Notes for James Joyce's* Ulysses (Berkeley: University of California Press).

Gilbert, Sandra M. (1980) 'Costumes of the Mind: Transvestism as Metaphor in Modern Literature', *Critical Inquiry*, 7/2: 391–417.

Gilmore, Leigh (2009) 'Obscenity, Modernity, Identity: Legalizing *The Well of Loneliness* and *Nightwood*', *Journal of the History of Sexuality*, 4/4: 603–24.

Gottfried, Roy K. (1980) *The Art of Joyce's Syntax in Ulysses* (London: Macmillan).

Grand, Sarah (1894) 'The Undefinable', *Cosmopolitan*, 17: 745–57.

Grimshaw, Tammy (2005) *Sexuality, Gender and Power in Iris Murdoch's Fiction* (Cranbury NJ: Associated University Presses).

Grosz, Elizabeth (1995) *Space, Time and Perversion* (New York: Routledge).

Halberstam, Judith (1998) *Female Masculinity* (Durham: Duke University Press).

Haraway, Donna (2003) *The Companion Species Manifesto: Dogs, People, and Significant Otherness* (Chicago: Prickly Paradigm Press).

Harland, Henry (ed.) (1895) *The Yellow Book V*.

Harmon, Maurice (ed.) (1998) *No Author Better Served: the Correspondence of Samuel Beckett and Alan Schneider* (Cambridge: Harvard University Press).

Harvey, Elizabeth D. (1992) *Ventriloquized Voices: Feminist Theory and English Renaissance Texts* (London: Routledge).

Heidegger, Martin (1995[1983]) *The Fundamental Concepts of Metaphysics: World, Finitude, Solitude*, trans. William McNeill and Nicholas Walker (Bloomington: Indiana University Press).

Heilmann, Ann (2000) *New Woman Fiction: Women Writing First-Wave Feminism* (Basingstoke and London: Palgrave).

—— and Mark Llewellyn (2010) *Neo-Victorianism: the Victorians in the Twenty-First Century, 1999–2009* (Houndmills: Palgrave Macmillan).

Heller, Louis G., Alexander Humez and Melcah Dror (1984) *The Private Lives of English Words* (London: Routledge).

Henke, Suzette (1978) *Joyce's Moraculous Sindbook: a Study of* Ulysses (Columbus: Ohio State University Press).

—— (1990) *James Joyce and the Politics of Desire* (New York: Routledge).

Herron, Tom (2000) 'ContamiNation: Patrick McCabe and Colm Tóibín's Pathographies of the Republic', in Liam Harte and Michael Parker (eds), *Contemporary Irish Fiction: Themes, Tropes, Theories* (Basingstoke: Macmillan).

Holmes, Frederick (1994) '*The Historical Imagination* and the Victorian Past: A.S. Byatt's *Possession*', *English Studies in Canada*, 20/3: 319–34. http//:www.guardian.co.uk/books/2002/oct/06/fiction.impacprize/print [accessed 20 January 2012].

Hughes, William and Andrew Smith (eds) (2009) *Queering the Gothic* (Manchester: Manchester University Press).

Hunter, Adrian (2007) *The Cambridge Introduction to the Short Story in English* (Cambridge: Cambridge University Press).

Irigaray, Luce (1985[1977]) *This Sex Which Is Not One*, trans. Catherine Porter (New York: Cornell University Press).

Jacobus, Mary (1981) 'Review of *The Madwoman in the Attic* and *Shakespeare's Sisters*', *Signs*, 6/3: 517–23.

James, Henry (1898) *The Turn of The Screw* (London: Penguin).

Jeffers, Jennifer M. (2002) *The Irish Novel at the End of the Twentieth Century* (Basingstoke: Palgrave Macmillan).

Johnson, Deborah (1987) *Iris Murdoch* (Brighton: Harvester Press).

Jones, Ernest (1920) *The Treatment of the Neuroses* (London: Baillière, Tindall and Cox).

Jouve, Nicole Ward (1994) 'Mother is a Figure of Speech', in Lorna Sage (ed.), *Flesh and the Mirror: Essays on the Art of Angela Carter* (London: Virago).

Joyce, James (1966[1957]) *Letters, Vol. 1*, ed. Stuart Gilbert (New York: Viking).

—— (1975) Richard Ellmann (ed.) *Selected Letters of James Joyce* (New York: Viking Press).

—— (1993[1922]) *Ulysses* (Oxford: Oxford University Press).

—— (2000) 'The Shade of Parnell' (1912), in *Occasional, Critical, and Political Writing* (Oxford: Oxford University Press), pp. 191–6.

Kahane, Claire (1995) *Passions of the Voice: Hysteria, Narrative and the Figure of the Speaking Woman, 1850–1915* (Baltimore and London: Johns Hopkins University Press).

Kaplan, Cora (2007) *Victoriana: Histories, Fictions, Criticisms* (Edinburgh: Edinburgh University Press).

Kenny, John (1998) 'Irish Writing and Writers: Some Recent Irish Writing' (Review), *Studies: an Irish Quarterly Review*, 87/348: 422–30.

Kenyon, Olga (1992) 'Angela Carter', in *The Writer's Imagination: Interviews with Major International Women Novelists* (Bradford: University of Bradford), pp. 23–33.

Killick, Katherine, and Joy Schaverien (1997) 'Introduction', in Katherine Killick and Joy Schaverien (eds), *Art, Psychotherapy and Psychosis* (London and New York: Routledge).

Kim, Rina (2010) *Women and Ireland as Beckett's Lost Others: Beyond Mourning and Melancholia* (Basingstoke: Palgrave Macmillan).

Kincaid, James R. (2002) 'The Nanny Diaries', *New York Times*, September 15, http://www.nytimes.com/2002/09/15/books/the-nanny-diaries.html [accessed 20 January 2012].

Klein, Melanie (1988) *Love, Guilt and Reparation and Other Works 1921–1945* (London: Virago Press).

Klett, Elizabeth (2009) *Cross-Gender Shakespeare and English National Identity: Wearing the Codpiece* (Basingstoke: Palgrave Macmillan).

Knowlson, James (1996) *Damned to Fame: the Life of Samuel Beckett* (New York: Simon & Schuster).

—— and Elizabeth Knowlson (eds) (2006) *Beckett Remembering Remembering Beckett: a Centenary Celebration* (New York: Arcade Publishing).

Koch-Rein, Anne (2005) 'Intersexuality – In the "I" of the Norm?': Queer field notes from Eugenides' *Middlesex*', in Yekani Haschemi and Beatrice Michaelis (eds), *Quer Durch Die Geistewissenschaften* (Berlin: Querverlag), pp. 238–52.

Kristeva, Julia (1980) *Desire in Language: a Semiotic Approach to Literature and Art*, ed. Leon S. Roudiez, trans. Thomas Gora, Alice Jardine and Leon S. Roudiez (Oxford: Blackwell).

—— (1982) *Powers of Horror: an Essay on Abjection*, trans. Leon S. Roudiez (New York: Columbia University Press).

—— (1989) *Black Sun: Depression and Melancholia*, trans. Leon S. Roudiez (New York: Columbia University Press).

Lacan, Jacques (2007) *Ecrits: the First Complete Edition in English*, trans. Bruce Fink (New York: W.W. Norton and Co Ltd.).

Lakoff, Robin (2004[1975]) *Language and Woman's Place: Text and Commentaries* (ed.) Mary Bucholtz (New York: Oxford University Press).

—— (1995) 'Cries and Whispers: the Shattering of the Silence', in K. Hall and M. Bucholtz (eds), *Gender Articulated: Language and the Socially Constructed Self* (New York: Routledge), pp. 23–50.

Laplanche, Jean and Jean Bertrad Pontalis (1988) *The Language of Psychoanalysis* (London: Karnac).

Ledger, Sally (1997) *The New Woman: Fiction and Feminism at the Fin de Siècle* (Manchester: Manchester University Press).

—— (2007) 'Wilde Women and *The Yellow Book*: the Sexual Politics of Aestheticism and Decadence', in *English Literature in Transition, 1880–1920*, 50/1: 5–26.

Lee, Alison (1996) 'Angela Carter's New Eve/lyn: De/Engendering Narrative', in Kathy Mezei (ed.), *Ambiguous Discourse: Feminist Narratology and British Women Writers* (Chapel Hill: University of North Carolina Press), pp. 238–49.

Lee, Hermione (1996) *Virginia Woolf* (London: Chatto & Windus).

Lee, Judith (1991) '*Nightwood*: The Sweetest Lie', in M.L. Broe (ed.), *Silence and Power: a Reevaluation of Djuna Barnes* (Carbondale: Southern Illinois University Press), pp. 207–20.

Leverson, Ada (1895) 'Suggestion', *The Yellow Book*, V: 249–57.

Lévi-Strauss Claude (2001[1978]) *Myth and Meaning* (London: Routledge).

Llewellyn, Mark (2004) '"Queer? I should say it is criminal!": Sarah Waters' *Affinity*', *Journal of Gender Studies*, 13/3: 203–14.

—— (2008) 'Breaking the Mould? Sarah Waters and the Politics of Genre', in Ann Heilmann and Mark Llewellyn (eds), *Metafiction and Metahistory in Contemporary Women's Writing* (Houndmills: Palgrave Macmillan), pp. 195–210.

—— (2009) 'Neo-Victorianism: on the Ethics and Aesthetics of Appropriation', *LIT: Literature, Interpretation, Theory*, 20/1–2: 27–44.

Lloyd, Moya (2007) *Judith Butler: from Norms to Politics* (Cambridge: Polity).

Lyons, F.S.L. (1977) *Charles Stewart Parnell* (Oxford: Oxford University Press).

Madden, Ed (2008) *Tiresian Poetics: Modernism, Sexuality, Voice 1888–2001* (Madison, NJ: Fairleigh Dickinson University Press).

Mahon, Peter (2007) 'Lacanian "Pussy": towards a Psychoanalytic Reading of Pat McCabe's *Breakfast on Pluto*', *Irish University Review*, 37/2: 441–71.

Marcus, Jane (1991) 'Laughing at Leviticus: *Nightwood* as Women's Circus Epic', in M.L. Broe (ed.), *Silence and Power: a Reevaluation of Djuna Barnes* (Southern Illinois University Press), pp. 221–51.

Marcus, Sharon (2007) *Between Women: Friendship, Desire, and Marriage in Victorian England* (New Jersey: Princeton University Press).

Martins, Susana S. (1999) 'Gender Trouble and Lesbian Desire in Djuna Barnes's *Nightwood*', *Frontiers: a Journal of Women Studies*, 20/3: 108–26.

Mayhew, Henry (1862) *The Criminal Prisons of London and Scenes of Prison Life* (London: Griffin, Bohn and Company).

McCabe, Patrick (1998) *Breakfast on Pluto* (London: Harper Perennial).

McWilliams, Ellen (2010) 'Madness and Mother Ireland in the Fiction of Patrick McCabe', *Irish Studies Review*, 18/4: 391–400.

Menegaldo, Gilles (1998) 'On Art and Life' (interview with Rose Tremain), *sources* (Easter): 101–19, http://www.paradigme.com/sources/SOURCES-PDF/Pages%20de%20Sources04-3-1.pdf [accessed 20 January 2012].

Michel, Frann (1989) 'Displacing Castration: *Nightwood*, *Ladies Almanack* and Feminine Writing', *Contemporary Literature*, 30/1: 33–58.

Mills, Sara (1995) *Feminist Stylistics* (London: Routledge).

Mitchell, Juliet (2000) *Mad Men and Medusas* (London: Penguin).

Moore, Lorrie (1995[1994]) *Who Will Run the Frog Hospital?* (London: Faber and Faber).

Moorhem, van Bran (2003) 'Bran van Moorhem interviews Jeffrey Eugenides' (interview with Jeffrey Eugenides), *3am Magazine*, p. 7, http://www.3ammagazine.com/litarchives/2003/sep/interview_jeffrey_eugenides.html [accessed 20 January 2012].

Murdoch, Iris (1958) *The Bell* (London: Chatto and Windus).

—— (1961) *A Severed Head* (London: Chatto and Windus).

—— (1997) *Existentialists and Mystics*, ed. Peter Conradi (London: Chatto and Windus).

—— (1999) 'Against Dryness', in Peter Conradi (ed.), *Existentialists and Mystics* (London: Penguin), pp. 287–97.

—— and J.B. Priestley (1964) *A Severed Head: a Play in Three Acts* (London: Chatto and Windus).

Neumark, Norie, Ross Gibson, and Theo van Leeuwen (eds) (2010) *Voice: Vocal Aesthetics in Digital Arts and Media* (Cambridge, Mass.: MIT Press).

Nolan, Emer (1994) *James Joyce and Nationalism* (New York: Routledge).

Oram, Alison (2001) *Lesbian History: Sources on Love and Sex Between Women, 1870–1970* (Florence, KY: Routledge).

Parker, Alan Michale and Mark Willhardt (eds) (1996) *The Routledge Anthology of Cross-Gendered Verse* (London: Routledge).

Pettitt, Lance (1997) 'Pigs and Provos, Prostitutes and Prejudice: Gay Representation in Irish Film, 1984–1995', in Éibhear Walshe (ed.), *Sex, Nation and Dissent in Irish* Writing (Cork: Cork University Press), pp. 252–84.

Poe, Edgar Allan (1994[1840]) *Selected Tales* (London: Penguin).

Pountney, Rosemary (1988) *Theatre of Shadows: Samuel Beckett's Drama 1956–1976* (Gerrards Cross: Colin Smythe).

Prince, Gerald (2003) *Dictionary of Narratology*, rev. edn. (Lincoln and London: University of Nebraska Press).

Punter, David (1984) 'Angela Carter: Supersessions of the Masculine', *Critique*, 25/4: 209–22.

—— (1985) *Hidden Script: Writing the Unconscious* (London: Routledge & Keegan Paul).

Pykett, Lynn (2000) 'Portraits of the Artist as a Young Woman: Representations of the Female Artist in the Women's Writing of the 1890s', in Nicola Thompson (ed.), *Victorian Women Novelists and the Woman Question* (Cambridge: Cambridge University Press), pp. 135–50.

Rabaté, Jean-Michel (1987) 'Fathers, Dead or Alive, in *Ulysses*', in Harold Bloom (ed.), *James Joyce's* Ulysses (New York: Chelsea), pp. 81–98.

Raitt, Suzanne (2002) *Vita and Virginia: the Work and Friendship of V. Sackville-West and Virginia Woolf* (Oxford: Clarendon Press).

Ramm, Ben (2005) 'Barking Up the Wrong Tree? The Significance of the Chienet in Old French Romance', *Parergon*, 22/1: 47–69.

Rank, Otto (1929) *The Trauma of Birth* (London: Kegan Paul, Trench, Trubner & Co., Ltd.).

Raymond, Janice (1979) The *Transsexual Empire: the Making of the She-Male* (Boston: Beacon Press).

—— (1996) 'The Politics of Transgenderism', in Richard Ekins and Dave King (eds), *Blending Genders: Social Aspects of Cross-Dressing and Sex Changing* (London: Routledge), pp. 215–23.

Restuccia, F.L. (1989) *Joyce and the Law of the Father* (New Haven: Yale University Press).

Richardson, Angelique (2002) 'Introduction', in *Women Who Did: Stories by Men and Women, 1890–1914* (London: Penguin), pp. xxxi–lxxxi.

—— and Chris Willis (eds) (2001) *The New Woman in Fiction and in Fact* (Basingstoke and New York: Palgrave).

Rivière, Joan (1929) 'Womanliness as Masquerade', *International Journal of Psychoanalysis*, 10: 303–13.

Roof, Judith (1994) 'Lesbian and Lyotard: Legitimation and the Politics of the Name', in L. Doan (ed.), *The Lesbian Postmodern* (New York: Columbia University Press).

Sage, Lorna (1994) *Angela Carter* (Plymouth: Northcote House Publishers).

Schaverien, Joy (1997) 'Transference and Transactional Objects in the Treatment of Psychosis', in Katherine Killick and Joy Schaverien (eds), *Art, Psychotherapy and Psychosis* (London and New York: Routledge).

Scott Bonnie K. (1984) *Joyce and Feminism* (Bloomington: Indiana University Press).

Serpell, James (1995) *The Domestic Dog* (Cambridge: Cambridge University Press).

Shainberg, Lawrence (1987) 'Exorcising Beckett', *The Paris Review*, 104: 100–36.

Shakespeare, William (1972) *King Lear*, ed. Kenneth Muir (Surrey and London: Arden).

Shostak, Debra (2008) '"Theory Uncompromised by Practicality": Hybridity in Jeffrey Eugenides' *Middlesex*', *Contemporary Literature*, 49/3: 383–412.

Showalter, Elaine (ed.) (1993) *Daughters of Decadence: Women Writers of the Fin de Siècle* (London: Virago).

—— (1982) 'Feminist Criticism in the Wilderness', in Elizabeth Abel (ed.), *Writing and Sexual Difference* (Brighton: Harvester Press), pp. 9–36.

Sifuentes, Zachary (2006) 'Strange Anatomy, Strange Sexuality: the Queer Body in Jeffrey Eugenides' *Middlesex*', in Richard Fantina and Thomas Calvin (eds), *Straight Writ Queer: Non-Normative Expressions of Heterosexuality in Literature* (Jefferson, NC: McFarland), pp. 145–57.

Silverman, Kaja (1988) *The Acoustic Mirror: the Female Voice in Psychoanalysis and Cinema* (Bloomington: Indiana University Press).

Sontag, Susan (1964) 'Notes on Camp', *Partisan Review*, XXXI: 515–30.

Spivak, Gayatri Chaktavorty (1988), 'Can the Subaltern Speak?', in Cary Nelson and Lawrence Grossberg (eds), *Marxism and the Interpretation of Culture* (Urbana: University of Illinois Press), pp. 271–313.

Sproles, Karyn Z. (2006) *Desiring Women: the Partnership of Virginia Woolf and Vita Sackville-West* (Toronto, Buffalo and London: University of Toronto Press).

Stephen, Karin (1933) *Psychoanalysis and Medicine: a Study of the Wish to Fall Ill* (Cambridge: Cambridge University Press).

Stone, Sandy (1991) 'The Empire Strikes Back: a Posttranssexual Manifesto', in Julia Epstein and Kristina Straud (eds), *Body Guards: The Cultural Politics of Gender Ambiguity* (New York: Routledge), pp. 208–304.

Sutherland, John (2002) 'Making It: *The Crimson Petal and the White* by Michel Faber', *Washington Post*, September 15, http://www.washingtonpost.com/ac2/wpdyn?pagename=article&node=&contentId=A12475-2002Sep13 [accessed 20 January 2012].

Talbot, Mary (2010[1998]) *Language and Gender* (Cambridge: Polity Press).

Taylor, Charles (2002) 'Review of *The Crimson Petal and the White*', *Salon*, http://dir.salon.com/story/books/review/2002/10/21/faber/index.html [accessed 20 January 2012].

Tennyson, Alfred (1883) *The Works of Alfred Tennyson: Poet Laureate* (London: Kegan Paul, Trench and Co.).

Todd, Janet (ed.) (1980) *Gender and Literary Voice* (New York: Holmes & Meier Publishers).

—— (ed.) (1981) *Men by Women* (New York: Holmes & Meier Publishers).

Tremain, Rose (1992) *Sacred Country* (London: Sinclair-Stevenson).

Trevenna, Joanne (2002) 'Gender as Performance: Questioning the "Butlerification" of Angela Carter's Fiction', *Journal of Gender Studies*, 11/3: 267–77.

Tyler, Carole-Anne (2003) *Female Impersonation* (London: Routledge).

Ussher, Jane M. (1997) *Fantasies of Femininity: Reframing the Boundaries of Sex* (Harmondsworth: Penguin).

Voigts-Virchow, Eckhart (2009) 'In-yer-Victorian-face: a Subcultural Hermeneutics of Neo-Victorianism', *LIT: Literature, Interpretation, Theory*, 20/1–2: 108–25.

Wallace, Clare (2004) 'Patrick McCabe: Transgression and Dysfunctional Irelands', in Neil Sammells (ed.), *Beyond Borders: IASIL Essays on Modern Irish Writing* (Bath: Sulis Press), pp. 143–56.

Waters, Sarah (1998) *Tipping the Velvet* (London: Virago Press).

—— (1999) *Affinity* (London: Virago).

—— (2002) *Fingersmith* (London: Virago).

—— (2009) *The Little Stranger* (London: Virago Press).

Waugh, Evelyn (1945) *Brideshead Revisited* (London: Penguin).

Weich, Dave (2002) 'Jeffrey Eugenides Has It Both Ways' (interview with Jeffrey Eugenides), Powells.com, p. 10, http://www.powells.com/authors/eugenides.html [accessed 20 January 2012].

Weil, Simone (1952) *The Need for Roots* (London: Routledge and Kegan Paul Ltd.).

Weller, Shane (2008) '"Some Experience of the Schizoid Voice": Samuel Beckett and the Language of Derangement', *Forum for Modern Language Studies*, 45/1: 32–50.

White, Chris (1999) (ed.) *Nineteenth-Century Writings on Homosexuality: a Sourcebook* (London and New York: Routledge).

Whitelaw, Billie (1995) *... Who He?* (London: Hodder and Stoughton).

Wilde, Oscar (2002) 'The Sphinx without a Secret', in Angelique Richardson (ed.), *Women Who Did: Stories by Men and Women, 1890–1914* (London: Penguin), pp. 3–8.

Williams, David (2007) 'Inappropriate/d Others or, The Difficulty of Being a Dog', *The Drama Review: TDR*, 51/1: 92–118.

Williams, Raymond (1977) *Marxism and Literature* (Oxford: Oxford University Press).

Wilson, Edmund (1961[1931]) *Axel's Castle: a Study in the Imaginative Literature of 1870–1930* (Glasgow: Collins Fontana).

Winfrey, Oprah (2007) 'A Conversation with *Middlesex* Author Jeffrey Eugenides' (interview with Jeffrey Eugenides), *Oprah's Book Club*, June 5, p. 4, http://www.oprah.com/oprahsbookclub/A-Conversation-with-Middlesex-Author-Jeffrey-Eugenides [accessed 20 January 2012].

Womack, Kenneth and Amy Mallori-Kani (2007) '"Why don't you just leave it up to nature?": An Adaptionist Reading of the Novels of Jeffrey Eugenides', *Mosaic* 40/3: 157–73.

Yeats, W.B. (1996[1989]) *Yeats's Poems*, ed. A. Norman Jeffares (London: Macmillan).

Zakresksi, Patricia (2006) *Representing Female Artistic Labour: 1848–1890: Refining Work for the Middle-Class Woman* (Aldershot: Ashgate).

Index